HONOR

HONOR

R. WRIGHT CAMPBELL

TOR

This is a work of fiction. All the characters and events portrayed in this book are fictional, and any resemblance to real people or incidents is purely coincidental.

HONOR

Copyright © 1987 by R. Wright Campbell

First printing: August 1987

A TOR Book

Published by Tom Doherty Associates, Inc.
49 West 24 Street
New York, N.Y. 10010

ISBN: 0-312-93020-8

Library of Congress Catalog Card Number: 86-51492

Printed in the United States of America

0   9   8   7   6   5   4   3   2   1

Foca Prison: 1983

Lieutenant Michael Karel had no idea what had prompted—no, compelled—him to travel the long distance to Foca Prison, especially during Christmas holiday week. It would be better to be at home stealing every happy moment he could with his two small children and his wife, Anya. She was planning a great round of celebrations and observances in spite of the fact that she had been born and raised during the era of official prohibition against religious piety. Was a belief in a supreme being, the trust that there was a fixed point in an otherwise chaotic universe, essential to human survival? Was it as necessary to certain individuals as love, honor, and compassion? He sometimes thought it odd that he, a policeman for so many years, could still wonder about such abstractions. It heartened him that the excess of murder and mayhem he'd cleaned up in a lifetime hadn't made him too callous and unfeeling. He was sure it was a consequence of his late second marriage and the two children who grew starry-eyed at stories of Father Christmas.

Perhaps that was why he was standing in the cold outside the isolated prison waiting for a man he scarcely knew to be given back his freedom. Senior Investigator Stevan Georgi, the man who was to be released after thirteen years, had never seen the three grandchildren born while he was behind bars.

Foca Prison was a modern gray fortress in the center of the Pannonian Plain near the apex of the triangle formed by the Danube and Tisza rivers. Towns could be seen on the horizon at three quadrants of the compass. There was a facility of sorts composed of a dormitory, a store, and a restaurant where visitors might stay while waiting for the uncertain moment when they would be allowed to go in to see a prisoner. Except for

1

that, there was no community nearby. It was as though no sensible human being would attempt to live so close to such isolation and misery, thereby making the isolation and misery of Foca the greater. Some of the fiercest fighting of the war had taken place in this wide valley. Some of the worst destruction. Many villages had been leveled, towns destroyed. Some had never been rebuilt. There had been no one left who loved the stones of the fallen houses enough to pile them up again. There had once been a sizable farming community where Foca Prison's granite walls rose forty feet from the barren earth. It was said that there was a well inside the walls that could not be used because it still ran with blood. It was a legend, but true in the way of legends. As true in its way as the national history that was read in the schools, that was remembered but could never really be part of a man's blood and bone.

There was snow on the ground. Karel's car was parked on the other side of the road opposite the first of the three gates through which one must pass to enter the prison, through which Georgi would have to pass to leave it. The gates were solid. There was no way for Karel to prepare himself for a confrontation. He had not, in fact, even fully decided if he would cross the road and introduce himself. What would be accomplished by it? What was being accomplished by his coming at all for that matter? He smiled wryly. A matter of honor, a small eternal verity, he thought.

The metal of the gates snapped like pistol shots. They seemed to tremble. They didn't open. Instead, a smaller door set in one of the gates squeaked open like the voice of a comedy mouse in some cinema cartoon. A man stood there in a badly cut gray suit and overcoat. He wore a felt hat as though it had been set on his head with a carpenter's level. It rode above his ears, and seemed to be far too small for him. He carried a cheap cardboard suitcase in his ungloved left hand. His face was clean-shaven except for gray mustaches trimmed to an old military fashion. His prison-issue spectacles were as round as coins, and appeared to be clouded over. He stepped over the lintel of the doorway, walked as far as the curb, and put down the suitcase. The door closed at his back.

Karel made his decision. He started across the road trying to think of what he could possibly say to a man Karel might have saved from thirteen years in Foca Prison.

= 1 =

The Policeman: 1970

It had been a mild winter, with none of the tree-shattering cold or cutting winds that annually crippled Belgrade. There had been very little snow. Day after day the street sweepers had leaned on their shovels and smoked after scraping up an inch or so, pushing it off into the openings in the curbs that dropped into the sewers. But the night before, a heavy snow had fallen. Although it was already nearly swept away on the business streets, there were patches of it on other major avenues and most was untouched on the residential streets. Around dawn the first real bite of winter chomped down, snapping the mild weather in two. The snow that had been left unswept developed a crust of ice that sparkled like diamonds flung on the ground.

Along the Ulica Marsala Tita the store windows were filled with consumer goods, evidence that the Socialist state had proven itself by providing a few of the luxuries the capitalistic West enjoyed. A good many of the windows had Christmas decorations behind the glass. The Communist government gave the church no special support, but it understood how church and state were inextricably intertwined in the history of the people. The true history that lived in the blood and bones.

At the end of the broad thoroughfare, toward the urban forest and park that lay to the south of Belgrade, the tall, square, gray buildings of government and socialist commerce thinned out and gave way to the mansions that had once housed the wealthy bourgeoisie and the lesser nobility. Prince Michael's Street entered the main avenue at an oblique angle. It was lined with larger mansions that had been converted to luxury apartments

3

after the war. The coveted accommodations were prizes given to favored bureaucrats, party officials, power brokers, exporters, and certain very successful gray marketeers, proof that there is no society without an angle, an edge, or an opportunity to be seized.

The man in the light gray overcoat with the rich black astrakhan collar and cuffs lay sprawled on his back. His homburg had fallen from his head and was on the slick ice five feet away. He had one glove on his hand, the other had dropped to the ground beside his briefcase. One could imagine him leaving the lobby of his apartment house, walking along the path to the gate, his briefcase tucked under his arm as he put on his gloves. One could imagine him watching his step on the icy walk. One could not imagine the dismay and terror he surely felt when he saw the gun.

There was a white silk scarf around his neck and a mess between his eyes. His blood was freezing around the back of his head.

"The gun had to be held right up against the bone to shatter his skull like that," Samuel said. His announcement was that of an expert. He was a senior medical examiner for the city. There were several policemen and officers in plain clothes on the scene. A small, compact man with brooding Oriental eyes and a thin upper lip stood beside the doctor and looked at the apartment block.

"I wonder what one has to do in order to live in such a place?" Sergeant Michael Karel said.

Samuel respected the policeman, even liked him, but he sometimes felt that Karel too often gave himself up to philosophical speculation. What did it matter what one had to do? The detective would never do it. He lived by the book, unimaginatively, taking no chances.

"I should guess that whoever murdered him was known to the dead man," Samuel said.

Karel regarded him with his soft, melting eyes. There were glints of amusement in them but his mouth was solemn. He knew that the doctor fancied himself a detective of sorts, able to break the most complex case with deductions made from the paring of a fingernail or the way a footprint had been impressed in clay. His flights of such fancies were often absurd.

"What makes you say that?" Karel murmured.

"In order to get so close."

"His head was lowered in attention to his glove," Karel said. "I have no doubt he was also watching his step on the icy ground. Someone could have easily been lurking behind one of the stone pillars that hold the gates or behind that thick stand of bushes along the fence. It would have been a matter of three strides for the killer to place himself directly in front of his victim. When the poor fellow looked up it would have taken a half second to place the muzzle of the pistol against his forehead and pull the trigger. It could easily have been a stranger killing."

"He wasn't robbed. You said so yourself."

"His briefcase wasn't taken. The coins and silver knife in his trousers pocket weren't disturbed. The billfold in the breast pocket of his jacket was left behind. But we can't be sure he wasn't robbed."

Samuel made a strangled sound of impatience and embarrassment. Never ask Karel about penguins, he thought, or you'll learn more about them than you ever wanted to know.

"We can't be sure of anything quite yet," Karel continued mildly. Then he added, in order to soothe Samuel's feelings, "It might have easily been a friend or acquaintance who pulled the trigger. It usually is."

He looked at the façade of the luxury apartment block again. It had once been the city residence of a count in the days of the monarchy. In the days of privilege for the few and poverty for the many. He knew that the arched tunnel at the end of the stone path led into a courtyard of grand dimensions. It had once been large enough for three dozen carriages to wait along the side, still leaving room enough for one to enter, discharge its passengers, and turn around. It had once received the glittering royal, noble, and aristocratic wastrels of Europe, come to attend balls and fetes where more money would be spent on the entertainment of a single night than would be expended in a year for the maintenance of the charity hospital for the poor. In its conference rooms and libraries self-important men would argue territoriality and the pain of wounded pride, sketching grand plans that would inevitably lead to war and the deaths of tens of thousands.

Now the courtyard was occupied by laundry sheds, drying lines, a play yard for the children of the occupants, and other makeshift buildings needed to serve the lives of fifty families where only one had lived before.

Karel's glance fell on a man in dirty boots and coveralls who stood beside the gate post with an air of surly importance. He was in conversation with a uniformed policeman. Karel didn't have to ask who he was. Janitors and custodians always looked the same. They carried their importance around on the rings of keys at their waists. There was no doubting who they considered the owners of the buildings in their charge. Karel walked over to the janitor, knowing that by doing so the man would feel honored. Karel would have won his cooperation.

"My name is Sergeant Karel. I have to ask you a few questions. You understand?"

"My name is Henick Ludu," the janitor said. "I understand. I'm the custodian of this building. I live in the gate house right there." He pointed out a small stone cottage with a round peaked roof like a large toy soldier's sentry box.

"Did you see the murder?" Karel asked.

"I was in the courtyard burning the week's trash. This is the only day of the week for burning. It makes it difficult. They collect the fats and wet garbage separately. Also the cans and glass bottles. But paper has to be burned. A whole week's trash from a building as large as this in one day. It is very foolish, but who wants to complain?"

"Did you hear the shot?"

"With the clanging of the cans, and opening and closing the incinerator door, who could hear a shot? Who would know it was a shot even if it was heard? It's a long time since the war. I forget what a shot sounds like."

"You've looked at the dead man's face?"

Ludu nodded and wrinkled his brow as though feeling the pain of the skull-shattering bullet.

"I shoveled the path from the door to the street not an hour before," he announced, as though suggesting that he'd only just missed saving the man's life—or witnessing his death—by a minute or two.

"Did you see anyone lurking about at that time?"

"Are you crazy? Only a fool or a janitor would be out in the cold at such an hour," Ludu snorted.

"Or a policeman," Karel said. "Or a killer. Was anyone walking past while you were shoveling the walk?"

"There may have been. Who remembers such things?"

"Were there any automobiles parked in the street?"

"A few. Yes, I think so."

"Any that were strange to you?"

"A black sedan was at the curb up the street."

"Did you have a good look at it?"

"I may have glanced at it. If you mean did I notice the plate, no, I didn't."

"Did your glance give you the impression that anyone was sitting in the car?"

"There might have been. The windows were frosted over. There may have been the shadow of someone sitting in it. I don't know. I wasn't expecting to have a tenant shot down on the walk, you understand."

"Can you identify the dead man for me?" Karel asked.

"Of course I can. Didn't I just say he was a tenant? It's Horvath. Jan Horvath. He lives just there," Ludu said, pointing to some windows on the third floor. "The five windows above the carvings of the saints to the left of the main archway."

There was a woman with white hair staring down on the scene.

"Is that woman his mother?"

"What? Oh, you've got the wrong apartment. That's old Madame Andric. I meant the windows just above."

Just then a woman pushed back the sheer curtains at the center window of the five.

"That's his wife. There's just Horvath, and her, and a small Pomeranian bitch," Ludu went on.

The wife was too far away for Karel to read the expression on her face but the attitude of her body, clenched fist to breast, spoke of righteous triumph, not of grief. Karel's superiors sometimes remarked among themselves that the sergeant was too apt to ignore cold facts in favor of intuitions. Karel shook his head in self-admonishment and looked over at the dead man again. The face was ghostly white where it wasn't stained with the horror of the bullet wound. Horvath looked like photographs of the soldier-dead scattered on the frozen battlefields of the last, liberating war. Samuel was still fussing over the corpse.

"I may have occasion to speak with you again, Ludu," Karel said. "You understand?"

Ludu said he did, and smiled importantly as Karel returned to the body in the snow.

"Will you close his eyes?" Karel said to Samuel.

"The lids are frozen, can't you see?" Samuel replied.

"Christ, I hate it when they look at me," Karel said. "You can take up the body when you please. I'm off to question the widow."

"I don't envy you that part of your job," Samuel said.

"I don't expect many tears this time," Karel said.

He was about to turn away and walk up the path toward the entrance to the apartment block when a black police sedan pulled up to the curb. Lieutenant Lutesh rolled down the window on the passenger's side and called Karel over.

"How is it going?" he asked.

"I've had a chat with the superintendent of the building. I'm about to question the new widow."

"Don't bother. Not for the moment."

Karel didn't say anything. His brows rose slightly. That was all the surprise he displayed.

"There's a question about jurisdiction," Lutesh explained.

= 2 =

Judge Anton Trevian's chambers in the Courts of Justice Building suited him. He was an old man, well past the age of retirement, but the respect paid him was so great that no one had yet dared suggest that he stand aside. Born to the old nobility, he had embraced communism when a young man and, in his middle years, had become one of the party's chief theorists. He'd fought with the Partisans as a common soldier during the war, making the example that even in battle no man should be placed above a comrade by reason of rank. Men became leaders, he insisted, because of their inherent ability to do so, or through virtue of the experience they acquired by survival.

He seemed to contain the physical qualities that might have served an artist in creating a portrait of a Royalist, yet had those which might have described a revolutionary peasant as well. He was short and blocky, had often been called the Little Bullock. He had a massive head crowned by a mane of white hair. His lip was decorated with a pair of black aristocratic mustaches that would have done honor to the old Kaiser. His feet were small and delicate, fit for dancing pumps, his hands as thick-fingered and gnarled as any farmer's. He wore conservative black suits without apparent style. The trousers seemed to bag more than a little at seat and knees so that he appeared somewhat shrunken when standing up, supported by a cane of native wood. The jacket was tailored to fit perfectly across his massive chest. He immediately became impressive, even forbidding, when seated.

His chambers were a mixture of the old and new, the Royalist and proletarian. He used an imperial eagle taken from a standard as a paperweight. There was a statue of a worker-soldier on the corner of his desk. The draperies that controlled the light coming through the tall windows were old velvet, the wastepaper basket near his feet of recently manufactured cardboard. He saw nothing strange in having a signed photograph of his dead king Alexander on the same wall as that of Tito. Neither did anyone question it. He was known as a man of impeccable honor, fidelity, and integrity. Who would dare ask him to deny a friendship?

None of the contradictions about himself were lost on him.

The Public Prosecutor had named Trevian the examining magistrate in the case of the unlawful death of one Jan Horvath. All he knew so far was that which was available to everyone who cared to read the daily paper. It lay neatly folded on the desk before him. There had been rumors, of course. There were always rumors in the track of any killing. They sprang up like weeds nurtured by blood, Trevian often said.

Each of the four men sitting in the chairs arranged before Trevian's desk had been provided with the drink that especially pleased him. *Sljivovica* for Lieutenant Peter Lutesh, chief of homicide for the Municipal Police. Harsh *rakia* for Director Dietrich Borodin of the Public Security Service, SJB. Polish vodka for Colonel Maxwell Bim, the commander of Military Counter-Intelligence, KOS. A glass of white wine for Senior Investigator Stevan Georgi, of the State Security Service, SDB, the once-dreaded Ozna. Trevian had a small pony of French brandy near his own hand.

He knew by an electric stirring along the back of his neck that this would be an important case. He sometimes believed the feeling to be a feral response to grave danger. The law was a fragile barrier against anarchy and chaos. He felt that one day a crime would be committed that would bring the world crashing down about their ears. Then only instinctive alarms and subtle intuitions would be of any use in survival.

"So, gentlemen," Trevian said, smiling brilliantly upon each one of them in turn, giving each a precisely measured portion of his welcome, "I am overwhelmed by the honor you pay me by coming to my chambers. But I must admit that I'm puzzled and confounded. What can there possibly be in this case of murder to attract the attention of three such distinguished law officers?'' He nodded toward Lutesh. ''I exclude our colleague, Lieutenant Lutesh, because homicide committed in the city is properly his concern.''

''What is there about it that provoked the Public Prosecutor into turning it over to an examining magistrate?'' Director Borodin asked. Trevian bestowed a smile and a nod upon the chief of the SJB. He made a mark on a sheet of paper with a large-barreled old-fashioned fountain pen.

''The identity of the victim,'' Trevian said.

''Exactly,'' Borodin said. ''This is no ordinary crime of murder.''

''Is there reason to suppose that Horvath was the subject of a kidnapping attempt that went astray?''

''There's no evidence of that,'' Borodin said.

''Could it be a terrorist attack?''

''That's possible.''

''Much is possible,'' Trevian agreed. ''In fact, I can think of very little that is not. However, would it be reasonable to look elsewhere for the motive?''

Borodin nodded.

''You've nothing to offer me that might suggest Horvath was engaged in any activities that might be construed as being, even generally, a matter of domestic espionage, sabotage, or subversion? No involvement in smuggling between republics and communes? No connection with nationally prohibited trade in drugs, arms, or gold?''

Borodin laughed, softly but with a certain expansiveness, as though Trevian's meticulous naming of possibilities had nothing to do with the real world of crime.

''Your honor, how can I answer any of that? It's quite clearly because we of the SJB believe that there may be something in the life and death of Horvath that bears upon national security that I'm here claiming jurisdiction. At least to put the case that for lack of any evidence to the contrary the SJB is the logical arm of the law to proceed with the investigation. After all, we have the facilities.''

''Facilities?''

"Laboratories, files, lines of communication, and cooperation with other countries."

"You suspect something about the corpse or the scene of the crime, otherwise unseen by the naked but probing eye of trained detectives, will give us a clue to the reason for the victim's murder?"

"I didn't say that, your honor."

"Of course you didn't, but you did say something of laboratories, and one makes conclusions from such remarks. Should I consider the emphasis was meant for the files? Do you suggest that Horvath was only one of a widespread organization, unidentified but suspected because of certain patterns of crime? Are you saying that a careful combing of your admittedly huge files will reveal such a conspiracy?"

"I couldn't possibly go so far," Borodin said less heartily. The old man's persistence was wearing through the thin veneer of Borodin's assumed expansiveness and threatened to reveal the fundamentally dangerous tyrant underneath.

"Then," Trevian went on with imperturbable good nature, "it's in the network of mutual cooperation the SJB enjoys with its counterparts in other nations that the power of your argument lies? The death of Horvath may well have international complications?"

"May have," Borodin said with sudden heat. "I don't claim that anything of the sort is a certainty."

"Thank you. Shall I have my clerk come in to pour you another brandy? You're welcome to do so for yourself, if you like."

Borodin first refused, then drank off the remains of his glass and got up to pour himself another after all as Trevian turned his benign gaze to Colonel Bim. He made another mark on the page.

"I requested this interview more out of courtesy than necessity," Colonel Bim said airily. "More to inform than to ask permission. Jan Horvath was an officer in the KOS. Any investigation of his murder clearly falls under our jurisdiction. For reasons of honor if no other."

"He was retired in nineteen sixty-two, was he not?"

"Nineteen sixty-five. I'm sure it was nineteen sixty-five,"

Colonel Bim said, smiling sweetly. "If Horvath was killed for motives extending from his service with us, we must surely be the instrument of vengeance. How could it be otherwise?"

"How, indeed," the old judge agreed, nodding his head in perfect rhythm to the drumroll of the colonel's arguments, "if it's vengeance we're after. How can we assume that a retired officer was a target of foreign espionage?"

"He was still carried on our table of organization in the event of a national emergency."

Trevian smiled sweetly. "Thank God we're not presently in a state of such emergency. Horvath wasn't on active duty when shot down this morning? He'd not been recalled?"

Colonel Bim waited a long moment before replying, thinking it through. He apparently saw no reason to go on beating his drum. He smiled.

"May I, too, have a second glass?" he said pointedly.

Borodin frowned sharply, not appreciating one bit the colonel's teasing, gracious ways. Judge Trevian frowned a trifle and pursed his lips, warning Colonel Bim not to insult the others. Then he smiled. They were old friends, and very easy with each other. They often played chess together. They were a nearly perfect match. Over the years perhaps not twelve victories separated their wins and losses. The oddity of their play, to those who had been occasional spectators, lay in the fact that one or the other would concede within no more than twenty moves when other players might not have done so in another twenty or more.

Senior Investigator Georgi was another dear friend. The senior investigator for the SDB and the old judge did not share chess. Georgi preferred to spend the evenings with the judge in discussions of obscure points of law and the novels of Franz Kafka, the novelist whose books dealt with the predicament of a solitary man hopelessly trying to come to terms with some remote and absolute power unknown to him, helplessly trying to contend with an incomprehensible and hostile universe. For a moment Georgi hesitated when Trevian's eyes fell upon him in his turn.

Should he even bother to make a claim of jurisdiction in the case? If he did would it seem foolish of him? If he did not would it seem suspect? His colleagues in the law were all watching him in their separate ways. Bim with amusement. Borodin with ill-concealed truculence. Lutesh, the least among them in place of rank and influence, gazed at him with sleepy eyes, more a real policeman than any of them. He was waiting patiently for them to sort things out so that he could get on with the job.

"I have no arguments or persuasions," Georgi finally said. "This case is unique. Apparently we all feel that. I've simply come to see how the examining magistrate intends to dispose of it."

"You make no special claims?" Trevian said.

"I expect it would do me no good. In point of law, if I quote my learned teacher correctly, 'No crime is to be considered a greater crime than it appears to be, unless there is powerful suspicion or real evidence that such an escalation does not offend common sense.' A man's been murdered. He was a soldier and is a reservist. How many men of his age in the country are not? There's no clue to the identity of the killer. How can we then assume that the killer's motive had to do with the suppression of evidence of crimes against the state or the security of the nation? Are we to assume a conspiracy without a hint that such a conspiracy exists? At the moment we've nothing more than a simple case of murder by a person, or persons, unknown, although the unfortunate victim is a man of many honors who enjoyed great esteem."

Judge Trevian nodded in pride and pleasure at his pupil's dissertation.

"Inspector Georgi has already anticipated my answer and my reasons for it in this jurisdictional dispute. Can the rest of you understand why it's my decision to allow the Municipal Police to get on with the investigation of this unlawful death?"

Borodin was already on his feet, anxious to get away from any lecture. Colonel Bim was eager to be gone as well. He examined the gold watch on his wrist with good-natured impatience, then looked at the judge as though prepared to give him one minute, but not the shred of another minute more.

Judge Trevian peered up at the two large men, then struggled to his own feet, shuffling around the corner of his desk in order to get closer to them, leaning on his cane, emphasizing the difference in stature between them. He was playing the old peasant daring the aristocratic officials to show unforgivable rudeness to a humble representative of the people. The old Royalist was having his fun with the Socialist police and turning the tables upside down.

"I am awarding the case to the Municipal Police because I know it will receive professional treatment as a homicide in the capable hands of Lieutenant Lutesh. It might have done in the equally capable hands of the SDB, the SJB, or the KOS, but the Metropolitan Police won't treat it as de facto evidence of a greater crime involving national security or some widespread conspiracy against the state. It won't be used, gentlemen, as an excuse for intruding into the personal lives of a good many people who may be guilty of nothing more than hoarding a few American dollars or bribing some official for a larger apartment. It will not be the key for the exercise of the unusual powers which your organizations can assume whenever there's a hint of danger to the government.

"Would any one of you like a last refreshment before you go?"

Karel waited on a bench in the corridor just down from the doors to Judge Trevian's chambers. He thought about his life and knew it to be a shambles. One woman was a burden. Two were a trial. If he could choose his way, he'd be a celibate policeman. Like a priest he'd be able to give all his energies to his purpose. In the priest's case, God, in his own, criminal apprehension. He never thought of justice. That was properly left to lawyers, judges, and legislators. He didn't have the stomach for splitting hairs. He didn't have the stomach for dealing with the consequences of his own passions either, but he was stuck with them and would finally have to reconcile his own dilemma.

The doors to the judge's chambers opened. Trevian's clerk, a man who always looked as though he'd sucked a lemon, held the door open as he bowed. Karel could practically hear the crackling of the man's dry bones. Borodin of the SJB came out first. His face was in momentary transition from a false smile of departure to a frown of displeasure. There was a chatter of farewells at his back but he didn't turn around to acknowledge any of it. He strode down the corridor, his boot-heels clacking on the marble floor. His bodyguards arranged themselves around him as they turned the corner.

Colonel Bim and Inspector Georgi emerged together. They shook hands with each other and with the judge. They smiled and put on their gloves, acting like two schoolboy rivals, each one afraid to turn his back on the other. They stepped out in opposite directions. An inconspicuous common soldier fell in behind Colonel Bim. Inspector Georgi was without an escort.

Karel's own boss, Lutesh, left Trevian's chambers. The door closed behind him. Karel stood up and watched his superior officer walk toward him. He couldn't tell much from the expression on Lutesh's face.

For all his unenthusiastic manner and apparent chronic boredom, Lutesh was a vigorous administrator and a working cop of formidable accomplishments. As he approached Karel, he toyed briefly with the idea of heading up the Horvath investigation personally. It would be good to be out in the field again. He often hungered for it and silently raged at being chained behind his desk. But he had a conscientious and skillful roster of investigators. They must have their chance for experience. The excellence they displayed as a group brought him valuable benefits. He was the head of homicide. There was no reason to believe that he could not one day be assistant chief of the entire force of Municipal Police. His wife's ambitions went even higher.

"We have the case," he said in his nasal voice. "It seems that Horvath was retired from the KOS. All those spy types wanted the case for one reason or another. Now we can get on with it. No one can fault us for having overstepped our authority even half an inch. But the interest these other services have displayed should be a warning to us."

"I understand," Karel said.

Lutesh smiled briefly, knowing that Karel did.

"Judge Trevian is the examining magistrate. That's good for us. He may want a good many reports but he's sure to back you up on any matter of search or disclosure you may request. Have you worked with him many times before?''

''A dozen perhaps.''

''This is different. It's a celebrity crime. At least it'll be considered so in those quarters I've mentioned.''

''I think that I'll know where to put my feet.''

''How will you proceed?''

''Horvath's wife first, of course. The old woman in the flat below. After that I'll interview Horvath's closest friends, the neighbors, and the tradesmen in the area where he may have transacted everyday business. Then there are the members of his many clubs. The newspaper printed quite a list. I'll pursue the members of the governing boards upon which Horvath might have sat before I try to question the membership. It might prove impossible to question the rank and file of every one of them.''

''Who do you want to help you on this one?''

''Samaja and Ulica,'' Karel said immediately. ''They can start on the neighbors and tradesmen.''

''Will they be enough?''

''At this stage we'll just be tossing our lines in anywhere. If the leads start piling up, then I'll have to look again.''

''Remember, I'm here to give you what you need,'' Lutesh said.

''I'll just follow the ripples Horvath's made in any ponds into which he's thrown a stone for a while,'' Karel said.

''You've heard some of the rumors, have you?''

''Oh, yes. They're making the rounds already. Horvath appears to have been a womanizer. He may have had a little more to do with the peddling of influence than a good Socialist should. There might even be matters of some smuggling or at least the import-export of goods not under license. The usual things that tattletales come up with when a man dies under violent or mysterious circumstances.''

''We hear them all,'' Lutesh agreed. ''But there's another rumor a little more dramatic than those.''

''Talk of vendetta, an affair of honor,'' Karel said. ''I've heard.''

''Do you know that eight out of ten murders in this country are still committed to settle old blood feuds?'' Lutesh said.

"I read the statistics but I wonder about them," Karel replied.

"Even so, it's a thought."

"I think I'll look first for an unhappy woman," Karel said.

"There are always a good deal of those," Lutesh replied. Then he smiled. "Win this one for us, and I'll do a favor for you. Anything within reason."

"A trip to Rome for the International Police Congress?"

Lutesh grinned broadly and slapped Karel on the back.

Karel went at once to the morgue. Samuel had performed a complete autopsy on the murdered man. There was nothing illuminating to be learned from it.

"When a man's brains have been splattered all over the pavement," Samuel said, "one can be reasonably sure he didn't die of poison. Still we are conscientious here in no-man's-land. The subject was a man in reasonably vigorous health, in the last half of his fiftieth decade. Some evidence of high blood pressure . . . which has now been relieved."

Samuel laughed but Karel didn't. Not only was he sick and tired of Samuel's pretensions to deductive excellence, but of his execrable sense of humor as well. He shifted his weight from one foot to the other, demonstrating his irritation and boredom.

"So, all right, I've got nothing new," Samuel said flatly. "The man was shot in the head and instantly died of it."

"Did his body have any scars?"

"An appendectomy, clumsily done. He'd been wounded. More than once. A bullet in the thigh and shrapnel in the ass."

At the property office Karel found nothing of interest among Horvath's effects. He took away the ring of keys and the address book. It was nearly brand new, the names, addresses, and telephone numbers penned in with the neatness that always starts a new directory but rarely ends it.

= 3 =

Karel wished his wife, Dika, would serve his dinner to him in the dining room. He'd often asked her to do so. For two or three meals they'd eat together at the blond Danish table of the set that had cost him three months' wages, using proper linen to wipe their mouths. Very soon she'd revert to serving the big meal of the day at the kitchen table, a rude affair of pine covered with a cloth of plastic-coated paper. He was forced to take his meal in sight of the sink, the cooker, and the hot water heater.

Sometimes he silently scolded her for returning him to the ways of his peasant roots. It only needed pigs and goats warming the house with their body heat to complete the picture, he told himself with bitter exaggeration. Of all the rewards his efforts had earned for them, the apartment that boasted four rooms and a bath seemed to him the clearest evidence of his success. Her reluctance to use the dining room diminished his accomplishment. He never scolded her aloud. It did no good, and only punished her for crimes he felt he'd committed, and was continuing to commit, against her.

When they'd been young, living on adjoining small holdings in the farmlands south of the Sava twenty-five miles from Banja Luka, a city often visited by earthquake, neither had harbored any ambitions beyond earning their daily bread, and one day raising a brood of children who would till the soil and keep the domestic beasts as their families had done for generations. He caught the thought. How could he know it to be true? Those expectations had been bred in the bone and fiber of his mother

19

and father, and Dika's mother and father. They'd had the centuries to instruct them. They'd planted the traditions in the heads of their children in turn when they were very small. But the war, the end of the monarchy, the entire disruption of the society had changed all that. A child no longer was born with its feet rooted in the earth like a tree or a stalk of wheat. Michael might have been born in that way but time had changed him, his parents' hopes for him, and his ambitions for himself. Not in a moment but in time.

Between the ages of ten and fourteen, Michael Karel had been given four years of schooling in the village. He was home during the seasons of planting and harvest. There was work to be done. It was so old a tradition in the villages that the schoolmasters and mistresses didn't even bother recording the absences. It was a matter of pride for Karel's father to say that his son was learning to read and write and add up sums. He didn't scorn such skills. He didn't believe that the farms would be nurtured by muscles and sweat alone. The new farmer would need to use his head. But when the government ordered that all children past the age of seven should be given at least eight years of schooling, he took Michael out of school altogether.

The peasants resisted the collectivization of the farms. By 1950 only sixteen per cent of the arable land in the province had been gathered into state farms or collectives. The farmers refused the attraction of pooling their cash resources to buy expensive tractors and harvesters. They saw the indebtedness created by the purchase of such machines as a subtle means for the government to win its way with them. But Michael's father also saw the machines moving across the fields in long powerful ranks, chewing up the farmers who resisted their benefits. In 1953 he apprenticed Michael to a blacksmith-mechanic and sent him to live in Sokolac a hundred and fifty miles away.

The main street of the county seat, Sokolac, was paved with stone. The roads bringing spruce logs from the forests were packed with wood chips so that the logs chained together behind horses and oxen wouldn't sink into the mud. There were hundreds of men and women laughing, cursing, and working to-

gether as equals. Some still carried the rifles and pistols they'd
used when they were Partisans and Chetniks fighting the Germans and each other. Those things were forgotten. They had a
new loyalty to the future. Michael had never before in his life
been so excited.

Mirka Vangel didn't look like a blacksmith. He had arms like
sticks and a chest one would expect to see on a consumptive.
His skin was very white but the smoke of the forge had tanned
his hands and arms brown up to the elbow. The soot had settled
in the creases of his neck and remained there as though they
were lines drawn with a pencil. He had small brown eyes like
olive pits. He laughed half the day and sang away the rest of it.
Apparently he pleasured himself and his wife a good deal of the
night. There were ten children and Dushanka was carrying
another in her belly.

Vangel embraced Michael when he walked through the door
out of the cold, and drew him toward the heat of the forge. He
knew Michael by the clothes he wore, Vangel said. By his
country clothes and his cleanliness.

"Thank God you've come," he said. "Dushanka is going to
have the child any day."

For a moment Michael wondered if Vangel thought he was a
visiting doctor or traveling male midwife.

"It would have made thirteen in the household," Vangel
continued. "Now that you've come we will only have to suffer
that danger a day or two, then we'll be fourteen. It's a bad year
when you have children and the household is thirteen. It takes
some time before it can be remedied. But now you're here."

By that Michael was made to understand that he was more
than an apprentice. He had been taken to Vangel's bosom as a
son. When he understood what was meant about thirteen he
volunteered to sleep in the forge until the baby was delivered.
Vangel wouldn't have it.

As it turned out, the fear of thirteen wasn't well founded
since the Vangel house was always crowded with half a dozen
members of his extended family, some introduced to Michael as
uncles and aunts, some as cousins, and some as brothers and
sisters.

That didn't necessarily mean that all were related. Michael

understood how a friend could be called a cousin, and a cousin a brother or sister. It was a tradition, for reasons both wise and practical, of the ancient tribes that had been nurtured on the farms and in the forests. So closely were families tied together in clans, and clans in tribes, and tribes in small nations of one people, that there had to be warnings that a danger of consanguinity might exist between two young people about to fall in love. Better safe than sorry. Bad blood too closely mingled made for idiots and defectives who would prove to be liabilities in the common struggle for survival. The custom had permeated the entire society, Michael thought, even in such a cosmopolitan melting pot as the county seat, where there was far less chance of cousin marrying cousin.

During the three years that he labored in Vangel's forge and improved his education in night school, he treated Vangel's daughters as sisters. He tried not to fall in love with one of them. Neither did he ever try to catch one in bed or behind the pile of scrap metal in the yard by the outhouse. Some of the family used the pile as a trysting place with girlfriends and boyfriends.

If Dika had been one of Vangel's daughters, would he have fallen in love with her? Karel mused. Surely not. His own determination not to betray Vangel's trust in him, or his status as a foster son among them, would have prevented it. If that were so, then what was the magic that formed between a certain man and a certain woman? It was called love and was more important, for a time at least, than anything else in the world. It was not some sweet madness but a careful recipe of wants, needs, and desires. The proper look at the proper time, the mouth that was available, the thighs that were ready to surrender, and the heart prepared to submit for matters of creature satisfaction, the cooling of the blood, the making of a nest, the creation of children, the preparation for age, and the unimagined death. The commitment was not a growing thing but a flash of lightning containing everything, the beginning, and the life, and the end.

One day a policeman in uniform came to the forge. He spoke to Michael and told him that Sokolac was growing into a small city. It needed more police. He wanted to offer Michael the chance to become a recruit and take three months' training. Michael wanted to know why they didn't enlist the men and women who had been fighters in the war, who were familiar with guns and had a liking for such things.

"Those are just the ones we don't want. The ones with experience at fighting and killing. If a drunk beats up another drunk we don't want some militiaman shooting them both down to keep the peace. If a man beats his wife because she's had it off with another man we don't want some policeman turning his back and telling him to beat her again. We're going to get these rifles and pistols off the streets. We don't want fighters doing it with gunfire."

Michael's father had financed his apprenticeship because he expected Michael would return and keep the machines they would need to make the farm flourish and succeed. He expected him to keep the books, and read the regulations, and resist collectivization by guile instead of dangerous stubbornness. Michael went home to confer with his father, who was a good man and wanted the best for his son. In the end it was agreed that Michael should join the police. His next oldest brother, Paul, came to the county seat and took up the hammer in Vangel's forge.

Michael no longer thought himself a son of the Vangel household. Dushanka suddenly became shy with him as though he were an honored, somewhat unwelcome, guest, and not the dirty blacksmith she'd seen naked in the tin bathtub a thousand times while she scrubbed his back as she scrubbed Mirka's back. Vangel cursed less around him. When they were in the tavern with the other men he waited for Michael to offer him a drink instead of humorously shaming him into buying a round for everyone. One night Michael asked Vangel if he no longer felt altogether comfortable with him.

"How can I say it? You're going to be a policeman. That's a good thing to be if one looks at it with this eye. Somebody has to keep the peace in a roistering place like this. Somebody has to look for the thieves and stop the murderers. But looking at it with this eye I see an enemy. It's always been that way with peasants and workers. Men in uniform are a danger to us even if we haven't done anything to worry about. It's in the bones I think. Old fears.''

''I understand. In my village it's the same.''

''So that's it, do you see?''

''Yes. I'll find another place to sleep. But will we be friends?''

''Cousins,'' Vangel assured him. He ordered Michael to buy a bottle. They took it into a quiet corner of the tavern and got drunk together. Vangel embraced Michael, and cried, and said how hard it was to lose a son.

It was viciously hard and lonely to live in the room Michael found underneath the eaves of a building that was a warehouse for the quantities of lumber that were required to build the growing city. Voles and rats nested in the timbers. He would listen to them scurrying about, playing with wood shavings or whatever it was they did to make so much skittering commotion. At such times he felt sorrier for himself than at other times.

He was very good at police work. He passed his training at the top of his class. Very early in his probationary period he was seen to have a gift for investigation. He was taken out of uniform after two years and made a detective in plain clothes. Everyone respected him. Even Vangel no longer seemed uncomfortable around him. He'd even given him information a time or two that led to the arrest of gangs of thieves that dealt in automobiles and metal parts. Michael was welcome at the Vangel dinner table and took some advantage of it. But he was very careful to wait for a specific invitation, though Dushanka insisted he was welcome at any time. He was very careful because he'd noticed how attractive Jasna Vangel had become, how grownup and full-breasted. He didn't want to resume his status as a Vangel son because he wanted very much to take Jasna behind the scrap pile and make love to her. He didn't think it would be dishonorable to do that to her without marriage as long as he could see himself a lover and not a brother. It was all up to him, in his head, and he would have to work at it.

It was a very hard game to play. He had to be just friendly enough toward her when in the company of any other members of the family for no one to suspect his feelings. Teasing would do his cause no good. Yet he had to take every opportunity he could get to touch her tenderly, to look into her eyes in a melting way, and to glance pointedly at her breasts while licking his lips. He knew she was a modern girl and no longer a virgin. She would know what all his actions meant, but like any other girl would demand a certain amount of flattery before surrendering herself to him. If she found him attractive. Sometimes in the night, lying on his cot under the slanting roof, listening to the small animals playing and making love in the piles of wood, he frightened himself with the thought that she would refuse him after he'd spent so much time and effort on her seduction. At twenty-two, Michael was ashamed to admit, even to himself, that he'd never had a woman. By any measure, old-fashioned or modern, that made him a very backward fellow.

It was Jasna who settled things and took the initiative. Following a meal, she simply asked him to come out in back with her to get some wood for the stove. She was afraid, she said, of the lizards and spiders that inhabited the pile and stalked around at night. When they were outside the kitchen door, she took his hand in hers and pulled him bodily toward the mountain of rusting scrap. She made a nest of leaves and rags as efficiently as though she were making a bed, then turned to him with her hands already at the buttons of her blouse and said, "I can't bear to see you suffer anymore."

She removed her blouse and pulled her shift up out of the waistband of her skirt so that she could remove it and expose her breasts. They were soft and large and sagged more than Michael thought a young woman's breasts should sag, no matter how heavy. He'd had dreams of snowy mounds topped with strawberries standing straight out like soldiers at attention. Her nipples were tan and had aureoles as large as saucers all around them.

He started to undo his shirt.

"No, no," she said. "Just take off your boots and trousers. Leave your shirt on. The less we have to put back on in a hurry the better."

"You don't think anyone will come?" he said fearfully.

"The children like to have a look and sometimes make fun.

It's just their way. But it's late and I don't think more than one at a time can make the excuse that they have to use the toilet behind the forge.''

She lifted up her skirt and quickly removed her cotton panties. She caught up the hem of her skirt and folded it upon itself so that it stayed bunched up around her waist and exposed her lower body to him. He knew what a woman's pubic triangle looked like, of course. How else could it have been in a crowded household where everyone took their baths in the middle of the kitchen near the fire? But he'd never really *looked* at one before. In the moonlight he couldn't tell if the hair of her muff was as fair as that on her head. It looked much darker, tinged with blue.

"Well, get on with it,'' she said. "Take off your underpants, too, if you like.''

He stared at her legs. They seemed washed with paler blue. She had her boots on. They looked like blocks of wood at the end of her slender ankles. Her shin bones were sharp and shiny. Her knees were round and bony. Her thighs were full.

She reached out and took his erection in her hand. The flesh of her palm felt rough and callused. "My God, you've got a weapon there, haven't you?'' She laughed easily. It was a rude sound. "Come on.''

He felt foolish as she tugged at him but he couldn't resist the pull of her hand. He put his arms around her and drew her close to him. When he kissed her on the neck she shuddered. Then he ran his mouth down to her breast and tongued her nipple.

"That's very nice,'' she said, "but we haven't got too much time for romance.''

He thrust his hand between her legs. The lips were swollen. A heavy smell rose up as though he'd pierced a ripe fruit that had already gone slightly sour.

"Put it in, for God's sake. Don't you know how to use your pistol?''

He was so awkward about it, and so quick to ejaculate, that she would have had to be a woman who thought herself irresistible to men, or a fool, not to know that she was Michael's first. She tried to hold his penis in her as it grew soft. She clutched him to her and thrust her tongue into his ear. She whispered into it, her breath cooling her spit.

"Am I the first? I can't believe it. Am I the first?"

Some instinct told Karel it would be worth the loss of pride to admit the truth. He nodded his head. She moaned and tore his shirt from him. She ran her tongue and lips all over his chest and belly. She took him into her mouth and made him hard again, trying to ruin him for any other woman he would ever know after her. Putting her mark on him in the name of some ancient rite she didn't even understand. The second time he penetrated her, he was far longer at it than the first.

When they were done he held her and whispered into her ear, "Marry me. Marry me."

She caught her breath. Then she laughed harshly and said, "You are such a fool, such a fool."

They did it every chance they got after that. But one night she told him she was doing it with his brother as well and that they'd better not mix Michael's seed with his brother's since she planned to marry Paul.

"But he's like your own family," Michael said. "He lives with you."

"Why do you think my father takes in apprentices?" she said. "What better way to test the nature of a son-in-law?"

Michael went back with them when Paul took Jasna home to have his family meet the girl he intended to marry. It was then that Karel noticed that Dika Donker, one of the daughters of the farmer on the next holding, had grown pretty and of age, even if she did have a funny name.

As it happened, all four got married together in the county offices. Jasna looked at Michael mischievously as she repeated the vows the county clerk recited. Michael wondered what his brother was getting himself into. Then he looked at Dika and wondered the same thing for himself.

He was given a small flat in a block of apartments constructed by the state for the housing of married police, firemen, and other county employees. It was on the ground floor. Dika had the privilege of keeping a small garden along the back wall. The building's incinerator was erected in one corner and a concrete pad accommodated the garbage bins. The flowers and vegetables planted closest to it received the heat of the fire that burned in it three times a week. They grew larger and more abundantly than those in the rest of the plot.

Dika worked hard in the garden and the house. The garden was without weeds or insects, the house was spotless. Envious neighbor-women slyly told her that a person could eat off her floors. They said they never saw a man's shirts hanging on the line so white on washday. She must boil them for hours. They were so nicely starched and ironed. But why did she starch his underwear? Why iron the sheets that would only become creased again after one using?

Michael worked hard and quietly at his job. Sometimes he'd come home and tell Dika about a case of murder. Even if he didn't describe the scene, Dika winced and hid her face in her hands. It wasn't long before Karel stopped telling her about his work. He felt it was just as well. Why should he bring such horrors home and put them on the kitchen table? But he found there wasn't much else to talk about with his wife. She wasn't one to gossip about the neighbors. There was just so much to be said of gardening and what might be happening back on the farm.

"They'll be sitting in the yard cutting up seed potatoes," she'd say. " 'One eye to a piece or the vines will fight,' my mother always warned us. It was such a sociable thing to do, cutting up the potatoes for the planting."

After it was dark they listened to the radio for a while and then were soon to bed. They sometimes made love, quietly and without invention. Dika treated the act warily, with a delicacy one didn't expect from a farm girl who knew what it was all about from watching the animals. She would never allow Michael to see her totally naked. If he was kissing her breasts she held her nightgown at her waist. If he mounted her she put the straps of the gown back over her shoulders and pulled the skirt up around her belly. When she embraced him her hands seemed to ride upon his back as though afraid to exert any pressure that might urge him on to greater vigor. In the first three years of their marriage she became pregnant three times but lost the fetuses each time within six weeks. After each miscarriage she made it clear in her quiet way that Michael's attentions were not wanted. The abstinence lasted as long as seven months. Michael sometimes went to a house near the freight yards where six women tried to satisfy the needs of the men who swarmed through the frontier town. There were many more women in the taverns and saloons but Michael feared to deal with them. It was too public an indiscretion.

In the fourth year Dika carried a child to term. The infant was delivered dead. Dika, wide-eyed, pale, and sleepless, hugged her thin arms around herself for two weeks. She wouldn't speak to Michael. She wouldn't look at him. He bought her a stuffed doll and placed it in her arms. She finally wept. Then she put the doll underneath the blanket, its head on the pillow, and lay down with her own head next to it.

When he took her home she sat in the window looking out into the garden that was all gone to weeds, rocking the doll in her lap. One day she put the doll in the corner on a little chair big enough for a child. She went out to plow up the garden and start again.

Michael worked long shifts. When he wasn't at work he had his nose in a book or took classes at the police academy. He became chief of detectives. There were only three of them but Sokolac was growing and the police force was growing with it. One day he could hope to be the head of a large division, perhaps even assistant chief of the organization.

Someone killed a man who traveled in hardware with one of the man's own nails. There wasn't much doubt about who did the job. A carpenter named Sendar had apparently taken a nail that was nearly as long as a spike and driven it through the man's skull. But first he drove it through the hand of his naked wife. When the police came she was lying on her belly on the bed, screaming wildly, her arm stretched out as far as it would go, her hand nailed to the dead man's head. There was a tool with an axe blade on one side and a hammer on the other lying on the floor. The carpenter was standing in the corner of the bedroom with tears running down his cheeks, his arms pinioned to his sides by two husky uniformed policemen.

Michael walked over to the three of them after first glancing at the scene on the bed.

"What are you doing?" he asked the officers. "Are you crazy? Why haven't you released that woman's hand? Why haven't you pulled out the nail?"

The older policeman said, "We didn't know if we should tamper with the evidence or not."

"Evidence? The man is clearly dead and the woman going mad. Let go his arm. Go over there and pull out the nail."

The officer looked shamed and bewildered.

"I have no tools," he said.

"Is this the house of a carpenter? There should be plenty of tools. Look on the floor just inside the door."

When the policeman let go the carpenter's arm to do as told, the carpenter lurched forward. Michael placed his palm flat on the man's chest.

"No," he said softly. "Take it easy. Stay where you are."

"She needs me," the carpenter declared.

"What will you do? Drag at her? If you try to embrace her you'll only cause her more pain." He looked at the second officer. "Did anyone send for a doctor?"

"Yes, sir. A boy was told to run and fetch him."

The doctor and the older policeman, holding a claw bar and some blocks of wood in his hands, came through the door together just then. They went to the bed and looked at the problem. The doctor placed his hand gently over the woman's eyes and she suddenly stopped screaming. She moaned like a dog instead. Michael and the carpenter watched as the policeman built a little bridge out of the wooden blocks around the woman's hand and the man's head. He set the claw under the head of the nail and pulled it out. The woman screamed and fainted.

"That's good," the doctor said.

Michael nodded to the older policeman, who wrapped the naked woman in the blanket and moved her to a chair beside a window which was filled with the faces of curious neighbors. The doctor asked for a basin of water and some clean rags. Michael took his hand away from the carpenter's chest and told him to go gently.

The carpenter went to his knees beside his wife and awkwardly cradled her as the doctor cleansed and bandaged her hand. When the woman woke up for a moment, the carpenter kissed her on the cheek.

It turned out not to be as simple as it had seemed at first glance. The carpenter, Sendar, said he'd come home to find his wife pinned to the man and could not be shaken from the story. A man named Lutesh came up from Belgrade. He was an officer in the Metropolitan Police there. He'd been sent because the dead man, the salesman of hardware, tacks, and nails, had been an important Communist, a hero of the war. People in high places wanted to be sure he got a fair shake.

"What is a fair shake?" Michael asked the city cop, who seemed bored with the whole affair. "This fellow came to our provincial town and seduced a simple man's wife. We're not sophisticates here."

"What's that supposed to mean?" Lutesh said dryly.

"She was easy prey."

Lutesh made a face meant to say that Michael was being silly. "Are you saying the city slicker assaulted the chastity of an innocent angel? Even if that were true, it provides no excuse for murder."

"Honor is the best excuse."

"That's no way for a policeman to talk. That's just foolishness. Do you condone what this carpenter did?"

"He says he didn't do it. He says he came home and found her screaming."

"Let's go and talk to him together," Lutesh suggested.

Sendar stuck to his story through all the clever questioning by the city detective. He said he loved his wife. He knew she went to bed with other men.

"But you'd finally had enough of that, hadn't you?" Lutesh said. "Finally got tired of having her pin the horns on you."

"Do you think I killed the man because of my honor?" Sendar said.

"Didn't you?"

"I would have killed *her* if that was the case."

"It looks like you've driven her mad. That's what you've served her with for sleeping around on you behind your back," Lutesh said flatly.

"Ah, no," the carpenter said, half weeping and half laughing. "She was half my age. What could a reasonable man expect?"

Lutesh and Michael left the carpenter in his cell still unconfessed.

"It would be easier if he'd admit the crime, but he'll hang for it all the same," Lutesh remarked. "He was apprehended at the scene. It was his axe that was used to hammer in the nail."

"That's just the point, isn't it?" Michael said. "The tool that was used."

"What do you mean?"

"The wrong tool. Not the sort of thing a carpenter would do. He says he always left that axe behind and never carried it on the job. I believe him. If he'd come home, caught them at it, and decided to drive the nail into them, he'd have taken the right tool from his kit for the job. He would have instinctively picked up a proper hammer for driving nails."

"If there was someone else who did the nailing and the killing, where's he gone? Why hasn't someone come forward and accused him? Those crowded yards and streets certainly don't lack for witnesses," Lutesh said.

"They don't trust you," Michael said. "You're the police-man from the city. They take a good deal of pride in taking care of their own problems and cleaning up their own messes."

"If that's the truth what can we do about it?"

"Well, we could go around and ask a lot of questions about this hardware salesman. We could get a lot of evasive answers and walk into a lot of walls."

"Won't they talk to you about it?"

"Not now that they've seen me with you. I don't think they will."

"What's to be done, then?"

"Nothing. In a day or two someone will be killed. Someone who knew the hardware salesman. Someone who'd slept with the carpenter's wife as well."

Later on, after Lutesh had gone back to the city, Michael went on with a quiet investigation. Things happened just as he predicted they would. A man named Petar was found stabbed to death in an alley alongside a tavern where the salesman had sometimes gone to drink. Petar had been the last of the lovers of the carpenter's wife. The last but one when the salesman was counted. But Petar hadn't killed the salesman for stealing into her bed. He'd killed him because the salesman had cheated him at cards. He probably meant to drive the axe into the salesman's head. Why he finally did what he did was something Michael could only guess at. A mad notion perhaps. Outraged jealousy. He might have felt himself dishonored by her infidelity to him.

Lutesh had been much impressed by Michael's handling of the affair. When asked by his superior for recommendations when a replacement to the homicide squad was needed, he named Michael Karel. The transfer was arranged. Neither man was sorry for it. They liked and respected each other. Karel knew that as Lutesh climbed the ranks he'd make certain that Karel climbed right behind him.

Only Dika had been the loser. The move to Belgrade was the worst thing in her life. Except for the terrible loss of the child. Karel tried never to think of that.

When had Dika stopped being pretty? Had it been when they'd made the first move off the land? Had it been when they'd moved to this apartment in the city, taking her away from her miserable little vegetable patch in Sokolac which she'd tended as lovingly as old grandmothers tended the altars in the churches? Certainly the last of her beauty had fled when she awakened in the hospital bed aware, even before she was told, that the product of her labor had been born without life or breath. That was when the light had gone out of her eyes. Though they'd always been wondering and sad, they had at least had some brilliance.

The meals she set before him were good enough. Simple fare. Strongly flavored beet and cabbage soup, black bread and fresh butter, and perhaps a breaded cutlet of veal or piece of beefsteak. She always served him first and watched him as he ate, while her own small bowl of soup grew cold.

Sometimes she made a hard effort to engage him in conversation. But she soon lost interest. Sometimes they discussed a movie they'd seen together. Once he got her to pretend that they would go to America on a visit one day to see what Hollywood was really like underneath the paint.

"It will be like a trashy woman," Dika said.

"But exciting all the same."

"Then it's trashy women that stir your blood, is it?"

"The only thing that stirs me more is a farm girl who knows her way around the barnyard and the hayloft."

He tried to make her laugh and pulled her down on his lap. He fondled her breasts. She angrily forced his hand away. That afternoon had occurred long ago.

Dika looked at Karel as he silently ate his meal. He wished that she would at least serve the big meal of the day in the dining room.

He wiped his mouth with his handkerchief and told her that he might not be home until very late. The murder of a very important man had been made his responsibility. There was no telling where it might lead. He was due for promotion to inspector soon and this could make the difference.

She said nothing. She merely looked at him. His ambitions were not hers. She took no pride in a husband who dealt with the dead and those who had violently torn their lives from them. She only dreamed of some injury happening to him. A gunshot wound. Not enough to kill or cripple, but enough to take him away from his profession and return him to the farm with a pension to make them secure as they grew old. It wouldn't take very much. Two aging people without children or grandchildren didn't need much to live well on a farm.

For no reason that he could explain Karel bent over and kissed Dika on the top of her dull, lifeless hair. It had been as yellow as butter once upon a time, he thought. Not only had she lost her prettiness but her youth as well. She was only thirty-one, yet she'd gone from youth to old age in one long tragic step. As his lips touched her hair he felt as he did when he kissed the head of his old mother after a visit home.

= 4 =

Karel took Rajco Ulica along with him to the apartment house. The detective was to question the old woman, Madame Andric, while Karel questioned Horvath's widow.

Hanna Horvath's physical presence was disturbing to Karel. When seen in the window, he'd read her posture as one of stiff and unyielding satisfaction. Now she seemed soft, her thighs and breasts full, the dip in the valley at the bottom of her belly, where the material of her skirt clung, ripe and inviting. From the moment that she'd opened the door to his summons, a little Pomeranian dog in her arms, she'd managed to flaunt herself in subtle ways.

"Will you have a drink, Sergeant Karel?"

"No thank you. Not while on duty."

"I've heard that often said in American films. I didn't know that it was really true."

"It is."

"Will you sit down, Sergeant Karel? Over here. The couch is more comfortable than the chair. Here, let me fix a pillow for your back."

"Mrs. Horvath, I regret that I have to make inquiries so soon after the death of your husband."

"It's good of you to be careful of my feelings but I understand it's something that must be done."

She sat down in the expensive overstuffed chair opposite him in such a way that her skirts revealed more of her legs than might be thought proper in any woman so newly met, let alone a wife so recently widowed. She held the dog on her lap.

Karel was unsure of his ground with her. He'd witnessed many times before, in women newly bereaved, the oddity of

35

behavior she was now displaying. The loss did something to their equilibrium, knocking their behavior askew. Some of the most respectable, against their own natures, suddenly began acting like sluts. Even as they awkwardly tried to be seductive, their eyes displayed their own dismay at what they were doing. Women were not alone in such anomalous behavior. Karel knew of cases where men forceably raped their sisters-in-law or cousins practically on the coffins of their own dead wives.

He still felt certain that he'd read the attitude of her body rightly when he'd seen her standing in the window early in the morning. But that could simply mean that she was carrying an extra burden of guilt and remorse with her now. Having been momentarily pleased at the death of a husband who'd wronged her in some way, she now found herself acting as though she were immoral, even evil.

"Fire away," she said. "They say that in the cinema, too. Fire away."

"Your husband was retired?"

"From the KOS, yes."

"But not retired altogether?"

"He was a vigorous man," she said with a certain bitter emphasis. "Not the sort who could be expected to lie back and do nothing. He would lie back, of course, but he would not do nothing."

"I beg your pardon."

"He pursued small business interests," she said.

"What did they entail?"

She shrugged and placed her hand flat against the swell of her bosom, inside the bodice of her soft woolen dress. She made the self-comforting gesture somehow provocative.

"Small matters of import and export."

She smiled. There was a stain of fresh lipstick on a tooth. It made her smile sexually provocative. The quality of wantonness about her was heightened by a certain look of sleepy slovenliness, of sensual disarray.

Karel reached into his pocket and pulled out a notebook. Hannah Horvath put the dog on the rug.

"Wait a moment," she said, leaving the chair and walking across the living room to a beautiful secretary desk standing against the wall. She opened the desktop and took something from one of the many pigeonholes. Returning with it, she sat down again and handed a small red book of imitation leather to Karel. It was stamped on the cover with a picture of a clump of trees, a souvenir of the forest park beyond the city where tourists went to marvel at the smell of pine, and locals went to picnic and make love on beds of needles.

"Open it," she said.

Karel did so. There was a tiny ballpoint pen tucked into a loop of the same plastic material.

"Clever isn't it?" she said. "Who would believe that the sale of such things as that could buy this sort of living."

"You don't believe that this luxury was purchased on the sale of such trivialities as this?" Karel said.

"I don't think about it. Can you understand that I don't even think about it? I'm a good wife." She made a small choking sound like a hiccup and corrected herself in mid-career. "I *was* a good wife. For twenty years I was a good, dutiful, patient, loving wife. I never asked questions. I admired my husband, and I loved him in every way I knew to do. And I never interfered in his private life."

She was on the edge of emotional disaster. The flood she'd held back all day, the real rage of loss, the guilty grief, was about to burst the dam and come flooding out in all its terrible manifestations and contradictions. She stared at Karel as though believing she'd already given too much of her shame away.

Karel lowered his head to the notebook so that she wouldn't be encouraged, by any compassion there might be in his eyes, to give way altogether. He tried to make a notation in the book. The shoddy little novelty didn't work.

"Doesn't your pen work?" she said in a certain tone of voice. Karel looked up. She was smiling seductively again, her tongue wetting her lips. Her eyes fell to his crotch. She was back inside her feminine fear of abandonment again. He was a male. If she gave enough of herself maybe he would protect her now that she was alone. It was understandably irrational.

Her innuendos and brazen manner made Karel nervous. Excited, too. How could he be unaware of the powerful promise that she offered in every gesture, in her very tone of voice, even though he knew it was the product of her unreasoning immediate terror? He laughed without the panache he would have wished. He plucked his own pen from his breast pocket. He made a useless note.

"I would like to have your permission to go through your husband's documents. Birth certificate, citations, awards, honors, bank records. That sort of thing."

"He didn't keep any papers here."

"Not that you know of."

"Well," she said, with a sarcastic twist of her mouth, "I would know that sort of thing, wouldn't I? After all I've been his wife for twenty years."

"Yes," Karel said flatly.

"I know what you're thinking," she said. "You're thinking that a wife doesn't really know everything there is to know about her husband. Perhaps a wife doesn't know very much at all."

"The same thing might be said about any husband," Karel said soothingly.

"I never did anything for which Jan might reproach me," she said, leaning forward in her chair, showing her bosom to Karel, unaware of it this time. "He couldn't say the same thing to me."

They sat there staring at each other like enemies.

"Well, what have you heard?" she demanded. "Who was he running around with?"

She wanted the name of a mistress so that she could focus her hate. If there was a woman, then she wanted a woman with a name so that her husband's betrayal would become real, brutal enough to excuse her anger at him for getting himself murdered and leaving her alone.

"Are you saying that you suspect that there is, at the moment, a special woman with whom your husband was involved?"

"You might ask the girl that works in his office. She's pretty enough in a trashy way. You can be sure he's been having it off with her. But as to a mistress with some excellence, I doubt if he'd been up to that lately."

"Then he was in the habit of keeping mistresses?" Karel said with deliberate bluntness.

She jerked her head sharply as though he'd physically struck her. A pin in her coiffure gave way and her heavy hair fell over her eye. She looked like a drunken woman all at once.

"A rejected mistress can be dangerous," Karel said.

"Are you suggesting that a jilted lady blew his brains out?"

"Or a husband. A boyfriend. Some man who may have felt his family name had been damaged."

"An affair of honor?"

"Yes."

"I don't think so. I don't think the bitches he chose to play with were the sort that were overwhelmed by passion for him. He wasn't the kind to inspire a woman to such risks and sacrifices. He picked foreigners who would be impressed by the influential people he knew. He courted shopgirls and secretaries who would consider themselves lucky to get an expensive dinner or some simple favor his connections could provide. He sometimes bedded married women, but only those whose husbands were glad to see them otherwise occupied so they could have their nights to themselves."

Her words had the sting of acid and the stink of hate. The poison came pouring out and Karel listened like a scavenger waiting patiently for a worthwhile scrap of meat.

When she was exhausted he said, "May I have the address of your husband's office?"

"It's stamped on the back," she said.

He read the imprint. "Hogamann is your husband's partner in this enterprise?"

"That's right. Denis Hogamann. Birds of a feather."

"Oh?"

"He chased women even harder than my husband did. He wasn't as good at it."

"How do you know this?"

"Because he tried to take me to bed. I turned him down. Of course, I would have turned him down even if I'd wanted another man. Hogamann is peculiarly unattractive."

"Were your husband and Hogamann cordial? Could there have been business rivalries and disputes?"

Hannah Horvath shrugged. She was worn out from the fierce struggle that had been fought inside her breast. She wanted nothing more than for Karel to leave her alone so she could sleep. The little dog whined, sensing her distress.

"Do you have a wedding certificate?"

She shook her head from side to side, not caring that her hair was loose and flying all about. "I told you I don't know where Jan kept our documents."

"I asked because the wife usually keeps the marriage certificate and the birth certificates of children, if any."

"We had no children," Hannah Horvath said, as though that were the question Karel asked.

"Where was your husband born?"

"In Zagreb."

"Did he go to school there?"

"School? I don't know. He never said."

"He never spoke of his childhood?"

"Never."

"But he was a native Croatian?" Karel said.

"Apparently."

"Do you know if, during the war, his sympathies were with the Ustasi?"

Her eyes sparkled with fear and panic. "Jesus, you're not going to try and put that mark on him, are you? You're not going to try and dig up something like that, are you?"

"I just want to know what was true. Did he support the Croatian Nationalists?"

"If you pin that on him—if you try to make it out that someone shot him down because of some old hatred festering since the war—the stain will be on me as well. Don't you see that? The Ozna will start looking me over and they'll never stop."

She writhed around in her agitation, causing her skirts to ride even higher on her legs. He could see the pink of her underwear. She clutched at her breast beneath the bodice of her dress.

"I'm a Serbian. I have no politics. I can prove that," she said. "My husband was a good Communist. He fought with the Partisans . . ."

"When?"

"What do you mean?"

"Was he with them from the beginning?"

"I don't know what you mean," she said.

"There were a good many who were first for the Chetniks or the Ustasi, and only with the Partisans at the end, when it

looked like they would come out on top. He may have betrayed
a lot of people along the way if he was a man to put on another
coat when the weather changed."

She stared at him as though he were accusing her of something.

"Your husband had been wounded?" he quickly asked.

"Yes."

"In the war?"

"Once in the war. He was struck by shrapnel in a battle
between the Partisans and Chetniks." There, she seemed to say,
he fought the Chetniks. How could he ever have been one of
them. "It was a battle fought at the River Drina," she elabo-
rated, adding credibility to her story.

Karel couldn't make up his mind if it was a lie or a genuine
memory suddenly recalled.

"And the other?" he said. "The bullet wound?"

"A hunting accident in Austria."

Karel put away the red plastic book and his pen, and stood up.

"Why did you remain with him?" he asked.

"I have expensive tastes, as you can see."

"Was that enough?"

"I knew him when he was younger. A young officer."

"When did you meet?"

"In nineteen fifty-two. In the summer."

"How old were you that year?"

"I was twenty-two. Can you believe it? I was beautiful and
twenty-two."

"And Horvath?"

She shrugged. "What do I know? I never knew my husband's
age. He told me he was thirty-three. I was sure he was older.
Vanity. What does it matter?" She preceded him to the door,
displaying her hips to him in a swaying, inviting walk one last
time. "I suppose . . ." she began, but then thought better of
whatever it was she meant to say. She used the door the way an
exotic dancer would use a theater curtain to half-conceal her
nakedness, looking at Karel and smiling.

"You're married, are you?" she said.

Karel felt that he had to save her pride. She was good-looking
but alone, scarcely in control, and very much afraid.

"Yes, I'm married," he said. "Happily."

= 5 =

Karel had been faithful to Dika for nearly all their years together. Even after renewed overtures following the death of the infant, and the abstinence that followed, were met with mere obedience and toleration. It had shamed him to suffer the appetites of the flesh and long for the release of sex. He'd been made to feel, by Dika's eloquent silence, the stiffening of her sinews, the inflexibility of her limbs, that his touch was a greedy and inconsiderate act of lust, and not an act of tenderness. He'd felt dirty because she'd made him feel as though he soiled her with an act that had never been meant for pleasure but only for procreation. The doctors had said that there would never be a chance of pregnancy again. The ruinous birth of the dead child had decided that. But had she really wanted him to live with her more as brother or friend than loving husband? Had he perhaps done something wrong when he'd tried to seduce her that first night, after months of waiting, as she lay on her back in the summer heat in her cotton nightdress? Had he been too urgent in his need for her? Had she sensed that his need was not so much for her but for any female body? When he'd tried to rouse her with techniques he'd never attempted before, had she been dismayed, shocked, even disgusted? Did she think herself a whore because she'd momentarily allowed herself to catch fire?

The harshest memory of that occasion, and the few that followed, had been the sight of her tears running out of her cowlike eyes across her broad cheeks, the touch of her cold hands and feet, and her stiff limbs clasping him weakly to her.

He'd become celibate in his body, then in his mind and heart, and finally in his spirit, until he chanced to meet Marta Barkai. She was a Jewess with the hot eyes of a desert princess and a fleshy pair of lips that hinted at Moorish blood. What was the day? He couldn't remember, and wondered why he should not remember a day so vitally beneficial to him. Was it because a day of such importance stands astride the normal passage of time so that one end of it is planted in inevitability and the other in magic? It seemed that meeting her was such an act of fate that, afterward, it was as if he'd known her forever. The moment that he'd first seen her was only the moment that he recognized the face of the infatuating creature that had always been waiting in the shadows of his mind.

Was it only her willingness to follow and sometimes lead him along pathways of the most outrageous sexual adventure? There was something in her erotic manner that challenged him to create designs he never thought were possible to his imagination. There was something in her straightforward pride in having him as a lover that flattered him immensely. She fondled his chest and arms, and stared into his eyes, as though assessing the value of a prize she'd won. She was naked in her pleasure for him, without shame. Her generosity with her emotions was unlike the secret, brooding miserliness he'd been taught were the foremost qualities of the Jew. It was well known that they gave their passion only to others of their kind. If they seemed to love otherwise it was all a pretense and a manipulation designed for profit. Yet he knew best and most vividly the feeling she gave him that he was mighty in sex and that she loved him.

Could it be her intelligence and wit that attracted him as much as the other? Having so little of his own, real education fascinated him, though he never completely trusted anyone who had too much of it. Marta had a degree. She did important work as a civilian employee of the KOS. Her security clearance was very high. Yet she was called a secretary, treated like a menial, and watched very closely. She was not allowed to emigrate or even to take a holiday abroad.

Minorities were guaranteed equality before the law. It forbade the "propagation of national, racial, and religious hatred and discord." The Constitution of 1946 said this. According to the census of 1931 there were about sixty-eight thousand Jews in Yugoslavia. After many were killed by the Nazis and Croatian Ustasi during the war, there were fifteen thousand left. Half went to Israel. Of the nine or ten thousand Jews living in Yugoslavia in 1970, most resided in the city. Even so thinly spread they felt the bitterness of anti-Semitism.

Sometimes Marta worked herself up into a rage about it. Sometimes she cried.

When Marta opened the door to him just after dark, she'd had scarcely time enough to remove her coat. She still wore her gloves. Karel's face was glowing from the cold. He looked like an apple-cheeked child. He embraced her even before greeting her, planting his cold mouth on hers and kicking the door shut with his heel. His ungloved fingers fumbled at the buttons of her sweater and blouse, the zipper of her skirt. He had trouble, as he always did, with the front closure of her brassiere. She feared he would tear it off. She protested laughingly as she backed off, lightly slapping his hands away as she unsnapped the clasp herself. Her eyes were filled with amused and excited wonder. He pursued her across the parlor to the couch. He threw off his overcoat and suit jacket, removed his tie, and practically tore the shirt from himself.

"Take that off," he said as he sat down on the floor. His eyes were on the small confining girdle she wore for extra warmth. He tore off his boots, unzipped and removed his trousers, lying on his back and kicking them off in a comic frenzy that excited her unduly. She removed the undergarment. He peeled off his shorts, then got to his knees. She started to unsnap the garters from the little belt that held her stockings.

"No, no, leave them on," he said. His voice emerged from his mouth as though his tongue had grown thick and clumsy. "Just the panties. Just take off the panties."

She obeyed. She stood in her stockings and black, short-heeled, strapped shoes. They were stained with the salt used to melt the snow on the footpaths. She still wore her gloves. She opened her legs to him as he crawled forward on his knees and buried his nose and mouth in her hair and flesh. He'd not removed his black socks.

They were like a couple in one of the dated pornographic

packets sold in the city at certain newspaper kiosks, old pictures
of sex performed by men and women long since dead. Amusing
photographs, one would think, that left most people with an odd
sense of sadness as though they had been secretly peeking at
lonely, needy creatures trying to find a measure of happiness, or
forgetfulness, in the vain pursuit of pleasures of the flesh. But
the suddenness of his assault, the sheer compliment implied in
his ravishing need of her body, thrilled Marta and filled her with
an exquisite turmoil. He brought her to climax with his mouth
and tongue within seconds. She stood there, knees slightly bent,
head thrown back, eyes closed, mouth opened wide, her hands
seeking to pull his head even closer to her. She shuddered until
she felt her legs letting go. She crumpled to the floor and lay
back with her knees thrust as wide as she could part them. She
groped for him and took his erection in her gloved hands. The
touch of leather sent a charge through him. She guided him into
her body. In a few moments he came as well.

They lay on the small daybed in the parlor, a light afghan
thrown over their nakedness against the chill that pervaded the
badly heated room. Her arms captured his head against her
breast. He touched the nipple of her breast with his tongue.

"Oh, my God, my peasant lover," she moaned. "You are
like a beast. Is that the way the bull takes the cow in the field?"

"That's the way it was done when the world was young," he
said, laughing softly. "Now the government technician comes
around and takes the semen from the bull and lines up the cows
and impregnates them with a syringe."

"How about the rooster with the hens?"

"He has a better time of it."

"My rooster," Marta said, hugging him violently.

She let him go.

"A cigarette," she said.

Karel scrambled out of the little nest they'd made and went to
get the packet of cigarettes and matches from the pocket of his
coat, an ashtray from the table beside the television set. His
body was white from the waist down, stained reddish-brown
above. The color given to his skin through the years of work in
the fields when he'd been a boy and youth would never go away
completely. She could see the chicken flesh the cold air raised

up on his thighs. She closed her eyes and imagined the smooth, evenly tanned, lightly oiled skin of young Israelis. Karel climbed back in beside her.

They lay back smoking, the ashtray lying on Marta's stomach.

"Now tell me what that was all about," she said.

"About my feelings for you. About the passion you arouse in me. About the desperation with which I love you," he said with such emphasis that while sounding like an outrageous burlesque of stage declarations, it possessed the power of truth.

"You might have seduced me more gently. You might have lifted me up and carried me to my nice bed with the new sheets you've bought me. You have no culture," she pouted.

"Culture is a trap," he said. He watched the smoke spiraling toward the ceiling. He thought about how contradictory his actions and feelings so often were. It was a common quality in people. The only sure thing about most individuals was that they could never be expected to do a certain thing in a certain way just because they'd done it that way a thousand times before. Their unpredictability was the only thing predictable about them. He shook his head, driving away the paradox. He was impatient with such thoughts that would insist upon rising in his brain at odd moments.

"What is it?" Marta said.

"I was thinking of the new case that's been put in my lap."

"What sort of case?"

"Murder. The murder of a man named Jan Horvath."

Her legs jerked slightly.

"You know him?"

"I read about it in the paper. Just the headline and the first few paragraphs."

"He worked for your organization."

"Some time ago, wasn't it?"

"He retired in nineteen sixty-five."

"A year before I went to work for them."

"You never met him?"

"I may have if he came back to visit any of his old friends. But the KOS isn't just one office. I don't even know where he may have worked. Inside or out. Here in Belgrade or in some other city. Even in some other country perhaps."

"Ah," Karel said thoughtfully.

"If that means you're thinking I might do a favor for you, put it out of your mind. Their files are sacred. I don't want any trouble."

"What do you take me for?" Karel protested.

"Is this an important case?" she asked after a while.

"It might be of the utmost importance to us."

She raised herself up on one elbow, the ashtray scattering its contents unheeded on the afghan which had fallen away to expose her naked breasts.

"In what way?" she asked, her voice sharply edged with excitement. "In what way valuable to us?"

Karel looked up at her face. All at once, it seemed less seductive than avaricious, the eyes narrowed, the full lips quivering as though prepared for battle. She was like an animal that sensed a victim, or a Jew ready to bargain. The thought came unbidden. He remembered his mother using the expression long ago when the Jewish peddlers came around twice a year with pots and pans and a thousand other things.

"How could it be useful to us?" she asked again, insisting with her staring eyes.

"I've been given the promise of Rome. An International Police Conference. That usually means the representative can take his wife."

"Do you mean it?"

"You could walk out of Yugoslavia on my arm," Karel said.

"Never to come back. Look, if there's any way I can help you on this case, short of breaking into confidential files, just tell me."

"No, no. It won't come to that. There was a small quarrel over jurisdiction in this case, and I don't suppose I can expect much cooperation from Borodin, or Colonel Bim, or Senior Investigator Georgi, but I expect I'll muddle through all the same."

= 6 =

Trevian liked Sergeant Michael Karel. He felt there was a great deal of simple honesty and honor in the man. He was a product of the farmlands. The land grew men who were sturdy, patient, and uncomplicated.

His nature was revealed in the way he stood on the rug in the hall, looking slightly shamefaced at the traces of snow melting off his boots, as though he were afraid of staining the rug although it was clearly put there for that very purpose. It was in the way he clutched his briefcase to his chest with both hands in a gesture that was respectful but also stubborn. It was in the simplicity of his apology for having arrived late for their first appointment.

"My fault. Entirely my fault," Trevian insisted. "We should have properly met in my chambers. Having you come to my home is an old man's indulgence."

"Still, I've interrupted your supper."

"Not interrupted, merely delayed," Trevian reassured him. "Nothing will be spoiled. When I'm alone, my supper is the lightest thing possible. A cup of soup with a cracker or two. Come into the library."

Karel followed the old aristocrat along the dark wood-paneled corridor to a room at the end of it. He noticed that Trevian wore simple carpet slippers. His gray sweater was threadbare and patched at the elbows. But the impression given was that the judge clung to the sweater because he had an affection for it and not because he couldn't afford a new one.

They'd worked together before. Karel knew that Trevian asked a thousand questions when he was assigned a case as the

48

examining magistrate. He also tended to digress and go off on speculative trails, as old men will do, eating up the minutes and hours. Karel never considered the questions intrusions on his job, or the digressions time wasted. He was very respectful. He always refused a glass twice before accepting it a third time. In his peasant way he understood the value of ritual between classes no matter what the Socialist theorists might say.

Trevian offered and Karel refused a brandy.

"How is your wife?" Trevian asked.

"Very well," Karel said.

"Dika. Is her name Dika?"

"Yes, sir."

"You'll please remember me to her?"

"She'll be pleased and flattered that you asked about her."

"She's a nice girl. A good woman," Trevian said with conviction, though he'd never met Dika. "A good wife?"

"Yes, a very good wife."

"Pretty."

Karel wished the old man would stop running on.

"Will you have a drink?" Trevian asked.

"No thank you, sir."

"Children?" Trevian said. "You have children?"

"Regrettably, no."

"Nor I."

The old man's eyes glazed over. He looked up at the mantel where the photograph of a little boy stood. He shook himself, reminding Karel of the shaggy dog dreaming beside a fire in the farmhouse of his youth. What had the dog's name been? Odd that he shouldn't be able to remember. He'd loved it well enough. It would come back to him. For a moment he thought that it might be nice for Dika if they got a dog. Perhaps a cat. At least some pet to help fill the empty pain she so transparently suffered. Karel became aware that Judge Trevian had addressed him.

"Sir?"

"Have I offered you a refreshment? Will you have one?"

"Thank you, yes."

Trevian poured two glasses of brandy. "What progress have you made?" he asked.

Karel picked up his bulky briefcase. The clasp fought with

him for a moment. Then he broke it loose. He felt embarrassed that the latch on his briefcase should be broken. He took out several thin files and was about to hand them over when Trevian raised a hand and smiled.

"No, no. My eyes are too old to read too much. Touch the high points for me as briefly as you can, will you?"

"In summary," Karel said, "I have so far interviewed Henick Ludu, the apartment house custodian—twice—Hannah Horvath, the murdered man's widow, and several other occupants of the dwelling. My associate has questioned one Madame Andric among several others."

"Yes, I know her," Trevian interrupted. "Many years ago, before the war, I owned a house on Prince Michael's Street."

"Ah," Karel said.

"It's of no importance," Trevian said, smiling at the memory. "Your associate questioned her?"

"And several others in the building. I single Madame Andric out because she'd been unable to sleep, and was sitting in the window around the time of the killing."

"What was her trouble? Why couldn't she sleep?" Trevian interrupted.

"She finds it frightening to lie down. A choking feeling rises in her chest."

"I had an aunt who complained of that," Trevian said. "Slept sitting up for twenty years. Tied her braids to the post on the chair for fear she'd slip down while sleeping and choke to death."

"Madame Andric may suffer the same distress. Something to do with congestion of the heart," Karel said. "Anyhow, she says she was awake and looking out the window on the morning of the murder."

"She saw it?"

"Unfortunately, no. It seems she got up to make herself a cup of tea. She thinks she may have heard the shot."

"Could she have done?"

"Perhaps. The chances are remote that she could hear anything behind closed windows that far away. The janitor claims not to have heard it, and he was in the courtyard."

"I don't suppose it matters. The time of the murder is sufficiently fixed, isn't it?"

"Yes, sir. There was no body when she left the window. When she returned with her tea, Horvath was lying there."

"Did she see anyone else in the area?"

"She's not certain how many people were in the street. There may have been two, there may have been three. Not counting Ludu the custodian, who came walking around the front of the building and spotted Horvath."

"What kind of people were they?" Trevian asked. "Men? Women? Tradesmen? Can she describe them?"

Karel shook his head. "No such luck. Madame Andric's old, and even with glasses I doubt she sees very well."

"Tell me what she thinks she saw all the same," Trevian said sharply, as though a little piqued at the reference to old age.

"A man carrying a walking stick. A woman."

"Old man, young woman? Together?"

"Separately."

"A walking stick or a cane?" Trevian said, touching the head of the cane leaning against the cushion of his chair.

"I don't know. The man was halfway up the street on the other side when Madame Andric noticed him. The woman was just turning the corner. A young woman in a hurry."

"Damned cold. Anyone would be in a hurry to get out of it," Trevian said.

"Yes," Karel agreed. "But if either of them had seen the murder, or even heard the shot, they might be in a hurry to get away so they wouldn't have to get involved in anything."

"And the third figure?"

"She thinks there may have been someone going into one of the houses along the road."

"Man or woman?"

"Madame Andric couldn't say."

"How long had she been sitting in the window before she got up to make the tea?"

"An hour she says. At least an hour."

"What else did she see? Any traffic on the street?"

"Nothing moving, but she did see a black sedan parked at the end of the avenue. Ludu remembers it as well."

"How long had it been parked there? Did it belong in the

neighborhood? Did either of them know the owner or was it a vehicle strange to them?''

A thousand questions just as Lutesh had warned him, Karel thought. Good questions, probing for details. The sort of questions he himself had asked of Ulica.

''She said it was a strange automobile. It drove up just as she sat down in the chair by the window the first time. It parked there and waited for a long time. More than half an hour. Then drove away. After a few minutes it was back, as though the driver had simply gone around the block and parked in the same place.''

''Was it there when she came back from her kitchen and she saw Horvath lying on the walk?''

Karel made a rueful face. ''She told my associate that she didn't know. She was too excited when she saw Horvath lying there.''

''Understandable. What do the movements of the car tell you?''

''They suggest that the killer parked on the street in the morning, knowing that Horvath would be leaving his apartment very early. He sat there—''

''Or she,'' Trevian interrupted. ''Plenty of women commit murder nowadays.'' He spoke with regret as though it were a phenomenon of modern times that he very much deplored. ''Give them their due.''

''The killer sat there in the cold gray morning and thought about what was intended. He or she decided to postpone the confrontation or give it up altogether, drove away, changed his or her mind, came back, and parked the car as before.''

''And then may have changed her mind again and drove off.''

''Or his,'' Karel said.

Trevian grinned. ''Yes. What else can you tell me?''

''The wife has made it clear that Horvath had girlfriends.''

''Mistresses?'' the judge interrupted, asking for clarification of the precise status of the women in Horvath's life.

''He was sleeping with the secretary he shared with his business partner.''

''Shared?''

"I meant in the office, not in bed."

Trevian concealed a smile of amusement by taking a sip from his glass. Karel was a very serious young man, almost stodgy in his insistence on delivering the facts without humorous embellishment. He never took the opportunity to deliver a double entendre or achieve an effect by a play on words. Was he always so solemn and precise, or was it Trevian's status that restricted a naturally playful nature that Karel might be hiding from him?

"He had no mistress at the time of his death so far as I can tell," Karel said. "No woman set up in an apartment or supported by him in any other way."

Trevian nodded with equal solemnity, accepting Karel's rough definition of a mistress. In his day, any courtesan worth her price would have been insulted to be told that all she was worth was free rent and household expenses.

"According to his wife," Karel went on, "the women he seduced were shopgirls, secretaries, or clerks. Or, sometimes, the wives of other men as eager for new experiences as he. That's all we know at the moment, but it's very early, of course."

"I compliment you on your accomplishment so far."

Karel understood that the interview was over. He began to pack away his files.

"I would ask you to stay for supper if . . ."

"I'm expected home."

"Of course you are," Trevian said. "My regards to your lovely wife. Will you pardon me if I don't rise and see you to the door?"

"Don't trouble yourself, sir," Karel said, and reached down to shake the old man's hand.

"It's warm by the fire," Trevian said. "Fears to lie down to sleep, does she?" he added thoughtfully. "The poor old dear." His thoughts were already gone from the case, his eyes on the picture of the child on the mantelpiece, his memories elsewhere.

= 7 =

Judge Trevian: 1898–1916

The picture of the small boy in a velvet suit standing on the mantel in a frame of scarlet watered silk and gold filigree was of Anton Trevian himself. A white collar covered the shoulders of the child he once was. He wore a large-brimmed hat with a round crown. Trevian remembered that there had been a flat ribbon that hung down in back. He'd been five when the photograph was taken shortly after the turn of the century.

There was a tiny rosette in the buttonhole of his lapel. It was an honor given him by the callous, willful, arbitrary, and unhappy king, Alexander, after a game of croquet. It wasn't long after that pleasantly illusory summer afternoon that Alexander and his queen, Draga, were assassinated in the palace of Belgrade. Twenty members of the court were murdered with them.

Anton's father, Count Trevian, wasn't among them. He was a particularly inoffensive man who avoided as much of his hereditary duties to the crown as he could manage, not because he reckoned that the Obrenovic Regime would be as short-lived as so many other Balkan dynasties, but because his interest in life didn't extend much furthur than the care of his estates in the country, his mansions in Belgrade, his books, and his butterflies. And sometimes—rarely—he managed to work up an enthusiasm for the son he felt had been responsible for the childbirth death of his beloved wife. He delivered this pronouncement in a melancholoy way as though he were not so much condemning Anton for murder, but acknowledging that fate had designed the infant to be the deus ex machina that took the Countess from him.

It may have been the punishment Anton suffered because of

his father's expressed belief that Anton was the hand of destiny, that decided him to study disciplines that offered some hope that man was, or could be, the master of his fate. He avoided religious instruction in favor of Marx. He refused fairy tales in favor of humanism. As he grew older he considered a career in medicine, then in engineering, and finally in the law.

He believed in the law. He was ready to defend the rule of law to the death. He defended the letter of it, but admitted to himself that he would probably break the law in small ways if other loyalties—to family or friends—came in conflict. Had the paradox been pointed out to him, he'd have found nothing strange in it.

"I never presume that a man's actions will be consistent with the evidence of the nature that he presents," he once said. "First of all, I doubt that anyone really knows what sort of man he is. Secondly, I doubt anyone's ability to do the same thing in the same way twice. Thirdly, I can never hope to know the complexity of the dynamic in which someone finds himself at any given moment. A drop of rain can be enough to destroy the balance of anything or anyone."

As a child he was considered melancholic, as a stripling unhealthily solemn, as a student argumentative, and as a young man tedious.

He'd been too young for the Balkan Wars of 1912 and 1913, but had been of the strong opinion that the only hope for Serbia lay in the creation of an alliance of all the South Slavs. He was underage for military service when the assassination at Sarajevo plunged all of Europe into war.

In 1914 his father died one autumn evening. He'd gone out to make a tour of the country estate. Apparently he'd made his way to the wood that bordered the northern perimeter. They found him leaning against a tree. He looked to be asleep. His pockets were filled with red and gold leaves.

Anton became Count Trevian. He immediately abrogated his title. It meant giving up the country estate which belonged to the family by right of succession and not by private deed. It meant the loss of a good deal that he loved, but he'd smelled the winds of change. He knew that monarchies would ultimately disappear from the continent. In effect he traded the luxury of the mansion—libraries, reception rooms, parlors, bedroom suites, servants' quarters, stables, outbuildings, garages, paddocks, gardens, kitchen plots, farms, forests, parks, and croquet lawns for the discreet notice and thoughtful respect of unnamed, unknown men whom he knew would one day rule a new nation.

He returned certain paintings and objets d'art to the palaces of the king and other nobles who claimed hereditary rights to them since the Trevians were a cadet branch of larger dynastic families. He presented others to museums and libraries. The horses and livestock were sold and the monies given to the Serbian Red Cross. He removed what furniture he thought useful to the smaller of two houses in Belgrade. The one in which he intended to live. He closed the other until he could make up his mind how to dispose of it.

When he came of age he joined the army. He was in the infantry when it at first successfully resisted repeated Austrian invasions. But they were soon driven back in retreat across Albania. With Allied help, the defeated Serbian Army reached the Island of Corfu.

Corfu lies in the Ionian Sea, separated from the coast of Epirus by a strait two to fifteen miles wide. The island is forty miles long and twenty wide. The north is mountainous, the center undulating, and the south low-lying. It is well-watered and fertile, the most beautiful of the Greek Isles. The prevalence of the olive trees has induced some writers to declare it a monotonous landscape. Others have claimed the soft dull green a soothing balm for the eye and soul. Myrtle, bay, ilex, and arbutus form a thick carpet of brushwood nearly everywhere. The weather is felicitous, life hard in many ways, yet curiously indolent in others.

Olive oil is the principal crop. The local wine doesn't travel well and is consumed at home. The people are very independent. They remember and boast about the fact that it was their fleet that engaged the Greeks in the first naval battle recorded in Greek history. The men of Corfu have ancient, lined faces before their time, giving them the look of wise men. Many live to be very old and actually become wise. The women age rapidly beneath the sun as well. But when they are young they are sometimes possessed of a beauty that stops the heart. They are full-bosomed when fourteen and are rarely virgins at that age, though public scorn of a daughter's or sister's chastity can be insult enough to start a vendetta that will last three hundred years.

Anton Trevian's battalion was bivouacked in the rocky fields northeast of the village of Cassopo. The troops were forbidden to visit the city of Corfu except under military orders or with a coveted weekend pass.

The men of his company chafed at the inactivity, the constant drill, the make-work and the discipline. Trevian found the routine punctuated by long hours of empty freedom to read, write, and think a luxury. He became an expert on the history of the islands, employing first those travel guides that were readily available and later the encyclopaedias and ancient histories kept in the libraries of the Greek churches within reach. He taught himself to read Greek, though he had less success with the spoken language. The first is a solitary, cerebral pursuit and the second an interchange that demands social intercourse with another human being. He was no better at such relationships than he'd ever been, the rough camaraderie of the army being nothing to his taste. He longed for a pass to Corfu as much as any of the other soldiers. He didn't want to get drunk in the tavernas or have a woman in one of the many brothels administered by the French which were inhabited by prostitutes imported from as far away as Algiers. He wanted to spend as many hours as he could among the books he was sure enriched the cathedral dedicated to Our Lady of the Cave.

During the reorganization of the shattered Serbian Army, some units were deactivated and their personnel transferred to fill up the ranks of other companies, brigades, and regiments. A private soldier, Enver Lazar, joined Trevian's company. From the first hour, he established himself as a master of mischief and manipulation among them. The simple farmers, tradesmen, and workers recognized in him the kind of clever fellow who could get things done. Even when he exploited them there was a certain entertainment in it, the scapegoat of one enterprise having the opportunity to laugh at another's discomfiture another time.

Trevian pretended not to notice him. He accomplished the tasks assigned to him with quiet efficiency, studied his books, and let it be known by the power of the quiet with which he surrounded himself that he didn't choose to be part of the fun. Predictably, the conquest that didn't come easily was the one that Lazar wanted.

He began to romance Trevian in a hundred small ways, little favors done without fuss or fanfare, a question asked about a point of debate, the occasional plea that Trevian, clearly the most objective man among them, adjudicate a quarrel. Lazar made Trevian the council chieftain of the company without anyone the wiser. He remained the king of fools who picked every pocket while they laughed at his capers.

Trevian was aware of everything Lazar was doing. He even vaguely understood the reasons why Lazar wanted his friendship. Still, he chose not to give it. He was flattered by the attention. Perhaps he felt it would be withdrawn if ever he should fall into Lazar's web of charm.

One day Lazar came to him with a triumphant expression that gave him the look of a bear who'd found a honey tree. Taking Trevian aside, where the others couldn't see or overhear, he showed not one but two three-day passes.

Trevian didn't ask how they'd been managed. He knew that there were people who could always manage the impossible. It was a talent that was born in the blood. His father had said that a good many peasants inherited the magic. How else could their kind survive the hard lives they sometimes had to live?

Trevian understood without discussion that there was a price to pay for the pass. If he accepted the lavish gift of the pass, it would mean that he must accept Lazar's companionship. And he would have admitted that he wasn't as self-sufficient as he pretended to be in the face of the bounty that Lazar could achieve by the quickness of his wit. But the vision of the books in the cathedral was too much for him. He looked Lazar directly in the eyes so that he would at least know that Trevian was aware of the debt he incurred, and plucked one of the two passes from Lazar's fingers.

• • •

Once in Corfu, Lazar was less pleased with their agreement and said so.

"There's not a soldier in the company who wouldn't have shined my boots, kept my kit, and done my kitchen duties when they came around for the pass I freely gave you," he declared.

"If you wanted to hire a serf or employ a servant you should have said so," Trevian replied.

"Look here, I didn't want the company of anyone else. You may think I'm a fool because you're a scholar. But I'm not a fool. I have a good head, and a good education for that matter. I wanted someone with whom I could hold intelligent conversation."

"Where?"

"Well, there are a hundred tavernas in the city. There are brothels that come highly recommended. Good, clean establishments run by the French authorities. The girls are inspected by the French army doctors. What could be better than that?"

"You don't need conversation in those places," Trevian pointed out with simple, infuriatingly somber logic.

"Well, I know I don't," Lazar said, nearly losing control of his temper. "It's not while a man drinks that he wants to talk about it. It's not while a man is engaged with a woman that he wants to hold a discourse on the Peloponnesian War. It's after he's done those things that he wants a friend to tell him what a good time they've had together."

"Do you feel that I owe you my company?" Trevian asked.

"Put that way, no. You owe me nothing." Lazar stopped Trevian as they walked along a narrow alley full of stone steps by placing his hand on Trevian's arm. He turned Trevian around to face him and grasped his shoulders between his hands. "You owe me nothing, Anton. So far as I'm concerned I only hope that I've made a friend. You owe me nothing."

"Let me go to the cathedral for three hours, then I'll go to a taverna with you for a meal," Trevian said.

"And a whorehouse?"

"I think not," Trevian said after careful, judicious thought.

Lazar sighed. "Very well. I'll come to get you at the cathedral just after the noon hour."

He turned around and walked away down the alley, springing

up on his toes like a small boy, his head jerking birdlike from side to side, looking for the worm of adventure.

Trevian was not a religious young man. His religion was the law, his breviary the precision of its statutes, his mass the trial. The great nave of the cathedral reminded him of the vast spaces of a central court. Huge chandeliers fashioned of iron and crystal hung on chains from the vaulted dome above his head. Hundreds of candles filled the air with the smell of wax, nearly stopping off the breath, bringing an odd muted giddiness to the mind. The light coming through the windows was filtered through colored glass and the dust of ages.

He was not entirely alone in the church, though he might have been, so sparsely were the old women in black scattered around the marble floor. Most stood with eyes lowered to their feet or raised to the mosaic of the virgin and two emperors that rose up on the wall behind the altar. A few knelt, suffering the greater discomfort of their supplications for His sake. Along the sides were several small benches, wide enough for two, meant to accommodate those too old or ill to stand during the celebration of the mass or while at prayer, and to allow those grown faint from extended worship to have a place to lie.

At first he hesitated about easing his tired legs by sitting on one of the benches. To stand or kneel inside these holy walls was the custom, a duty of the faithful. It would have been a discourtesy not to obey the rules. He found himself thinking that there might be hypocrisy lying at the heart of his obedience to such custom. He wasn't one of the faithful. Not at all. He grew impatient with himself for chewing over such a dry bone. In the end he decided to sit down on the bench that enjoyed the coolest, deepest shadows closest to the door. He immersed himself in his guidebook and history.

In a matter of minutes, the gloom, the murmurs of the praying old women, the smell of incense and candlewax, and the occasional scraping of a foot which echoed from every corner like the tolling of a bell, put him into a trancelike state. He had no idea how long the girl had been sitting there when he first became aware of the softness of her body pressing against his hip and thigh. When he started and quickly turned his head to look at her, the young woman smiled tentatively and murmured something in French.

Her smile was brilliant, her glance downcast and demure. There was a small dimple just under the corner of her mouth and another at the point of her chin. Her cheeks were as round and rosy as a child's, her complexion like the petal of a flower. The hair that peeped out from beneath a colorful scarf tied about her head was blond, perhaps reddish, perhaps the color of honey. Her eyebrows had been plucked. They were slender arches above eyes that seemed to wait for some reply.

Is this how it happens? Trevian wondered. Does one fall in love, after having so little interest in women, so little experience of them, all at once, in a foreign church, while one is an outcast from home?

His French was very small. He understood that she'd expressed an apology, saying something about taking the bench without realizing that it was occupied since she'd come into the darkness from the glare of the sun upon the plaza.

He excused her in French that was broken and halting. He apologized for taking up so much of the bench and moved aside a trifle. She laid her hand on his sleeve, smiled, and shook her head. Their whispers attracted the disapproval of the old women. They clucked their tongues softly at the young couple, warning them that they'd do better to be at their prayers than at flirtation, lest they grow old and die before they'd made their peace with God.

Out in the sunshine she began to laugh aloud, clutching the knot of her scarf at the chin and pretending to be one of the Corfu crones.

"Ahhh," Trevian breathed, enchanted by the quality of her enjoyment. He became so bold as to suggest a glass of wine at some sidewalk taverna. She took him instead to one that conducted business from a shack on a hillside. The tables were scattered along the slope, their legs cut to the proper length to accommodate the changing elevations. The chairs stood on little platforms made of stone. The waiter walked along paths of steps made of pebbles set in wooden forms. Bushes ablaze with fleshy-petaled blossoms grew everywhere.

Her name was Felice Marchand. She was twenty-one and was a civilian employee of the French military in the division of records. She was unable to accurately convey the reasons and circumstances that had brought her to Corfu. She found it beautiful but lonely. She'd gone to the cathedral seeking solace, though she was not a member of any Orthodox faith.

Trevian found it surprisingly easy to talk with her for the very reason that she didn't speak his language, he spoke very little of hers, and they had no other in common. The expression of his thoughts became an exercise in qualities the very opposite of dissertations upon the law. He was forced to tell Felice in gestures, expressions, and few words, benchmarks to the feelings in his heart, that he'd been smitten by her. She didn't laugh, but smiled, touched his hand, then turned her head away.

Trevian didn't meet Lazar at the cathedral that afternoon. Neither did they meet that evening. Trevian and Felice dined alone at a little restaurant within sight of the sea. He spent all next day with Felice, who took time off from her work, pleading illness. They ate that night in rooms she'd found and engaged behind a shoemaker's shop. It was on a sheepskin thrown upon a pile of hides that they made love. It was the first time for Trevian. She admitted that it was the second for her, though she assured him that he shouldn't be jealous of the French boy she'd slept with back in Limoges, because he had been going off to war.

When he returned to the bivouac, Trevian found Lazar lying on his back on his bunk reading a cheaply printed periodical that featured pictures of ladies in partial undress. He pretended to be angry only for a moment because Trevian had failed to make their meeting. When Trevian told him the story of the miraculous introduction to a living angel in the cathedral, Lazar grinned, clapped his hands, threw the magazine aside, and demanded to be told the details.

"Was she beautiful?"

"I said she was an angel."

"Provocative?"

"Demure."

"Challenging?"

"Modest."

"Fine tits?"

Trevian blushed and turned his head away.

"What's this? What's this?" Lazar demanded. "Did you make love to her?"

Trevian was torn. He wanted to protect and cherish the affair. He wanted to boast about it and share his feelings of triumph and wonder. "We made love," he said.

"Where?"

"Behind a shoemaker's shop on a pile of leather."

Lazar yipped like a dog. "I knew it. I always knew you were a sneaky devil. It's as they say, still waters run deep."

"Nothing like that," Trevian protested. "We made love in a proper way."

"Oh?"

"We're going to be married."

Lazar stopped laughing as though someone had broken the hinges of his jaw. His teeth snapped shut and he turned as white as a sheet.

"What did you say, my innocent?"

"I've asked Felice to marry me."

"Here, sit down on Pavelic's bunk," Lazar said. He took Trevian's hands in his own. "What madness is this? You make love to a girl once—"

"A good many times," Trevian interrupted.

"Who cares if it were a million. Several times, then. Over the course of three days. You meet a girl in time of war. A time when you're filled with a sense of your own mortality."

"Are you playing uncle?" Trevian asked, amused at his friend's uncharacteristic intensity.

"I'm telling you that you, a lawyer . . ."

"A student of the law."

"A man of reason, of judicious action . . ."

"I've thought it all out," Trevian said before Lazar could go on. "I've thought it all out very carefully, and I mean to be married."

"She said she'd have you?"

"Yes."

Lazar stood up as though his bones were charged with electricity and walked stiff-legged up and down before the two cots. "Whore," he said.

"What did you say?" Trevian asked, but he'd heard well enough.

Lazar sat down and took Trevian's hands again. "I meant it as an entertainment."

Trevian understood.

"As a joke you mean. As a way to amuse yourself at my expense," Trevian said, his voice sounding strange to him.

"Never. No, never. I'm too fond of you for that. I only meant to prick your balloon of pomposity a bit. You act too old for your years. You act as though you've settled everything to your satisfaction, though you've never been drunk, or gone hungry to bed, or had a woman. I just wanted to scratch you a little. At the same time I wanted to give you a good time. It was a good time, wasn't it? She was good, wasn't she?"

"How should I know?" Trevian said coldly. "How should a man with so little experience know?"

"For God's sake, don't execute me for a favor. I did you a favor. At no small cost to me, I might tell you."

Trevian reached into his pocket.

"How much were the whore's services?" he asked.

"For Christ's sake, it was a gift."

"Thank you," Trevian said, and walked away.

They didn't speak with each other for a week. Then one day Trevian went to Lazar and told him that he knew all along that Felice was a prostitute. How could any sensible man have believed that a retreating army would have burdened itself with women keeping records. Lazar knew that Trevian was lying. But he slapped his friend on the back and embraced him as though he hadn't seen through the lie.

"So you were just punishing me. I must say you're good at keeping a straight face and playing the game out."

"Say no more about it," Trevian said.

= 8 =

When Anton Trevian and Enver Lazar were mustered out of the army at the end of the Great War, they were still together and still friends.

There's an old Bosnian saying, "Trust the dog that has bitten but has not yet been beaten." It's the kind of folk wisdom that causes dispute. One side argues that a dog that's been allowed to bite without punishment will consider itself immune to the consequences of its acts. It becomes a bad dog, not to be trusted under any circumstances. Others, who understand better the power of the undelivered but eternally threatened blow, hold that such an unpunished dog will always be anxious, and will do what it can to prevent the delivery of the punishment. Scholars maintain that the saying is a corruption of the tale of the sword of Damocles and that the analogy doesn't travel well.

Trevian knew that Lazar was aware of the injury he'd done to an innocent and unsuspecting victim. Lazar had a code of fairness of his own. He'd sneak every advantage from a stranger, toss a coin on an acquaintance, but would never knowingly do an injury to a friend unless his own life and ultimate well-being were at stake. It was never a question of moral right or wrong, merely of closeness.

Trevian also knew that Lazar would consider himself in-debted to Trevian until Trevian committed a similarly thought-less act. Since he never intended to do so, but to bind Lazar even closer to him with acts of kindness and consideration, Trevian felt that he'd always have a faithful paladin if ever he should need one. He knew that no matter how many favors he asked of Lazar, they would never count against the fundamental debt owed to him. In Lazar's account books one would have nothing to do with the other.

What Trevian didn't understand quite so well was that Lazar would welcome the moral obligation he'd created for himself. It gave him a reason for living that he would have had to seek elsewhere.

Both men, different as they were from each other, were simply looking for a dependable friend, and both considered themselves lucky when Lazar announced that he intended to follow Trevian into the study of the law.

An observer might have been fascinated by the interplay between them. Trevian sought the philosophy upon which the law was founded. Lazar looked for the pragmatic manipulation of its many gears and levers. Trevian pursued purity of intention and application. Lazar delighted in the loophole, the exception, and the edge. Trevian dreamed of justice, and Lazar of profitable advantage.

In their second year at the University of Ljubijana, Lazar fell in love with a bright young woman. The romance was passionate. Lazar called Vladamira his fiancée. They invented a hundred ways to excite their senses but she would never allow Lazar to penetrate her. She had her price. He finally decided to pay it.

"I'm going to marry," he told Trevian.

Trevian made no comment, unless one interpreted his silence as comment.

"I love her very much," Lazar went on. "Well, what do you think?"

"How many girls have you known since we enrolled in school?" Trevian asked.

"I don't count women as though they were trophies," Lazar said, suggesting that he was so great a hunter that he couldn't number all his kills.

"More than a few?" Trevian asked. "A good many? As many as you could talk into lying down and opening their legs for you?"

"That's not how it is with Vladamira. She won't let me do that to her."

Trevian didn't say another word. He merely smiled. The delicacy of his friend's language amused him. He was not too much surprised when, despite his good advice, the overheated and long-frustrated Lazar invited him to a wedding.

Neither was he much surprised when the marriage, such as it was, fell apart after a year of hot sex quickly cooled down, intimate quarters quickly grown crowded, and long conversations quickly reduced to observations on the weather.

In his fourth year Trevian, in his turn, fell in love. The girl was beautiful. It surprised him that she should find him attractive. She was a student of the law, a rare thing for a young woman to be. He manufactured stories in which he saw himself and his wife sharing a practice. He saw the city, the building, and the offices themselves, paneled in rich polished woods, brass lamps on two desks, and shelves of books bound in red leather lining the walls. He decided to ask her to be his wife without ever mentioning his feelings for her to Lazar. He was afraid that somehow Lazar would spoil it for him.

When he asked her to marry him and told her about his plans for them she seemed startled, then sympathetic. She told him that she'd always admired him for his intelligence and wisdom, but that she'd never entertained any thoughts about being his wife. He may have turned pale. His feeling of rejection was that great. She was a kind young woman and took him into her bed, making love to him in a thoughtful way. It wasn't marriage but it was something, Trevian comforted himself.

Upon graduation he and Lazar set up offices in Split. Lazar wanted to go to Belgrade or Trieste straight off, but Trevian argued that a smaller city would afford young lawyers greater opportunities for practice. Lazar was always quick to give up an argument with Trevian. He wouldn't have admitted it, but he was afraid that if he beat Trevian down he would have to give up his feeling of superiority. He wanted success, honor, and money, but he wanted as much fun as he could manage as well. He found it among the young women of the provincial city. He made love to tourists on the castle walls and married one of them, an English girl whose name was Felicity. The marriage lasted not quite a summer.

Trevian and Lazar were successful otherwise. Businessmen

learned very soon that Trevian would do a job of research that would confound all but the most learned judges. They learned that Lazar could be depended upon to find little cracks through which an illicit act might slip, and a corner in which an unethical one might hide. Lazar set up estates that took every advantage of the law. Trevian settled them with patient rectitude. They took their share of divorce cases. Trevian captured a few important corporation accounts. Lazar defended a few distinguished criminals.

In 1930 they opened a new practice in Belgrade. Trevian surprised Lazar by showing him the two mansions he owned, the one that had been closed for so many years, and the smaller one that he'd visited from time to time. Each one wanted to keep a separate establishment. Lazar considered it generous when Trevian offered him the larger of the two houses for his use. It would cost him nothing. He had only to staff and maintain it. Trevian kept the smaller of the houses for himself. Neither one of them could afford to open an entire mansion. They both began by living in a single wing. Trevian's apartment contained seven rooms, including servants' quarters, and Lazar's contained twelve.

When Trevian revealed that his family had once been counts and that he'd given up the title, Lazar called him a fool and insisted that Trevian call up old family acquaintances to enhance their chances for big city success.

Trevian did so. There was no way that the two young attorneys could fail to make their names and fortunes. They were welcomed everywhere. Scarcely a party or social function of any consequence failed to include them on the guest list. There seemed to be a good deal of pleasure among the aristocracy that a prodigal son had returned. There was even some talk of restoring Trevian's title. Had anyone cared to ask, they would have discovered that Trevian was not in agreement with the royal dictatorship which Alexander I of Serbia had proclaimed.

"The tricky bandages these power brokers use to bind the wounds of the nation are ridiculous," Trevian told Lazar. "Nothing will work but Socialist democracy."

"Keep those opinions to yourself," Lazar advised, secretly dismayed that Trevian could refuse a title in so cavalier a manner when he himself longed for such honors and titles with burning hunger. He had initiated a romantic liaison with the younger daughter of an impoverished noble family who looked kindly upon the young lawyer as a suitor. It would only take, he thought, an association with a newly reconstituted baron to make his suit a certainty.

When Alexander I was assassinated at Marseilles by a Macedonian Irredentist, the two young lawyers argued far into the night. Trevian maintained that the assassination, which he believed to be the first of many to come, proved his case that monarchies were doomed. The fact that young King Peter had immediately assumed the throne and the nation continued to be ruled by a royal regency was ample proof, so far as Lazar was concerned, that most European countries would continue to be ruled by royal dynasties for quite some time.

Trevian withdrew from a good deal of their royal and aristocratic associations. Such self-serving prudence was viewed by some as careful modesty. His attempt to isolate himself from any political philosophy recommended him, in certain quarters, for possible public office.

Lazar married his young aristocrat. He increased the number of rooms and redecorated the flat he still enjoyed rent free in Trevian's mansion. For a time he and his wife entertained lavishly but Trevian sensed a spot of blight in the pretty fruit of their marriage. When Lazar was too often seen about the clubs and theaters of the city, romancing actresses and entertainers, he knew that his friend had failed once again in finding excitement and fulfillment in legitimacy.

= 9 =

In the month of March, in the year 1940, Anton Trevian, at the age of forty-one, was already being considered for a place on the King's Bench and his partner, Enver Lazar, was being talked about for a post in the Office of the Attorney General.

The coup d'etat that tumbled the regent from power and placed it in the hands of General Dusan Simovic did nothing to spoil those possibilities. The steel fist of the German Army smashing across the border and through the Yugoslavian Army changed everything.

Lazar, because of the special favor that had been shown him by the deposed regent Prince Paul, was viewed with some suspicion by the followers of King Peter, the new premier, Simovic, and his vice-premier, Macek. There wasn't much danger of his being scooped up along with others who were loyal to Prince Paul and his government, but neither was he apt to be trusted for any important post. He found himself in the infantry as a private soldier, no consideration at all being given to his status as a veteran of the First World War or as a member of the bar.

Trevian was offered a commission in the Office of the Inspector General. He refused and volunteered as a private soldier, with the quiet explanation that in her time of greatest trial Yugoslavia needed every fighting man she could find, not more administrators. He said he knew how to carry a gun and would do so, forgetting altogether, in the storm of patriotism that charged his heart and bowels, that he was no longer the young man who'd fought in the first Great War.

But all such reluctances on the one hand, and brave gestures on the other, were made academic within a matter of nine days when King Peter's government fled to Palestine and Yugoslavia fell.

Trevian and Lazar, cut loose from their units by defeat, made their separate ways back to Belgrade, instinctively seeking their suite of offices as the place from which they might rally their personal resources and decide what they must do in order to survive and, ultimately, prevail.

It was Palm Sunday when the two lawyers, dressed in a motley of army issue and civilian rags, arrived separately at Terrazzia Square. It would one day come to be known as Bloody Sunday. The German bombers came in low over the rooftops. There were not many guns to threaten their dominance, no Yugoslavian fighter planes to deny them the sky. The Hotel Srpski Krajl was blazing. People were fleeing that and other buildings. The side streets disgorged larger mobs. They moved through the square on their way toward the river, riding bicycles and dragging carts piled high with household goods. Horses pulled wagons that looked like small swaying hills of trash. Men and women trod on the feet of one another and cursed without anger.

Trevian sought cover at the base of the Albania Building, the glistening white structure of white stone and chrome in which Trevian and Lazar, Attorneys at Law, kept their offices. The bombs fell all around, some bursting in the air, knocking people down. Many lay as they fell. The wall of stone behind which Trevian crouched shuddered and sang out with a mournful note like that of a church tower bell. When he placed his hand on it he could feel the dying vibrations for a long while.

Then the planes were past. No more bombs fell. The masses of people had cleared the square as though by some magic, syphoned off along the streets that fed the riverfront. But those who had fallen still lay there. Trevian got up from his knees. He walked along the street. He passed a shop that had once sold jewelry. The show window had fragmented away. There were boxes lying in the shards of glass. He kicked one aside. Watches, rings, and bracelets spilled out. He didn't bother to pick them up. In the sky the engines of bombers could be heard like the buzzing of a million insects. It was difficult to know if they were leaving or if new flights were on their way.

A trolley car lay on its side in the center of Terrazzia, like a great beast that had been slain.

Trevian stepped off the sidewalk and wandered through the bodies that lay in the square. Others were doing as he, looking here and there, bending, searching the faces of the dead, sometimes trying to call a corpse back to life. A woman in a bright green headscarf held a child to her breast and rocked it back and forth. When she stood up with the child in her arms her knees left bloodstains on the bricks.

The faces of the dead were bluish-white from the cold. Trevian examined a corpse, trying to find out what had killed the man. There was no blood, no wound. Concussion had killed him with a blow from an invisible fist.

Another survivor knelt beside Trevian. Trevian looked up to see Lazar smiling pitiably at him. They embraced and began to cry, remarking about the miracle that had brought them together at that moment, in that place, alive. Both alive.

The white bulk of the Albania stood untouched except for broken windows. Why had the German bombers missed such a target?

Lazar laughed in the furious hope that it was an omen of good fortune. He drank from a glass of brandy poured full from the cut glass decanter that Trevian kept on the sideboard. Trevian poured his glass a third. It said something about the difference between them. In distress, Lazar wanted plenty of everything to assure him that things would be all right. Trevian wanted what he'd always had in exactly the right proportions to prove to him that there were constants in the universe.

They talked about the consequences of Yugoslavia's defeat.

"Mihailovic. Do you know of him?" Lazar asked.

"I know the name."

"He's forming an army, the Royal Army of the Fatherland, in the Sumadija Mountains."

Trevian sipped his glass of brandy as though testing its qualities, rolling the drops on his tongue, licking his lips afterward with the slow sweeping motions of a cat.

"We can't stay here, I don't think," Lazar said. "We probably would find ourselves being denounced soon enough because of our past associations with the government. We wouldn't be safe."

"Would you stay on if you could be safe?"

"What do you mean? Are you posing me a hypothetical question in the face of the facts?"

"Would you stay on if it meant collaborating . . ."

"No!" Lazar said explosively.

". . . cooperating," Trevian amended. "Or even lying low and pretending to be a common citizen?"

Lazar shook his head and made a strangled sound of impatience, waving his free hand in the air between them as though washing such thoughts from Trevian's brain, the words from his tongue.

"I just said that I'm considering joining this Colonel Mihailovic in the mountains, didn't I?"

"Yes," Trevian agreed, and fell silent again.

"What are you thinking?" Lazar asked.

"I'll join the Partisans."

"The Communists?"

"They aren't all Communists. In fact, very few are Communists. They are the people."

The bombs began to fall again. As though sharing the same unspoken thought, neither man sought the comparative safety beneath the desks. They sat where they were in their leather chairs as the wave of bombers went overhead and disgorged its bombs. They couldn't speak above the din but looked at each other as though reading the mind of the other. When the flight was gone, and their motors reduced to the buzz of another insect swarm, Lazar was the first to speak.

"When will we leave to join these Partisans?"

"Soon," Trevian said, smiling. Then he said, "At once."

"I have no convictions of my own," Lazar said. "Is that how it seems?"

"I think you have the conviction that you'll always do what

is right if you can. And that simple conviction, no matter how far it might seem to lead you astray, may be better than my own.''

''Your philosophical convictions?''

Trevian tapped the tip of his forefinger on the bone of his skull between his eyes. ''My personal honor,'' he said, ''which even I cannot define.''

Lazar stood up and went to the decanter to fill his glass again.

''I can't go with you right away. I must look after my wife if she's anywhere to be found.''

When he arrived at his borrowed mansion Lazar found it smashed flat. There were refugees living in the ruins. One of them had heard that the aristocrat who'd lived in the house had been in it when the bomb fell. She might be dead or only injured. She was nowhere to be found.

Trevian and Lazar joined a group of men and women, some armed with hand guns and rifles, who had gathered of their own accord in the forest park south of the city. A man named Stoyan Vojeslav seemed to be the leader. In ordinary life he'd been a plumber, a man burdened with a wife who thought herself too good for him, and seven children who ate like wild pigs. There had always been the belief in him that he was made for better things. He was forever looking for an opportunity to show what a great man he was truly meant to be. He suspected that the German invasion might be fate's way of testing him.

He was suspicious of Trevian and Lazar. They were too well dressed for one thing. Lazar was altogether too cordial after his initial nervousness wore off. He seemed like a tricky fellow, an organizer who might challenge Vojeslav's preeminence among them. The other was perhaps even more threatening to him. The one called Trevian was quiet, orderly in his thoughts and slow in his responses. Within an hour an old woman had gone to cry on his breast as Trevian sat by the fire. A small child went to him and gave him her hand. Those were things a man could claim as marks of leadership if he pleased, a danger to Vojeslav's power over these simple people.

Still and all the newcomers were men in the vigor of their

manhood. They had weapons and seemed familiar with their use. Being a careful man, Vojeslav appointed Trevian his lieutenant in charge of the commissary and Lazar his lieutenant in charge of reconnaissance. In that way one would be kept busy feeding his growing force and the other would probably be shot by the enemy early in their campaign to leave Belgrade and join with other Partisans in the Julien Alps.

The Communists were well prepared for guerrilla warfare but hesitated to commit themselves to vigorous resistance because of the German-Soviet nonaggression pact. They saw in Yugo-slavia's defeat their opportunity to take power. Then the German forces turned Hitler's fury against Russia, and Tito moved swiftly to gain control of the population by urging a program of sacrifice in the name of liberation. He restrained the passions of the Serbs and Croats, and encouraged the Macedon-ians, Montenegrans, and Slovenes to fight side by side with the Serbs and Croats with promises that all ethnic groups would be equal in the new Yugoslavia the Communists meant to build after victory.

The little band led by Vojeslav contacted and were absorbed by a larger Partisan group. Vojeslav was not given rank. Neither was he given any authority. Instead, the quiet one, Trevian, was asked to join in council.

By the end of August 1941 the success of the resistance forces had inspired a popular uprising that liberated a large part of Serbia. Tito and Mihailovic met to discuss common action. Trevian and Lazar were there.

Trevian was brought to Tito's attention and was offered a place at headquarters. He hesitated about accepting the post and did, in fact, nearly decline it. Lazar urged him to accept the promotion. Tito decided the matter by sending word that every man or woman must serve where most needed and best used. There was more vanity in refusal than acceptance. Trevian was transferred.

Though officers had already taken to devising little marks and badges, worn to identify themselves, Trevian insisted upon keeping his rank of private. It was his way of maintaining that he held no rank at all. He wore a red star cut from a woman's petticoat stitched to his cap.

When Tito and Mihailovic sat down to confer, Trevian, though not in the first rank of advisers, was in the second. Colonels and generals often turned their heads over their shoulders and asked questions of him. As he whispered his council into their ears, they looked straight ahead at the Chetniks, as though the officers of the Royal Army of the Fatherland were enemies.

The bloody success of the guerrilla warfare had resulted in the most extreme and brutal forms of German reprisal against civilians. The population of whole villages were dragged from their beds and forced to stand by as their houses and barns were burned to the ground, promising them a brutal and killing winter. In some villages squads of German soldiers and Croatian Ustasi slaughtered all the men. In some they chose their victims at random, men, women, and children alike. In others they first marked the doors of this dwelling and that for reasons of their own. It was an opportunity for a good many old blood feuds to be settled, and for a good many more to be initiated. Mihailovic was appalled by the extent of the bloodshed and destruction. He didn't agree with the Partisan slogan, "Attack the enemy wherever, whenever, and however you can without counting the cost."

When asked for his advice about how the fighting should be conducted in view of that difference of opinion, Trevian felt his heart lurch. He hated the thought that an opinion of his could have the effect of murdering thousands of his countrymen and women. He would have urged restraint but couldn't do so.

"If we don't slaughter the enemy whenever they are exposed to us, they'll take hostages everywhere and hold them ransom for the good behavior of men and women fighting to liberate the nation. We'll have armies ordered *not* to destroy the enemy. How can that be? Is there such a creature that pulls its own claws and fangs before battle? That isn't a dog of war but an old toothless hound fit for nothing but dozing by the fire."

Before the end of the year the differences between the Chetniks and the Partisans broke out into open warfare. It became as necessary for Tito's high command to know the plans and movements of Mihailovic's forces as to know those of the Germans and Italians. Trevian was asked if he would accept a dangerous mission. Would he infiltrate the main body of the Chetniks? Would he put himself as close as he could to Mihailovic? This time he had the option to refuse because everyone recognized the extraordinary dangers involved in the activities of a spy. Since he was given the right to say no, he could do nothing else but say yes. He wasn't to go alone. He would have a companion. Lazar insisted that he would be that comrade.

The two old friends went together into the enemy camp.

= 10 =

The Policeman: 1970

Karel had met the type a hundred times before. They came in many shapes and sizes but had two traits in common. They never looked a man directly in the eye. They had smiles that clicked on and off like electric light bulbs. He sometimes joked that men like Denis Hogamann never looked at you because they were too busy searching for pennies in the gutter. They could never decide whether they should be solemn or ingratiating, and managed to confuse themselves and everyone around them with smiles that never rested.

Hogamann happened to be a large man. He sweated profusely. His office was hotter than comfort demanded. He was wedged into a chair too small for him behind a desk that was too large for the room. It was covered with two telephones and a scattering of all sorts of novelties.

There was another desk in the suite, and a reception counter that had been hammered together out of plywood, an attempt to isolate the secretary's duties from those of the receptionist, though the same girl served both functions. Karel had asked for and received her name, Nin Babaja. She'd been frightened by his manner, although he'd done nothing more than show his credentials. She sat at the desk in the farthest corner of the room, pretending to be writing in some ledger while her nearest ear shifted like a tiny radar dish in order to hear every remark that passed between her employer and the detective.

"In answer to your first question," Hogamann said right off, "no, Horvath had no enemies."

"I haven't asked a question yet," Karel interrupted softly.

"Isn't that the usual first question the police ask when a man's been shot down in the street?" Hogamann rattled on. His smile flashed on and off like a faulty neon sign, a flickering that captured the attention and made it difficult to study his eyes.

"Go on, then," Karel said.

Hogamann began to stammer. "I mean to say that my friend had no enemies bitter enough to blow his brains out."

Karel never flinched but kept his steady gaze on Hogamann's mouth.

"He was well liked by everyone," Hogamann went on. "Horvath was a very sociable fellow. A joiner. Why, he had more memberships and served on the board of more organizations than I can even count."

"He was the outside man," Karel said flatly.

"What?"

"He was the hail-fellow-well-met who made the contacts, shook the hands, greased the rails, traded the favors, and generally handled the public relations without which your enterprise wouldn't have prospered."

"Prospered?" Hogamann repeated like a raven.

"And you're the inside man. You know your way around permits, and export documents, and bills of lading, and maybe which dockers are approachable and which are not."

"See here, we've done nothing criminal. We have all the necessary permissions to trade in various souvenirs and promotional items."

Karel leaned forward and poked around in the mess of key rings, notebooks, plastic whistles, ballpoint pens, and other trivialities.

"I find it hard to believe that Horvath lived in such style on the proceeds of such junk as this," Karel said.

"He had his pension. He was a National Hero of the War. He was still active in the reserve. An officer."

"Still," Karel said doubtfully. "Where do you live?"

"In Kasan District," Hogamann said hesitantly.

"A very good neighborhood," Karel said.

"Yes. My wife prefers it to the city."

"In a luxury flat?"

"In a villa."

"Oh, that's something, isn't it?"

"We have three children."

"Yes, one wants the best for one's children."

He was thoughtful for a moment. Hogamann noted the sudden softening of the detective's eyes. He wondered what he'd said that had gotten to the man. Something about the children?

"Two boys and a girl," Hogamann said, expanding on his advantage. "The girl is seven. The boys four and twelve."

Hogamann saw the detective's eyes chill again. Well, he thought, it wasn't anything about the children. What did I say that made him ease off there for a moment?

"What sort of car do you drive?" Karel asked.

"A Chrysler."

"That's an expensive car."

"It's five years old."

"You have a place in town besides your suburban villa, don't you?"

"No more than a bare room. Practically a closet. Just someplace to lay my head if the pressure of business demands that I sleep over in the city for a night or two."

"No, it's quite a nice little flat. Two rooms and a kitchen with private bath. A little place of entertainment. I can guess what sort of entertainment."

Karel glanced over at the secretary. The shell of her ear had turned red.

"Hogamann," Karel said, "I want you to tell me the truth about your dealings. I want to know how you and Horvath made your big money. I don't give a damn about any Coca-Cola, or French perfume, or small German kitchen appliances you may be smuggling in. I have no interest in American cigarettes, English whiskey, or Swiss chocolate. I'm interested in homicide. But I'll have to know what illicit and illegal contacts you and Horvath have made over the years. It could well be that somewhere among them stands our murderer. You'd better not try to conceal the identities of any officials in high places who trade you documentation for gifts of money, goods, or women."

Hogamann laughed nervously, a staccato sound like the clearing of his throat.

"Officials in high places? My God, we're not dealing in arms

or chemicals or heavy machinery. A little trade in luxury
goods, that's all we've done. Officials in high places aren't
necessary for that.''

"Officials, administrators, or common clerks. I don't care
what they are. I want their names.''

"You say your only interest is homicide? Then will you
give me your word that you won't use the names I give you to
cause trouble for these people?''

"It would be tempting to ruin your credibility, Hogamann,
because I don't like your sort. If I scooped up a few of your
colleagues, who would ever trust you again? It could damage
your business. You might have to live less well, even go to
work for a living. Certainly you would have to give up a good
many of your fancies. The only promise I'll make to you is that
if you *don't* tell me what I ask of you, I'll make your life so
unbearable you'll soon wish you had. At the same time I'll tell
you that we in the police are often kind to those who cooperate
with us because it makes our own lives easier. Surely you've
seen that on the same American television shows that informed
you about the first question detectives classically ask in murder
cases. I might add that you're not out from under a cloud of
suspicion. You had a good deal to gain by Horvath's death.''

"What? What could I possibly have to gain? He was the man
with the contacts. I can only hope to maintain them. What could
I possibly gain?''

Karel looked pointedly at the secretary sitting in the corner
with her back turned toward them.

"I think you've already been quick to take a profit,'' Karel
said. "And then there's the Widow Horvath, who'll be in need
of comfort from the man who now runs the business that had
provided her such a fine life.''

Hogamann began to protest, his face growing red, but in his
eyes was the realization that the prospect of bedding Horvath's
widow might be an easier matter than seducing Horvath's wife.

"Which is Horvath's desk?'' Karel asked.

Hogamann made a thumbing gesture over his shoulder toward
the desk where the girl sat.

"What about a private file? Did he keep a locked drawer in
one of these cabinets?''

Hogamann shook his head, watching Karel as he took Horvath's ring of keys from his pocket and walked across the room to Horvath's desk. The girl stood up in some confusion, as though she feared Karel had come to strike or scold her. The flush made her face a pretty picture and Karel smiled at her to reassure her. One of the keys easily opened the top drawer. Karel sat down in the chair. He glanced up at the girl, who was backed up against the plywood counter. She hurried away to the other side of the office.

There were not many things in the drawer. A worn wallet with about twenty thousand dinars in small bills in it. Several programs for theatrical presentations. A pair of hardly used keys for a bank deposit box on a novelty key ring, a little flashlight that no longer worked when squeezed. Three address books much thumbed, the covers worn out along the spines and some pages loose. The kind of books that were saved after the information was transferred over to a new one in case a name or number, having no immediate value, might be needed sometime in the future.

Karel left the wallet after very carefully inspecting it a second time. He put the keys and little directories into his pocket. Then he left the office without another word.

He waited for Nin Babaja in a little park across the street from the office block. He suspected that Hogamann had already taken her to bed. He might have driven her home, but on this afternoon, when a police sergeant had visited, he doubted if either of them had the stomach for making their affair even slightly public. Not that it mattered, but he thought that if he wanted to convince someone that he wasn't having it off with a certain woman from the office he'd do nothing to avoid being seen with her in any innocent situation. Karel often watched people at cocktail parties. If a man and a woman knew each other well, yet made it a point not to touch, that was evidence that something was either going on or soon would be.

Babaja looked modern and smart when she left the building. She wore an unbuttoned coat with the belt loosely tied. The cold spell had been short-lived and there was a hint of spring in the air. The scarf she'd brought along for her hair was around her neck. Her mouth was freshly painted. It seemed to Karel to be as bright as Horvath's blood on the icy pavement. He crossed the street and stopped her.

"There's not a thing for you to be afraid of," he reassured her. "There's nothing your bosses might have done that will rub off on you."

"I just wanted the job," she said.

He led her across the street, placing his hand under her elbow.

"Why this job in particular?" Karel asked.

"It had a certain . . . shine."

"Is that your description?" Karel asked as he walked her to the bench he'd occupied. She sat down with her feet close together, playing the schoolgirl. He sat beside her.

"No. That's how Jan Horvath described it to me," she said. "He promised there was a certain amount of shine and glitter in the business."

"And does it glitter?"

She made a wry face. "There were some parties at the consulates and embassies. Either Horvath or Hogamann would take me."

"And presents? There were presents?"

She made another face. "Small presents. These old lovers like Horvath don't like to pay off in cash or even a month's rent. It makes it seem to them that they're buying the girl's favors, do you see? They want to convince themselves she's doing it for love. Small presents. A coat perhaps. A pair of stockings, a bit of costume jewelry, or a dinner out, that's okay. In fact, a girl can get fat but not rich on respectable affairs with older men."

"Why do you do it then?"

"Should I work in some government office? Should I work in a shop or restaurant? Should I marry some worker and make babies? One of these days I'll go to the summer coast and see what I can do for myself with the tourists, but I hear the competition is keen. You don't believe the slogans, do you?"

"What slogans?"

"That this is a worker's paradise."

Karel didn't answer. Whatever answer he gave would be wrong in its own way.

"This is limbo, like they tell about it in the Bible," she said. "Not good, not bad, everybody the same. Or nearly everybody. The rules don't apply to the Horvaths and the Hogamanns. They get around them somehow." She fell silent, thinking about it. Statements that tried to deal with the big picture didn't mean much to her. Her world was small. It extended only to the reach of her arms and a few modest daydreams of a foreign lover by the sea. "Hogamann," she said. "I don't think he's going to make it now that Horvath's gone."

"Did Horvath ever talk about his past to you?"

"Nothing I haven't heard a hundred times before from every man his age I happen to meet."

"What's that?"

"Well, they say if you go to Germany you'll never meet someone who was a Nazi. They all fought against them in the underground. In this country you'll never meet a man over fifty who didn't fight with the Partisans. Every damn one of them was a hero. Maybe he was. He had wounds, you know."

"Yes. In his thigh and rump. Did he say how he got them?"

"The one in his leg he once said he got in Spain fighting against Franco."

"And the other?"

"With the Partisans. He didn't say what battle, just that it happened in the Black Mountains."

"Did he name a sector, town, or village?"

"Budva. He mentioned that once or twice, I think. And Podgorica. Once he mentioned that town, I think. How am I to know? One doesn't really listen."

"Did he keep anything at your flat?" Karel asked.

"Like clothes, you mean? Yes, he kept a change of clothes and a bathrobe. No extra money, if that's what you're thinking."

"I wouldn't care a bit if he'd left a fortune cached with you. I don't give a damn about his love affairs or his crooked deals. I want to find his murderer. That's all. What I want to know is if he left any personal papers or documents with you."

"No, no, nothing like that," she said quickly, frightened by his outburst.

"I'm sorry for yelling at you," Karel said. "Who am I to be calling the kettle black?"

"What?" she murmured in dismay.

He didn't bother to explain.

He sorted through the names of half a dozen clerks and minor officials. A customs agent. A clerk who issued licenses for import-export. Another who had limited control over the shipment of works of art. It was that one Karel decided to put to use.

The public got indignant over different things at different times, depending on how they were manipulated by the state-owned press, radio, and television. The flight of national treasures from the country was a drum beaten from time to time. Ironically enough, the treasures they most deplored losing were religious icons, products of a faith the state actively rejected.

Actually, there were three industries dealing with the paintings and carvings. The first was the manufacture of counterfeits, some of them very well done. These were sold clandestinely to tourists through contacts made by friendly hotel clerks or guides. They were passed through customs with amazing ease, the inspectors having the knowledge of an expert, and a fine sense of humor. They often discussed the number of proud amateur smugglers who were returning home that day to other parts of Europe, Great Britain, or America with a genuine imitation tucked away in their dirty underwear.

The second industry had its base in some of the lesser-known museums, a few of the monasteries and churches, and several of the antique shops in Belgrade and other principal cities. It was a different game with more serious consequences for the sinning traveler. Nothing really bad. A body search, an hour's humiliation, perhaps a missed air flight, the confiscation of the genuine and valuable artifact, and a good deal of fright. Still, they had the story to take back with them of the close call they'd had with a prison sentence behind the Iron Curtain, and the helpful inspector who'd allowed them to escape for the equivalent of a hundred dollars or so.

The third enterprise was run by professionals. On one side

were important buyers from principal museums and private collectors with considerable wealth. On the other were the owners of icons taken from family tombs and hidden treasure troves and turned over to traffickers who knew how to get the icons out without discovery. In the middle were such men as Albert Hebrang, who was the director in charge of export permits for private persons given permission to leave the country in its service and privileged to take along works of art, even those designated national treasures, to their posts in consulates and embassies.

Hebrang knew he was in for it the moment Karel showed his badge and mentioned Hogamann's name. He turned as white as the yet unmelted snow outside in the small park that faced the windows of his office. It was a drab room furnished almost entirely with green filing cabinets reaching almost to the ceiling. A wheeled ladder gave him access to any drawer. There was a small desk beside the one dirty window, and a chair that was losing the stuffing out of the seat pad. There was the smell of dust and old bones about the place. The same dust seemed to have coated Hebrang. He even peered through glasses misted with it.

"You had a friend in Jan Horvath," Karel said.

"I knew him, yes."

"Did business with him. I won't play with you," Karel warned.

Hebrang was too easy. He collapsed on the spot, falling into his chair with the look of a very sick man on his face.

"I did no one any harm," he pleaded. "I allowed a few trinkets through the net of customs officials. Icons, antiques, a few paintings."

"Trinkets," Karel said.

"Have you ever been to the government warehouses?" Hebrang asked shrilly. "Have you ever been to some of the remote monasteries and chapels? I'll show you rooms in the Duke's Palace crammed with tapestries black with mildew, sedan chairs rotting away, paintings gnawed at by rats feeding on the glue. I'll show you a chapel in a remote province where a Titian suffers on a wall moldy with damp every spring and washed with rain water every winter. Do you think anyone cares for these

treasures? Has anyone minded enough to even catalog them?
The government is like a child that doesn't want a toy but
doesn't want anyone else to have it either. They make propa-
ganda out of their publicized intention of preserving the nation's patrimony, but what do they do to act upon it?''

"What do they do?'' Karel asked mildly.

"I'm not criticizing the authorities,'' Hebrang said in sudden
fright. "Don't misunderstand my words.''

"Just complaining about some of the bureaucrats like yourself who run things?''

Hebrang was in complete confusion and on the run. He knew
he was being baited unmercifully but didn't really know why.
What did the policeman want, a confession? He had the evidence of his dealings with Horvath. Was he just playing cat and
mouse for the pleasure of it?

"Compose yourself, my friend,'' Karel said smoothly, hating
the sound of oil in his voice. He'd never before applied fear and
coercion for his own purposes. "I just wanted to make the
point that all the laws and good intentions in the world don't
mean much when there isn't a structure of administration to
make them work. Isn't it so?''

"Yes,'' Hebrang agreed doubtfully.

"I mean to say that a simple clerk can throw a wrench into
the works in all innocence and make all the heavy laws and
great pronouncements of purpose just so many words on paper.''

Hebrang didn't reply this time but the color returned to his
face. He was no longer afraid.

My God, Karel thought, how difficult it is to fool these clever
foxes. This man is a survivor. He'll not only endure but prevail.
He'll feast even if others starve. He can read the temper of the
wind with a wet finger. He knows I want something from him.
I'm no longer a danger to him and he can afford to be less
subservient with me. He'll wait now until he hears what I have
to say, giving nothing more away. He was altogether too sure of
himself all of a sudden. That would never do. He needed
another jolt of terror. Something to keep him honest. A threat
that wasn't easily put aside.

"I'm concerned about Horvath's murder, not his schemes,''

Karel said. "I want to know if there was any reason why you might want to kill him . . ."

Hebrang started to protest, the color fading from his cheeks again, but Karel raised his hand and smiled.

". . . or knew of anyone else dealing with Horvath and Hogamann who might want one or both of them dead."

Hebrang shook his head solemnly from side to side, his eyes as round as teacups.

Karel sighed. "I want you to do me a service," he said.

A sly smile touched Hebrang's mouth.

"I want you to secure a blank passport for me," Karel said.

"Just how am I supposed to do that?" Hebrang protested, waving his hands in the air.

"I have the feeling that it won't be too difficult for you. Thieves talk to thieves, and clerks to clerks. One hand washes the other, don't you know? I'll just bet there's quite a fancy little trade in blank documents going on."

Hebrang stared at Karel for a moment, then opened the top drawer of his desk, rummaged in it, and came up with a small packet of shiny new passports. There may have been five or six of them. He removed one from beneath the rubber band.

"You'd better give me two," Karel said, "in case the first gets spoiled."

Hebrang snapped another passport out of the packet as though paying Karel his bribe with a new banknote.

"Jan Horvath was a member in good standing?" Karel said to Obradov, the commander of the one hundred and third chapter of the Veteran's Union.

"Very good standing," the old soldier agreed.

"He was active?"

Obradov hesitated, a careful man who never spoke without thinking things over.

"He was exceptional in that he was willing to do the dull work. Clerical matters. Keeping the service records and payment of dues."

"He was the secretary-treasurer?"

"He may have been. At one time or another. The books will

show. I merely meant that he was always willing to take home a briefcase stuffed with such trivia and put it down in ledgers in an orderly manner. He was very conscientious. I remember once he stayed three hours after a meeting because of a small amount of petty cash that didn't show up in the receipts. The treasurer was ready to let it go. It was such a small amount that I even volunteered to make it up out of my own pocket if Horvath would only let it go. But he wouldn't. He worried the records like a dog with a bone until he found the error."

"You mention service records. Are these duplicates of official service records which are on file elsewhere?"

"No, no. Just our own forms we ask the membership to fill out. Informal documents."

"I'd like to see the record of Jan Horvath."

Obradov went over to a wooden filing cabinet that looked as though it wasn't much used. He opened a drawer and fished around for five minutes. Finally he turned around with a sheepish look on his face.

"Not here, it seems. Or at least not in its proper place."

"You said that Horvath kept the files?"

"Others did as well. It was my responsibility really. Mine and whoever holds the post of secretary at the moment. Of course, there's no telling how long Horvath's record has been missing or mislaid."

"Do you know much about his service record?"

"I know that he was a member of the Counter-Intelligence. I remember we used to chide him about that. You know. Accusing him of spying on us. It was all meant in a friendly way and that's the way he took it. He was quick to laugh at a joke or any good-natured teasing. We didn't really think he was spying, of course. Who would there be to spy on except a lot of old soldiers boasting about their days of hardship and glory? Our chapter doesn't get many of the younger military men. There are other, more fashionable, chapters of the Veteran's Union. Do you belong?"

"I never spent any time in the service," Karel said. "There was no war and I was excused my conscription duty because of my job."

"Policemen are soldiers anyway," Obradov said, smiling in a complimentary fashion.

"Was he with the Counter-Intelligence during the war?" Karel asked.

"Was there even such a thing? Our war was fought in such confusion. The Chetniks over there. The Ustasi over there. The Germans over there. And the Partisans over here." He tapped his chest, making it clear with whom he'd served from the very beginning. "By the time it was over, of course, we were all fellow countrymen again."

"After the executions," Karel murmured.

"Well, yes, after the invaders were driven out, and after the collaborators were punished. How could we have survived otherwise?"

"Horvath?" Karel said, bringing them back on track.

"He was a career officer. I mean to say he apparently stayed on in the army during the reconstruction of the country. I'd say that was the time of greatest need for something like the KOS. I've no idea where his loyalties lay before the invasion and occupation."

He regarded Karel with a very careful, knowing eye. The eye of an old man who knew that honesty and candor were not necessarily proof against official harassment and suspicion. He'd be very good at cards, giving nothing away he didn't mean to give away.

"What do you have to tell me?" Karel said abruptly.

"What makes you think I have anything more to tell you?"

"There's always something a little more," Karel said. "You've given me facts—"

"That's all you've asked of me," Obradov interrupted in a soft, reasonable tone of voice.

"Now I'm asking you for impressions. What is it that you didn't like about Horvath? What is it that you mistrusted?"

"He smiled too much, he spoke too loudly, he volunteered too often."

Karel smiled to himself. Old soldiers never trusted anyone who volunteered. It was sucking up to superiors, making good marks for the record. But it wasn't much with which to condemn a man.

"Is that all?"

"I think he was a liar. Perhaps a monumental liar."

"You've evidence of that?"

Obradov shook his head.

"A feeling. How does one explain such a feeling? Here was a man who was quick with anecdotes and stories. He'd tell everyone that he'd done this and that, been here and there. His life seemed to be filled with a variety of jobs, experiences, and women. Enough to fill a dozen lives." He tapped a finger to his forehead. "If one had a memory for detail, his dates began to collide with one another. After a while it seemed pretty clear that a good deal of what he told about himself was invention."

"Perhaps he was just the usual sort of braggart."

"That's possible, of course, but he also evaded direct questions about certain times of his life. I don't mean the sort of probing questions that might be offensive. The casual sort people might ask. He never gave a satisfactory report of his youth. He said that he'd gone to university. He didn't say where."

"Where was he during the war?"

"There you have it," Obradov said, smiling in a clever, triumphant way. "What else do old veterans talk about than their wartime experiences? He never said with whom he fought, or where he fought."

"Do you think he might have been a Chetnik or a member of the Ustasi?"

Obradov shrugged. "Who knows? He might have been. All his cheerful poking through the files may have been his way of making certain that no ghost from his past popped up to surprise him."

The office of the International Red Cross was in a building occupied by any number of minor government agencies. Though it wasn't a state organization, it had not been able to escape official regulation.

When Karel entered the office he saw three people, two women, and a man, staring at the clock on the wall, waiting for the day to end. The man was a scarecrow, as thin as a rail. His bony wrists jutted out of the cuffs of his shirt like bundles of sticks. The fingers were twisted with arthritis. One of the women looked like a chicken, her sweater ruffled up around her neck to keep out the chill. The other woman was stout and had the face of an aging cherub, all rosy and round.

He had to clear his throat twice before they became aware of him. Then they started a marvelous fuss, twittering to one another all at the same time. The hen ushered him over to a chair at the cherub's desk, gently dragging his coat from him as they went. The man rattled off introductions and asked Karel if he'd care for a cup of tea all in the same breath. The only name that fixed itself on Karel's memory was that of the cherub. She was Madame Niko.

Karel found himself seated under her beaming attention, a cup of tea at hand, while the hen and the scarecrow hovered over him in smiling expectation. He was clearly an event in their drab lives. Karel displayed his credentials, causing a new round of twittering.

"It's about our friend Horvath," Madame Niko said.

"Yes. I must ask some questions."

The scarecrow brought the hen a chair, then drew up another for himself. They waited with open mouths.

"He was a volunteer?" Karel said.

"More," Madame Niko said.

"Yes?"

"He was an inspiration. He'd served the Red Cross on the battleground, you know."

"In the war?"

"Before the war. Before the second Great War. In Spain."

"Did he tell you that?"

"Yes, he told me one evening after a monthly meeting. It was a social event. We had things to eat and a lot to drink for those who wanted it."

"And he told you that he'd served in Spain?"

"He told me, yes."

"Just like that?"

"Like what?"

"Without being asked. Without there being a conversation that might have naturally led to such a revelation."

"People talk to me sometimes," Madame Niko said, and

colored prettily. It made her blue eyes seem bluer, and Karel looked more closely. It was then he saw that the lady was nearly as old as Obradov and certainly just as shrewd.

"I was a nurse during the war. I didn't learn my skills on the spot. I was a graduate of the Royal Nursing School."

"But not a Royalist?"

"Who gives a damn about such things?" she said. "I said I was a nurse. I'd still be working at it except I'm thought too old. I'm a nurse, and people talk to nurses. Horvath had a bit too much to drink that evening. He was feeling lost and sorry for himself, I think."

"Have you any idea why?"

"We all feel that way sometime or other. Don't you feel that way?"

Karel almost said that he did. Almost began to give the reasons why: the failed marriage, the dead child, the lost love, the troubling affair with Marta. Yes, clearly people talked to Madame Niko.

= 11 =

Karel waited until they reached the bedroom before placing his hands on Marta's breasts and buttocks. He gave her small pats as though preparing to offer her some surprise. He stood in the corner of her bedroom as she pulled down the shade and drew the curtains.

"Why are you standing over there so far away?" she said.

"I want to watch you take off your clothes."

"All right," she said agreeably. She took off her jacket and removed the broad leather belt that cinched her in at the waist. The muscles of her belly relaxed. Karel noted with affectionate amusement that his mistress might grow a little pot if she were not very careful. She unzipped her skirt and let it fall to the floor in a woolen puddle. When she bent forward to pick it up, her heavy breasts pushed against the harness of her brassiere. Karel sat down in the boudoir chair.

"Aren't you going to get undressed?" she said.

He smiled. "Get on with it."

Marta sat down on the edge of the bed and took off each shoe in turn, raising her legs one by one and resting the ankle of one on the knee of the other. When Dika changed her shoes, she leaned over and barely lifted each foot from the floor to take them off.

"At least take off your overcoat," Marta said. Her smile was tremulous. A wary look had crept into her eyes.

Karel took a bottle of brandy from his pocket. "French," he said. He reached into his other pocket and pulled out a slim box wrapped in foil. "Swiss chocolates."

"This is a celebration?" she said. It was only half a question.

"Perhaps. Get naked," he insisted. He unwrapped the candy and uncorked the bottle.

"Don't you want me to leave on the belt and stockings?"

"No, no. Everything. Take off everything and lie on the bed."

She shook her head so that her hair became disarrayed and wild, giving her a wanton look. She quickly removed her stockings, panties, and the garter belt. She took off the brassiere last. She smoothed the flesh of her breasts and belly with the flats of her hands as though trying to rub the red marks of the undergarments away. Then she lay down on the bed as she'd been told.

Karel stood up. "Open your legs," he said. He brought the bottle and the box with him to the bed and put them down on the side table. She watched him like a prisoner wondering what her captor meant to do. He chose a candy with a soft center. He leaned over to examine her muff, parting the hair gently with his fingers. He poured a little brandy along the fold of flesh. She jumped and giggled a bit. He could see the vein beating in the hollow of her groin. He inserted the chocolate between the lips of her vagina, then poured a little more brandy on top of it. He lowered his head.

"My God," she gasped. "You could be arrested and imprisoned for this. Don't you know that you're breaking the law?"

He sat up, chewing the candy, his grinning lips glistening with brandy. He got out of his clothes in a hurry, scattering them everywhere.

"What is it? What is it?" she demanded. "You must tell me what it is that makes you crazy."

"I've taken the first step on our journey," he said.

"Tell me," Marta demanded.

"When I've done with you," Karel said, and stopped her mouth with his own.

When they were finished, the sun was throwing the last slanting rays of day across the bed. Marta placed herself beneath Karel's arm, her mouth close to his nipple so that when she spoke her breath would gently excite it.

"Now tell me what you've done," she said.

"Find my jacket and look into the breast pocket. Bring back what you find there."

She left the bed. She passed through a bar of light. It turned her flesh to honey. She bent over to retrieve his jacket from the floor where he'd thrown it. Her buttocks were rosy from lying in the bed. She took out the brand-new passports and turned around, leafing through them with her fingers.

"I get it, yes. This is what you meant when you said there were possibilities in this murder case," she said.

"Horvath dealt with a good many minor officials who had access to documents of one sort or another."

"Someone at the passport office?" she said. "Was Horvath getting people out of the country?"

There was something sharp and eager about her expression when she asked the question, as though she were angry about something.

"No, no," Karel said. "The man who gave me those works in another department of the government altogether. But these clerks are forever trading favors."

"Then why haven't you simply approached one of them before?"

"Because there was nothing with which I could threaten any one of them," Karel said. "Now get into bed and let me tell you."

She got back into the bed. They arranged the covers about themselves.

"Look here," he said, "this will be filled out very carefully. Then you must learn something about my wife's past. The trick is to learn some of the facts, but not necessarily all of the facts. Then if any questions are asked, you can respond with enough of the truth to show in your eyes and at the corners of your mouth."

"The corners of my mouth?"

"Perhaps I shouldn't have mentioned that. Liars can sometimes look you directly in the eyes but the corners of their mouths give them away."

"There's a trembling there?"

"No. A rigidity. Little pale marks that turn the corners of the mouth down a trifle. Don't concern yourself about it. My wife's father's name was Savo Donker.''

Marta suppressed a giggle.

"What is it?" Karel asked.

"Your wife's name was Dika Donker.''

"I used to think it funny, too," Karel said. But now he didn't laugh. Just hearing the name of his wife brought her sad face to his mind. He shuddered when he thought of the panic she'd feel when she realized that he'd betrayed her. He was taking the first steps in a plan to desert her, to dishonor her and himself with the people who knew them.

"Be good and learn your lessons," Karel admonished Marta.

She composed her face as he told her other things about Dika's family. Her mother's maiden name. The names of her grandparents, brothers and sisters. Facts that the officials of the passport control might have in hand or could be able to get easily enough if they chose to do so for whatever reason such petty satraps decided to harass travelers.

Marta commended the facts to memory with astonishing ease and accuracy. Karel complimented her.

"Carry on if you like," she said. "I can remember a good deal more. How about the names of friends and neighbors? How about the names of great-grandparents?"

"No, that's good enough. Sometimes to appear to know too much is very suspicious.''

"I can see that. People really know a great deal less about themselves than other people think they know.''

"That's exactly it.''

She reached out for him and kissed him long and tenderly.

"I have to meet with Samaja and Ulica," he said.

She kissed him again. They made love, without gymnastics or even much fire, for no more than twenty minutes, laughing together like conspiring children. The start of dangerous ventures are often humorous.

"What have you got for me?" Karel asked Samaja and Ulica at the end of the day.

"Not much more than yesterday," Ulica said. "I've talked to

all the local tradesmen and shopkeepers. They say unanimously that Horvath was a dependable client or customer, patient with delay and apt to pay his bills right on the dot. He didn't have any particular friendships or associations with any of them except for a tobacconist who belongs to one of the same veteran's clubs. They were somewhat friendly because Horvath had a taste for a certain brand of Russian cigarettes that come wrapped in black paper, and they'd get into conversations about the differences in tobaccos from time to time. Nothing more intimate than that. By and large they didn't know more or less about Horvath than anyone might who had dealings with one of us. No one could believe that Horvath could have had any enemies. Certainly none vicious or bold enough to murder him.''

"Universal dismay,'' Karel said. "Predictable.''

Samaja and Ulica nodded as one, patient soldiers of the law who knew that most investigations were nothing but dry commonplaces hiding a precious clue that might lead to the discovery of a perpetrator. Their eyes revealed the kind of patience that certain factory workers, picking through parts looking for defects, reveal. Except there was a sharp wariness in the corners, a certain cynicism in the depths of the policemen's eyes.

"I've interviewed every occupant in the apartment house and in those on either side,'' Samaja said. "Most had no more than a nodding acquaintance with Horvath and his wife. You know the sort of thing. Good-mornings in the elevator, a brief exchange of words in the hallway. A professor and his wife lives one side of the Horvaths. The husband says he didn't much like Horvath. No particular reason. They'd never had a dispute over anything. Just that the professor felt that Horvath was not to be trusted. The wife made some mention of the fact that she suspected anyone who owned an apartment furnished in such luxury as the Horvaths flaunted. On the other side live a husband and wife. Both are doctors. They have three children. They socialized a bit, mostly because Hannah Horvath was willing to watch the children when emergencies arose that had both doctors on the run. They expressed their shock and dismay. Neighbors above and below had no complaints. The custodian of the building seemed to like Horvath for favors done for him. Little things that needed influence.''

Karel went into his pockets and pulled out the address books and the pair of keys. He handed the book taken from Horvath's body and the last of the old books, the green one, to Ulica.

"Check these names against each other. Make a list for yourself of any names in the green book that aren't in the new one." He handed over the other two books. "Do the same with each one of these, comparing it to the one that came after it. You'll end up with three lists. Take them back to front in point of time and check them out."

"I understand," Ulica said.

"Then give me back the newest book. I'll keep checking the listings out while you do the others." He tossed the two keys toward Samaja. "You may have trouble with these. There's no identification tag. No way of telling which bank has the deposit box they'll open. Do your best."

The detectives stood up. Karel had a sudden pang of sadness. It took him a moment to realize that he'd soon never see them again, and he'd never have the chance to say good-bye.

Karel was dismayed to see what Dika had done in preparation for the evening meal. She'd drawn the curtains against the scene outside the window and set the table in the dining room with finger bowls and candles. The table was artfully laid. Karel suspected she'd found some reference in a magazine of homemaking somewhere.

Dika was dressed in a peasant-style dress of fine material, the blouse heavily embroidered around a yoke that was cut to expose her shoulders. Her full skirt was cinched in at the waist with a broad belt. She'd done her hair up in two braided coils at her ears, a style that had once pleased him. There was a touch of artificial color on her lips and cheeks. She appeared shy with him when he stopped short in the middle of the room. He clutched his briefcase to his chest in his two hands and stared at the room, the table and her costume.

"Is it a celebration?" he finally found the voice to say.

"Does there have to be a reason?" she said with a certain fluting edge to her voice that revealed the strain she felt. Had she been afraid that he would laugh at her?

"No, of course not," Karel said as she took the briefcase from him, placed it on the floor beside the door, then helped him off with his coat. "I just thought I might have forgotten something. It's not your birthday?"

She laughed. "Sit down at the table. I'll pour you an aperitif."

"It's not *my* birthday, is it?" he went on, taking his chair.

"No, no. It's nothing. Nothing."

She came back from the sideboard with two small glasses filled with a green liqueur. She placed his glass in the middle of the service plate, then took her own to her place at the opposite end of the table.

"You're sure. Not an anniversary?" he said.

For a moment it seemed to him that her eyes filled with tears. They sparkled in the candlelight and threatened to spill over on her rouged cheeks.

"Drink up," she said.

The aperitif was sweet and sticky. It left a film on his lips. When he tried to smile as she served the soup his mouth felt stiff. It made him uncomfortable as though his body was pointing out to him that he was shamming when he tried to make Dika believe he was pleased with her efforts. He wasn't pleased at all. Though she continued to play a clumsy charade of mystery throughout the meal, he had a fair idea of what it was all about. At least an apprehension. After he poured himself a second cup of coffee he tried to get a reasonable response from her again.

"What's this all about, Dika?" he said with a little laugh lifting the edge of the sentence. "You really must not keep me in the dark any longer."

"I just woke up," she said. "I just this morning woke up."

"I don't understand," he said, knowing that he understood only too well.

"I don't mean I awakened from a night's sleep. After you'd gone off to work I awakened from another sort of sleep. How could you have stood to be alone these years?"

Karel instinctively shoved his chair back a few inches. He raised his hands as though defending himself against a physical attack and shook his head furiously.

"No, no," he said. "Please don't do this, Dika."

She reached across the table. Their hands fought in the air like pigeons as she tried to capture his in her own.

"Eight years," she said. "How terrible it's been for you."

"And for you. I understood. Please. I understood."

"Have you? If you have, it's because you're so good. So very good."

He tried to pull his hands away. She was surprisingly powerful. She wouldn't let go. If he struggled any harder he would drag her across the table. She was staring into his face with eyes that seemed to be starting from her head. Unattractive eyes like those of a madwoman.

"I don't blame you. I don't blame you one bit," she said.

"What are you talking about?"

"I understand how it is for a man. You needed women. You needed a woman."

"You don't know what you're saying," Karel protested.

"I forgive you all of them," she declared piously.

"What are you talking about? What women are you talking about? For what women am I to be forgiven?" He protested more loudly and vigorously than he should if he really meant to assert his innocence. He heard his own voice ringing off the walls and ceilings like the voices of the guilty criminals who protested their innocence by shouted assurances as shrill as a Klaxon screaming guilty, guilty, guilty. Karel tried to stand, not caring if he overturned the tables, chairs, or even knocked Dika to the floor. He couldn't believe her strength. She left her chair and rushed around the table, never letting go of him. She threw herself onto his knees, throwing him back into his chair.

"You won't have to lie in bed next to a stick again," she whispered. It came out louder than it was meant to do.

He felt a wave of revulsion ripple through his bowels and turn his stomach over.

"My God, don't do this," he begged.

She rocked her body against him. She released one of his hands and pulled down the shoulder of her blouse so that one breast was nearly exposed.

"I beg you not to do this, Dika."

"I'll give you whatever she gives you. I'll do whatever she does to please you."

"Please, please, please," he moaned. He felt a wet coolness on his cheeks. He was startled by the tears. He couldn't remember the last time he'd cried. Years ago. Certainly many years ago.

She pulled his head down to her naked breast. He'd lost the strength to resist her. She held his face against it. He breathed her skin, heavy with the scent of perfume and powder. He felt sickened by it, and saddened by the spectacle of her humiliation. He rocked his head from side to side, trying to deny the disgust he felt.

"Yes, yes," she said. "Suck it. Bite it. What will I do for you? What do you want me to do to you?"

She pulled up her skirts. She moved around on his lap so that she could reach down between her own legs and grope for his penis. There was no erection there. Suddenly she became aware of herself. She stood up. He felt relieved of a demon. She stood with her back to him, rearranging her skirts and her blouse.

"What's the matter, Dika?" he said. "Tell me what the matter is?"

It sounded comedic even to his own ears. After such a passionate if clumsy attempt at seduction, to ask in a calm voice such a question was a comedy turn worthy of the nightclub stage.

"Are you going to tell me there have been no women in these eight years since the infant was born dead?"

"There were no women for eight years."

"There's a woman now," she said. "I can smell her on your clothes. I still wash and iron your shirts and underwear, you know. I still brush out your suits and polish your boots. I still do some of the things a wife is meant to do."

"You've been a good wife," Karel said, marveling at the steadiness of his voice. He got to his feet. "That was a good meal."

"Who is she?" Dika said.

"I have more work to do this evening," Karel said. "This case, this murder, is very difficult. I may stay on at headquarters until morning. It will give you the morning to sleep in if you like."

"Murder," Dika repeated, as though it was a word she'd never heard before.

"We have a great deal to think about and talk about. Yes, we'll think about it and then we'll talk."

"Yes."

"Calmly, I mean."

She went to the window.

"It's not as though our marriage died only yesterday," he said.

"How long will the winter last, do you think?" Dika asked quietly as she looked out the window at the trees that were dripping water from the melting ice that had sheathed the branches and twigs.

"Spring is already here, I think," he said.

= 12 =

Karel arranged an appointment with Colonel Bim. He was shown into the office of the chief of the KOS by a homely female corporal. Bim could never be accused of staffing with women who might be tempting in bed.

Bim rose from behind his desk, smiled, and extended his hand.

"I'll assume that you're here in the matter of Major Horvath," Bim said without wasting a moment on courtesies. He seemed upset.

"I'd like to see his dossier."

"I can save you a considerable amount of time. The answer is no."

Karel was caught off guard by the swiftness of the refusal.

"May I ask why the file won't be made available to me?"

"All our personnel files are confidential."

"I have a security clearance."

"Not one that the KOS recognizes if it doesn't choose to do so."

"Would there be any use in my asking Lieutenant Lutesh to make the request?"

"I've looked at Horvath's file and there's nothing in it that will help you in your investigation."

"Why not allow me to decide that, sir?"

"I'm afraid you must accept my decision, Sergeant."

"I'm concerned with his history before nineteen fifty-two. You can sanitize the file if you like."

"Are you bargaining with me, Sergeant?"

"I'm trying to pursue a murder case. I should think the KOS would like the murder of their comrade solved."

"It would."

"Then I should expect a willingness to cooperate with the proper authorities."

"We take care of our own, Sergeant. We require help from no one."

There was something precious and thin-lipped about the declaration. Something foolish and old-fashioned. So far as Karel knew of Bim's nature, his attitude was definitely out of character. The head of KOS was usually much smoother, using affability as a smoke screen behind which he could exercise any sleight of hand he might feel the occasion warranted. Karel was left with the feeling that Bim was uncharacteristically flustered by something that had surprised him shortly before Karel's arrival.

He nodded and got to his feet.

"I'll accept the fact that you won't cooperate with me, sir, but I trust you have no intention of throwing any blocks in my path?"

Bim took a deep breath. It seemed to restore both his confidence and his good nature. He laughed and waved his arms in an expansive gesture.

"You've caught me at a bad time," he apologized. "Don't take my refusal as final. Let me look into Horvath's file in greater detail. I'll get back to you." He walked Karel to the door with a friendly arm linked through Karel's elbow. "If you see Judge Trevian before I do, please give him my regards."

Karel expected to get less cooperation from Borodin of the SJB than he had from Colonel Bim. In fact, he didn't expect that Borodin would even see him. He was proved right in that. When he called for an interview, he was told to seek an appointment with Slobodan Saloman, the Assistant Director.

Karel didn't like the man on first sight. He was bald except for a yoke of black hair that ringed the back of his skull and spilled over his ears. He wore a pince-nez. It seemed a professional affectation. Saloman kept his hands folded on the desktop.

"I know all about you, Sergeant Karel," Saloman said right off, as though Karel were a criminal accused of some heinous crime. "You people argued for this case and now you're out crying for help."

"Cooperation between law enforcement and investigative agencies should be the rule, not the exception," Karel said mildly.

"I agree. Why don't you cooperate with us and tell us what you've discovered about this Horvath fellow?"

"He was a child in Zagreb. We assume he went to high school, and maybe to a university, but we don't know where. He was wounded. Twice. One might have been a hunting wound or both may have been the result of war. He may have fought in Spain. He may have been with the Ustasi or no more than a sympathizer."

A connecting door opened. Borodin walked in. Karel began to stand up. Borodin waved him back, planted his hip on the edge of the desk, and smiled benignly. He had a cigarette in one hand, a slim folio in the other.

"The only thing we can say for certain about his past is that he was an officer in the KOS in nineteen fifty-two. He retired from active service in nineteen sixty-two, transferring in the rank of major to the army reserve," Karel finished.

"And that's what you know?" Saloman said, making no attempt to conceal his amused contempt.

"He chased after women," Karel said without a smile.

The two directors of the SJB were silent for a moment, then burst into laughter. Saloman was just a beat behind Borodin. Very quick with his nose, Karel thought.

Borodin opened the file folder and started to quote from it.

"Since his retirement Horvath has been engaged in any number of clandestine activites involving the import of luxury goods and the export of national treasures, principally icons and other religious artifacts."

"If I may ask, sir, why hasn't the SJB moved against him?"

Borodin smiled. "He was more useful as an informer and unpaid agent."

Karel wondered if Horvath's greatest value hadn't been in revealing secrets held by the KOS. There was as much intelligence-gathering activity conducted between agency and agency as against foreign powers.

Borodin extracted a sheet of paper from the file and placed it in Karel's lap. It was a discharge for one Lieutenant First Class Ivan Boreta from the Headquarters Company of the Third Command of the Corps of National Defense of Yugoslavia, an elite uniformed troop, numbering about seventy-five thousand, formed immediately after the war. It had been separate from the army and the police. Its primary missions had been to overcome all remnants of organized political resistance, prevent sabotage, and guard Tito and his high command. In time it had lost much of its purpose, was reduced to one-third its size, and was transformed into a special frontier guard force under the authority of the army. Ivan Boreta's age was noted as being thirty-six. The date of the discharge was February 1952.

Borodin then handed Karel the enlistment paper of one Captain Jan Horvath. He'd joined the Counter-Intelligence, the KOS, fourteen days after Boreta's discharge.

"Note that this Horvath enlisted in the rank of captain," Borodin said, as though he knew exactly where Karel's eyes were on the paper. "No remarks about transfer or special qualifications."

Horvath had been taken into the Quarantine Barracks of the KOS at Nis, apparently to await assignment.

The third document was a copy of a letter dated 1947. The month and day were illegible. The name of the man or organization to which it had been sent had been cut off the top. The signature at the bottom had been clumsily inked over with a broad nib. The letter read: "I know that the man calling himself Ivan Napica is a traitor, a spy, and a murderer. I have evidence that I would like to put before you. Please do not ignore me. I am a poor man but I am proud, and my son has been killed by a dishonorable man."

"Have your laboratories looked past the ink blot at the signature?"

"They couldn't make it out."

"Where did this document come from?"

"The files of the Secret Police."

"From a dossier on Horvath?"

"From a dossier on Napica."

"You think that Ivan Boreta, Ivan Napica, and Jan Horvath were the same man?"

"I think you may discover that this Horvath wore a great many faces and used a great many names."

"How did you make the connection?"

"Ah," Borodin said, and grinned, refusing to give away his methods.

"Have you any documents that forge the links and fill in the gaps?"

"In your business it's important that evidence makes a neat package. In ours it doesn't. We can live comfortably with reasonable conjecture, intelligent projection, and logical synthesis."

"Ah," Karel said.

"Besides," Borodin said, grinning, "someone had censored the records at the KOS. Interesting that, isn't it?"

"Thank you," Karel said. Borodin reached for the documents. Karel handed them over and stood up.

"We cooperate," Saloman said expansively. With his boss there, he stood up and reached out to shake Karel's hand.

= 13 =

Jan Horvath: 1933–1941

Ivan Lukac didn't want to be a merchant like his father, grand-father, and great-grandfather. He loved to count things, keep records and estimate profit, but he felt it degrading to wait on people.

Great-grandfather Fila Lukac had started with a wagon and a horse, traveling the dirt roads of the countryside selling pots, pans, needles, cloth, spices, and other goods. The peasants could tell the day of the month from the moment of Lukac the Peddler's arrival. They sometimes paid him with livestock, grain, or the favors of their daughters. He managed to get what few coins they might have as well. In hard years, after brutal winters or wet springs, he gathered up picture frames, small icons, and other family treasures. Most were redeemed when a good harvest improved the fortunes of the farmers. Some were never claimed.

With the pawn goods Lukac the Peddler had collected during a lifetime, his son, Ivan's grandfather, opened a shop in a town close to the Italian border where a good many tourists came to buy. It was a grand trade in fine goods. In the shop next door he opened another business selling shoddy imitations. In time he opened a third that sold cheap mass-produced items to the locals. In this way Lukac profited from all classes and all tastes.

Upon his death, Ivan's father, Edvard, inherited everything. He sold out all the shops and took his family to Zagreb in Croatia, where he opened the largest department store in the city, bought a fine house in the rich section of the town, and immediately established himself as a man of civic responsibility. He had eight sons, the youngest Ivan, and one daughter who was simple-minded. As each son came of age Edvard Lukac gave him the means to start a mercantile enterprise in another city. The father provided the lease, the stock, and a house suitable to a young man who expected to have a wife and children. In Ivan's case things were to be different. He was told that he was to be the family treasure. He could decide for himself what he wanted to do with his life. He could be a doctor, an artist, a writer, anything he chose to be. He expected and feared that he was meant to be supported so long as he took personal charge of his sister.

That's how he accurately perceived his father's plan for him. He looked for something that would spare him that but which would still elicit his father's support.

His father served on councils and committees, not because he felt a need to serve the community but because it gave him access to important people that could help him in his financial dealings. Ivan learned the subtleties of opportunism and duplicity at his father's knee. The elder Lukac always put self, business, family, and fortune before any other considerations. He had been all for the Austro-Hungarian monarchy that had occupied his country until the Great War brought changes that couldn't be ignored. At the end of it he found himself serving on the legation that was sent to the prince regent of Serbia to petition him to create and rule the union of states that formed a newly created nation. The new king Alexander gave Lukac a title as a reward. Lukac's commercial enterprises flourished.

Ivan thought of politics as a career through which he might distinguish himself and confound his father's plan for him to become his sister's caretaker. The politician has many of the qualities of the merchant. He promises much and delivers as little as he can. He sells by way of slogans. He has no loyalty to a product unless the public continues to want it. If sales slump, the shelves are cleared to make room for whatever it might be that will make the public want to buy again.

When he was seventeen, and enrolled in the University of Zagreb, Ivan was approached by a group of young Croatian

Nationalists. The leader was a boy named Serge Skela. He was dark, tall, and intense in a way that disconcerted many, intimidated many, and charmed a good many more. Ivan had admired him for a long time and wanted to emulate him. But he was afraid of his political activities.

"You have to understand the way it is," Skela said when Ivan refused to listen to his proposition. "Didn't you find it better to join up with this group or that in the other schools you have attended?"

"I didn't go to school. I was tutored privately at home."

"An only child?"

"One of nine."

"And private tutors for all. Your family must be very rich."

"Oh, no. We lived in reduced circumstances," Ivan quickly replied, smelling danger as heavy as the spoor of a bear in the atmosphere. Why was he afraid? Skela made no open threat. Not every student in the university was approached to join the Nationalists. It was considered to be an honor by some. No harm had ever come to any who'd been asked and refused. Was it even fear he felt? Or was it excitement because someone he'd long admired was trying to recruit him into a cause they would share.

"What does your father do?" Skela asked.

The smell of danger sharpened. Ivan suddenly realized that he had no skills in dealing with people in the real world. His experience had been that of a chess player fighting wars in the safety of the library before the fire.

"He's a priest," Ivan heard himself lie, thinking that Skela would not expect the son of a priest to be an activist in any cause except that of Christ.

Skela looked thoughtful. "We have no priests or sons of priests with us," he said. "I think it might be a good thing. The girls in particular will like the thought that our cause has a priest to pray over it."

"But I'm not a priest, and my father is old and no longer serves mass," Ivan said desperately, trying to retrieve a portion of the lie.

"Ah, ah, ah," Skela said soothingly, throwing his arm around the smaller boy's shoulders. "You know the words, don't you? You know how to make the motions, don't you? I don't believe any of that moaning and mumbling myself—no offense—but still I have an idea it can be made useful. We'll find a way. If nothing else it will make us both very popular with the girls.''

"What do you mean?"

"Women are very pious, don't you know? Haven't you heard how they lie down for the priests? They tell the girls that they'll be shown the key to heaven.'' He laughed abruptly. ''I suppose that's just what they are shown if you look at it in a certain way.''

"I don't understand."

"Don't be a dolt. They just want a good reason to spread their legs for a scratch when they begin to itch. They want to know they're giving up something for a good cause. National independence is a good cause. We'll call them the comforters of the soldiers.''

He thought his words over, captured by his own inventiveness.

"The blessing of a priest will make it even better.''

"For the soldiers?''

"We're the soldiers,'' Skela said, ''and we're going to sleep with a lot of girls.''

Ivan was netted. The hook of flattery was firmly in his mouth. He was one of them. He'd told an incredible lie and found himself one of them, like it or not.

"What is this organization I've joined?'' he asked.

"The Ustasi,'' Skela replied.

The Secret Police hated and deplored the Ustasi. They came to take Ivan away for questioning sometime after his initiation. He'd long since confessed his spontaneous lie to Skela. They'd laughed about it. Skela admitted that he hadn't believed a word of it, but knew that it would serve his purpose better to pretend to believe that he did. It didn't surprise Ivan that both of them had acted more effectively with lies than they might have done with truth. But now the lie was paying him back.

"You call yourself a priest?'' the interrogator said.

Ivan sat painfully erect on the hard, wooden chair. He wanted to present as strong a portrait of a polite and obedient young man as he could.

"Not a priest. The son of a priest."

"Why is that? Why would someone do such a thing?"

"It was a joke."

"You joke about religion, do you? You joke about God? Do you joke about the King as well?"

"I didn't mean it was a joke meant to make anyone laugh."

"What was it meant to do?"

"To make someone leave me alone."

"Someone was threatening you? With what were you being threatened?"

"Not threatened. I was being urged to join a group I didn't want to join."

"What group?"

"Just a student group."

The interrogator punched him in the stomach then. It happened so suddenly that Ivan started to cry, not from pain alone, but from the shock of terror.

"That's to let you know you can't play schoolboy games with me," the interrogator said calmly. "You can't play at words with me. If I ask a question I want an intelligent response. Right away. I don't want to have to dig around in the dunghill of your mind. What group?"

"The Croatian Nationalists."

"There we are. That wasn't difficult, was it? The truth isn't difficult."

Ivan was suddenly afraid that the truth would kill him if he wasn't very careful.

"I want you to call someone for me," Ivan suddenly heard himself saying. Fear rose up like sour water in his mouth. What was his unconstrained tongue doing to him now? "I want you to call my father. His name is Edvard Lukac."

He waited for another blow. The interrogator stared at him. He leaned back against the wall and lit a cigarette.

"Do you smoke?" he said.

"Yes," Ivan replied.

The interrogator gave him his own cigarette and then left the cell.

Ivan was left alone. When the cigarette was finished he didn't know what to do with the butt. He spit in his palm and snuffed it out, then put the spent end in his pocket. If he dropped it underfoot he was afraid the interrogator would use that as an excuse to strike him again. Hours passed. He never left his chair, though he'd not been told he couldn't do so. He was quaking inside when the interrogator returned, all grins and bonhomie.

"Well, I suppose it's the sort of thing schoolboys do, isn't it?" he said expansively. "The sort of thing an innocent young man of good family and good heart might be trapped into. Would you like to stretch your legs or are you comfortable there?"

Ivan's legs, rump, and back cried out for relief from the hard chair but he shook his head and said that he was all right.

"Relax. Lean back. No need to sit so stiff and formal with me," the interrogator said, drawing up another chair for himself. He straddled it and folded his hands on the back of it.

"All you have to do right now is tell me who recruited you into that gang."

Ivan hesitated for a moment. There was no courage in him. All at once he hated Skela for having put him into the position where he'd been forced to find that out. He gave Skela away without another moment's hesitation, though he felt that someone had cut his throat. He felt sorry for himself.

"No one will know—" he began to say.

"No one will know that it was you gave him away," the interrogator interrupted. "What do you think, we're fools? We already know the name of your leader and more than half the membership. We just wanted to know where your loyalties lay."

"With the King, of course. With the King."

"Who could doubt that after talking with the man who vouched for your father. You were duped into joining, or bullied into it."

"Yes," Ivan said.

"Now, I don't want to bully you into anything," the interrogator said silkily. "That other—that love tap—was just a momentary expression of my impatience. You understand? Of course you do."

"I'll resign from the organization right away," Ivan said, anticipating what the interrogator intended to demand of him.

"No, you won't. I mean we'd much rather that you didn't. We want you to stay right where you are among them. In fact it might not be a bad idea if you became even more active. Pretend that the threats we made to you only strengthened your resolve. Do you get my meaning?"

Ivan sat there without moving. He wanted to cry. He knew he was being forced into doing something against his will once more. They were using his fear against him again. He didn't know what he could do to fight against it. He couldn't bear it if they hit him again. He would weep or shit himself. Forever after he'd have to wear that garment of unbearable shame.

The interrogator watched the boy struggle with himself. The natural independence of youth resented what was being asked of him. But he was scared spitless. He was only looking for a way to convince himself that what he was going to do he was going to do out of conviction, or at least accommodation, and not because of terror. For a moment he wondered if it was even worthwhile recruiting a coward and weakling like this boy into the service. Were jellyfish known to grow spines? No, but they were known to grow very wily.

His stomach growled. He'd missed his midday meal. He would develop a headache if he didn't eat soon and that would never do. There were more students to question. If he felt out of sorts they would only irritate him too much. He might damage one of them to no purpose. He reached out and grasped Ivan's wrist in his hand. The boy started and cringed away.

"Hey, why think about it? You'll do as you're told. We both know it."

Ivan played the game. He even came to like it. Sitting and drinking among his comrades in the kafanas, knowing that a word from him could make their lives as miserable as he chose to make them, gave him a great sense of power. He sometimes wondered how many of the members had been turned around just as he'd been turned. Which of them was a spy like himself? Everyone wondered about the loyalty of everyone else. Everyone treated everyone else with friendly suspicion. Even the girls who easily gave their bodies to nearly everyone in the name of comradeship might be doing nothing more than lulling a man into an indiscretion. That was all right. Two could play that game. Amid the groping, writhing, and lovemaking, a good deal of low-grade espionage was conducted with nothing much ever really found out.

Ivan continued in his pose as a priest's son. He knew it lent a certain piquancy to his seductions. The girls were thrilled by the idea that they were being dandled by a semi-holy fellow who might also be a vicious spy. He might even be a patriot in the cause of Croatian nationalism as well. It was like playacting. They could all be as many characters as they liked as long as they kept their roles apart, never speaking with the wrong voice at the wrong time. Students and young workers were given to such dramatics. There were even a few serious revolutionaries among them. Every now and then a student would be taken away for questioning. Occasionally one would not return to class or kafana. If inquiries were made they were turned aside. If anyone continued to question a disappearance there might be a knock on the door in the middle of the small hours of a dark morning.

There was a girl in their group, Riva Vakuf, who was called *mala lisico,* the little fox, because she had hair that was the color and texture of a fox's brush. It was combed straight back from her brow and bound so tightly with a metal ring that it seemed to pull at her temples and lift the corners of her eyes. The tail of hair hung down her back nearly to her waist. It glinted each time she moved her head. Ivan longed to smell and taste it.

The young women of the movement were generally easy enough with their favors. Except for the little fox. She held herself to herself, giving nothing away, not even a touch, not even a comradely kiss at the beginning or end of meetings. Not every man wanted her. Ivan couldn't understand that. He believed someone so beautiful should have a fascination for everyone.

Skela, arrogant and amused because he wasn't stricken, laughed at Ivan.

"Riva is a fanatic," he said. "Fanatics don't make good bed partners. You should know that by now. All the passion left her body and went to her brain. She wants to be had by the revolution. I think she would join anyone, even the Communists, if there was no other cause around. It's a wonder she hasn't joined the church and become a nun.''

Ivan wanted to smash Skela in the mouth for talking that way but was afraid Skela would beat him up. Or he might simply laugh and brush Ivan's blows aside.

He mooned about after the little fox. She sometimes acted amused, sometimes irritated. Once she told him in the harshest language that if she ever came in heat like a bitch she would inform him. Until then—if ever—he must stop sniffing around her like a dog. She said this in front of everyone before a meeting in a kafana, a time when good fellowship ran highest. Everyone laughed at Ivan's expense.

The next day he informed on her, claiming that she was one of the student agitators who had broken into the university files and destroyed a good many private documents in protest because the university, at the government's request, kept dossiers on the political activities of the students. When she was taken away, he became terribly afraid and remorseful.

The name of his father had once saved him a beating. They'd never mentioned that incident between them. Ivan expected that his father knew he spied for the government. Ivan didn't know if he approved. He'd discovered, much to his confusion, that people never showed the same face twice a day. A person would say one thing, mean another, and act in yet another way altogether. Even the simplest matter was a tangle. Was it any wonder that the affairs of governments and nations were a tangle as well? What was a man to do except protect himself as best he could? Every dog for himself.

He wanted Riva punished for humiliating him. He wanted her to go to bed with him. He wanted to make her understand. He wanted to make her love him.

When he went to his father asking that he intervene in the matter of his girlfriend, the senior Lukac made a good deal of it, turning the request over in his mind as though he expected it would cost him more than he wanted to spend.

Finally he said, ''Once before I spent a little of my store of influence in your behalf. Why not? You're my son and it was my duty as a father to protect you from your errors. My name is valuable to me. You have a stake in it for it's your name as well. This girlfriend of yours—what does that mean?''

"Sir?"

"What is a girlfriend? It's been a long time since I was young. I know what I meant when I called a young woman a girlfriend. I want to know what you mean. Is she your lover?''

"No, sir."

"Not a candidate for marriage?"

"It's never been discussed. Not even hinted at. It's not the same to call her my girlfriend as you might have meant when you were my age.''

"That's what I'm asking."

"She's a friend."

"Like a man would be a friend? A comrade?''

"Yes. A comrade."

"In this Croatian nationalist group you were asked to infiltrate?''

Ivan noted that his father put his association with the movement the wrong way round and made it sound as though Ivan had been first an agent for the government who then risked his life to enlist in a dangerous enterprise. The turning of a sentence, the shading of the truth.

"She's on the Central Committee."

"Exactly."

Ivan had no idea what that meant. He waited to be informed.

"She was a leader. She took her chances. To apply pressure for her release would compromise her. She wouldn't thank you for that.''

Ivan realized his father intended to do nothing in Riva's behalf. He intended to save the precious store of influence he possessed. The little fox could well be one of those who never returned from the interrogation cells. Something in his brain ran around like a squirrel in a cage. His father, all unknowingly, had just given Ivan a lever, a weapon to use against his reasoning, if only he could get his hand on it. He had to speak or the moment would be lost. Something clicked. It had the effect of the bulb above the heads of comic characters in American cartoons.

"That's just it, Father, don't you see? She'll have to tell me things to repay the debt she will feel she owes me. She'll have to satisfy her honor. Her honor is like a man's."

"She'll hate you for it," his father said.

"I understood the sacrifices that would have to be made when I accepted the job I do," Ivan said sanctimoniously.

His father exercised his influence and Riva was released without real harm having been done to her. She was cautious around Ivan. But, then, she acted fearfully toward a lot of the members of the group for many days. She didn't know who had informed on her, or even if it was someone inside the group. She didn't know who had effected her release. She was politically sophisticated. She understood how little such organizations as the Secret Police cared about brutality applied to the innocent. They reasoned that no brutality was ever wasted. It always served as a lesson. Someone had called in a debt or asked a favor to keep her safe from torture. She'd been given just a taste. It had been enough to weaken her bowels and shame her.

Some of her fire had been blown out.

Ivan was good with children and cats. He'd learned that they were not to be forced into friendliness and affection. Helpless creatures that they were, they were best courted by inattention. He never forced an embrace or a conversation on a cat or a child. He simply sat as quietly as he knew how, ignoring them as they sniffed at his cuffs or peered at him sidelong. When he felt the tug of teeth or fingers on his sleeve, a nose pushed into the cup of his hand, or a little hand placed in his, he knew that he'd piqued the curiosity that captured cat and child. He knew this very well because he was himself captured by people who ignored him.

He started to treat the little fox like a cat or a child. He no longer chased her or even looked at her except with a certain bland kindliness. It was as though he'd put aside his childish infatuation and become a compassionate adult overnight. He realized that having twice exercised power over her, once by dropping her in the boiling soup, and once by plucking her out, he no longer was a prisoner of his lust for her. He could look at her in a different, more confident way.

Riva made up her mind that Ivan was the one who'd first

betrayed then saved her. She didn't know why. She knew that he was called the Priest. She herself had once laughingly, mockingly, called him Father when he'd made overtures to her, telling him that it wasn't becoming for a priest to beg for favors from an unmarried girl. That was before she'd raged at him, insulting him, leading him to act against her. Now she took to looking at him when she thought he wasn't watching. One night in the kafana she made a point of sitting next to him. She put her thigh against his. When she reached across the table for a cigarette or the wine bottle she allowed her breast to brush his arm. She glanced up at him with her foxy eyes and shaded them seductively with the fur of her lashes. When they left that night she went along to his room without a word. He made himself a pot of tea and poured her a cup when it was ready. He acted as though she was there, but not there. He made small remarks about the chill of the room, the possibility of rain, and the lateness of the hour as though he were talking to himself. He undressed in the toilet down the hall and came back wearing a robe. He got into bed and turned off the light. He said good night as though talking to a cat or the room in general.

She undressed in the dark and climbed into bed with him naked. Her body was very small and fine-boned. Her limbs were restless as she opened his robe and put her mouth on his chest. He recognized her. He arranged himself so that she lay in the cradle of his arms. They began to kiss each other, exploring their mouths with their tongues.

"Was it you?" she whispered.

He lay as still as death, thinking out the best answer to her question.

"Was it you who arranged my release?" she asked.

He nodded his head and cupped her small breast in his hand. It was not much larger than a teacup. The nipple was long and rubbery in his mouth. She gasped softly.

"Was it you?" she whispered again. "Was it you who betrayed me to the police?"

He was still for a long time, then he said, "Yes, it was I," letting her know because it demonstrated the power that he had over her.

She gasped again and struggled to help him mount her. She was in a frenzy.

The next morning, while she still slept, he cut off and saved a lock of her hair as a token of his power over her.

Ivan learned when to smile and when to frown, when to overwhelm an adversary with a flood of words and when to disarm him with silence. He learned exactly how to find the key to any girl's seduction. He learned that even with a key not every man could seduce every woman. He accepted the fact that he was not outstandingly attractive and that he would have to pay for what he got from women one way or another.

As graduation approached he gave a good deal of thought about what his degree in political science could do for him by way of establishing a career. It had been a neutral discipline designed to occupy students until they could decide what to make of their educations. His father said that he would, of course, work for the government as though he once again had no knowledge of Ivan's employment with the Royal Secret Police. He made suggestions about the clerks of court, the judiciary, and the foreign service. Ivan waited for his contact with the Secret Police to make him a real offer. When it came, it was not as much as he'd hoped for, but it was something.

"We've arranged for you to have a post with the Office of the International Red Cross," they told him. "It may seem tame to you after the excitement of student action but we can assure you the work is sensitive and vital. These people that volunteer to serve the helpless and needy are most often liberal in their political persuasions. Stands to reason, doesn't it?"

Ivan didn't answer. He'd learned in conversations with anyone from the Secret Police that they had the interrogator's trick of engaging you in what seemed a conversation by forcing answers to innocuous questions out of you when all the while they were telling you, in no uncertain terms, just exactly what you would do.

"We need them, certainly," the liaison went on. "They're a necessary bunch in time of disaster, earthquakes and the like. It will be a nice safe post for you, a place to learn how to set a broken arm and staunch a wound. Who knows, that might come in handy one day.

"We have a new name for you. Ivan Kosho. How do you like it? Just the last name changed. Makes it easier to remember and less chance of not responding to a friend when they call for your attention. Papers are being made out for you in that name. You'll have to pretend that you're a Moslem. An irreligious one if you like. There's not a lot to know in order to play the part."

So that was the first time Ivan Lukac gave up his name.

When he was sent to Spain to monitor the activities of Yugoslavian Red Cross units serving the wounded of the vicious civil war, he had some chances to apply the first-aid lessons. He wasn't particularly good at it. The blood and filth frightened and offended him. He couldn't understand why the Secret Police would have sent him into a war-ravaged country where Red Cross units were made up of volunteers from many countries. There were no political dissidents among them as far as he could see. They were simply good, foolish people doing a dangerous job. He didn't like being one of them.

He didn't know that the Secret Police didn't really trust him. They thought him weak and foolish, apt to break when the least pressure was applied, a baby who had cried for Papa the first time he was punched in the belly. They didn't forget such things.

On the other hand he was a man in place when the order came down that a certain political dissident named Joze Kropenick, then fighting with an International Brigade on the side of the Communists, had been marked for assassination. Ivan Kosho was assigned to a medical aid unit serving the sector where Kropenick was known to be fighting. Ivan could move about at will with considerably more freedom than any soldier could exercise. He was approached by a control agent and given the order. It was a test.

He accepted the job. What else could he have done? He concealed the gun the agent gave him in his kit. Then he became afraid that another medic might find it. In the end he slept with the gun under his pillow. When he was awake he carried it inside his tunic. The hardness of it against his belly frightened yet excited him. It recalled the feeling of Riva's hard little fists pummeling him as he rode her to climax. He had a picture of the man he was to murder in his tunic as well. After a week of fear he reasoned that the chances of his ever confronting the man in the confusion of the battle area were very few. Even if he came face to face with Kropenick, how could he be sure that he would recognize him? War made great changes in the face of a man.

He began to feel adventurous. He sat with his comrades in the medical unit drinking tea around the fire and hugged the pistol to his chest, smiling to himself, complimenting himself upon his courage until one or another would ask him if he was dreaming of his girl at home. It was a great pleasure to imagine himself a hard killer, a secret hero, when there was no danger in it.

Then one day he miraculously came upon Kropenick in a shell-gutted field. He was moving across an area that had been passed over by artillery and the attack of infantry units in company with two others, when he saw Kropenick lying in the bloody mud, his eyes rolled back in his head, all but unconscious. One hand had been blown away. Ivan bent over and peered into the wounded man's face. He didn't even have to check his memory with the photograph. He straightened up. Looking off, he saw that the rest of his party had gone down a dry riverbed toward the sound of screaming men in need of them.

Suddenly his hands were wet. He was painfully aware of the need to urinate. He took the gun from inside his tunic. Now that the moment had come he wondered if he could really do it. A crow cried out, startling him. It was the spur he needed, that sound, like Riva laughing at him before he'd taught her a lesson. He put the muzzle of the pistol to Kropenick's face and pulled the trigger. He took Kropenick's pay card to prove that he'd done the murder. Afterward he would often try to remember if he'd first felt the bullet strike his thigh or heard the report of the gun. He looked around to see who was shooting at him, but all he saw were the dead. Clutching his leg, he ran away.

$= 14 =$

Once blooded, the man who called himself Ivan Kosho had found it no easier to take another's life. It was never enjoyment for him. He loathed and feared the killers among them who took real delight in murder. They weren't the worst of the brutes he had to fraternize with from time to time. There were the interrogators, men and women who enjoyed inflicting pain. They chilled his heart. He thought them depraved. He sometimes thought that he'd rather die than become one of them. He'd much rather kill. It wasn't always clean but it was usually swift, over and done before the eyes could inform the belly what the hand had done. He trained himself to be very cool and efficient. Within a few years he was considered a top assassin. He became adept in the use of a hand gun. He would have enjoyed becoming expert with a rifle but couldn't develop the eye or hand for it. He wasn't skillful with a knife, hating the close encounter it demanded. He studied the characteristics of poisons. There was really not a good deal of call for his services, but enough to excuse him from most other duties.

Over the years he operated in several countries under different names, always traveling as a tourist because he had no gift of language and could never have maintained an undercover role. For a while he thought of himself exclusively as Ivan Lukac, but with so many identities his sense of self became blurred. He began to think of himself as Ivan Kosho, for that was how he was known among his comrades in the Secret Police. He had less and less to do with the past, visiting his father in Zagreb less frequently, and scarcely ever dropping in on his brothers, who had prosperous shops in other cities.

He established no permanent relationships with women. He told himself that his profession prohibited love and devotion. In fact, it suited him. His conquest of Riva, long ago, had taught him important lessons about the nature of women. His experiences thereafter were totted up in an account book, the facts distorted to fit the premise that women were attracted first to power, then to mystery, and then to physicality. Somewhere very low on the list they counted love. He had to buy a good many of his feminine companions. That was understandable. He moved around so much. It was difficult for him to meet women in the ordinary way.

The women he bought were of two sorts. Prostitutes, openly mercenary, and therefore entitled to very little consideration, or girls of the lower and lower-middle classes who claimed to be looking for love and romance, but were really looking for excitement or security. Small gifts, dinners, or weekends at some seaside resort bought them. It bought him the illusion of affection.

The ultimate intentions of the German Nazis and Italian Fascists to rule Europe had become quite clear by 1940. Prince Paul, regent in the name of Alexander's son, Peter Karadjordjevic, who'd not yet reached his majority, maneuvered as skillfully as he could to maintain Yugoslavia's neutrality. Public opinion was outraged when Italy attacked Greece and Germany invaded Romania, but the government could do nothing.

Early in 1941 Premier Cvetkovic was summoned to Berchtesgaden. Ivan went along as one of several bodyguards. He was afraid of the dangers involved, but felt proud that he'd been named to play a part in an historical conference.

Hitler suggested that Yugoslavia, Bulgaria, and Turkey join the Tripartite Pact between Germany, Italy, and Japan. Even though they feared for Yugoslavia's territorial integrity, Prince Paul and Cvetkovic were resigned to their helplessness. They had neither the internal strength nor the foreign support to effectively oppose Hitler's will. Ivan was with Cvetkovic again when the premier went to Vienna to sign the agreement on March 25, 1941.

Upon their return two days later they found Belgrade in an uproar.

Ivan was allowed to return to his apartment to refresh himself after the journey, and dress himself in clean clothes. He was expected to return to Cvetkovic's side at the palace by the fall of evening. Late in the afternoon, while he was in bed with a whore selected from his little book of numbers, he was visited by two officers of the Serbian Air Force.

They treated him with a great deal of courtesy.

"Ivan Kosho," the younger of them said. "We've been told that you're a practical man, one who knows how to read the handwriting on the wall."

The older man laughed sharply. It was like the barking of a hunting dog. "One who doesn't have to be hit over the head twice, so to speak," he said.

"What is this all about?" Ivan asked politely. He was pleased that his voice was even, that the hand holding his cigarette didn't tremble. He was even pleased that they were interviewing him while he was in his dressing gown. It was an expensive garment of satin brocade purchased in Vienna.

"It's about good sense," they said. "It's about the political realities. We have a King only a few years under the age of his majority. Do we need a prince regent as well?"

"Coup d'etat?" Ivan said.

"Succinctly put," the younger man said with honeyed admiration.

"Who leads you?"

The officers looked at each other. Conspiracy breeds caution. Then they realized that they'd have to kill Ivan if he refused to help them, so why shouldn't he know the name?

"General of the Army Dusan Simovic."

Ivan knew that they'd kill him if he refused. He also knew he could lie to them, agree to join their conspiracy to overthrow the government and inform on them as soon as he reached the palace. But if Simovic led them, there was every chance that the coup would be successful with or without him.

"What do you want me to do?" he asked.

"Nothing," they said.

"What do you mean?"

"We simply want you to do nothing. When we come to arrest Premier Cvetkovic we would like you to stand aside."

Ivan thought about it. There were other things to consider. With the fall of the government he could be out of a job.

"I could take a more active part," he said.

The officers were pleased but wary.

"You'd help us?"

"Yes. I've made the offer."

"Even knowing that your life would be forfeit if we fail?"

Ivan nodded. He'd never before felt so alive, so excited. He wondered if the whore had her ear at the bedroom door listening to the conversation, learning what a daring and dangerous man he was.

"Would it do us any good to approach the bodyguard that works with you?"

Ivan shook his head. "Bartul can't be bought, persuaded, or frightened off," he said. "He's very stupid and very loyal."

"Will he fight?"

"Against any odds."

"We would like this coup to be as bloodless as possible, but if this Bartul is the kind of man you say he is, he'll have to be eliminated. Try to do it in such a way that Cvetkovic doesn't suspect you. It might be useful to make it appear that you resisted us."

"I understand," Ivan said.

They shook hands and the officers left.

Ivan went into the bedroom. The whore was sitting up in bed, the sheets pulled up to hide her breasts. Her eyes were as round as saucers and she was breathing heavily. She didn't pretend not to have eavesdropped. She was aware that Ivan knew she wouldn't have missed the opportunity.

"My God, are you such a man?" she whispered in a storm of excitement and arousal.

Ivan took off the robe of silk brocade and fell on her. He'd never performed so magnificently.

When General Simovic's soldiers invaded the palace, Ivan and another, Bartul, were with Cvetkovic in a small anteroom. The premier had grown friendly with his bodyguards during their private hours together. He clearly favored Ivan over Bartul. Bartul never smiled. He scarcely ever turned his head on the thick neck that rose from powerful shoulders like the trunk of a tree rooted in stone. He didn't care if he was liked. He didn't know what friendship meant but worshipped loyalty with religious fervor.

When they heard the commotion along the corridors approaching the room, Bartul immediately drew out his gun. He never took chances. He walked toward the door. The moment the summons sounded on it Ivan shot Bartul in the back.

Then he quickly shouted out, "We surrender!"

The door burst open and the younger of the two officers who had visited him that afternoon came in at the head of a small squad of armed men.

"Put down your gun," he ordered Ivan.

Ivan allowed the gun to fall to the floor. Two soldiers pinned his arms behind his back. Two others took Cvetkovic in charge. As they escorted the premier out the door, he rubbed his hand along the paneling of the door, proving to himself that the shot had not been fired from the other side. He looked at Ivan with condemnation. The soldiers played out the game according to orders anyway, leading Ivan off as though he were a prisoner.

Ivan Kosho was given a commission in the army. He was given a new name.

The new premier Simovic tried to assure the Germans that Yugoslavia intended to honor the Vienna agreement, but on April 6, without a declaration of war, the German Air Force began the bombing of Belgrade and the German Army smashed across the border from Bulgaria.

The Yugoslav Communists saw in the defeat of Yugoslavia their opportunity to come to power. Croatian animosity toward the Serbian-dominated government was unrelenting and many welcomed the German invasion. The army's equipment was poor, communications inadequate, and the troops badly disposed. Early defeat was inevitable. King Peter and the government fled to Palestine. On April 17 the Yugoslav High Command capitulated.

Ivan Kosho, who had been operating under the assumed name provided as protection against any future reprisals by adherents of Prince Paul or Premier Cvetkovic, chose still another one. As Ivan Napica he joined an element of a new Royal Army of the Fatherland under the leadership of Colonel Draza Mihailovic. They became known as the Chetniks after the Serb peasant-soldier bands who had fought a guerrilla war against the Ottoman occupation of Serbia from the fifteenth to nineteenth centuries. The Chetniks were strongly anti-Communist.

The Communists were only a small part of the Partisans but the supporters of Tito occupied all of the command positions. Many had fought in the Spanish Civil War.

Tito and Mihailovic met to discuss common action. Mihailovic couldn't agree with Tito's slogan, ''Attack the enemy wherever you can, however you can.'' He believed it presented too bloody a price in Nazi reprisals. Before the end of 1941 their differences broke out into open conflict.

In late December a band of Partisans and a larger unit of Chetniks attacked one another in the valley formed by a small tributary of the Drina near the town of Priboj. In the ensuing battle the better arms and greater numbers of the Chetniks overpowered the Partisans. Among the captured wounded were Stephano Merin and Bosa Kvadir. They were tied up along with several others and thrown into a makeshift prisoner compound. There were two guards to watch them.

None of the captured Partisans held out much hope for their lives. In the fluid, mobile nature of the kind of war both Partisan and Chetnik fought against the Germans, prisoners were a burden. Sometimes they were taken to some town which was held against the invaders, collected there, and used to trade when it was possible. Most often they were interrogated until an excuse was found to shoot them all. The hope that they might survive made their plight terrible. If they were sure to be shot, then fate had already decided for them. If there was the least glimmer of hope, then they could still discuss a strategy to save themselves.

''Could we make up a valuable story and feed it to them?'' one suggested.

''How could we expect everyone to remember the details of

it? There are some among us who are scarcely mental giants,'' another said.

"The only sure way would be to join them,'' still another advised.

"They would never believe it.''

"There's no hope,'' Stephano Merin said.

"Why do you say that?'' Bosa Kvadir, who was not a brave man, asked angrily. He would hate anyone who took away his shred of hope.

"I know one of the officers among them,'' Stephano said. "He was in the University of Zagreb when I was there. He was known to be a government spy. I saw him there, and I saw him in Spain. He was with a Red Cross unit.''

"See there? He must be a good man,'' Kvadir said.

"I saw him put a pistol to the head of a wounded Yugoslav and pull the trigger,'' Stephano said flatly.

"Was it an act of mercy, do you think?'' Kvadir said.

Why did everyone try to find a good explanation for an evil act, Merin wondered. To capture hope, of course, he answered himself.

"The man could have been saved,'' Merin said. "I'd looked at him minutes before. He could have been saved. This man, Ivan Lukac, killed him like a hunter kills his prey.''

"How can you be sure it wasn't an act of mercy?''

"He took his identity card from the dead man's pocket. As though it were proof. As though it were a trophy.''

So it was agreed that there wasn't much hope if such a man was with the Chetnik unit.

Bosa Kvadir was one of the very first to be questioned.

The officer Stephano Merin had called Ivan Lukac told the sentry to remove the ropes that bound Kvadir's arms behind his back. He sat him near the fire on a tree stump large enough to be a banquet table. He smiled and offered Kvadir a cigarette.

"My name is Captain Ivan Napica,'' he said. "Are you afraid?''

"Yes,'' Kvadir said like the croaking of a frog. His spit had turned to glue. It coated his tongue and threatened to choke

him. All the water in his body had gone to his bladder. He
wanted to piss like fury.

"Why be afraid?"

"I don't know."

"Of what do you have to be afraid?"

"I've done nothing," Kvadir said. "I've just done what I've
been told. I tried to be a good soldier and obey orders."

"But you're not a soldier, are you?"

"What?"

"You're not really a soldier. You're a member of a bunch of
ragtag irregulars. Just because you cut out a red star and pin it
to your hat doesn't make you a soldier, does it?"

Kvadir didn't know what to say.

"We're soldiers. We belong to the legal Royal Yugoslavian
Army of the Fatherland. Isn't that so?" Napica said.

The smiling devil of an officer was trying to trap him into a
political debate, Kvadir thought. He was no good at it. Someone said, "This is what will be good for you," and talked of
more food and a warmer house, and Kvadir agreed. Of course
he wanted those things. He felt the piss running down his leg.

The captain laughed. "You are afraid," he said. He removed
the pistol from its holster. Kvadir fell on his knees in the mud
made from his own piss.

"Someone here knows you," he screamed, in a low, soft
voice. It was like the sharp keening of a wind through the bare
branches of winter trees.

"What is that you say?"

"Stephano Merin knows you. He says that your name is
really Ivan Lukac and that you were a spy in Zagreb. He says
that he saw you murder a Yugoslav on a battlefield in Spain."

"Get up, get up," Ivan said almost abstractedly. He was
thinking back to his youth. Had he ever known anyone named
Stephano Merin? He couldn't remember any such name. Of
course, he'd been visible to everyone. He might have been
known to many and himself known very few. He looked down
at the groveling coward who'd managed to put himself back on
the stump. He felt a sudden foolish desire to let the man live.
He reminded him of something or someone. He couldn't put his
finger on it but it made him feel sympathetic.

"Do you know how to be silent?" he asked.

Kvadir nodded his head like a madman. Tears he didn't know were in him spilled out of his eyes in torrents and ran down his filthy cheeks.

"You just spilled your guts to me," Ivan pointed out.

Kvadir moaned and rocked his head from side to side.

Ivan bent to one knee beside the man and put his arm around Kvadir's shoulders. "Be a man," he said.

"I can't help it," Kvadir said.

"I understand," Ivan said, quite gently. He put the pistol back into the holster.

"What does this Stephano Merin look like? Describe him to me."

When Kvadir was done, Ivan said, "Listen to me. I want you to go to my tent. It's the third one along the row." He took his handkerchief from his pocket and tied it around Kvadir's arm. "This is your pass if anyone challenges you. Go into the tent and stay there. Go on now."

Kvadir shambled off. Ivan looked at the soldier standing off about twenty yards. The soldier's eyes made no comment on what he'd seen. He didn't care, it was the officer's business. Napica called the sentry over and described Stephano Merin.

"I want him next," he said. "Leave his arms tied behind his back."

When the sentry came back with Merin, Ivan asked for the sentry's rifle. "Have a smoke," he said in a friendly, generous way. When the guard was gone, Ivan turned to Merin. Now that he could connect a face with a name, he remembered Stephano Merin. He'd been known at the university as a great hero in the mountains he'd come from. A special man.

"I know you," Ivan said.

Merin shrugged.

"I remember you," Ivan said. "Do you remember me?"

Merin said nothing.

"How do you intend to play the game?" Ivan asked.

"What is the game?"

"We want information about you Partisans."

Merin looked at the earth, shifting his eyes from side to side as though counting the dead. "You know everything there is to know about us," he said.

"You weren't operating entirely on your own. Don't take me for a fool. Do you take me for a fool?"

Merin shrugged again.

Ivan felt a tremor in his hands. It surprised him. He wasn't in a rage. He wasn't trembling with frustration. Suddenly he knew why he was unable to control his hands. He was afraid. He was afraid of a man whose arms and hands were tied behind his back. He was afraid of a man who was weakened from a wound in his thigh. The blood had soaked Merin's trousers and was caked there like a crust of bread. Why was he afraid? He crouched down and peered into Merin's face, trying to find the reason in his prisoner's eyes.

Merin never flinched. Neither did he play a game of war with glances. He merely stared back at Ivan as blandly as though they were new acquaintances introduced at a party or on the street. It was a neutral look, unremarkable in every way. Except there were glints of disdain and amusement in the eyes like tiny biting insects trapped in amber.

"Are you afraid of me?" Merin asked softly.

Ivan gathered saliva and spat into Merin's face.

Merin laughed outright.

"You've got that the wrong way around," he said. "In the cinema it's the prisoner who defies his captor by spitting into his face."

Ivan slapped him then.

"Coward," Merin said, without the slightest change of inflection or tone.

Ivan slapped him again and again. He closed his fingers and made fists. He punched at Merin's face until the Partisan decided not to bear it any longer and, tipping over to the side, fell to the ground. He lay there with his head twisted so that he could look up at the silently raging Ivan and grin at him. Fresh blood stained his mouth and chin.

Ivan wrestled him into a sitting position. Merin leaned against the huge tree stump. He lay his head against it as though he enjoyed the roughness of the bark on his cheek. He smelled the wood.

"What are you doing?" Ivan said.

"Getting a good smell into my nose," Merin said.

"It reminds you of the air of Montenegro?"

"Yes."

"Those were good days," Ivan said. "You were admired by everyone."

"Yes," Merin said without vanity.

"Do you remember me now?" Ivan said.

"Oh, I remembered you from the first."

"Did you remember me when you saw me in Spain?"

"Where is Bosa Kvadir?" Merin asked. "I didn't hear a shot. Did you give him his life for telling you about Spain? Will you shoot him later on to hide your shame? What a dirty coward you were then. When I shot you in the leg, you didn't stand and fight. What a dirty coward you are now."

The fury that Ivan thought had been expended in the blows to Merin's face roared up through his belly and chest like a fire. He swung the stock of the sentry's rifle against Merin's jaw, stunning him like a butcher stuns an ox before slaughter. He arranged one of Merin's legs on the tree stump. The edge of the stump bit into Merin's calf but he didn't feel it. Ivan grasped the barrel of the rifle with both hands. He raised it over his head, paused to gather all his force, then brought the stock crashing down on the shin bone.

The thud of the blow was mixed with a snap like that of a dry branch breaking. Merin screamed, the pain waking him from his unconsciousness.

The prisoners in the compound stiffened at the sound. One bit his lip until it bled. Another shit his pants. They feared they would get some of the same. In Napica's tent Kvadir started to cry.

Ivan arranged the other leg on the tree stump, holding it there with a boot on Merin's thigh. He swung the rifle stock again and broke the leg. Merin's second scream was not as loud as the first. It was muffled by the sickness that flooded through the cavities of his body.

Kvadir stood up. He tested his legs. They were weak but charged with an electric energy that made him feel he could run forever without pause. He knew that the Chetnik captain had thought him completely cowed. He had no idea that extreme terror can drive weak men to feats of strength, daring, endurance, and cunning greater than those accomplished by brave men in control of all their senses. He peeked out of the flap of the tent. The Chetniks he could see were all looking toward the source of the screams, made nervous by something they didn't understand. Kvadir slipped out of the tent. He made his way to the edge of the encampment. No one challenged him. He began to walk into the dark. Merin screamed again. Kvadir ran.

The screaming was too much for Ivan. He hadn't intended to reduce the man to that. Why wouldn't he stop? He realized that the screams of pain were also screams of rage and condemnation. Merin screamed coward at him in words drawn out like the howls of an animal, bitten off at the end as though each word was a bite out of Napica's flesh.

"Cowaaaard! Cowaaaard!"

Ivan smashed the butt of the rifle into Merin's open mouth. Broken teeth fell out. Blood gushed. It boiled on his lips as Merin continued to scream his accusations. Would nothing stop him?

Ivan saw that the stock of the rifle was broken. It dangled by a web of splinters from the barrel. He tore it away. He placed the muzzle of the barrel against Merin's forehead and pulled the trigger.

= 15 =

The Policeman: 1970

Karel was about to reach for the phone and seek a late afternoon appointment with someone at the Secret Police when a call came from Ulica saying that he'd unearthed someone interesting. Horvath had confided something to the old nurse, Madame Niko, when he'd been drunk, and had rattled on to Babaja. There was sure to have been others. Like everyone else, Horvath had needed someone to talk to, and Ulica had unearthed another confidant.

Karel met Ulica at the Hotel Splendide, a government-run luxury establishment designed for the comfort and pleasure of visiting dignitaries and businessmen. There was a swimming pool on the first floor and a small nightclub in the basement where female nudity was featured, though such exploitation was officially frowned upon. The only legal casino in the city occupied a mezzanine floor. It boasted French croupiers and American blackjack dealers. The posted stakes were very low, but a great deal of money was wagered among those who knew the high signs. There were three restaurants and two bars. Ulica escorted Karel to the smaller of the last.

It was dark even in the afternoon. The bar accommodated seven stools. There were banquettes on one side and along the back. The largest of them occupied the corner of the room. Several girls and women sat on the padded benches. It was too early to hope for any trade. They were there warming up their smiles and comparing notes. They all looked at Karel when he walked in. When they saw Ulica with him they lost interest, except for a tall redhead who slid out from under the table and walked over to the bar to join the detectives.

Karel couldn't restrain his sexual speculation about her. The whore's hips were wide and her belly hard. What sort of ride would she give a man? He almost extended his hand to cover his confusion. Ever since he'd met Marta Barkai he looked at every attractive woman as a candidate for bed. For a fleeting moment he wondered if he was going a little crazy for women's flesh. He did such mad things with Marta.

"This is Sonia Plovic," Ulica said. "Tell the sergeant what you told me."

Sonia looked at him resentfully. There was also a touch of fear. Ulica was known to be rough. He had no time for good manners with thieves and whores. He made them feel like dirt, then ground them underfoot unless they gave him what he wanted. Karel reached out and touched her hand to take her attention.

"Please sit down. It's very early in the day, I know, but would you like a cocktail?"

She smiled, showing pretty teeth.

"An orange juice maybe."

Karel glanced over at the bartender leaning against the wall in the corner of the bar. He came over and Karel ordered two glasses of orange juice. Ulica had a beer. Karel gestured with his chin toward the girls on the banquette.

"Enjoy your beer. Have a chat," he said to the detective.

When Ulica went away Sonia seemed to relax. She slid herself onto the barstool.

"He frightens me," she said.

"Do I frighten you?"

Sonia looked into Karel's eyes.

"No. You're a man who really likes women."

"I hope you don't think that means you can twist me around your finger," Karel said, and laughed. He made Sonia feel as though they were afternoon companions.

"No. You're a harder man to deal with than he is, when all is said and done. I can see that. You're not all charm and sweetness."

"That's no reason we can't be friends. Tell me about Jan Horvath. How well did you know him?"

"Very well. Would you believe it, he's been coming to me for nearly twenty-five years."

"Regularly?"

"From time to time. Sometimes as much as a year would pass between visits. Then I knew he'd found himself a mistress he was keeping in a comfortable flat somewhere."

"He never offered such an arrangement to you?"

"Why should he? I'm here for the price. I don't have to be romanced. I couldn't play the part of the respectable woman waiting to be seduced." She touched her fingers to the corners of her eyes. The nails were painted red. "Can't you see. I've been at it a long time."

"But in the beginning. When he first met you."

"I'd been at it for a long time even then," she said dryly.

"If he kept coming back to you, I'll assume there was something special that you gave him."

"Motherly tits and barley soup," she said.

He grinned.

"I'm no acrobat. Never was. You should know. For all the promises anyone may make, there's not much one woman can do that another can't. There's no magic in one man that isn't in another for that matter. In the beginning he might have been bowled over by the color of my muff. This hair is natural, do you see? I've got a natural redhead's milk-white skin and pale freckles all across my shoulders and sprayed over my ass. Men like that."

"I shouldn't wonder," Karel said.

She stared at the backs of her hands. They were anything but milk white. The liver spots showed up even in the gloom. She sighed.

"The novelty wears off soon enough. No matter how hard you try, a person uses up all the tricks and inventions. In the end it's just a little human kindness one wants, isn't it?"

Karel knew that she was right. He wondered how soon it would be before he and Marta ran out of new stimulations. Would quiet, gentle love replace it? Would he stop wanting to perform prodigies of sex on her body?

"Jan Horvath liked to talk to me. There were times in fact when he hired my services for the night and never did more than lay his head on my breasts or belly."

"What did you talk about?"

"What do we all like to talk about when we're low? Youth. Even childhood if those years were best. Even when they were not so good. It's easy to pretend they were."

"Do you think Horvath made up a past to talk about?"

"We all lie but I think he usually spoke the truth as he remembered it."

"He told you where he was born?"

"Some town near the Italian border. I don't remember that he ever told me which one exactly. But he described to me how the summer air smelled, and how his governess gave him a glass of olive oil for his constipation. Later on, after his family moved, he had a horse of his own. His father was a merchant, and very well off. But Horvath hated the idea of running a shop. He saw himself doing other things. Then the war came along and broke everybody's magic mirrors."

"Did he ever go home for a visit?"

"Oh, yes. It was how I first met him. He'd been on a visit home. Then he'd taken a short holiday in Trieste."

"Was Horvath the only name by which you knew him?"

She looked at him with real admiration. "You are clever, aren't you," she said. "I wonder how you could know that he used other names."

"Names?"

"Yes. More than one. When I first met him his name was Ivan Napica. That was in Trieste."

"When he was there on holiday."

"That's what he told me. He may have had other reasons for being there. Sometimes my clients want to talk about their jobs, sometimes not."

"Go on."

"Later on, when we fell in with each other again in Belgrade, I heard him called Boreta by the reservations captain in a restaurant. I joked with him about it, making what I thought was an amusing fuss about me being taken out by a spy. He laughed right along and said that his wife was suspicious. He said he wouldn't put it past her to check every restaurant in town to see if he'd arranged for a table for two persons. And, for that matter, every hotel as well to see if he'd booked a room.''

"What about the next change of name? What did you say when you saw that he was calling himself Horvath?''

"I didn't even bother asking for a story. What for? He could do what he pleased about names so far as I was concerned. I knew more than one fellow who had changed his name. I learned not to ask why. Some people carry around new secrets. A lot more carry around old ones.''

"Did he hint at having a burden of them?''

"Not in so many words. You know how it is. Someone wants to get rid of the pressure of the past. Old regrets. Old sins. Old mistakes. They start to talk about it. Then they stop. Start again from a different point of view. They look at you as though they are suddenly afraid that you're a spy sent to trap them. They stop talking altogether. Then they have another drink or the memories come back too powerfully for them to resist. The talk begins again. They deliver up their past to you in little bits and pieces. Not all of the pieces fit. You have to imagine a good deal.''

"I think you'd be better at that than most.''

"I am, yes. It's this business that I'm in. It's not always this men want,'' she said, pointing to her crotch. "Sometimes it's this and this,'' she went on, touching her heart and her ear. "I've had as much training listening as the other.''

"What do you think his secrets were about?''

"The war. I got the feeling that he'd done shameful things during the war. Dangerous things. I think he feared for his life from time to time. I mean he didn't go about looking over his shoulder. Still, there would be times when he seemed apprehensive as though he'd spied the ghost that would kill him one day.''

"As though he feared someone's revenge?''

"That's putting words to it,'' Sonia said, "and that's further than I'd care to go. But it could be. He talked in his sleep sometimes. All garbled up the way nightmare conversations usually are, but in his dreams he was clearly being hunted.''

Karel felt his pulses quicken.

"Did he ever cry out a name?"

"From time to time he'd speak some names quite clearly. I remember Kvadir, I think. Other times he said the names Napica and Boreta. But the name he screamed out the most often, and with the greatest anguish, was Merin."

Karel took a bill from his wallet and placed it on the bar to pay for the drinks. He started to remove another larger one. Sonia tapped his wrist.

"Please, no," she said.

"I'm sorry. I thought you might like to have the rest of the evening for yourself."

"Only if you'd like to spend it with me," she said, lifting the sentence so that it became a question.

"I have a wife."

"So did Ivan. So do most of my customers."

"I have a mistress."

"Oh," Sonia said, and smiled, "that's another matter."

= 16 =

For many months after buying the little black automobile for himself, Karel had taken extraordinary pleasure in driving around at any hour of the day or night for no other reason than to have the pleasure of turning the wheel and listening to the engine hum. Next to his apartment and the furniture, the automobile was the symbol of his great success.

But after a while it became old hat, just another convenience that broke down, ate gas and oil, and required more care than he sometimes wanted to give it. Like a wife, an impish voice whispered in his head. He tried to shake it away, but the imp insisted on elaborating on its first comedic effect. Surely, it said, the analogy fit Dika to the skin. Might it not, one day soon, fit Marta as well?

As he drove through the nearly empty streets he suddenly felt that while all the people of the city were comfortably at home, or meeting with friends in some kafana or restaurant, he alone was forced to wander through the town listening to a mocking voice he couldn't still. He began to sing.

He drove along the length of the Ulica Marsala Tita in the direction of the Metropolitan Police building. He made a turn in the middle of the thoroughfare and drove back to Prince Michael's Street. He pulled up in front of the luxury block of flats where Jan Horvath had lived, and where Hannah Horvath still lived. There were dim lights on in the windows of her flat. Was she watching television, scarcely knowing what was transpiring on the screen? Was she sitting down to a lonely dinner for one? Was she already preparing herself for bed?

He felt a sudden, sharp, charging sensation in his groin. His scrotum cringed with pleasure. Hannah Horvath had a figure that was very lush and mature, full of curves and juices. The body of a mature woman. Not the stiff board of a body he'd lived with so many years even when Dika had been at her best. Not even like the sharp, angular, though heavy-breasted body of Marta Barkai. Hannah's was a good, rich, comfortable, almost motherly body. He thought of the prostitute in the bar. Sonia Plovic had said something sardonic and amusing about motherly tits and barley soup. They went together in a way that had an attractive hint of incest about it. He laughed dryly to himself. The farm boy had apparently grown quite sophisticated.

He left the car and locked it. Then he walked across the icy road, telling himself that he just meant to surprise Hannah Horvath with some questions about her late husband.

He rang the bell and waited. When minutes had passed, he rang the bell again. He thought he heard a muffled voice shouting from another room. More minutes later the judas hole set in the door slid back.

Hannah Horvath opened the door. Her hair was disheveled. There was a flush on her face, neck, and chest but it wasn't the flush of sleep. Her eyes were bright, almost feverish.

Karel's eyes fell to her bosom. He hadn't meant to look at her, had even struggled against it for a moment. Her breasts swelled invitingly in the open vee of her robe. Hannah Horvath frowned and drew her robe together up high at the throat.

"What is it?" she said snappishly.

"My regrets. I have a few more questions."

"Don't you work a normal day?"

Karel almost said that killers didn't work normal hours, but it would have been too dramatic, too cinematic.

"It's not yet even suppertime," he said instead.

She knew there was no defense against any questions he wished to ask of her. She'd simply wanted to file her protest, to let him know that she wasn't pleased by his intrusion. She stepped back and swung the door wider, turning her head toward the door that led to the next room as she did so. She waved her hand impatiently, as though asking Karel to sit down, ask his questions, and have done with it.

He sat on the edge of the sofa as though his visit would be very brief. She sat in the chair opposite as she had before.

"Why didn't you tell me your husband had changed his name?" he said.

She started, looked away, then placed her hands on her lap with the fingers spread out as if she were examining the backs of her hands.

"The subject was never raised."

"It's the sort of thing we would expect you to assume would be of interest to us."

She raised her head and smiled at him.

"In the films, witnesses are told never to assume anything. Never to volunteer anything. They're told to simply answer the questions with no more than a yes or no."

Yes, the films, Karel thought. More than we know, we live by the rules and manners set down by films. Certain people more than others. This childish woman of forty, for example, who had been willing to suffer any humiliation at the hands of her husband as long as he provided well for her. A petulant woman, desperately afraid, now that her breadwinner was dead, that she would have to give up some of her luxuries. But everybody lived by the example of films more or less. Except the farmers, and the hunters. Except men at war, perhaps.

"I take you for an intelligent woman," Karel said. "I don't think I have to lead you step by step to the information that will enable us to find the person who murdered your husband in front of his own front door."

He was deliberately manipulating the images, offering an old-fashioned domestic touch meant to tug at the heartstrings. The entrance to the apartment house lobby was scarcely a front door. Front doors conjured up pictures of cottages.

Hannah Horvath stared at him as though examining the picture he drew for her and deciding whether she wanted to live up to it.

"When I was introduced to my husband it was as Ivan Boreta. Just weeks after, he told me his name was really Jan Horvath and that's how we'd be known."

"In what month did you meet him?"

"January. On New Year's Day."

"Did he explain the reason for the change?"

"Not in detail. He'd been an officer in the KNOJ. Do you know . . ."

"Yes," Karel said. "The Corps of National Defense of Yugoslavia."

"There were changes being made to it. It was going to be cut by two-thirds. It was to become some sort of special frontier guard. Ivan . . . Jan . . ."

"Yes, yes. I understand," Karel said.

"My husband felt that with the reduction and change of purpose in the KNOJ his opportunities for advancement were effectively diminished, perhaps cut off altogether. He was fortunate in having friends in high places. He managed a transfer to the Military Counter-Intelligence. He explained that it was their policy to transfer new officers and to establish them in new identities."

"For what reason?"

"I assumed for reason of security," she said, and spread her hands out in the air on either side of her face, asking him to examine her ignorance of such clandestine complications.

"Did he ever tell you that he'd been called by another name before you met?"

She hesitated. A small frown appeared on her forehead between her eyes. She rubbed it away with her fingertips as though unconsciously aware that she must do everything to preserve what beauty was left to her now that she was alone.

"I suppose it can't matter now," she said in a sudden rush of words. "Once, shortly after our marriage, we were on holiday in Dubrovnik. A hearty man approached my husband in the lobby of the Imperial Hotel. He tried to embrace him and called him Ivan Kosho. Both names, you know. In that excessive display of familiarity some people use. My husband laughed and pushed the man away, then took him aside. They laughed and slapped each other on the back. The man apologized for the case of mistaken identity. I wondered what Jan had told him, that I was a woman he'd brought to Dalmatia for a dirty weekend? Jan came back and said the fool was drunk and had mistaken him for someone else. Do you see?" she finished.

Karel made no reply.

"Do you see," she said again musingly, "sometimes a good, obedient wife may not even know the name of the husband she lives with for twenty years. It's the way the world sometimes is. But I remarked at the time how strange it was that in this case of mistaken identity the stranger should have hit upon my husband's true first name. A double coincidence."

"Was your husband also amused by the oddity?"

"We talked no more about it. Ever."

Behind the door leading to the adjoining room a little dog yipped. Hannah Horvath coughed as though she'd been startled by it or as though she meant to cover the sound. The dog yipped again. She smiled nervously and told the dog to hush. The sound of its mistress's voice aroused the dog to a frenzy of barking. Karel looked at the lower edge of the door where the light from inside the room spilled out onto the living room carpet. He could see the shadow made by the Pomeranian as it stuck its nose into the crack and whined.

"Is that all?" Hannah Horvath said, standing up.

Karel took his eyes away from the door, then looked again. In the last split second he had noticed something out of the corner of his eye. The shadow of the little dog had disappeared. It no longer snuffled at the crack. Karel strode across the room and flung the door wide.

Hogamann, covered by nothing but the little dog he cradled against his chest, trying to keep it quiet, stood there looking ludicrous.

Karel felt a wash of irritation that was close to jealousy. He also felt disgust and anger. If she was going to take a lover in such a hurry, she might have done better for herself, he thought. Like me, he wryly added.

"Get under the blankets," Karel said, "you'll catch a chill."

He closed the door on Hogamann. He smiled at Hannah Horvath and nodded, then started across the living room to the door. She scurried after him, clutching the robe at her throat, looking up at him as though she were his wife or girlfriend caught out in sin.

"You must understand . . ." she said, and would have said more except that Karel stopped her.

"You've nothing with which to reproach yourself," he said in his kindliest voice. "My God, don't I know what it's like to feel lonely and deprived?"

He left the apartment. In his car he paused a moment and smiled to himself with perverse satisfaction. He doubted if Hannah Horvath would allow the paunchy Hogamann to mount another amorous attack on her that night.

= 17 =

Karel brought a camera to Marta's apartment to take the picture for the false passport. She took out her lipstick and refreshed the paint on her mouth as he set the camera up on the table.

"Don't get too flashy," Karel said. "Wipe off some of that lipstick." He arranged a chair the proper distance from the lens and brought a floor lamp closer.

"Aren't policemen's wives supposed to be pretty?" Marta asked as she sat down.

Her impishness was lost on Karel. He peered through the viewfinder. "Sit up straighter," he said. "I think it might be smart if you tried to look as plain as possible. Beautiful women draw attention. Sometimes clerks and minor officials like to engage them in conversation just to have the pleasure of flirting with them."

Marta wiped the lipstick from her mouth with a tissue. "So you think my beauty could be our undoing," she teased.

Karel went to get a pillow from the couch and brought it back.

"Here, sit on this," he said. "It will make you sit taller." He looked through the viewfinder again and grunted approval. He went over to adjust the lampshade. The bulb illuminated her face with the same harsh light used by passport photographers. Karel seemed pleased with the effect.

"Ready?"

Marta smiled brilliantly.

"No, no. Not such a great smile. Try not to be so friendly and provocative. That's better. A reluctant smile. The kind of

148

smile Dika would put on just because she was told to do so by the photographer.''

"As though I had a cramp?'' Marta said.

"Exactly.'' Karel snapped the picture. "One more just to be sure.'' He took a second picture.

"Hold on,'' Marta said as he started to pick up the camera to rewind and remove the roll of film. "How many shots are left?''

"Nearly the whole roll of twenty-four.''

"Go on, then,'' she said, and started unbuttoning her blouse.

"What are you doing?'' Karel protested.

"Oh, go on, take my picture. Pretend that I'm an exotic dancer.''

She undid the second button and pulled the material away from her bosom to expose her breasts welling over the cups of her brassiere.

"We really have better things to do,'' Karel said, but snapped the shutter all the same.

Marta began to hum under her breath. It was a racy, growling version of a burlesque song she'd heard in some American film or other. She opened up her blouse, holding the sides out and moving the cloth back and forth across her shoulders before slipping her arms out of the sleeves and tossing the garment on the floor. "Take my picture. Take my picture,'' she said. Karel snapped the shutter again. She lifted her buttocks from the chair by pressing against her thighs and unzipped her skirt. She dragged the hem up past her stocking tops, then lifted the entire skirt up and over her head, holding her one arm posed after she'd flung the skirt aside. "Snap it,'' she said. The shutter clicked.

"This is foolishness,'' Karel said. He could hear the rough edges of desire in his voice. He could feel the stirring in his groin as he watched the sexual flush spread across Marta's chest and rise along the column of her neck. Her eyes were brilliant, her mouth wet with the flickering of her tongue.

She began to sing more loudly, making up filthy lyrics to the song. She turned her knees away from him, showing him her back as she unsnapped her brassiere. She teased him with flashes of her breasts before allowing the undergarment to fall. Karel clicked the shutter. He imagined it to be the winking of a voyeur's eye. She shook her breasts at him. "Take a picture of my tits," she said. "Pick up the camera. Move around me. Do as the pornographers do. Love my body with the camera."

Karel obeyed her. He moved around her, going in close, retreating, changing the focus, snapping the lever over to advance the frame, pressing the shutter release as she slid her panties down her legs. She posed her limbs, this way, that way. She opened them up to the camera's eye. He took closeups. She spread herself with her fingers. She placed her fingers into her body.

She started to laugh. It made her flesh tremble. Her belly convulsed with joy. Her breasts shook. The nipples had grown and were as hard as pebbles. The pulse was beating in the well of her throat.

"Oh, my God, we're going to be free," she moaned as she reached out for him. Karel snapped the last picture of her face. It was distorted with a fearful ecstacy.

"Take your clothes off," she whispered.

Karel nearly tore them from himself. Was there no end to her power over him? It seemed that she could find some way to excite him whenever she pleased. She pretended that she was under his care and protection—that she needed him immensely, more than she could say—but it was he who needed her. He sometimes felt as though his reason was threatened.

There were times when Karel wasn't sure that Marta was altogether rational. It was as though her reason was unbalanced by a rage of expectation about her much-desired escape. It was difficult to pin down from her conversation exactly what she thought she would be escaping. Paranoia walked hand in hand with hope. She wanted so desperately to leave the country and start a new life elsewhere that she believed everyone was plotting against her. She saw agents of the SJB everywhere. She always called it Ozna. She spoke often of "The Terror." Karel doubted if a small Jewish child would have ever been the object of the political purge that took place after the war.

What did Karel know about Marta Barkai? Not much really.

She admitted to being thirty-two. He thought she might be a year or two older. He had no evidence that she indulged in such small deceptions but that's what he suspected. If asked, he would have said it had something to do with a policeman's instinct.

Karel knew that Marta had been born in Sarajevo. She called herself one of the survivors and sometimes worked herself up into a mild hysteria talking about the Holocaust. According to a census taken in 1931 there had been sixty-eight thousand Jews in Yugoslavia. At the end of World War Two, after the Nazis and the Croatian Ustasi were through butchering them, there were only fifteen thousand left. It was something to remember.

The Barkai family had come to the Balkans from Spain four hundred and fifty years ago. Since the forming of the nation, they considered themselves Yugoslavians and Jews in that order. Yaacov Barkai worked as a tailor. His wife, Dara, kept the house. They had five children. Marta was the youngest. It wasn't all that easy being a Jew in the days before the war. A Jewish name was enough to attract the rotten viciousness of bigotry. Yaacov barely made enough to keep a roof over their heads and food on the table. Still, they were pious people, reverent to their God, and they found a certain happiness in the community of Jews that lived in the narrow alleys of the city shoulder to shoulder with poor Moslems and Serbs.

At the bottom of a hill was a beautiful Greek Orthodox Church. Higher up were the minarets of a mosque. Surrounded by them, like an afterthought, was a gray stone shul.

The outside was unprepossessing, but inside there was a chandelier made of glass prisms.

Marta enjoyed watching the pieces of glass pick up and reflect the light, sending it glancing into her eyes like little knives of light.

Marta was probably no more than five when the Germans invaded. She grew wild-eyed as she told the story of how she'd lost her family. It occurred in April of 1941.

When the Nazis crashed through Sarajevo they looted every Jewish home in the city no matter how poor it was. They carted everything away that had even the smallest value. They stripped the Barkai home and shop of threadbare rugs, rotting curtains, and the bolts of cloth from which they made their living.

The Ustasi from Croatia came with the Germans and were worse than the Germans. They shot down Barkai's two oldest sons out of hand, just like that, for no reason anyone could determine. Put them up against a privy wall and shot them down.

One day Ustasi and Nazis went to the temple and broke all the windows with stones, laughing like bad children as they did so. They broke through the door. They first shattered the prisms of the chandelier, then threw a loop of rope around it and pulled it out of the ceiling in a rain of plaster.

Then they rounded up the Jews. They said they were sending them to places where the Jews could work for the good of themselves and the glory of Germany. Places like Dachau and Treblinka which sounded no more terrible than any other strange place. They placed the Jews, men, women, and children, into the ruined temple to await transportation to these other places. They packed them into the small building until there was no more room. Even after people had no room left in which to breathe, the guards and dogs drove the Jews into the temple. They were refused food. They were told to drink their tears when they cried for water. When they began to die they couldn't be laid down on the floor. There was no room. Marta's mother died. Her father held Marta in his arms up off the floor, and was forced to look into his dead wife's face because he couldn't turn around. Then he died and Marta slipped out of his arms. Her sisters tried to shelter her. The cantor's wife helped. She gave the children little bits of food she'd concealed in her pocket. She managed to bring them water from the faucet that was turned on and off as the guards pleased.

At the end of fifteen days transportation arrived to take the survivors away. They were taken to a temporary camp outside of Zagreb. The Germans hadn't yet begun their horrors there. There was a special cruelty in that. One Jewish settlement was destroyed, another given a reprieve that could last a week, a month, or even longer.

Some prisoners dug a tunnel under the fence. It was too narrow to admit even a small man. They were unable to enlarge it. They had no timbers to support the sides and roof, and no skills in such a special art. They sent Marta and her sister Ruth out through the tunnel. The other sister had already died.

They found shelter with a Christian family. Ruth took ill and died because the family was afraid to call a doctor. When Marta became ill they were so afraid for her life that they finally did what they'd been afraid to do for Ruth. The doctor came and then reported the family for sheltering a Jew. Before the Ustasi came to take them, the Christian family sent Marta away with a friend who was making her way to the mountains to join the Partisans. Marta stayed among them until the end of the war.

Once when she was nearly ten she carried a message to a Partisan agent who was working in Belgrade. She remembered that better than most things.

"There was snow on the ground but no fresh snow was falling. The sky was gray as though it was an overcast day and not the middle of the night. The streetlamps, however, were out. There were no lights anywhere. The boulevard didn't have one automobile or cart on it as far as I could see in either direction. Every light standard had been used as a gallows. There was a Jew or a Gypsy hanging on every one of them. They turned slowly in a wind that blew up from the river."

Her eyes started from her head. Flecks of spittle gathered at the corners of her mouth. She seemed in danger of being overcome by the terror of her memories. Karel grabbed her wrists and told her that she must not believe that every one of the hanged had been a Jew or Gypsy.

"They were Serbians, civilians, and soldiers. Partisans. Some Jews perhaps."

He tried to make the horror less by telling her that the slaughter had not been directed only against the Jews. The Germans had been lashing out right and left. They wanted to kill any Slav no matter what faith they had. It didn't matter. The Germans wanted to kill Yugoslavs. How stupid it seemed to him to try to comfort someone's fears by telling them that a horror was general and not specific.

"No, no," she said, "everyone wants to kill Jews."

The woman who'd saved her through the war was Rebecca Levin. Marta started calling her auntie from the very start. Aunt

Rebecca. Rebecca often came back from a fight with the Germans, Ustasi, or Chetniks. She took Marta on her lap and petted her even when she was grown and serving as a runner. Rebecca's husband and daughter had been killed by the Germans while walking across the street.

Rebecca took Marta to live with a distant relation who had survived the war in Belgrade by covering up any evidence that she was a Jew. She had a large house which they turned into a sort of boarding hotel.

There was a lot of rebuilding to be done in Belgrade. Workers came to the city who'd never been away from their farms and mountains before. The countryside was ravaged. There was work in the cities. Keeping rooms and cooking was not the only work the women were called upon to do. They were formed into labor brigades and set to work clearing the streets of rubble. The committee of the local *rejoni* met in the house. It was decided under the rule limiting private holdings that the house was to be divided and half given to the commune. It made no great difference to anyone since it was there that they already kept their files and held their meetings.

A partition was constructed in a hallway on the ground floor so that the kitchen entrance was now the entrance to the private apartment and the front door the entrance to the offices of the *rejoni*. Marta's aunt and the woman who had once owned the house continued to make the beds, clean the rooms, and feed the workers who occupied them. But since they cleaned the offices as well and fed the officials a lunch, they were excused from working in the streets clearing away the fallen bricks and stones.

That's the way Marta grew up. In something like a boarding house with the advantage of political leaders close to hand to take care of any little request that might make life easier. They saw to it that she went to the best school. They arranged that she should have extra coupons for clothes. She was like a mascot to them and they wanted her to look her best so that they could be proud of her. Little matters of class and caste.

She was a good but not brilliant student. The people in the combination boarding house and district headquarters had hopes for her. Some wanted her to be a doctor, some a lawyer. No one said anything about her being a Jew. Her aunt Rebecca was proud of her faith. Even the distant relative who had owned the house no longer tried to hide it. A good many Jews had fought with the Partisans and that wasn't yet forgotten.

Marta also grew attractive if not beautiful. Her breasts were the best feature of her figure, large and upstanding, apt to tremble when she laughed. Her mouth was the feature of her face that first drew attention. The members of the committee all secretly dreamed about taking her to bed, but each one protected her as though she were a woman of his own family. She had twenty uncles who endeavored to keep her virgin.

When she was seventeen she fell in love and allowed the boy, a university student like herself, to take her. She was smart in most things, but ignorant in the matters of contraception. When she became pregnant she didn't blame the young man, only herself. She proceeded to have an abortion without consulting Rebecca or anyone else. The doctor who performed the curettement told her that her organs were immature. She must take great care if she ever intended bearing children. The night of the operation she began to bleed excessively. She waited a long time before seeking help. When she went into the dark hallways of the house meaning to rouse Rebecca, she fainted on the carpet. So everyone found out what she'd done.

The men who'd kept their hands off her were disappointed and enraged. Among themselves a few even said that they regretted not having taken her maidenhead since she had apparently been so eager to give it away. They withdrew their enthusiasm and support in small ways. Without their influence the paths to medicine and law were closed to her because she didn't stand high enough academically. Her confidence in herself was broken. She began to think of herself as a victim even though a good many people had risked themselves and given of themselves to help her and nurture her. She mistrusted her power as an individual. But she never underestimated the power of her breasts and her mouth, and the clever things she taught herself to do in bed.

Sometimes she made the men she allowed to make love to her pay a curious price. Before they could have her they had to listen to her troubles, her complaints about the injuries done her in the past, and the new terrors that waited for her just around tomorrow's corner.

She insisted that there was a program against the Jews after the war, even after the horrors of the death camp had been revealed. She said that the Ozna had been almost as bad as the Gestapo, looking for Jews everywhere, claiming that they had financed Hitler.

"Blame the Jews for everything," Marta said bitterly.

"Hush, hush," Karel said, "there's none of that true. There were political arrests made. The party had to be cleansed."

"Cleansed of Jews," she said.

"No, no."

He obtained a copy of the Constitution of the Federal Republic of Yugoslavia, written in 1946, and read a passage of it to her. It forbade the "propagation of national, racial, and religious hatred and discord." It guaranteed the rights of all minorities.

Marta smiled as though Karel were ignorant or innocent. She put her hand alongside his cheek and patted his face gently.

"If that's the case, why do they refuse me a passport? Why do they forbid me to leave the country?"

"It has nothing to do with your being a Jewess," Karel said reasonably. "It's because you chose to take employment in the KOS."

She'd left the university before she'd completed her third year. Without a degree or a discipline the best she could do was secretarial work. Nearly every job of that description was with the government in one way or another. She successively found employment with the Confederation of Trade Unions, Yugoslav Radiotelevision, the Socialist Alliance of Working People, and the League of Communists of Yugoslavia. Her first boss got her an apartment, another access to many clubs, the next a small automobile, and still another provided her with the means to buy imported luxury goods. There were other jobs in between of such short duration that she never thought of them as part of her career. She saw herself as an executive secretary of exceptional skills. Each employer in turn stole her from the one before through flattery and promises. Though such frequent changes of job were officially frowned upon, she soon learned that certain people had a gift for pushing buttons. It was a matter of finding the right man for the right button.

When an executive in the KOS saw her, coveted her, and offered her a job, she accepted without seeming to give the matter another thought. If pressed hard enough, and if she were given a long enough time to listen to herself, she might have explained that by becoming part of the intelligence community she, a Jewess, would be safe from terror and destruction forever. Karel warned her to stop reading the morbid works of Kafka, to which she was inordinately devoted.

"I was recruited when I was too ignorant to know any better," she said.

"Marta, what are you saying? You make it sound as though you're some sort of clandestine agent. A spy. You're a secretary whose work sometimes deals with sensitive matters."

She smiled as though that was all a common policeman would know about it.

= 18 =

The last few days had been conducted in such a way that everything was managed to Karel's satisfaction. He rose from the couch in the living room very early in the morning. He didn't even bother to make himself an eye-opening cup of coffee before creeping out of the house. He suspected that Dika awakened as early as he, but wasn't yet ready to challenge the shaky truce that existed between them. He felt cowardly closing the door softly behind him and practically creeping down the stairs.

During the morning and afternoon he pursued the case of Jan Horvath. His register of cases had been cleared of all others. But no matter how hard he worked, how many people he questioned, he'd yet to turn up any hard evidence that might point to a perpetrator. He still hadn't managed an interview at the offices of the Secret Police, though a meeting with Senior Investigator Georgi was promised at any moment. Every day, late in the afternoon, Karel decided that he'd call Marta and tell her that he wasn't stopping by to see her that day. He never got so far as to actually pick up the phone. As dusk approached he was always dismayed to discover an appetite for her growing in him. He had to see her. Twice they made furious love. They talked about their escape to Rome and other far places. He'd not yet told her that Dika suspected their affair.

Well after dark he presented himself at the door of Judge Trevian's apartment in the great mansion that, in other times, had once belonged entirely to the old man. The ancient manservant, Doder, himself an anachronism as startling as any of the imperial decorations inside the flat, showed Karel into the library where a fire blazed on the hearth. Trevian sat in his chair and gestured toward the one opposite, inclining his head in gracious invitation. Karel very soon came to think of the hour spent with Trevian as a quiet respite at the end of the day. Their sessions nearly always began with exactly the same words.

"What have you to report?" Trevian asked.

Karel shook his head. "Very little, I'm afraid."

"Will you have a brandy?"

"No, thank you."

Trevian observed the younger man closely. He sat in his chair with his folders spread out on the briefcase on his lap in the same way he always arranged them. Yet there was something different about his manner. It had something to do with the awkward placement of the detective's feet, or a special, extra sadness in his dark eyes. Whatever it was that troubled him was surely a personal matter. Trevian couldn't imagine Karel becoming emotionally or egotistically involved with a case in hand. He was almost the perfect policeman, neutral and bland, unwilling or unable to judge an act but calmly prepared to clean up the consequences of it.

"Of all the possible motives for Horvath's killing, barring the act of a casual madman, we can reasonably reduce them to four. Murder because of differences over business. Murder of passion by or because of a woman. A professional execution due to some act committed by Horvath while in service. Revenge for an insult to someone's honor or an act committed in the past, probably during the war."

Trevian interrupted to ask Karel if he would like a glass of refreshment. Karel refused. Trevian nodded.

"As you know," Karel continued, "Horvath was in partnership with a man named Hogamann in any number of petty rackets. Smuggling this and that. Peddling influence. Trading in blank documents for import and export. A good deal of it had to do with religious objects of art. I don't see evidence of drugs, foreign currency in quantity, precious stones or metals—none of the enterprises in which the serious criminal organizations engage."

"And the woman?" Trevian asked.

"If this had been a killing committed in the middle of a quarrel, in a bedroom during a fit of passion, or even in a restaurant at the height of the dinner hour, I might believe that uncontrollable jealousy, or despair based upon lost love, had motivated it. But this was deliberate, efficient, and swift. His own wife made the observation that Horvath was scarcely the kind of man that a woman would kill out of passion or despair. He played around a lot. He was having it off with his secretary."

"You don't suppose she could have . . ." Trevian started to say as he rose from his chair.

"No, sir," Karel replied, without waiting for the completed sentence. "She certainly wasn't plunged into despair for love of Horvath. She's already taken up with his partner, Hogamann."

"Will you have that brandy now?" Trevian said, even as he poured them. "This business partner sounds to be an interesting case," he went on.

"He's a womanizer as well. Not as successful as Horvath, but busily at it all the same."

"Cases of retarded development, of course," Trevian said as he handed Karel the glass of brandy, then reseated himself. "A pair of adolescents."

Karel felt his cheeks color. He felt as though Trevian were commenting upon his nature. He hoped the old man wouldn't notice the change in his complexion.

"He's also been quick to crawl into the widow's bed," Karel said.

Trevian opened his mouth to speak. Karel was sure he was going to say, "You don't suppose . . ." again. He went on without pause. "But neither of those benefits would be enough motive for Hogamann to have done Horvath in. Not so far as I can see."

"You make it sound like this fellow Hogamann would have liked to have lived his partner's life," Trevian mused.

"I think that's a fair statement of the impression he conveys."

"Do you really think we should let this Hogamann get away with his illicit dealings?" Judge Trevian asked.

"Without Horvath making the contacts in high places, Hogamann can't do very much."

"Perhaps you're right. Have we finished with women?"

"No, sir. It seems that Horvath was also well known to the prostitutes of the city. Not the girls that are available to anyone with the price in pocket, but the not-quite prostitutes that work the best hotels. They don't sell themselves indiscriminately. 'Foreigners' girls' they're called. Their ultimate hope is to meet, please and marry some rich foreigner and leave the country. But on the whole they're ready to offer themselves to anyone with hard currency to spend who's willing to provide them with the better things money can buy."

"You've mined this territory?" Trevian asked.

"A good man did the legwork. He knew what to look for and when to call me in. It can be very hard-going with professional women."

"No one trusts the police?" Trevian said, smiling wryly.

"Except perhaps real criminals who know what to expect from us," Karel replied.

"Yes, there's something comforting about dealing with the experienced ones, isn't there? I mean the old-timers who know when a crime is a crime, and know the rules. Once the women of a certain class were thought to be conducting an honorable business enterprise or committing their lives to a valuable profession. Then we decided to make criminals of them."

Karel wondered if Trevian had ever known the whores who sold themselves for the price of a glass of *rakia*. He wouldn't have thought the life of a prostitute such a gracious and pleasant one if he had.

"The woman I was called in to interview was an older prostitute," Karel went on. "Not one of the flashy young ones but one who has been working on her back for more years than she'd like to count. It seems that Horvath made a friend of her. I suppose he needed someone to relax with from time to time. Someone with whom he didn't have to put on airs or pretend to be more vigorous than he really felt."

"Someone upon whose bosom he could lay his head and speak of all the old dreams that never came to pass," Trevian said.

"Exactly right. This prostitute, this Sonia Plovic, served that purpose for him."

"Did you get anything worthwhile from her?"

"Yes. She confirmed information I already had in hand that Jan Horvath had used the name Ivan Boreta."

Trevian's eyes widened a trifle and his jaw fell half an inch.

"You say this information confirmed something you already had?" Trevian stammered.

"Yes, sir," Karel said. What had there been about the name Boreta that had given the old judge momentary pause? He'd almost lost his poise. "Borodin of the SJB showed me documents suggesting that Horvath was once called Boreta, and before that, Napica. Sonia Plovic confirmed that she'd known Horvath first as Napica, and once overheard him called Boreta."

"A slippery fellow."

"A leopard that often changed his spots."

"You think there are more aliases?"

"Probably a good deal of them. A second interview with Madame Horvath not only strengthened the probability that Horvath once lived as Boreta, but revealed the name Kosho as well. I doubt if any of them were the dead man's real name. I think we'll discover, if we ever *really* discover most of the truth, that Horvath had been an active agent in one clandestine organization and another for many years, and operated under false identities for reasons of his own as well."

"Then this might have properly been put into the hands of one of the intelligence organizations after all," Trevian said.

"I don't think this was a killing because of any clandestine espionage activities. We've no reason to suppose that Horvath wasn't truly retired from service of any kind for the last eight years."

"There's not a good deal that can be done about it now in any case," Trevian remarked thoughtfully. "I've committed myself to you and the Metropolitan Police. We'll stay the course."

Doder shuffled into the room. He cleared his throat and, when they turned to see what was wanted, he looked pointedly at the clock on the mantel. Then he shuffled out again.

"He's informing me that I'm to have a guest tonight and that the hour draws near."

Karel gathered up his papers even as he started to stand.

"No, no, sit back. Finish your report," Trevian said.

"I have nothing else, sir."

"Give me your considered opinion then. Having cast doubts upon the possibility of murder for profit, doubting it to be a crime of passion, and assuming that it's not a professional execution—though I must say it has all the marks of one— we're left with an affair of honor and revenge. Is that your reading of it, then?"

"I think Horvath's murder was the end result of a blood feud. If we can piece together the histories of all the Ivans he ever was—if we can, above all, discover the original Ivan—I think we'll be close enough to his killer to lay a finger on him."

Trevian turned his eyes to the fire. Karel stood up.

"Vendetta," Trevian murmured, then arose to show Karel to the door.

Lazar and Karel passed each other practically on the doorstep. Trevian was saying good-bye to one as the other started climbing the stairs. He made no attempt to introduce them. Lazar looked shrewdly at the policeman, and Karel politely stood aside to allow him to go by, though there was more than enough room on the steps for them to pass abreast. Then he hurried down to his automobile, unlocked it, got behind the wheel, and drove off.

Doder took Lazar's hat, scarf, and coat.

"Was that young Karel?" Lazar asked Trevian.

"Yes, do you know him?"

"I recognized him. I expect we've met once or twice, here and there, but never been introduced."

"I should have done," Trevian apologized.

Lazar waved a hand to say that it was of no consequence.

Trevian led Lazar into the parlor. He replenished the fire even though the room was warm. Lazar settled himself in the chair closest to the fire.

Though they were almost the same age Lazar looked fifteen years older than Trevian. He was dried up and shriveled around the eyes and mouth. His eyes often ran with unbidden tears. His hands trembled with constant palsy. In the mornings his pillow was often wet with the drool from his slack, toothless mouth.

He looked like a shark with his false teeth in place. When he laughed it was shocking. It was the laugh of a man half his age. A hearty laugh with not a trace of prissy refinement. He loved dirty jokes and even at his age frequented the prostitutes who hung about the more expensive tourist hotels. Whores who were supposed to be otherwise gainfully employed at honorable tasks in this classless society. Prostitutes who weren't supposed to be visible at all since such women were the product of the dire poverty possible only in capitalist countries.

"What progress has this Sergeant Karel made in the case of Jan Horvath?" Lazar asked.

"He's brought me startling news. No, perhaps not so startling when one comes to think of it. Napica was destined to die violently."

"What are you saying?"

"This Horvath is our bad penny. He's turned up again in a new disguise."

"I'll be damned."

"Possibly."

"Are you saying that you think his murder had something to do with the cover-up of the war crimes that never came to trial?"

"Karel seems to have decided that vendetta is the best possible motive."

"Then you, as the examining magistrate, will have to subtly convince him otherwise."

"I'm not sure that I can do that."

"You have a very delicate sense of honor, Anton."

"Is that a bad thing to have?"

"I merely wish that I could understand its workings. How you place one demand upon it over another."

"It's a sensitive balance, I admit. One that I must struggle with every time conflict arises. But in this matter, at this time, I simply meant that I doubt I have the power to lead this detective down the garden path. He's very good at what he does."

"Why in hell did you give jurisdiction over the case to the Metropolitan Police?"

"How was I to know that Horvath was our own blackmailer?"

"Worst luck. The intelligence bunch could have been ex-pected to cooperate with us if given the proper motivation."

"Proper payment you mean."

"Don't be self-righteous. There's danger to both of us in this."

"I'm much aware of that."

"And if Karel begins sniffing around old graves?" Lazar said challengingly.

Doder came in then to announce dinner.

It was a simple meal, the kind of food Trevian had enjoyed when a boy. Cabbage soup with a dollop of sour cream rising up out of the center of the dish and coarse black bread that Doder had baked himself from flour he'd milled by hand.

= 19 =

Karel hoped Dika would be asleep when he finally went home after spending an uncomfortable night in the ready room at the homicide offices. The night detectives had made fun of him, demanding to know if his wife had kicked him out because he wanted too much of her or gave her too little. False dawn was washing the gray skies above Belgrade when he parked the car in front of his block of flats. Now he stood in the doorway between the living room and bedroom, in the terrible quiet of early morning, in the terrible moment when it would suddenly become dark again for another hour.

His clothes clung to him like the wet hide of an animal. He smelled his armpit. His body was stale. There was a bad taste in his mouth. Why had he come home at all? What had compelled him to leave the cot at the office and come home? Had he hoped to find that Dika had died in her sleep or had gone away? Had he hoped to step through the door into the hollowness of empty rooms?

He could barely see the slight mound she made under the covers of their bed. He couldn't hear her breathing. He took off his clothes where he stood, staring at her, afraid that she might awaken. All at once he needed a shower very badly. He remembered what Dika had said about smelling Marta on him. Was that why he wanted to bathe himself, to wash Marta's scent away? The dark after false dawn entered through the window. He crept toward the bedroom.

"I'm awake," Dika said. "What are you doing? Why have you come home?"

"I needed to bathe. I needed a change of clothes," he said.

"There's fresh underwear and stockings in the drawer," she said.

"I know."

"Will you take all of it?"

"What do you mean "

"Will you take all of your things and go live with her?"

Perhaps that was just what he should do. Take what he needed and go to Marta's. Live with her. Forget about escaping the country and starting a new life. Why not start a new life together right where they were? Perhaps he should talk to Marta about it now that the cat was out of the bag. Perhaps they should all three act sensibly in this. Dika seemed prepared to do so. Her voice was calm. It didn't seem to have much anger or reproach in it.

"Are you thinking about it?" Dika asked.

"I don't know what to say."

"Then you don't deny that there's another woman?"

"I don't think we should bring her into this."

She laughed. It was harsh and bitter. "My God, you are a fool," she said.

"What happened between us really has nothing to do with her," he said.

"Are you naked?" she asked.

"I was going in to wash myself."

"You're going to catch a chill. Then you won't be able to think or make the right decision."

He hadn't felt cold until she'd asked the question. Now he shivered and gooseflesh rose up on his arms, legs, and buttocks.

"Get under the covers," she said.

He hesitated.

"I promise not to molest you," she said.

Karel laughed. It wasn't like her to make that sort of joke anymore. He crept across the rug and slipped beneath the covers. The bed was warm from her body. When her flesh touched his it seemed to be burning. She was naked. The thought that she had lain there, alone in the dark, available to all the demons that may have peopled her prudish nightmares, excited Karel. He felt himself growing. Then he felt her hand on him.

"Listen, you said . . ." he began.

"Be quiet," she interrupted. "Isn't this a game for liars?"

She began to stroke his erection.

"What can happen in one hour in the middle of the night doesn't really have much to do with it," he murmured.

"Here, be quiet, and stick it into me," she said.

It was better than it had ever been with her, Karel thought. But was it enough? Was it anything like the outrageous sexual inventions he had become addicted to with Marta?

He shuddered and Dika clutched her to him with her legs and arms, wrapping him in her flesh and bones. She rocked him in the cradle of her pelvis. He withdrew and left the bed, hurrying to the toilet to relieve his bladder which was suddenly painfully full.

"Was it good, was it good?" she called after him.

He didn't know what to answer.

= 20 =

The State Security Service, the SDB, had once been called the Administration for State Security, the UDB. Before that it had been the Department for the Protection of the Nation under the authority of the Commissariat of National Defense. That had been back in 1945 and 1946. But nearly everyone, even those who could not remember "The Terror" when the agents of the UDB purged the society of post-war dissidents and Irredentists, still called it Ozna.

Stevan Georgi read the letter which Karel had secured from the examining magistrate, Judge Trevian, in hopes that it would dissuade any other authority from throwing up a barrier against his investigation as Colonel Bim had done. It urged the cooperation of anyone to whom Sergeant Michael Karel applied for help. Georgi smiled and ran his finger over the heavy engraving at the top of Trevian's letterhead.

"You didn't have to go to this trouble on our account," he said. "We're ready to help you in any way we can."

"The letter isn't just for the Secret Police," Karel said.

"Within reason," Georgi added as though he hadn't heard Karel's comment.

"I beg your pardon?" Karel said.

"I said we're ready to help in any way we can within reason."

"Yes. Well, I've come to find out that Jan Horvath had lived and worked under other names. Horvath was a comparatively recent alias."

"You're sure Horvath is an alias as well?"

"I know that in three previous incarnations he was called Ivan."

"Isn't it possible, then," Georgi said, "that his retirement name was his real name?"

"I have an idea that he wanted to take on a new life altogether. A new life, a wife, business interests, and an entirely new name that wouldn't jar anyone's memory about the past."

"In order to protect himself from the interest any foreign agents, intent upon settling old scores, might have in one of his previous incarnations?"

"Some old score, yes, but a domestic one. More like vendetta than professional revenge."

Georgi nodded and flicked a finger as though closing one subject and opening another.

"Besides the KOS, how many other organizations do you think Horvath belonged to during his career?"

"I know that he was a member of the Corps of National Defense of Yugoslavia."

"The old KNOJ, yes."

"I have hopes that his association with other services will show up in Ozna records," Karel said.

"Please," Georgi said, raising a hand.

"Pardon?"

"Not Ozna. That acronym, under which the Secret Police operated right after the war, when a good deal of violence and terror had to be applied in order to purge the society of subversive and dangerous elements, is best forgotten. The State Security Service, if you will. Or the SDB should suit in conversations between fellow professionals."

Georgi didn't seem offended. He seemed amused by the necessity of instructing the municipal policeman about SDB public relations policy. Karel had the feeling that the dissertation was not meant to scold or inform him, but to give Georgi time to think.

"I understand," Karel said. "Whatever the name under which your service has operated, now and in the past, it's always been the principal investigative arm for the examination of the histories of such applicants as I've described."

"You're right, of course. But you must understand that the

war and its aftermath was a time of great confusion. Any man who had the will and wit to do so could have obtained the necessary documentation to prove himself to be nearly anyone he wished to be. So long as that person was dead, unidentified, and without family. There wasn't a city hall or church that wasn't a treasure trove for anyone wanting to use the war as cover for a private disappearance. You'd be surprised how many long-lost husbands, fathers, sons, and brothers suddenly make an appearance, surfacing after thirty years of living another life.''

''We've had a case or two like that ourselves,'' Karel said. ''But if Horvath had always been a professional he would have left a very different kind of trail. His tracks will appear in official and unofficial rosters and in files flagged with every change of identity he assumed. If I'm right in my speculations, he'll show up under some other identity back in the service of the regency or as a member of the Ustasi.''

Georgi leaned forward and touched a button on an intercommunication device.

''I'll have our files searched. It might not be much more than you've already discovered for yourself. You understand that?''

''Yes, of course,'' Karel said, getting to his feet.

Georgi stood up and extended his hand. The door at Karel's back was opened by Georgi's aide.

''And you understand,'' Georgi said, ''that I'll have to review the material before turning any of it over to you? One never knows what sensitive stuff lies in the bellies of some of these fish.''

Karel had the feeling that he'd been put off in yet another way. Intelligence types worked with different styles but were essentially all the same, reluctant to give away any scrap of information.

= 21 =

The Senior Investigator: 1938–1942

The people of Montenegro are very proud. They boast that they are the only Yugoslavs who retained their political independence after the Turkish conquest of the Balkans. They had remained an independent principality until the end of the Great War, when the Assembly voted to join the new Yugoslav State of their own free will.

When a boy of the mountains is five years of age he is given his first jacket made of sheepskin turned inside out and embroidered with patterns of a million stitches. It is fashioned by the loving hands of the women of his family. Each five years it is replaced until he receives the last magnificent garment when he is twenty. It is the measure of the love and respect he has gathered. Legend has it that once upon a time if a woman's husband fell in battle she tried to retrieve his bloody shirt to give to her son. Red thread figured prominently in the embroidery.

When he is seven he is given a mountain pony by his father, uncle, or older brother. It is not much smaller than the horses they themselves ride. The sturdy breed grows no larger. The beasts can go for miles, even through passes drifted chest high with snow, forcing their way through on stout, chunky legs, stride after stride, seemingly forever. They've been known to carry on even when their eyelids are frozen shut from the ice formed by the breath rising from their nostrils.

At nine a boy is given a gun, a pistol, or a rifle. Any firearm will do. A family treasure in good working order is more highly valued than a new one. A trophy of combat is most highly valued of all.

Some boys are marked for greatness when very young. They stand out above their brothers, cousins, and all the other boys of all the families and clans in and around the village. Stephano Merin was such a boy who grew to be such a youth in the village of Kalog. He distinguished himself in games, in mock battles, in his studies, and was admitted to adult conversations. He was sent to the closest town where there was a school providing eight years of education. He graduated with honors. He was loved and respected by everyone for his courage, fairness, and humility.

His father, Zoran, was laughingly accused of puffing up like a valley adder when he spoke of his son. His mother, Magda, and sisters, Tessa and Dinna, were accused by the father of doting on Stephano too much. His brother Otto loved and obeyed him in most things. But it was his little brother, Milan, sixteen years younger, who adored him without reservation. He would have gladly followed Stephano right down into the mouth of Hell.

Stephano went to the secondary school at Gtad for four years, and then to Zagreb to study law. He learned about republics and nations, continents and the dynamics that ran the world, things that had always been of small interest and concern to mountain people. There was the family, there was the clan, there were the People, and that was all. Except for honor. Honor above all.

Stephano learned to think in bigger ways about more complicated matters. He learned of the civil war in Spain. He went home to the mountains and engaged his father and the elders of the clan in a long consultation. They urged him not to be foolish, not to fight a stranger's fight. These people a world away in Spain had no claim upon his honor or his courage. His loyalty was promised to his own people. If things grew worse and war came again, as it had twenty-five years before, his strength and prowess would be needed right at home. He told them he thought the war had already begun and that by fighting in Spain he would be one of the first fighting to defend the mountains. His father would have forbidden him to go but that would have been dishonorable.

Stephano went to Spain with one of the twelve volunteer international brigades that were recruited in the U.S.S.R. and elsewhere. He saw a good deal of fighting and lost a lot of friends from his own country and countries like England, the United States, Poland, Russia, and France. He was wounded and sent back home.

Milan was just nine. He had his embroidered sheepskin vest and his horse. His adored brother Stephano, the hero, gave him his gun. It was a Spanish pistol taken from an enemy in hand-to-hand combat, the most glorious weapon of all.

The older brother, who was a man, told the younger, who was still a boy, a hundred stories of blood and bravery. There was one story he didn't tell because the memory of it troubled him.

Stephano had been cut off from his company by a sudden assault of tanks manned by Germans in a narrow salient along the Ebro near Barcelona. He was almost out of ammunition. There were no more than five cartridges for his rifle left. He carried two grenades hooked to the empty bandolier across his chest. He knew he must not use them unless he was driven into a fight for his life.

Dead comrades were strewn around him on every side. Two or three were horribly wounded. One raised an arm without a hand and cried out for help. Stephano hurried to the man's side. It was a countryman, Joze Kropenick. He was not a man of the mountains but the plains, a gentle man who had once said with stunned surprise that he had never imagined what war was really like. At the time Stephano had thought the man a fool, and wondered what sort of outing anyone would think war was apt to be. Stephano took the grenades from the bandolier and laid them aside. He cut a length of the belt for a tourniquet and placed it around the wounded man's upper arm, twisting it tight with the sheath of his bayonet. The wounded man began to cry out of relief and gratitude. He expected he was saved. Stephano gave him a drink of water from his own canteen and a cigarette from his own packet. His comrade sucked the smoke into his lungs. Stephano smiled and told the man to loosen the tourniquet every minute while he went to help the others.

Stephano went off to do what he could for the next one. A

random shell burst overhead. The concussion pounded him into the ground, into oblivion. When he awakened he saw a party of men moving through the battlefield. One of them carried a flag of truce. All wore white arm bands with red crosses on them. They were a lifesaving detachment of volunteers who took no sides. Still, Stephano was afraid to show himself. He knew the amount of treachery that took place in the horrible confusion of war. Friends easily became enemies. Enemies were not surely known.

He watched and waited, counting the number of searchers. There were three. One moved off a little way from the rest. The pair passed through a gully along a streambed dried up by a dam created by an explosion up along the tree line. The solitary man walked among the dead and wounded, peering into faces. He came closer and closer. Stephano stared at him in surprise. It was a man he'd known at the university. His name was Ivan Lukac. They weren't friends, but were slightly known to each other. Stephano felt himself truly out of danger. He was about to stand up and make himself known when Lukac stopped and bent down to peer closer into the face of Joze Kropenick. Lukac looked around to make certain that he was unobserved. He took a pistol from inside his tunic and put the muzzle of it to Kropenick's head. He pulled the trigger. The pistol shot was muffled. It sounded like the snapping of a dead branch. Lukac took something from the dead man's pocket. Stephano's head was swimming, but he aimed his rifle and shot at the murderer. Then he passed out. When he came to the second time Lukac was gone.

Stephano went back to see Kropenick. Half his face was blown away. He rummaged in the man's pocket and came up with some family pictures and a letter from home.

Stephano found the remnants of his brigade. Seven days later he was wounded. He made his way to Tirana by ship. He traveled along the coast in any transportation that came his way. He left the seashore and journeyed into the farmlands, going to the village where Joze Kropenick had lived. There was a family left behind. A large family of peasants who worked the land of a distant landlord. There were twenty or more living all together with their animals in a farmhouse suitable for five.

Their fields were covered with a sparse stand of ripening wheat. The autumn evening grew still as they sat down to eat. There was a saffron glow along the line of the horizon.

The smell of the hut made Stephano sick. He was used to the smell of pine and wood smoke in the open air. The potato soup tasted like the paste made of flour the soldiers prepared to fix the unglued Spanish stamps to their letters home. He was used to game and fish, sweet berries, nuts, and autumn vegetables. Not in Spain, of course, but home in the mountains.

He told the grandfather what had happened on the distant battlefield. The old man showed no rage and swore no vengeance. Stephano was dismayed.

"Your son was murdered as he lay in his own blood. I have given you the name of the man. What will you do?"

The old farmer's eyes were as pale as gruel, one eye gone milky with cataract.

"Where does this murderer live?"

"I don't know. He went to university in Zagreb."

"Why did he kill my son do you suppose?"

"I don't know," Stephano admitted.

"My son had no arm?"

"No hand or wrist."

"He had other wounds?"

"Perhaps."

"This party of men who searched the battlefield, were they men of mercy?"

"They wore the red cross."

"Could it be that this man who shot my son was performing an act of mercy?"

Stephano couldn't believe his ears. He felt very angry and would have struck the old man.

"Shouldn't you know that for certain before you forgive your son's killer?"

The old man shrugged. Water spilled over from the lid of the blind eye. He wiped it away with a hand that looked like the root of a tree.

"Have you no sense of honor?" Stephano persisted.

Thunder sounded across the level plain. The family all looked to the grandfather. There was anxiety on their faces and trust in their eyes. The air seemed dry enough to snap.

"A storm is on the way. The grain must be taken in," the grandfather said. He looked at Stephano with eyes that had seen a thousand disasters and never wept. Perhaps a son had been murdered. There was a whole family that must be led through pestilence, accident, and starvation.

Stephano worked beside the family as they hurried to bring in the wheat before the rains should spoil it.

When the Germans threatened to invade the country in 1941, Stephano was among the first of the mountain men to join the army of the king. He led a dozen comrades out of the stony chasms and scarps into the valley. They brought themselves and their horses to the Fortieth Royal Cavalry and enlisted as troopers. Their horses were assigned to the pack train where they carried burdens out of proportion to their size. The men were given army mounts, larger animals of uniform color, either chestnut or black.

There were other troopers gathered from everywhere. The officers were noblemen, young lords who had polished manners and lazy drawls. Everything was a bore to them, even war. It was all a foolish pose. Underneath they were excited and frightened. They were also very skillful on horseback and very brave.

They camped along the railroad line between Prahovo and Nis in the valley of the Nisava along the Bulgarian border. It was there the German armor first struck in force. The men of the Fortieth were all that was between the armor and the central plain from which the columns could shoot out in three spearheads driving toward Belgrade, Sarajevo, and the country to the north.

Does a man decide to be a hero? How does a man decide such a thing? Why is one man a hero and not another? Are all heroes lonely men? Does a man learn to be a hero by imitating another one? Stephano was a very brave man. He was a hero of the Spanish War. He was a hero to Milan and to all who knew him. When he chose a hero for himself he chose Lieutenant Sasha Petrovic. He managed to become his sergeant. He rode at Petrovic's right hand. Everyone wondered why Stephano, so dark and bold, had chosen the pale, slender, effeminate aristocrat to emulate. Most of the officers and soldiers thought Petrovic a fool and even worse, a homosexual.

They were camped on the edge of the valley, facing the border and the road the German armor was taking. Petrovic was the officer of the day, Stephano his orderly. They were crouched by a campfire, wrapped in army blankets against the chill that was in the April air.

"There's no need, Sergeant, for you to ride with me when the battle is joined," Petrovic said.

"Why should I not, sir?"

"You've heard the rumors about me?"

"I never listen to rumor. I read books for myself. I read the faces of the men I meet for myself."

"It's true. I prefer the intimate company of men."

"That's your affair."

"This isn't an overture. I simply wanted you to know. Men who are about to challenge death have superstitions about the persons with whom they will face it."

"I'm prepared to face it with a man I believe will be a hero," Stephano said.

"Why do you say that?"

"I trust your honor," Stephano said.

"My honor depends much on what cause I might be called upon to serve. In time of peace there can be no real challenge to it. How foolish that a country must go to war in order for Petrovic to prove his honor."

The next morning the grinding and clanking of the tank treads could be heard coming through the riverbed leading to the valley. The bed was wide, flat, and dry. It wouldn't carry water until the late spring rains which were not expected until May, a month away. A messenger on horseback arrived. The armor was an hour off. It had smashed through the artillery massed on the heights with scarcely a pause. Guns and horses were shattered. The artillery men were dead by the hundreds.

When the probing armored scout cars broke out into the clearings, the Fortieth was massed rank on rank, armed with sabers, lances, side arms and light carbines. A few men had grenades. A few more, old hands from Spain, had fashioned makeshift bombs out of powder, cans, and nails.

Stephano was mounted alongside Petrovic. The lieutenant looked at his sergeant.

"I was once in your mountains," he said.

"Did the people know you were a noble?" Stephano asked.

"I was traveling incognito."

"Lucky for you. They might have made rough sport of you. We don't much like nobility and aristocrats."

"I was aware of that," Petrovic said, and smiled. "I spent a night with one of your women. A girl of eighteen or so. She came to turn down the bed I was offered in a hunting lodge and stayed the night."

"I thought your preferences lay elsewhere, sir," Stephano said.

"That's so, but there was something about her that made me rise to the occasion," Petrovic said. He waited for Stephano to laugh at his small joke. "For one night I thought that there was hope for a different life."

"Why didn't you stay on in the mountains?"

"Ah. We all have our family duties. Our class obligations. We all do what we must do. Do you know the Polish Cavalry forged a golden myth when the Germans attacked? It's said they flung themselves against the armor without pause or reflection."

"They would have been damned fools to do anything like that."

"I don't think they were damned fools. They had good terrain for horses, just as we do. The tanks had been slowed down in the hilly, rocky land. It was crisscrossed by the gullies of dry streams. Thick stands of bush and bracken grew everywhere. It was a proper use of horse even against armor. Just as this battle will be."

"At the walk! Forward!" the colonel's adjutant cried out. It was taken up by the officers of the Fortieth. The ranks of mounted men started forward at the walk. A trumpeter sounded the change of gait. "At the trot!" They passed quickly through the trot to the canter. The trumpet called again. "At the gallop! Chaaaarge!" The horses broke into full gallop. Officers and troopers lay over the necks of their horses. They gave out the shattering cry that had terrified the armies of a dozen invaders throughout the ages. But men in tanks couldn't hear them and the gray-clad soldiers following in the treads feared bayonets, not war cries. Lances were lowered and sabers flashed in whirling arcs above the heads of the officers.

The cannon on the tanks opened fire. Men and horses fell all around, bone-shattered, disembowled. Stephano caught a glimpse out of the corner of his eye of Petrovic grinning like a demon bound for hell. His slender body was bent at the waist but otherwise erect, the sword arm outstretched, the point of his saber pointed straight at the heart of a monster of steel. His mouth was open in a joyous cry. The white teeth gleamed. The blond mustaches were defiant.

The brigade broke through the tanks and then smashed through the scattered ranks of the German foot soldiers. But the tanks and armored vehicles spun around on their tracks. The cannon- ade pinned the survivors of the charge between the walls of a defile that ended in a cul de sac. Stephano, Petrovic, and twenty more faced certain destruction or surrender. The only alternative left to them was to charge back again into the mouths of the guns.

Petrovic looked at Stephano and grinned. He mouthed some words that Stephano couldn't hear above the gunfire. Petrovic raised his saber, waited until he felt that all his men could see it, then brought it slashing down, ordering the charge. The troop came off the granite walls like a salvo of living shot. Petrovic was at the head of the charge as before, Stephano riding right beside his shoulder. Petrovic seemed elated, joyous, finally certain of some purpose. Stephano thought that he'd never seen a man quite so handsome. The next moment there was a bloody stump between Petrovic's shoulders, his head all blown away. His body still sat the saddle, legs clasped around the barrel of the horse. Stephano saw the legs spur the animal. It rode directly into the breastplate of a tank. The horse and headless body crashed to the ground. The tank treads splintered the bones of horse and man.

Stephano left his mount on the run and clung to the turret of the war machine. He pulled the pin on the grenade he clutched in his right hand and threw it into the ventilating duct. The muffled explosion inside the tank sounded like the cough of a beast. The machine swerved crazily about on the axis of a single tread. Stephano was thrown free.

The Fortieth lost that day. Lost nearly all its men and horses. Lost in spite of the fact that they made the monsters pause to chew their bones and drink their blood. Killed more than a few of them. Killed a good many of the gray-clad German troops as well. The Fortieth rose up off the battlefield when the juggernaut had gone through on the way to the central plain. They were a handful. Stephano was alive.

The colonel took the Order of the Royal Fleece from his own tunic. It had been given to him by the old king's own hand for outstanding gallantry during a decisive battle of the Great War. He gave it to Stephano and kissed him on both cheeks. On a day of extraordinary courage Stephano Merin was a hero among heroes.

The royal army collapsed in three weeks. Stephano returned to the mountains.

In July, as the Germans began the occupation of the country, the Communists mounted an insurrection meant to wrest power from the monarchy. It was not a last desperate attempt to form a government that might negotiate a less destructive peace with Germany. It was a seizure of the opportunity the foreign invasion afforded to achieve that which they had been unable to achieve before in spite of years of subversion and agitation. The new government would not negotiate with the invaders. It was founded in the Partisan movement which swept up patriots who intended to fight the enemy until they were driven from the land. The government moved from place to place, into a city for a few months, then back into the mountain caves. They fought with captured arms and, later, weapons supplied by the British.

Stephano and Otto, valuable fighters who had already been seasoned in blood and fire, formed a Partisan band. Stephano made contact with the Communist leadership. His men were absorbed into a regiment. He was named its political commissar.

Not all patriots responded to the call of the Reds. There were a good many who remained loyal to the king. These Chetnik forces went into the hills and mountains, too. They were led by a colonel called Mihailovic. Chetnik fought German and Communist. Communist fought German and Chetnik. The Germans fought everyone and continued to pile victory upon victory. In time promises were made and compacts formed between the Germans and the Chetniks. After that the Chetniks sometimes fought only against the Communists. In Croatia the Fascist Ustasi committed atrocities against the Serbs.

Stephano and Otto fought all through the fall and winter. In a battle with Royalist guerrillas at the end of December in 1942 Otto was killed, Stephano wounded and captured. A Partisan, Bosa Kvadir, returning to the mountain village where he and the Merin brothers had lived, brought back the story of Otto's death and Stephano's capture.

The father, mother, sisters, and Milan, the surviving brother, thirteen now, sat around the table in the kitchen as the veteran warmed his hands around a cup of tea laced with brandy and told his story.

"Were they together when Otto was shot?" Zoran asked.

"Shoulder to shoulder," the soldier answered.

"Was Stephano already wounded?"

"The raking fire that did for one did for the other."

"Stephano fought on in spite of the wound?"

"As long as I could see them, he remained on his knees beside his brother's body, firing his machine pistol until there was no more ammunition in the magazine. I lost sight of him just as he fell and was taken. I had my own fight to fight."

"Ahhh," the family sighed. They understood.

"But you heard afterward that Stephano had been captured alive?" Zoran said.

"Yes, that's the way it was."

Zoran smiled bravely and placed his hand upon his wife's hand.

"Then we can expect that he'll come home."

But Stephano Merin never did come home.

There were only eighty houses in Milan's village. Three hundred and fifty people. Maybe three times that many sheep and goats.

There had been seven in his family, twelve in the family of one of his father's brothers, and nine in the family of a second brother. Twenty-eight Merins in all until Stephano and Otto were killed.

When the Germans came roaring up out of the valley into the village there was a Ustasi and a Chetnik with them. One villager said the Chetnik's name was Lukac. Another said he was wrong, his name was Napica. The Ustasi and the Chetnik went through the streets chalking the doors. One person was taken from each house that had a chalk mark on the door. The houses of the Merins were marked with many crosses and all were taken to the village square with the others who had been gathered up. No one knew why the Merins should be receiving special attention.

The marked men, women, and children were placed in the center of the square and the Germans opened up with rifles and machine guns. There was a great deal of screaming and confusion. The people broke for the woods. The German soldiers didn't want to pursue them into the trees. They knew the Partisans were hiding deep inside the woods and there were some fine snipers among them.

Of the twenty-six that bore the name of Merin nine survived. It was a miracle. Of Milan's immediate family all but Dinna lived. Zoran wanted to go back to look for her body when night fell, but his brother and Milan restrained him. At midnight the sky was lit up with the fires of their burning houses. In the morning the Germans screwed up their courage and swept through the fringes of the forest. They were unopposed. The Partisans were elsewhere. The Germans killed some of those who had escaped before. The rest scattered through the trees, running for their lives. Milan was somehow parted from the rest.

He suffered cold and hunger for seven days, then went back to the village. The few standing buildings were empty. He went to the square and saw the mound of bodies. The Germans had covered the corpses with hay. Perhaps they had meant to burn them and had been prevented from doing so, or had decided otherwise. Milan heaved the frozen bodies apart. He found Dinna clutching the small child of a cousin to her breast. She'd been trying to protect it. He had to carry them both to a hut without a roof. He built a fire and warmed the corpses, thinking that it would part them. In the end he buried them together. He made a wooden cross and marked his sister's name and the name of his cousin's child on it. In case his father and uncle came they would know that someone had returned to do what he could to preserve something of Dinna's dignity and the family's honor. Then he went off to find a band of Partisans.

In the Merin family it was said that Zoran died three times. The first death came when Bosa Kvadir came to tell them that Otto was dead and Stephano wounded and captured. But the hope of Stephano's return lifted Zoran's heart and he recovered from all the other deaths to some degree. When the months slipped by and became years, his eyes took on a distant look, that appearance that mountain men call seeking one's final home.

Bosa Kvadir returned to the village on some errand. Zoran invited him to the house for a meal. When it was nearly done he said, "Bosa Kvadir, I want to hear you tell me again about the death of Otto and the capture of Stephano." Kvadir had been laughing when those words were spoken. His face became solemn, puzzled, and frightened from one second to another. Milan would always remember that.

Everyone was excused from the table, even Magda, and Zoran was left alone with Kvadir. In the next bedroom they crowded all together on the bed, wondering what was going on. Once they heard Zoran cry out as though in pain.

When they were allowed back into the kitchen where they lived, Kvadir was gone and Zoran sat staring into the fire looking very grim.

Perhaps he told what new thing he'd learned to his wife, but neither he nor she ever told their surviving children anything about it.

Zoran made several trips to the capital. He stayed weeks on end. When he returned he was shrunken and defeated. He said nothing about the battles that he'd clearly fought. He opened the gate of the paddock and allowed his horse to run out of the pasture and into the hills beyond. He gave orders that it should not be recaptured or ever again be ridden. It was then he began to refuse meat and boiled grain. He declared that Stephano would never come home. Zoran waited for the third and final death.

Milan was nineteen when it came. He was the surviving son, the last son, the head of the family. He was strong and willing, but had no education. Before his withdrawal from the world Zoran had always spoken of the need for education. The old ways would surely be blown away in the storm of war and the winds of its aftermath. That was why Stephano had taken to the law. That was why Otto and Milan had been meant to follow their brother into higher education. The war had come. Otto was dead. Stephano was dead. There would be no opportunity for Milan to seek an education.

At Zoran's funeral Magda's brother-in-law, their uncle by marriage, husband of Magda's eldest sister who had died in childbirth, came from Belgrade to show his respect. His name was Alexander Georgi. He was well off. He'd managed to save his fortune throughout the war. Now that the Communists were taking power he'd already made the necessary friends to secure a good portion of his property for himself. He'd given up a few apartment houses and two country villas, but he still had a large house all to himself and small apartments in each of three buildings confiscated for public housing. He had a store of gold coins and silver plate. What he didn't have was a son. Three marriages had produced six daughters, but no sons. He'd out-lived all his wives. Four of his daughters had died at one time or another. The two surviving, the oldest and the youngest of the six, took care of him. He acted the autocrat with his daughters, but loved them to distraction. It was because of the oldest, child of his first wife, Magda's sister, that he'd maintained contact through the years.

The funeral visit was the first he'd made to Magda and her family in twelve years. When he saw Milan after so long a separation he remarked upon the fact that he had Magda's eyes and nose and mouth. Since his wife had shared those features, he declared that Milan could easily be mistaken for her son, therefore his son as well.

Before returning to the city he sat down with Magda and offered to take Milan to the city as his ward. He would give him the best education. He would house, feed, and clothe him. If his daughters remained unmarried Milan would share equally with them upon Georgi's death. If either or both married they would be given dowries and give up all but affectionate rights in Georgi's final estate. He would send money to Magda each year to make up for the loss of the son who would have taken up his place as the head of her household. She agreed to everything in principle. Georgi had always been a good trader, adept at saving the worst for last in any negotiation when his adversary had already agreed to everything else.

"For this I only wish that Milan should formally take my name, Alexander Georgi. I don't want my name to die with me."

Magda called Milan, Tessa, and Tessa's husband to a family council. Milan refused his uncle's offer out of hand, though it was clear he longed for the chance to follow in Stephano's footsteps and take up the study of the law. If Georgi was so concerned about the death of his family name what of the name of Merin? he asked.

Tessa said, "A name is only a name. Blood is blood. You'll always be your father's son and the brother of your brothers."

Her husband didn't agree with her pronouncement, but he was too wise to contradict her.

"I'm the man of the family," Milan said.

"Mother will come to live with us," Tessa said. Her husband nodded his head.

His mother captured Milan's hand in hers and made him look into her eyes as she'd done when he'd been a small boy. They'd called it reading the truth.

"All right, then," she said softly. "You know what dreams your father had for his sons. You're the last. You're the head of this family, it's for you to make the decision. What should we do?"

He thought for a long time. Then he said, "I'll take the name Stevan Merin Georgi. That will have to be enough for my uncle."

Milan's formative years coincided with the years of Communist innocence. All things were thought possible. The new broom was to sweep very clean indeed.

It was hard for old customs and traditions to die out simply because someone declared that they should do so. It was hard sometimes to choose between loyalty to family and loyalty to the party. Not everyone was asked to do so but the best and brightest were seduced, flattered, and persuaded into becoming active party members. It wasn't very hard to convince Stevan Merin Georgi where the bright future of the nation lay, he'd heard too much of the promise of a people's government from his brother, who had been intelligent and good and a hero.

Life in his uncle's household was pleasant. The oldest daughter, Fran, was not pretty but she had a naturally loving heart. She made much over Stevan as though he were truly a younger brother, or even a son of her own. She ran the house, giving orders to her young sister, Clara, and a servant couple who went to Georgi from time to time seeking more money or more of anything. They insisted that the new government had declared everyone equal. They were workers, not servants. There were no longer servants and masters. They worked for Georgi because they chose to but they wanted to better themselves. What did he intend doing about it?

"Are you saying that you're ready to trade me some of your wages for the luxurious room I give you?" Georgi asked.

"Why should we do that?"

"Because, though work of any sort is not all that hard to find—I will in fact help you to get work on the demolition and road-building crews—work in private homes is very scarce. There aren't too many private homes left, you understand. I'm certain that I'll be able to find a couple prepared to work for less than I presently pay you. I'll charge them for their food and bed as well. All in all I'll come out much better for it. And then, of course . . ."

"Of course what?" both recited like good little parrots.

"I was going to say that of course there is the matter of loyalty and trust and mutual concern that has grown up between your family and mine over the years."

Nodding their heads cheerfully they said, "The honor of your house is the honor of our house."

That would be all of that for another month or two. It was a happy household.

•　　•　　•

For two years the newly named Stevan got used to city life. He became a brother to the sisters, until one day when he came upon Clara in her bath.

Clara was two years younger than Stevan, and very pretty. He wasn't quite sure what constituted beauty in a woman, but he often lay in bed staring at the ceiling, convinced that Clara was beautiful. Her mouth particularly fascinated him. He'd never seen lips so round and full. They looked like the surfaces of four separate cherries. Her cheeks and arms, and what he'd seen of her thighs and breasts by happy accident, were round ripe fruits as well. Just thinking of her produced an erection. He had to be very careful not to let his mind wander to her during recitations lest he be called upon to stand and give some answer. It wasn't long before he admitted to himself that he was in love with her. They were cousins. Marriage was impossible.

He threw himself into his studies with such zeal that he astonished his instructors and his fellow students. He lost weight and became absentminded and secretive. He spent most of his time at his books. In his dreams Clara came to torment him with erotic temptations. When awake he avoided her until she could no longer pretend that there was nothing wrong between them. She often cried and begged her sister to talk with Stevan and find out what was wrong. Fran knew exactly what was wrong. Though she'd never been courted, she recognized the look of stifled passion. She also understood the desire that rose up in young men when placed in proximity to a pretty girl. She waited a year before she spoke with Stevan. She wanted to be sure that it was love, not lust, that motivated him. When she felt sure enough she went to her father and explained the situation between Stevan and Clara.

Alexander Georgi seemed surprised by the revelation. He'd thought his foster son was simply haunted with the need and desire to emulate his dead brother, to be all that Stephano would have been and more. He called Stevan into his study.

"I've noticed," he said, "that you work too long and too hard over your books."

Stevan smiled wanly but made no reply.

"Do you ever join the other students in the kafanas?" his uncle went on.

"Sometimes."

"Are there as many pretty girls available as there were when I was a young man?"

"A few."

"Have you had much to do with them?"

"Sir."

"You're twenty-one, isn't it so?"

"Just twenty-two."

"And a man."

"Do I understand you, sir?"

"Do you?"

Stevan smiled. Mountain children know a good deal about sexual matters when still very young. A man of twenty-two, no matter what his background, couldn't be innocent. Stevan knew exactly what his uncle's questions meant.

"I've had my share of women," he said.

"Everything worked out all right?"

"I had no complaints from them."

"Did you have any *about* them?"

Stevan shrugged. "They did everything they were supposed to do."

"Do you think you've learned enough to treat a respectable woman properly?"

"I don't know what you mean."

Alexander Georgi was the sort of man who went to the very heart of any negotiation. He knew exactly what he wanted and how much he was willing to give. As soon as possible he endeavored to find out the same things about the other fellow. "How do you feel about Clara?" he asked Stevan bluntly.

Stevan's face turned white. He wondered how his feelings for his cousin had been found out. His uncle placed his hand on top of Stevan's.

"I wanted you for a son," he said. "How much better it would be if you were to love and marry my daughter. There's nothing dangerous in the relationship between you. Were you to have children by Fran there might be doubt because she's the daughter of your mother's sister. But none of your blood is in Clara. She's the daughter of my last wife."

"Still and all, aren't we cousins?"

"The church might frown a little on such a marriage. But the church isn't much listened to anymore. I doubt if any political commissar would find such a marriage illegal or immoral. If you wish to court her, you have my permission. Well?"

"I would," Stevan said without hesitation.

"That's settled, then. I think a year's courtship would be suitable. It means you must be very careful not to find yourself alone with Clara. Whenever you are together, Fran, myself, or one of the servants must be in the room. You understand?"

Stevan was amused that his uncle should accept the confiscation of so much of his property and the change in the entire government of the nation as an understandable, if not entirely acceptable, consequence of the war and modern times, yet still cling to old morals and customs.

Within a week he and Clara were in bed together.

Recruiting young men and women for clandestine organizations, licit or illicit, antigovernment or government-sanctioned, is fraught with inherent peril. The game of double agent, turned agent, and implanted agent is more complex than a game of chess played by grand masters. There are a good many people in high places who think it a great deal more foolish. They reason that if the principal trait of the good agent is blind loyalty and unquestioning obedience, and any slightest deviation from that ideal suspect, then it doesn't much matter which side of a moral, philosophical or political position recruits him since it will ultimately be the individual who most impresses or puts the fear of hell into his bones that will control him. Still, it's part of the charade for candidates to be as carefully vetted as it is humanly possible to do.

The committee in charge of making recommendations to the governing body of the Secret Police had hesitated over Stevan Merin Georgi. They understood the taking of a version of his dead brother's first name. After all, that brother had been more than once a hero and it was clearly taken as a mark of respect meant to do his brother's memory great honor. There was a slightly sour note struck by the fact that one of the legends about the fallen hero had to do with a medal given after a battle when he was a soldier in the Fortieth Royal Cavalry. But a great many men had fought with the Royalists when the Germans first invaded. There was no powerful reason to believe that the sympathies toward the Communist cause shown by Stephano Merin after the fall of the monarchy were false. The medal was merely a sour note.

There was the matter of Zoran Merin's attitude about the death of his son. There'd been rumors about it. It had been said that Stephano had been tied up with other captured Partisans. After they'd been brutally interrogated, they'd been marched to a clearing in a forest and forced to kneel on the leaves with their hands still pinioned behind their backs. One by one they'd been executed. Zoran had pursued an investigation of his own. It was only after the greatest difficulty and a final flat refusal to give over any documents to the vengeful father that a lid was finally put on the case. Had the father confided in his youngest and only surviving son? The clans of the mountains put great store in personal and family honor. They didn't hesitate to kill in order to exact revenge. The new government wanted no part of such private feuds. It wanted order and conformity to the laws it set down. Would the Secret Police come to harbor a fox in their breast? Would he use them to further his own vendetta? Or could they harness any disdain and rage he might feel toward the bureaucracy and channel it for their own benefit? It was a lot to speculate about. A sour note.

It was finally decided that he was a likely candidate for the Secret Police. A recruiting officer was sent to the school to interview Stevan in private. There was a good deal of flattery of very good quality. Stevan saw no reason why he shouldn't take the offer.

One week after his graduation with academic honors he was married. The week after that Clara and he moved into Alexander Georgi's own wing of the house, and a week after that he was sworn into the service of the Secret Police with the rank of cadet recruit.

If Alexander Georgi thought that his newly promoted foster son and son-in-law, Investigator Georgi, could be of service to him in his constant endeavors to maintain what property he still had, and obtain compensation from the government for that which had been taken away, he soon discovered that he'd not thought it through. Investigator Georgi, however, had done so very thoroughly.

He reasoned that there'd be no better test of his loyalty to the Secret Police than his willingness to gather information about his own relatives that might well be used against them. Long before he was asked to initiate such a probe into his father-in-law's affairs he informed Alexander Georgi that it might be wise to convert all the real estate and other tangible property he owned into such easily convertible and concealable wealth as gems, gold, stamps, and works of art not of native origin. He delivered this appraisal in such fashion that if questioned he could honestly say that he'd never forewarned anyone or conspired to thwart the intentions of the state.

After conducting a painstaking investigation as ordered, he handed in a detailed report on his father-in-law's affairs. Alexander Georgi appeared landless, except for one half of a large house. In addition, he had no more than a modest bank account. Stevan had depended upon Alexander to do a good job of concealment, creating confusion in a set of books that had once been as carefully kept as any in the most efficient bank. He'd not been disappointed. In the end, when the authorities moved to confiscate what they could of Alexander Georgi's remaining property, it was necessary for Stevan and Clara to move into a two-room flat with shared kitchen and bath in a modern block. Alexander moved back into his old suite of rooms, his servants were made the superintendents of the newly created apartment house and received their wages from the government. When they came to their old master to complain about their fate, he forgave them for any sins they might ever have committed against him and, upon supplementing their income in a small way, found that he had acquired more loyal and conscientious servants than he had ever before enjoyed.

Clara knew of the care Stevan had taken of her father. She thanked him for it in many ways and was devoted to him all the more. Stevan accepted her compliments, but wondered if he would have done as much if Alexander Georgi had been only a father-in-law and not an uncle of his clan.

Stevan Georgi had proved himself when he was a lieutenant and continued to do so as he climbed through the ranks with patient if unspectacular service. Some of his colleagues thought him a humorless man too much given to home and hearth. His subordinates learned that he was unforgiving of any action taken behind his back, but would join any one of them at the wall if they came under attack for anything they did with his full knowledge and consent. He was considered a good boss, but not necessarily a kind or understanding one. His superiors discovered that he would bend a rule, but never betray a trust, shade the truth, but never abuse it. He was not to be asked to join in any conspiracy, no matter how petty, but if support were required to achieve a desired result by procedures not strictly according to the book he might be persuaded to cooperate. He would do a favor without asking for one in kind, but he would never forget a favor done for him. With it all, there was something about him that caused everyone to deal with him with some reservation.

"I simply don't know who he really is," one colleague said.

"The thing that frightens me is that *he* might not know who he is either," replied another.

As he climbed the ranks, his family grew proportionately. First there was a girl, then another, and finally a boy was born. Each of them was born about five years apart. The family's accommodations expanded to suit. The two-room flat gave way to three with bath, then four, and finally five with a bath, separate toilet, and a long narrow enclosed terrace. Georgi was allowed a small sedan for his private use. They had a television set and went twice a year on holiday, once to the mountains and once to the seaside, depending upon the season. He was considered a very successful man. There was promise of more to come.

= 22 =

The Policeman: 1970

Karel's briefcase was growing bulky with the transcripts of interviews collected by Samaja, Ulica, and himself. He accepted Trevian's offer of a brandy at once. Trevian and Karel had become old friends and such careful courtesies no longer pertained. But Trevian still started each evening's discussion by saying, "What have you to report?"

"We've located the third person that Madame Andric said she might have seen going into one of the houses along the way."

"What about the other two, the old man and the young woman?"

"Not yet, but the interview with the third party may have brought us a trifle closer. The person Madame Andric thought she might have seen is one Frederick Uzden. He's a dentist. One morning a month he visits a children's school that's not too far away and works on the children's teeth. He must get up very early to accomplish this volunteer work so that he can be back home to have his breakfast and open his surgery at the regular morning hour."

"Then he was coming home from this monthly service when Madame Andric saw him?"

"Yes, sir."

"And must have seen the old man and the young woman."

Karel smiled. "He remembered the woman but not the man."

"Understandable," Trevian said.

"He was able to give a description of the woman. Madame Andric was right when she judged, from her walk, that she was young. Uzden says that she was in her early thirties. Her hair was covered by the hood of her coat so he couldn't tell the color, but he said her eyes were dark brown, and her cheeks and

194

nose very thin. She was olive-skinned, her cheeks rosy with the cold. Her mouth, he said, was very red as well, like ripe fruit. He didn't think she used lipstick.''

"Did he say good morning? Did she reply? Did he hear her voice?''

Karel shook his head regretfully.

"That's all of it, except that he turned around to watch her as she walked away and remarked to himself that her legs were thin in comparison to her breasts.''

"He could tell that even when she was bundled in a coat?'' Trevian said incredulously.

"He seems to fancy himself a connoisseur of such matters,'' Karel said, "but I have similar doubts as to the accuracy of that particular observation.''

"Did he have to pass the dead man on his way to his door?''

"No, sir. He heard the shot, however, just before he turned the corner into his street.''

"He said that? He said that he heard the shot?''

"No. It was only after he read in the paper that Horvath was dead that he realized it must have been a shot he heard. At the time he thought it might have been a backfire or a window slamming. It was that kind of sound, he said, flat, and not all that loud.''

"Has the laboratory identified the kind of gun that fired the bullet?''

"Not precisely. They believe the gun used was of some foreign manufacture. There's a good many such weapons floating around the city, souvenirs from the war most likely.''

"It isn't really very much, is it?'' Trevian said sympathetically.

"Most investigations into murder begin with a fishing expedition,'' Karel said. "A thousand questions asked, a thousand answers sorted out. Sometimes we get lucky and have an early strike, the hook snags something out there in the dark water. Even if it can't be immediately seen, one has only to gather in the line to see what's been caught. It's a step-by-step affair, simple and fairly neat. Not every answer to every question drops into one's lap. There are even some tag ends that have to be left unexplained or unresolved except to say that it was the way of human nature. Then there's another sort.''

"Without nibbles?"

"No, with too many. Or rather with the sight of a hundred shadowy shapes out there under the surface, any one of which might be a fish." Karel flushed as though embarrassed by something he'd said. "I'm sure you don't need instruction about how the police conduct murder cases, sir," Karel said, thinking that he might have been boring the magistrate.

"Perhaps not, but I enjoy it," Trevian said.

"Well, then, there's one other element we've not discussed or even mentioned seriously. There's always the possibility that this was a casual homicide, a stranger killing. Some madman—or woman—walking the streets taking vengeance against anyone for crimes against themselves that exist only in their minds."

Trevian grunted. He reached out for the decanter and refilled their glasses.

"I think I may have cleared up one small puzzle for us," he said.

"What would that be?"

"Colonel Bim's extraordinary performance when you asked for his cooperation. It was so out of character for him to treat you harshly and undiplomatically. He's a good friend of mine, and his nature is well known to me. It wasn't like him at all."

"You've discovered an explanation for his actions?"

"Of a sort. We discussed it over dinner. It seems difficult to believe, but when Bim asked for Horvath's dossier to be brought to him—a dossier on one of their own retired members, mind you—it was missing. You can imagine his humiliation and dismay."

"Missing?"

"Lost, strayed, or stolen. Missing all the same."

"Surely they must have duplicate copies kept on microfilm."

"Snipped out of the reel. Incredible, isn't it?"

Karel felt at a loss, all at sea. It was a complication that introduced an incredible spectrum of speculation. What could it possibly mean? He hadn't the vaguest idea. He felt that he'd been slapped back from a chosen path and was at the very beginning of a new mystery manufactured in some wonderland.

= 23 =

Karel squeezed a lemon into a saucer. With an artist's brush he dampened the edges of the passport's page with the juice. When it was dry he put it into the warm oven. In a few minutes the edges had become discolored as though from age and use.

He repeated the process with the counterfeit birth certificate he'd forged. Yugoslavs leaving the country usually had all the documentation they could gather up just to make certain that nothing was asked of them they couldn't produce. It had an official stamp from the health service at the bottom. The ink Karel had used to make the imprint from a used stamp acquired in a small junk store dealing in odd and illicit items had been diluted. The impression looked as though it had faded with time.

The pages of the passport were filled with little signatures, dates, and visa stamps which nearly matched the few that appeared on his own passport. It gave the impression that his wife had accompanied her policeman husband on some of his holidays and official trips. The stamps for such impressions could not be purchased anywhere, but had been easily carved from raw potato, an old forger's trick. The one thing he couldn't reproduce was the embossment produced by the official seal at the passport office which was stamped across both photo and page. It was very difficult to fake. He would have to make demands on Hebrang for help with that.

He was taking such care aging the material under the theory that brand-new passports were given a much closer look than those that looked as though they'd been often used.

197

Karel sat at the kitchen table rubbing his hand along the back of the passport, transferring some of his oils to the pages so that they would take on the odor of papers that had been handled for a long time. Marta sat across from him reading Kafka's novel *The Trial* for yet another time.

"Dika knows about you," Karel said.

Marta started.

"How's that?" she said. "How does she know me?"

"I don't mean that she knows your name, just that another woman is in my life."

"What does she intend doing about it?"

"I don't think she knows herself."

"Well, what did she say? Did she scream and cry and carry on?"

"She tried to seduce me. Not once but twice."

Marta laughed.

"What's funny?" Karel asked, annoyed, even angry, for no particular reason he could think of.

"Nothing. Just the thought of a wife having to seduce her husband."

"It was a very serious thing to Dika. Very hard to do. She isn't comfortable playing the role of a slut."

The tag ends of Marta's laughter stopped.

"Hey! What is that supposed to mean?" she said. "Is that a reference to me?"

"No. That didn't come out the way I meant it. I simply meant that Dika would think acting provocative and seductive was sluttish."

"But you don't?"

"Of course not. I enjoy a bold woman. You know that."

"Yes, I do," she said, laughing sharply. She made a face as she slid down in her chair.

Karel jumped as her toes slid between his legs and collided softly with his testicles. "My God," he said.

"Shall I bring you off with my feet?" Marta said.

He grabbed her ankle and thrust her foot away, smiling but wanting the nonsense to go no further.

"That's enough. Here I am committing forgery. Here I am

about to defraud the state of the services of two valuable civil servants.''

"You and me," Marta interrupted with a grin.

"And you play evil mischief with my concentration.''

Marta subsided. The joke was too small to carry much weight.

"Did she succeed?" she said.

"What?''

"Am I speaking too softly for you?" Marta said with mild sarcasm. "You heard me, didn't you?''

"Well," Karel said, pretending to be engrossed in his task, staring at his moving hand.

"Tell me a lie," Marta said.

He looked up at her. She was grinning, but there was anger behind it.

"Tell me how you fought her off.''

"I refused her the first time," Karel said with a certain careful dignity.

"And the second?''

"I decided it was better not to challenge her. I don't want her complaining too much to the neighbors or writing letters home. I don't want her demanding a divorce on the spot, forcing the issue and spoiling everything.''

"So you went to bed with her for our sake?''

"Yes!" Karel shouted.

"But you made certain you didn't enjoy it?''

"It was no particular pleasure.''

"Still you rose to the occasion." She put her hand to her mouth. "Ah, don't mind me. I'm being a bitch. What else could you do?''

"Besides," Karel said cautiously, "I felt sorry for her somehow.''

The corners of Marta's mouth lifted derisively again. "And you thought you'd just give her a little joy with your thing. Oh, my God, slap me in the mouth. There I go again. So, has she asked you for a divorce?" she asked in a careful voice.

"It hasn't yet come to that.''

"Has she asked you to leave the house?''

"No. But that will come. How could it be otherwise?''

"What will you do? Will you come move in with me?''

"Good Christ, no. That's all we'd need—to draw that kind of attention to ourselves at this time. I can hear the gossip and the speculation. Don't think any policeman of any sort isn't being watched all the time. Just a little scandal and the lights will go on full. And then, when we arrive at the airport with our passports in hand, the official looks us over, and maybe has somebody standing by who knows my wife."

"Are we being too careful about all of this?" Marta said in a voice of sudden impatience, weariness, and despair. "If I simply applied again for a holiday out of the country, do you suppose they might not just give it to me?"

Karel rubbed the sheet of paper and regarded his mistress as objectively as he could. She was energetic, but was she stubborn? She was passionate, but was she patient? She knew how difficult it was for anyone who held the sort of sensitive position she held, who was in on so many secrets as she was, to obtain a passport.

"No, of course they wouldn't," Marta said, answering her own wishful question before Karel could do so.

$=24=$

Jan Horvath: 1943–1947

The man known as Ivan Napica couldn't understand why one murder out of all the murders he ever committed should persist in his dreams. No, not dreams, but nightmares, rages of terror and conscience he'd never experienced before. Why should he remember the screams of the Partisan fighter and Montenegran hero, Stephano Merin? He'd shot others. He'd even tortured a good many men and women because he was told to do so or had to do it in order to accomplish one thing or another. It had never been a personal matter but simply one of expediency and profit. For long stretches of time he could go about his business without distress, sleeping nights as well as any man could who was engaged in guerrilla warfare, who was trying to judge which of the many factions in the turmoil would come to the top at the end of it all. Then one night Merin would come back to visit his dreams, laughing in Ivan's face with his broken teeth and bloody mouth, flailing at him with broken limbs that flopped about at horrible angles.

It was the eyes. Yes, it was the mocking eyes that were the most terrible aspect of the night-riding demon that tormented him. The eyes of the hero calling him a coward and worse.

Ivan nursed the pain of it until he volunteered for an assignment to lead a German armored column that was sweeping through the villages of Montenegro, burning villages and massacring the population in reprisal for the killings committed upon them by the Partisans. He'd reasoned it out that Bosa Kvadir, after his escape, would have run back to report the death of Stephano Merin in a way that would make himself look good. He would have acted to protect himself against the possibility that other Partisans had gone uncaptured in that fight along the Drina and, from hiding, might have witnessed what happened after. Kvadir would tell his own version of the story. No matter how that story might be tailored, he might name Captain Ivan Napica as the Chetnik officer who interrogated the prisoners. It would leave the mouths of the Merin family and filter through the mountains and hills. It would lose its color, but not its power. Weak and inaccurate as it might become, the story would always carry weight as long as there were Merins to confirm any part of it.

"If a man is the subject of a hundred rumors he may be the victim of ninety-nine lies, but the shred of truth in the hundredth tale will bring him down." Better to stop any tales. Better to stop the mouths of the Merin family with dirt. Better to ferret out Bosa Kvadir and kill him. Was such a thing possible? Of course it was. Normal men stayed close to friends and home. Ivan did not. He roamed as he pleased. He could take on a face, an attitude, a new identity, whenever he chose to do so. He could ask questions and never answer them. Other men gathered like sheep. Ivan went alone like an outlaw wolf.

When he rode into the village where Stephano Merin's fame had become legend, he marked the doors of this house and that with a piece of chalk. He pretended to make a game of it with the Ustasi who rode with them. He laughed with the German officers. They called him the roller of dice. In an amusing pretense of frenzy he marked the door of the Merin house with more crosses than there could be people in the house.

As the villagers were gathered up to be herded into the square for execution he asked one, and another, and another, if a man named Bosa Kvadir had been there. In their fear, hoping to save their lives by cooperation, they told him that such a man had been there to speak with Zoran Merin about the capture of his son but had gone away soon after.

Was the son alive, then? Ivan asked.

Some said yes, some said it had been reported by other soldiers that Stephano Merin had been butchered like a steer with a bullet to the brain after being smashed and broken.

My God, Ivan thought, surely Bosa Kvadir never admitted to

knowing that. How had the truth found its way from the valley of the Drina to the Black Mountains? He was afraid of the power of the truth.

He was even more afraid when the Germans bungled the massacre and some of the villagers, Merins among them, ran out of the square where they were to have been slaughtered and ran into the forests.

The Germans piled the ones they'd slaughtered to one side of the square. Ivan and the Ustasi were told to gather up straw and machine oil so that the corpses could be burned, leaving their relatives nothing to honor with ceremony and burial. While about the task he looked into all the faces, trying to find the eyes of Stephano Merin.

He left with the main body of the column because he had to direct them to the next village marked for punishment.

The German soldiers left behind to finish up the job found five bottles of brandy and two women cowering in the dusty corners. They got drunk and took turns with the women, then killed them with bayonets thrust up between their legs. They threw the bodies on the pile with the rest but forgot about burning them.

Ivan knew that Chetnik power was broken. British and American aid had been curtailed in 1943. It was withdrawn altogether in 1944. Draza Mihailovic fought on, though Tito had been made marshal of Yugoslavia by the National Liberation Committee and it was clear that there would be no place for the Chetniks in any government that dictated the course of the nation after the war was won. There was no doubt it would be won. Losses suffered elsewhere, strong resistance from the Yugoslavians, and continued pressure from the Russians had already forced a withdrawal of Axis military units from the country.

Before long, sensible men would reorganize their priorities. Ivan had backed the wrong horse but the damage done was not irreparable. If he kept an eye on the main chance, an opportunity would come his way. That was a cardinal tenet of his faith. A forceful man put himself in the way of a good fate.

On August 30, 1944, seeing victory imminent and wishing to

seek conciliation, Tito presented an invitation to the Chetniks, the Ustasi, and the Slovenian Home Guards to join the Partisans by September 15. Their opposition to the Partisans and collaboration with the occupation would be forgiven. Tito's agents were everywhere, trying to appraise the sincerity of the reactions the invitation was expected to produce.

A simple thing caught out Trevian and Lazar who, by posing as medical aides, had infiltrated the Chetniks nearly to the heart of Mihailovic's headquarters. Someone who'd know them as lawyers in Belgrade also knew that they'd thrown in their lot with the Partisans. Since the informer was himself twice a turncoat he found it easy to go to Napica and turn them in.

Trevian and Lazar were taken to the first-aid tent located at the very edge of the camp.

"What a lot of time we'll save," the Chetnik captain said amiably, "if you'll put aside any intention of denying who and what you are and answer my questions with that obedience which will do us all a great deal of good."

Lazar laughed outright. Trevian studied Ivan with the intensity of a biologist reckoning the identity of a new species.

"Very well. Now I know which one is the fool," Ivan said. He gave his attention to Trevian. "Your laughing friend is the sort who'd die laughing just for the effect he'd think it made. There's no one to impress here. Except for me. One word and they'll put you up against the side of the hill with your hands tied behind your back and shoot you out of hand. No trial. No conversation. Were you in the last war?"

Trevian nodded.

"No blindfolds, last words, or final cigarette as in the cinema." He glanced at Lazar. "None of that romantic crap. Just death from the muzzle of a couple of rifles. Got it? And maybe a lot of pain up front if it strikes my fancy to give it to you.

"Now, how close are you to the top?"

"Very close," Trevian said.

"Tell him nothing," Lazar said in sudden fury.

"I'm not planning any dramatic assassination of Tito, or Rankovic, or Djilas. I want to know just how much you can do for me. Are you professionals at this business?"

Trevian shook his head.

"Not even talented amateurs," he said.

"It amazes me that you people have managed to come out on top in all this," Ivan said.

Trevian's eyebrows lifted a shade. Their captor had just given it away that he intended to save their lives.

"What's the offer you're making?" Trevian said.

Lazar looked at his friend in some surprise. What had Trevian read in the man's attitude that he had not?

The Chetnik captain was smiling.

"It's going to be a pleasure doing business with you," he said. "Can you put me in the way of information that would allow me to join up with a Partisan outfit? Can you feed me enough details about some battle, a month of marching, a half dozen men killed whom another soldier might have known? I want the sort of thing that will make it believable for me to present myself as a Partisan fighter who got separated from his company in the confusion of battle. Unable to make contact with my own unit, I'll say, I simply wandered in to the first Partisan army I stumbled on. It won't take anything too elaborate. I might not even be asked to prove myself, but one never knows. In my business it pays to have a story tucked under the tongue and another in one's back pocket."

"And what do we get in return?" Lazar asked.

"Your lives."

"Someone pointed us out to you as spies," Trevian said.

Ivan laughed. "That's no problem. I never trusted that man anyway."

"The informer might have told a good many others."

"I doubt that, but even if he had I'm ready to support the claim that the damned fool was mistaken. My word in such matters is as good as gold around here. Better. Gold alone couldn't save you right now."

"Are we to stay here?" Lazar asked.

"Hey, don't be a damned fool. When you've told me all I want to know, point your noses toward your own lines and get the hell out of here as fast as you can."

"How do we know you won't shoot us in the back?"

"If this were a moving picture I'd say you don't and that you'll just have to take the chance."

"If we do as you ask are we quits?" Trevian asked.

Ivan smiled and hesitated. Finally he shrugged elaborately.

"Why not? Are you afraid that I might come after you for favors in future? Forget it. I'm no petty blackmailer. Why do you hesitate?"

Trevian didn't answer and Lazar just stared at his friend, not knowing why he didn't simply take the offer and have done with it.

"I'll let you gnaw on it together for five minutes," Ivan said. "There will be a guard outside the tent. He can see your shadows so there's no good trying to slip out the back. If you blow out the lantern he'll have orders to machine-gun it to ribbons. I think I've covered everything."

When he was gone Lazar took Trevian's hands.

"What's going on?" he asked. "Why haven't we just said yes? Don't you trust him? Do you think he intends to shoot us down after we've given him what he wants?"

"No," Trevian said.

"What is it, then?" Lazar asked in bemusement.

"He'll let us go. Oh, yes, he'll let us get away safely. This man, this kind of man, deals in dishonor. His own and that of anyone that he can entrap. He brushes aside the chance that he'll ever come to us for help in future."

"I think it very doubtful that we'll ever even come face to face with him again."

"What is this? Is Yugoslavia the United States? Is it even England with a dozen major cities? There's Zagreb, Sarajevo, and Trieste. But for any ambitious man there's mostly Belgrade. And if we survive this war will we sink into obscurity or will we not become, as he knows we'll become, men of some prestige and influence?"

"So he'll come to us. What good will it do him? We'll tell him what to do to himself."

"If he's desperate enough he'll tell the world that we let a war criminal get away from the justice of the people."

"And drop himself in the soup?"

"This one is the sort who has no name or face because he takes on any name or face that pleases him. No. He'd be more likely to drop *us* into the soup and then disappear to re-emerge some other time, some other place, as Ivan this or that, complete with a biography, a fictional family, dead, a fictional village, destroyed, and a fictional record of valor.''

Lazar still gripped Trevian's hands.

"So what are you telling me?' he said. ''That you intend to refuse this offer. To die for some obscure, contorted idea of honor?''

"I think we should consider trying to overcome and capture him when he returns. Even kill him if we have to.''

"The guard.''

"I don't believe there's any guard paying special attention to us at this moment while this fellow's making his deal.''

"No! Why take the chance? The bloody war's coming to a close and we're alive. I intend to take this opportunity to come out the other side safely, if not as gallantly as you might wish. If you play your own game and get yourself shot it'll be for nothing, understand?''

"You're settled in your mind about this?''

"I'm determined.''

"Very well, then.''

Trevian tried to take his hands away but Lazar still clung to them.

"Does this mean that you'll reproach me with this for the rest of our lives?''

Trevian shook his head.

"No, no. That would be the most dishonorable thing of all for me to do. I wanted to discuss the possibilities with you. We've done so. The decision belongs to both of us.''

= 25 =

The Policeman: 1970

One day Karel realized that all his preparations for their escape from the country had really been a game to occupy Marta. A game played to occupy her with a fiction of escape so that her manufactured fears wouldn't get out of hand and truly drive her mad. The request for the passports obtained from Hebrang might be considered compromising, but were Hebrang to talk, or anyone to ask, he could easily say that he was gathering evidence against the dishonest clerk. So far Karel hadn't done anything that couldn't be explained away.

Forging the passport that placed Marta's face in the place reserved for Dika Karel had almost been fun. He considered it a test of his own skills of observation to see if he could go just far enough in creating an authentic look without going too far.

Now there was the matter of the official seal which marked both photograph and page, welding them together where the steel jaws of the embosser pinched the papers together. There was no getting around the illegal act he must ask Hebrang to commit in his behalf.

"I want a favor from you," Karel said.

Hebrang hadn't bothered to rise when Karel came into the office. He remained seated in his chair as though aware that he had the upper hand. He'd had time to think about Karel's use for blank passports and had put something together that made him feel confident and arrogant. He nodded his head.

Karel smiled and sat on the corner of Hebrang's desk. He looked at the toe of his polished half boot as it swung in a small arc. He seemed to be admiring its shine.

"What do you think is going on, Hebrang?" he asked.

"What do you mean?"

"Well, why do you think I asked for the blank passports?"

"To make one that appeared genuine."

"Why would I do that?"

"Because there's someone who wants to get out of the country and isn't being allowed to do so."

"Me?"

"It could be you. After all, you have special skills the government wouldn't want taken elsewhere."

"That's old news, isn't it? I mean there haven't been heavy restrictions against free travel for a long time. Isn't that what the papers say?"

"That's the official line, of course."

"I see," Karel said. "You pretend to know what's really going on behind the scene."

"Well, no. What favor do you want done?"

Karel swung the toe of his boot into Hebrang's shin. Hebrang yelled.

"You shouldn't even think subversive thoughts about the honesty of your government and the ultimate good of its purpose, whatever that might be. Do you understand? Things aren't always what they seem."

"I understand," Hebrang said.

Karel dropped the passport on the desk.

"I want you to have this stamped."

"How am I supposed to do that?"

"Don't play the fool with me. You would have had to have a contact inside the passport office to get your hands on the blanks. Use that same contact to get this stamped. Better yet, tell him to lend it to you while you sit at his desk. Tell him to turn his back so that he'll be able to say he never saw you do it in case he's questioned."

Hebrang's face grew pale and his eyes wide.

"Are you saying there's danger of that?"

"Not if you keep your mouth shut," Karel said. "You just tell your contact that. The smell of danger will keep him honest."

"Oh, he'd never inform on me."

"Nor you on me. Isn't it so?"

= 26 =

Samaja and Ulica were still tracing down the leads available in the lists taken from the address books and keys, and those that led from interviews in seemingly never-ending bifurcations. They were still conducting an investigation into a conventional killing, a civil matter without political overtones.

Karel thought about the new possibilities opened up by the revelation of the missing KOS file. It would have been no simple matter to steal the dossier and invade the microfilm files as well. It meant that someone inside the Military Counter-Intelligence had done the jobs, one or both. Either the KOS had been penetrated or someone with access to the files had been coerced, blackmailed, or bullied. Could it have been Borodin of the SJB or Georgi of the Secret Police? Could it even be Colonel Bim pretending that his files had been invaded when he'd done the job himself? Of all the bloody tangles of intrigue, plot, and counterplot left over from the war, none were so complicated as those surrounding the executives of the intelligence organizations. The top ranks were filled by men who'd changed their spots a dozen times, who'd made their careers on duplicity and mystery.

Colonel Bim had the habit of secrecy. It was part of his physiology. Without the practice of it he would develop ulcers and die. Hearty handclasps, sophisticated dirty jokes, and polite laughter were his means of dissembling. Inside he was a man always in conversation with himself.

Just before the war with Germany he'd been a student in Nuremberg. One side of his family was German, and he'd been sent there with a head start in the language to take up the study of engineering. He'd been approached by the SS and asked if he would like to join his destiny to that of his spiritual homeland. They seemed ready to forgive the unfortunate fact that he'd been born in a backward nation. So far as they were concerned, he was a German.

At the first opportunity Bim made contact with officials from his embassy in Berlin, taking perfect care that none of the German agents set to watch him were aware of the interview he'd arranged. He was asked to return to a certain restaurant in three days' time. Under cover of the crowd of beer-drinking students, a female member of his country's espionage apparatus, flown in with direct orders from home, recruited him into the service. He was ordered to accept the proposition offered him by the Nazis.

He was taken into the SS. During the war he rose to the rank of major among them. His training gained him access to the inner circles of the party. He had a picture of himself wearing the black uniform of the SS with silver flashes at the collar. He was standing at a table with several other men similarly uniformed. They were raising steins of beer. He was laughing. He kept the photograph in a locked trunk but sometimes took it out to look at it. It reminded him of the time when he lived in constant, unremitting terror.

When the war was nearly over Bim was contacted by another agent from home. He was asked to allow himself to be captured by the Americans and to insinuate himself into their security organization. They expected the Americans would be as practical as the Russians, and would use the best trained of the German specialists to mount the cold war against the new enemy. The United States and the U.S.S.R. would square off to see which would inform the conscience of the new generation and mold the destiny of the world. Bim refused. Not because he admired the Americans. Not because he feared the Russians. But because he'd been afraid to spend a night with a woman, or have one drink too many, or confide in a friend, for far too long. Ozna lost interest in him. He found employment with the Military Counter-Intelligence.

Had he not done so he had every reason to believe that he might well have been scooped up and liquidated as a potential traitor during "The Terror." It made him wary even now. He sometimes wondered why he'd lost his courage when he'd been asked to carry on. It was a memory that shamed him. It was the sort of thing that made a man uneasy and suspicious. Of all the rivals he feared in his own organization, and in the wider espionage establishment, those who had the true gift of secrecy and silence frightened him most.

Borodin was another sort of beast altogether. He could be expected to be more violent and direct if ever he decided to go after an enemy. He fancied the technique of terrorists like those under whom he'd obtained his early training in the U.S.S.R. He'd been a foreign recruit in the OGPU as far back as 1935, when he was only twenty-five. He was far enough away from the director, Genrikh Grigorevitch Yagoda, to escape any suspicion when Yagoda was purged, placed on trial, stood self-confessed as a murderer and foreign spy, and was shot to death in the cells of Lubyanka. By 1938 he was looked upon with favor by Lavrenti Beria, the man who took Yezhov's, Yagoda's successor, place in the newly named NKVD when Yezhov was purged in his turn. It was Beria who sent Borodin back to Yugoslavia with credentials that placed him among the leadership of the National Liberation Committee, that same committee that ultimately named Tito marshal of Yugoslavia in 1944. He was appointed to the directorship of the SJB from the moment of its formation, and of all the intelligence chiefs was longest at his job. In 1948, when Tito broke sharply with the U.S.S.R. and set Yugoslavia on a path away from the policies of the Soviet bloc, Borodin's security was in doubt. But, apparently, he satisfied Tito that he had no loyalty to Russian communism, and that his loyalties lay completely with Tito and Yugoslavia. There were, however, still those who believed that Tito nurtured a viper in his bosom, but they were afraid to openly say so.

No one doubted Georgi's devotion to the nation. His love of silence and secrecy was more a matter of policy than a personal attribute, though he displayed a soothing quietude of manner that was a subtle negation of personality. The cleverest observers understood that he'd chosen to exercise his strength from a subordinate post, and generally believed that he could have wrested the top spot from his bumblingly inefficient director any time he chose to do so. Dante Kosmaj was truly the invisible man. He left everything concerning administration in the field up to Georgi. All internal matters were handled by another senior, Petrova Gora. He spent his time in the pursuit of school-girls and raising prize poultry at his farm outside Belgrade. Some of those who watched suspected that Georgi hesitated in order to conceal something from his past which might be uncovered were he to step into the spotlight. They knew the man Georgi *seemed* to be. They speculated about the man he might be if he were entirely himself. Lately, it were as though, they said, someone else lived inside the body of Stevan Georgi, next to the heart, and often engaged him in silent conversation even when Georgi was out in public. Not self talking to self but two people inside a single body. There was something about the cast of his eyes at such times that was most disquieting. It was as though Georgi were looking for someone to kill, not in some hotly dramatic way but with cold disregard of that someone's humanity.

Karel thought of Trevian as well. There was something in the examining magistrate's conduct of this investigation most unlike the vigor with which he usually pursued the cases put before him. Perhaps it was simply old age finally come to sit on his shoulder.

= 27 =

The Judge: 1944–47

There's a quality about wartime that is best described as a determined test of each individual's entire span of competencies. That is not to say that every man or woman is actually challenged to the utmost—Providence still protects some and abuses others—but it is meant to convey the thought that war, being an unnatural state, an interruption of the normal tenor of most lives, forces the development of certain skills that will prove only minimally useful when peacetime comes again. To have been a sapper affords a farmer no practical advantage in raising a crop. To have been a rifleman is of little use to the baker who returns to his ovens.

There are certain attributes, however, that are transferrable from one state of existence to the other. Effective consultation and the exercise of diplomacy are two that find favor at the bargaining table in any negotiations. Lawyers find ready employment no matter what the condition of society may be. Dissemblance and duplicity, also, are traits that can profit any who know well how to use them. Spies are rarely without a job of some sort in or out of time of war.

In October of 1944 Trevian and Lazar entered Belgrade two days after Tito had returned from Romania to the city. They were present when he angrily asked his questions of his subordinates. Why was nothing being done about the suffering of the people? Why was the city still swarming with all kinds of informers, spies, and provocateurs? Why were groups of Mihailovic's men known to be operating almost without restraint?

It was pointed out to him that the agents of Ozna were

methodically tracking down every suspicious person. Arrests, trials, and executions were being conducted under the strictest adherence to the rule of law. No one must be able to accuse the new government of drumhead justice. Tito said that the rot must be cut out by the most expeditious and effective means. Trials for all? Justice for all? Impossible.

Trevian was asked his opinion. He thought long and carefully, and then he said, "There is no way that enough courts can be formed and so constituted that thousands of decisions can be sent down. There is such bitterness among our people against the German agents and collaborators, after the terrible burning and killing so bloodily done, that deliberative justice will enrage them to the point where they might take matters into their own hands. Then the guns of the soldiers would have to be turned against our own long-suffering people. It's certain that there will be a good many whose crimes are so petty that not even the harshest courts would condemn them to death, but who will die all the same. It's in the nature of revolutions that men are often guilty not of having done something, but of having belonged to something. Leaders and women, the very young and very old, however, must be given trials as a note of the respect to civilized values which the new government intends to make the mark of its administration of justice."

It was decided that Trevian should sit as chief justice of one of several courts composed of men who had been judges, prosecutors and professors of philosophy in civilian life. Lazar was assigned the post of advocate for the state to Trevian's court.

In time Trevian came to regret his recommendation for such special examinations. Lazar chided him for having allowed his humanitarian feelings to prompt him to create a situation that was despicable. The trials were usually arbitrary, brief, contradictory, confused, impassioned, argumentative, badly reasoned, and essentially unjust. Pressure and influence were brought to bear upon the courts in any number of ways, bribery of high officials being not the least of them. Trials that should have encompassed days took hours. The court calendars became clogged even so. The trials were attracting the wrong kind of attention.

In a silent but desperate attempt to fairly administer his concept of justice, Trevian worked twelve, sixteen, then twenty hours a day, reading and rereading badly kept trial transcripts, depositions, and other documents until his eyes felt as though they were burning out of his head. He never tried to enlist Lazar in his special effort, though Lazar often made it clear that he would refuse to enter into such madness even if he were asked.

"I won't try to drain the ocean with a tea strainer," he said. He would bring his friend pots of tea at two o'clock in the morning. He would bring cool, wet cloths and place them on Trevian's eyes. Once he knelt down, removed Trevian's boots, and massaged his swollen feet.

"We must believe, at least, in the *possibility* of justice and honor," Trevian sometimes murmured in his exhausted sleep. Lazar, overhearing him, knew that Trevian would have refused Napica's bargain and allowed himself to die if he alone had been in jeopardy.

One day, by some curious, almost unbelievable accident, an officer of the Red Army, who'd fought for the liberation of Belgrade, was brought before Trevian's tribunal accused of rape and murder. Witnesses testified that in the outskirts of the city the drunken officer had smashed his way into a pharmacy, killed the owner, and raped the wife. Five thousand Yugoslavs attended the funeral in protest of the outrage. In order to quell the temper of the crowd, members of the newly formed Corps of National Defense of Yugoslavia, the KNOJ, broke into the Russian headquarters and placed the officer in protective custody.

How and why the officer, one Captain Korneyev, should have been brought to the center of the city and placed in a detention cage along with suspected saboteurs and provocateurs awaiting trial was unknown to anyone. It was but the first of a series of procedural and administrative gaffes that finally stood him up before Trevian and four other judges. Once there, the court could find no way of shuffling their responsibility off to anyone else. No one would have Korneyev. Neither did Trevian feel that they could simply let the crime go unremarked. The simple people who had attended the funeral of the pharmacist were aware that the Russian had been brought to trial. That they didn't know it had come about by error no longer had a bearing on the situation. Tito's infant government was being watched and everyone knew it. The case became the kind of cause célèbre that suddenly rises up out of the general confusion of far more important matters and captures everyone's attention and concern.

After an exchange of notes, letters, demands, and explanations, it was decided that the Politburo, two prominent Yugoslav commanders, the chief justice of the trial court, and the chief prosecutor would meet with the head of the Soviet military mission and his principal aides. It wasn't a pleasant confrontation. Trevian's restrained explication of the case was met with scarcely concealed disinterest. Tito's recommendations for effective Soviet discipline of officers and men produced offensive anger.

Impulsively Lazar spoke up. "The worst of this matter is that our political enemies are taking advantage of this crime. The Red Army and the National Army of Liberation are considered brothers in arms. The actions of one reflect upon the other. Critics are comparing the assaults of Red Army soldiers upon civilians with the civilized behavior of British officers."

The head of the Soviet military mission leapt to his feet and began to roar. His tirade might have been distilled into the single statement that he would not countenance an insult that attempted to compare the Red Army with the armies of any capitalist country.

The confrontation was effectively brought to an end. Later that day Captain Korneyev was released into the custody of the Red Army. Three days later Trevian's court was officially informed that he had been executed for crimes against the Yugoslav people. Three days after that the activities of Trevian's court and all other panels were indefinitely suspended. A bargain had been struck. Both sides had delivered.

Trevian and Lazar were summoned to Tito's headquarters to receive commendations. As they walked up the steps of Tito's villa and through the doors, they passed between soldiers of the KNOJ, that elite group criticized by a good many as a restoration of hated royal pomp.

The ceremony was brief. Tito congratulated Lazar on his vigorous prosecution of justice and Trevian upon his patience and wisdom. They were asked to take service with Military Counter-Intelligence which would play an important role in the establishment of justice in the new Yugoslavia. Then they shared a cup of coffee and talked of the beauty of Dubrovnik and the Adriatic. There was, Tito said, a villa called Scheherazade, a fairy-tale construction on the face of a cliff overlooking the sea. He was thinking of taking it for a summer home. He hoped that one day they would come and spend a holiday weekend with him.

Back at their offices, which had survived the occupation almost intact, they shared a bottle of brandy.

"Did you see him?" Lazar asked.

"See who?" Trevian replied.

"That fellow Napica."

Trevian straightened up in his chair. "What are you talking about?"

"He was one of the honor guard standing at the door."

"My God."

"Indeed. Do you know, I rather admire the fellow," Lazar said.

Lazar was neither so insouciant or amused in the autumn of 1947 when Trevian, then assigned as the civilian member of a panel of military men convened at necessary intervals by the Office of the Military Counter-Intelligence, called him for a conference in the offices they still maintained together. Trevian refreshed his friend's memory of the constitution and intent of the judicial board. It was meant to conduct preliminary examinations into accusations of war crimes as defined under Articles 125–128 of the Yugoslav Criminal Code and make recommendations to the Politburo that might lead to court-martials of members of the armed forces.

A war criminal was deemed unworthy of any sort of social protection. It was a legal curiosity of the procedure of which Trevian was a part that, though it was supposed to be a merely investigatory and deliberative body, its recommendation for indictment virtually carried the weight of conviction. Therefore, it was at the very outset that libertarians like Milovan Djilas successfully argued for civil rights protection in the person of a civilian jurist.

"That bird you once admired for his brass and impudence has come home to roost," Trevian said.

There was no need for him to qualify the subject of his conversation further.

"I know to whom you refer," Lazar said, "but the name escapes me."

"It was Napica when he made his bargain with us. Now his name is Ivan Boreta and he's an officer in the KNOJ."

Lazar raised his eyebrows and waited for Trevian to go on.

"A man named Zoran Merin, a citizen of Montenegro, has brought charges against Ivan Boreta, claiming him to be one Ivan Napica, also known as Kosho or Lukac . . ."

"My God!" Lazar exclaimed.

"Not a proper oath for a good Communist," Trevian remarked dryly, "but I think it expresses my feelings, too. This man changes his identity with considerable ease."

"Extraordinary."

"Yes. I'm reminded of the creature from Greek mythology. The many-headed Hydra. When the hero cut off one head, two more grew back in its place."

"What charge has this Zoran Merin brought against . . . ?"

". . . Boreta, Ivan Boreta."

"Yes, Ivan Boreta."

"He claims that one day in the week before Christmas in nineteen forty-two his son, Stephano Merin, was wounded and captured while fighting with a Partisan company against a brigade of Chetniks at a bend of the River Drina. Our . . . lifesaver . . ." His mouth twisted as though he'd bitten down on a rotten bit of meat or fruit. "Our benefactor was the officer in charge of prisoner interrogation. Apparently, he first tortured and then shot Stephano Merin."

"What sort of testimony does Merin have to support these charges?"

"Not much if one were to be talking about the conduct of a criminal or civil trial. But you must remember that we're looking at the possibility of a court-martial and that, as you well know, is another legal matter altogether, conducted under rules of procedure and evidence very much different. Even now feelings run high when it comes to war crimes and such atrocities as are herein described.''

He tapped his finger on a single typewritten page lying in the center of his desk. Lazar looked at it as if he'd not seen it before, as though it were a creature that might strike out at him.

"If I were sitting in judgment on Merin's case I would probably throw it out for reasons of insufficient evidence. That would be the case that a prosecutor such as yourself would put to me. One witness, and that a man who heard only screams and a shot, but didn't actually see the murder. Some corroborative evidence from other Partisan survivors of that interrogation who didn't actually see the killing either.''

"Was the body of the murdered man buried at the site?''

"Merin says that it was and he's probably right. It's part of what we're expected to do in our investigation. That is to say we have the means to send out soldiers and bulldozers, and look for the grave.''

Lazar made a sound of skepticism.

"Oh, it would be difficult to find perhaps,'' Trevian said, "but not impossible.''

"This Ivan Boreta has been taken into custody?''

"Only house arrest. And not very severe at that. It seems he's very well liked by his superior officers.''

"Does he know you're sitting on the board?''

"Yes,'' Trevian said just as a knock sounded on the paneled door.

Lazar started and turned his head sharply.

"Come in,'' Trevian said.

The door opened and Ivan walked in. He was smiling. His hand was outstretched as though they were old friends newly remet.

"Good to see you. You both seem prosperous and not much changed. Enver Lazar, isn't it? Who could forget? I've followed your career in the courts with great interest. And you, Judge Trevian. Who hasn't heard of the wisdom and patience of Judge Anton Trevian?''

When he'd finished shaking hands, he didn't take the empty chair standing in front of Trevian's desk. He stood there looking very smart in his major's uniform as though waiting for comments on his appearance.

"You seem to have done very well for yourself, too," Lazar said, matching Ivan's urbanity with his own.

"I survive," Ivan said.

He gestured to the empty chair as though asking permission. When Trevian nodded, Ivan sat down. He took a brilliantly white handkerchief from his sleeve and wiped his mouth.

"A drink?" Trevian said.

"I admire your manners," Ivan said. "You don't really feel politely inclined toward me."

"Very well. Say what you have to say," Trevian replied evenly.

"That's right, let's drop the other shoe," Ivan said.

"Pardon?"

"I'm here to claim the rest of the debt you owe me."

"I don't think we owe you anything," Lazar said. "You've lived unmolested for more than six years."

"Why should it have been otherwise?"

"Because we saw you when you were a member of Tito's guards."

"I thought you did," Ivan said easily. "When you didn't acknowledge me I expected my simple change of appearance had been successful. It did, in fact, give me a good deal of confidence."

"We didn't inform on you."

"It would have been dangerous for you if you had," Ivan said.

"I doubt you would have suspected us. After all, we didn't blink an eye when we passed you."

"I would have thrashed about quite a lot if I'd been lifted. You can bet on that. I would have tried everything and anything."

He took a dull silver cigarette case from the breast pocket of his tunic and offered its contents of black Russian cigarettes to Trevian and Lazar. They wordlessly refused.

"I don't think you would have informed on us," Trevian said. "I don't think you would have given up the influence you might hope we could exert in your behalf."

"And there you are," Ivan said, slapping his knees loudly

with his open palms. "I'm here to do exactly that, to call on your influence."

"I'm not sure I can manage it," Trevian said. "After all, I'm only one of five judges sitting in judgment of the merits of the case brought against you."

"But the most honored of them. The civilian judge. The aristocrat who gave up a title and joined the common men. A theorist, a councillor, and a confidante of the great."

"Still and all, the others won't blindly follow my unsupported recommendation."

"Support it then. Construct a persuasive argument."

There was the ring of challenge in the words. There were also sharp points of threat and command. Trevian stared at Ivan impassively.

"Shall I help you choose your themes?" Ivan said.

Trevian stood up. His face was set, his hands cupped but motionless as though he feared they would do violence to the smiling man sitting before him, legs carelessly crossed, a black, pungent Russian cigarette dangling from his fingers.

Ivan uttered a strange laugh as if he'd been momentarily frightened and then, remembering his adversary, had quickly recovered. He leaned over and smashed his cigarette out in the ashtray, then stood up as though in a sudden hurry.

"That's a foolish suggestion, of course," he said. "Sending a boy to do a man's work. Is there anyone suited to telling Judge Anton Trevian how to compose a brief?"

Lazar stood up as well. "This is the end of it," he said, a trifle shrilly.

Ivan slowly turned his head and shoulders toward Lazar. He looked at him as though he were a strange intruder. His eyelids descended a fraction, measuring Lazar's insignificance.

"Of course," he said, "we'll be even."

"Quits," Lazar yipped.

"Yes, 'quits,'" Ivan said and smiled. Lying was among the easier things he did, something that he sometimes chose not to do very well. Let them know that he would damned well call upon them anytime he chose. Let them respect the fact that he wouldn't cry for help over minor matters but that he would surely call if pushed to the wall. Let them damned well know that they were all dishonorable men. Only the quantity, and perhaps the quality, of their betrayals were different.

Ivan paused in the doorway. "Prosecutor Lazar," he said, "you've been investigating the fate of your wife."

"Yes," Lazar said sharply.

"She died in the bombing," Ivan said, and left.

Lazar sat down and stared at his hands. They were trembling.

"You're free to go on with your life again," Trevian said softly. "You're free to marry again if you like."

"He never meant it when he said we'd be quits on what we owe him," Lazar said. "But if he thinks he's got us in his grip forever and ever, he's much mistaken."

"Oh?"

"Oh, no. He won't be allowed to extort anything he wants from us over and over again. This will be the last time. I promise you."

"How can you say that?"

"I'll kill him if I have to," Lazar said, and somehow Trevian believed his old friend meant it.

= *28* =

The Policeman: 1970

There must be at least two persons involved in an act of murder. At first the victim is usually the one about which most can be easily discovered. Even if his past is lost in the natural mists of time or the more impenetrable fogs of intentional design; even if he has changed his name and identity so often that some of the characters he chose to be have disappeared forever, leaving gaps of months or years in his biography. Enough can be learned of his recent past to at least allow certain presumptions about his activities and associations. If the short-term dossier reveals no motive for his killing, the task becomes more difficult.

Karel had begun to doubt that he would ever clear up Horvath's murder. Some hand had smudged the victim's past. A past that was as tangled as any Karel had ever investigated or even heard about. Jan Horvath had once been Ivan Boreta, and before that Ivan Napica and Ivan Kosho. And before that what had he called himself? What had he done? What crimes had he committed under aliases? What murders for himself or for some clandestine organization?

Karel placed his hand on a thick file that lay on his desk like a small gray tombstone. It contained the names of all the known officers of the Royal Army of the Fatherland that had been led by Draza Mihailovic. Ozna had painstakingly compiled it after the war to help them in their search for the leaders of all those fighting forces that had collaborated with the Germans or opposed the Communists. After the execution of Mihailovic, the hunt for Chetniks had become less intense. The common soldiers were forgiven and worked alongside Partisans in the rebuilding of the nation. A good many of the officers simply faded into the crowd. But the names by which they had once been known remained. And the name Ivan Napica was there, enlisted in the Chetniks in August of 1941. Come from where? How did a man step out of nowhere into a position of command as a full captain? Who had exercised influence in his behalf?

Karel opened the drawer of his desk and took out the items he'd found in Horvath's desk drawer at the offices he shared with Hogamann. Ljubo Samaja had failed to turn up the bank box for the keys. Karel had put him to checking out more likely leads. It might well be that the box was in another country filled with the monies Horvath had made with his illicit operations. Rajco Ulica had just the day before informed Karel that he'd exhausted all the names on the list taken from the green address book found on Horvath's body without turning up anything new. Just the names of a few more whores, a few more foreign importers, and a few more officials who might have done him a favor or even shared in the action of his dealings. Now he was patiently examining the names on the next list farther back in time, names that hadn't been transferred to the green book or the one that came after. The keys and the four small directories sat in a row on Karel's desktop. One had been black, but was now worn almost gray. One was faded red. The third was the green one. The fourth and last was shiny black. He idly leafed through the pages, one after the other.

He heard himself sigh as though he were an invisible presence in the room, observing himself. He wondered if he were unconsciously slackening his own efforts. If the case remained unresolved, the conference in Rome might come and go without him. He'd be unable to carry through the plan for taking Marta out of the country with him as his wife. He wouldn't have to face the shame he knew he'd certainly feel for abandoning Dika without explanation. He might, in fact, have to face the new relationship she was trying to thrust upon him, and perhaps find a solution, even a renewal.

= 29 =

"You seem lost somewhere tonight, Michael," Marta said.

He took his eyes from his book, realizing that he hadn't been reading the page for the last few minutes. She sat at the other end of the couch knitting. A domestic couple. They'd spent such hours together more often since Dika's perpetually reproachful glances and silences had driven Karel out of the house more and more.

He shook his head slightly and smiled. "Sorry. Did you say something?"

"Nothing important. I just remarked that you were gathering wool."

He regarded her sitting there, reading glasses perched on the end of her sharp nose. This is the way we'll be with each other more often than pantingly entangled in each other's limbs, he thought. This will more certainly be the product of our passion than sweating bodies and pounding hearts.

"More like gathering up clouds that won't be packed away neatly in a box," he said.

"This Horvath murder?"

"It's going nowhere. I suspect it's a vengeance killing. I know that in my bones, but that doesn't tell me much. It doesn't point me in any direction. Except . . ."

"Yes?" Marta said when he hesitated.

"Except toward the past."

"You think that's where the answer lies?"

"I'm sure of it. But I can't sort it out."

"Does it matter very much? I mean, was this Horvath an estimable man?"

Karel shook his head.

"A reprehensible one. People whose lives are shrouded in mystery have usually done something to be ashamed of, something that makes them a target of someone they've injured terribly. I think that's true."

"Then, so what if his killer isn't found?"

Karel almost started to give her the lecture about justice being the government's as it might once have been the Lord's. He almost started to express his deepest feelings about people who killed other people, no matter what reasons they thought they might have for doing so. He stopped himself. He knew that she would be impatient with such abstractions. A bad man had been shot down by someone who probably had good reason for killing him. So much for that.

"The offer made to me by Lieutenant Lutesh was that I'd be sent to the police conference in Rome as the Yugoslav representative if I successfully cleared up Horvath's murder."

"Surely that was just his way of telling you that he'd already decided to let you go. A little teasing joke."

"I don't think so."

"But that would be rewarding you as though you were a child. That would be suggesting that you wouldn't do your best unless there was a sweet promised to you at the end."

"No. I don't think it was meant that way either. He knows me. He knows I always give every case the best I've got."

"Well, I should hope he knows it," Marta said.

"But I don't think I'll be sent to Rome if I fail in this. He doesn't know I won't be coming back. I wouldn't be able to simply put the investigation down and pick it up again upon my return."

"And if you don't go to Rome . . ."

"We'll have to find another way to get you out of the country."

She regarded him fiercely for a long moment, then her eyes softened.

"Without you?" she said.

"If necessary."

She tossed her knitting and her glasses aside and threw herself into his lap. She kissed him with an intensity that bruised his lips, telling him that she loved him.

He was immediately aroused. It somehow shamed him. What was all that ruminating about quiet, dull, domestic contentment all about? She'd only to kiss him, place her hand upon him, show him a bit of her breast or thigh, in order to arouse him. Could any attractive woman do the same? Hannah Horvath would surely have seduced him if her night fears and loneliness hadn't already moved her to toss back the covers of her bed and let Hogamann slip in. His wife had found him an easy conquest when she decided to have him, even though he knew that strict refusal of her overtures would have been much the better, kinder course. He was helpless before Marta's tongue and lips, the pressure of her breasts and the weight of her thighs. She was the authoress of his reawakened passion and he feared he might never get enough of her.

She touched the lobe of his ear with her lips, then gently allowed her tongue to swarm into the shell of it. He lurched slightly and almost pulled his head away but she clasped him tighter with her arms and moved one hand to hold his head in place.

He'd never quite understood the kind of love that could lead to murder. If a man or woman claimed to have killed because the object of their affection had threatened to leave, Karel looked upon them with cynical doubt. Even if no other motive was found, he really couldn't accept murder in the name of love. But now, as he held Marta on his lap, moving to the bidding of her touch, he could understand a little of it. Would he, however, really kill her if she left him? He was surprised to realize that he truly didn't know.

She pushed him away saying, "No, no. Later. In a little while." Then he realized that he'd been undressing her. She got off his knees and moved back along the couch. Both were flushed. Her hands fluttered at the open bosom of her blouse and she laughed nervously as though they were not yet lovers but very close to becoming so.

"What are you going to do?" she said, as though looking for something to say to cover her agitation and sweet confusion.

"Do?"

"About the Horvath investigation."

"I intend to keep digging as far as the things in hand will let me."

"Things in hand? What would they be?"

"Not much. A key to a bank box we can't locate. Four small address books, three of them filled with old numbers. The fact, but not the possession, of missing and censored dossiers at the SJB, SDB, and Secret Police."

The erection she'd caused to grow wouldn't subside even now that her body no longer touched him. His mind was on the backs of her thighs. He thought of taking her that way from behind so that he could hold the bones of her hips and look down at himself entering her. He envisioned the moons of her buttocks trembling beneath his blows.

He became aware that she'd said something. "What?" he said like a man of impaired mental capacities.

Her laughter sang out like a trumpet. He looked into her eyes and saw that she was perfectly aware of what his thoughts were about. That, perhaps, was the greatest part of her hold over him. She knew, she always knew, when she'd aroused him even if it were only with a glance or the sight of the tip of her tongue licking cream from her lip. She rushed into his arms and started dragging the clothes from him.

"My God, you're in pain," she said when he was half exposed. "Let Nanny do something about that."

= 30 =

The Senior Investigator: 1969–1970

In 1969 a rumor concerning Stephano Merin and his death reached Senior Investigator Georgi's ears. It was started because of something altogether unconnected to his brother but not unconnected to the war. A woman named Natalia Jova had boasted in the mountain district where the Merin family lived that a powerful friend of hers, Ivan Lukac, now known as Jan Horvath, had arranged for her to receive a monthly veteran's pension though she'd never fought in the war. When Horvath's name appeared on everybody's lips it stirred up old memories, suspicions, and accusations, things that Stevan Georgi had never heard before.

Everyone in the district seemed to know that Stephano Merin, the war hero, had been wounded and captured. He'd later died under unexplained circumstances. Now the rumor circulated that a Chetnik officer, Ivan Lukac, also known as Ivan Kosho, had been the hero's executioner. The rumor said that before his own brains were blown out, Stephano Merin accused Lukac of having, in similar fashion, executed a helpless man on a battlefield in Spain many years before. The rumor said the man named Lukac was no longer known by that name but was an important figure in Belgrade who lived as Jan Horvath.

Stevan Georgi went to Titograd which had been Podgorica during and before the war. It was not a great city as cities go, but it was a large city for Montenegro. He never bothered to use his authority or influence to find Natalia Jova. He simply looked in the telephone directory. Nor did he bother to call her first. He went to her apartment at the supper hour. She wasn't at home. The next morning he was on her doorstep. Still she was away.

He went to question the janitor of the building. When asked about Natalia Jova, the old man licked his lips and made a face of pleasure.

"I wish I had the price," he said.

"She's not at home," Georgi said.

"That happens," the janitor said, and grinned and winked.

"Where does she work?"

The janitor looked at Georgi as though he didn't believe such innocence.

"Here and there," he said. "Are you a cop?"

"What makes you say that?" Georgi asked innocently, and smiled.

"You have the way about you. They come around from time to time."

"What for?"

"To harass her. To keep her frightened and paying up. You know how it is."

"So you don't know where she might be when she's not at home?"

"I didn't say that. She goes to the Metropole Hotel bar when she's working and to the Prince's Kafana when looking for her own fun."

Georgi gave him a small tip. No matter how you try to build a society, it always comes back to that, a coin, a bribe, a gratuity for services rendered.

There were only two main streets. Neither place was hard to find. They were only half a block away one from the other. He went to the hotel first. There was a woman sitting at a small table sipping a drink. She looked at him and smiled. He went over and sat down.

"You don't waste any time, do you?" she said.

"Will you have a drink, Natalia?"

"You know me, do you? I don't remember seeing you before."

"We have a mutual friend. He told me to look you up whenever I was in Titograd. He told me you would show me a good time."

"Yes?"

"Jan Horvath. You know, Ivan Lukac."

Her face paled. The blood receded from her cheeks and brow and seemed to settle in her neck and bosom which glowed with it. Her lipstick and eye makeup were suddenly very harsh in contrast.

"What have I said to startle you?" Georgi said.

"Nothing. How do you know that Horvath was called Lukac?"

"We're old, old friends." He watched her carefully.

"He told me to be careful never to mention both of his names in the same breath," she said.

"And have you done as he asked?"

She was clearly frightened.

"That's not why you're here, is it?" she whined. "I mean, I didn't broadcast it all over town. I just mentioned it to a girlfriend or two. Especially Sophie. She got on my back. She said that I was growing old and probably couldn't make my way on my own much longer. She said I would die an old whore without a friend or a place to lay my head. She's young and full of herself. She thinks she'll never grow old. You understand?"

She was leaning forward, peering into Georgi's face, asking for his sympathy.

"So what did you tell her?" Georgi asked as amiably as he knew how to do.

"Just that I had a friend all right. I had a friend who was very important and who'd made very sure that I wouldn't end up begging."

"And you told her his name in order to support the truth of your story?"

"That's right. That's exactly the way it was. When Sophie went on to sneer at me and ask me how anyone was to know about some man named Horvath living in Belgrade, I told her who Horvath really was."

"And who was he?"

"Well, you know. He was Ivan Lukac, a very important man in Belgrade."

"Important in what way?"

She frowned. It was getting to her that Georgi probably didn't have much of anything to do with Horvath if he knew so little.

Or was the good-looking fellow just playing cat and mouse with her?

"How did Horvath—or Lukac, take your pick—make sure you would never want for anything?" Georgi asked.

"Who the hell are you?" she said, leaning back in her chair and starting to gather up her gloves and purse.

"I told you. I'm a friend."

"Why all these questions?"

"I'm just making conversation."

"The hell you say," Natalia said accusingly. Her lips grew thin as she determined that she wouldn't say any more.

"It's no good taking that tone of voice with me," Georgi said evenly. "I'm not here to do you any harm."

"How do I know that?"

"Believe it or not as you please," Georgi said. His voice had developed an odd chilling edge as though he'd honed it like a razor. He realized once again, with regret, that his training didn't suit him for this kind of interrogation. "Just answer the questions I put to you," he went on, "and you'll be safe enough."

She winced.

"Play games with me and we'll see if we can find you someplace else to work besides this nice hotel bar. What favor did Horvath do for you?"

"He got me a veteran's pension."

"You're too young to have fought in the war."

She smiled, simpered, and preened herself.

"For Christ's sake," Georgi said, "that wasn't a compliment."

"Well, it's true all the same. I am too young."

"One way or another, what he did in your behalf was illegal."

"I didn't ask him to do it," she protested. "It was his own idea."

"Why did he want to do the favor for you?"

"You know," she said coyly.

"Tell me."

"Favor for favor."

"Services rendered?"

"He occupied all my time whenever he came to town."

"Are you saying that he arranged for the government to give you a pension rather than pay you your regular fee?"

"We got to be friends, do you see? I couldn't charge a friend. It's a matter of honor with me not to charge good friends."

"You don't have very many of them, do you?"

"Good friends? Well," she said, grinning tentatively, "I couldn't afford too damned many, could I? I'd be likely to starve to death if I gave it all away."

"How long have you been receiving the pension?"

"Three years."

"And why have you just started bragging about it?"

"I told you. Because of Sophie. Because she frightened me by what she said. I wanted . . ."

She was having difficulty thinking through her feelings.

"Yes?" Georgi said.

"I wanted to hear myself say that I would be all right," Natalia finally said.

"Why did Horvath come back to Titograd?"

"To see his brothers." She paused. Georgi could see her thinking what else she could volunteer that might placate him. "They used to own a big department store in Zagreb," she said.

"What do they do now?"

Natalia shrugged. "Who knows for sure? One, I think, works for the travel agency. Another at the power plant."

Georgi stood up. "That's all," he said.

She reached up and put her hand on his sleeve.

"You wouldn't want to stay and talk awhile, or maybe come to my room?"

"I don't think so."

"I'd make you a price."

"I'm like Horvath," he said. "I don't like to pay for it."

"No money. I don't want money."

"What do you want?"

"A promise?"

"Of what?"

"That you won't do anything to get me arrested."

"I promise. I give you that for nothing."

"And . . ."

There is always an *and*, Georgi thought. Always a small escalation of demands or requests. That's why good men become impatient and turn into tyrants and terrorists. People should be grateful for the smallest crumb when it's given to them by gift and not by right. But when they get a little bit, they always want a little bit more. He smiled, waiting for her to try to wheedle what more she could from him.

"Yes?" he said.

"You won't have that pension taken away from me, will you?"

"What do I care?" Georgi said. "Should I be the ruin of such a little thief?"

"You're a good fellow," Natalia said. "If not tonight, any-time you're in town, come look me up. It won't cost you anything."

Georgi found Barta Lukac behind the counter of Putnik, the national travel agency. It was a small office with an air of despair about it. No grand tours were booked out of it. Just the usual holiday excursions.

Barta Lukac wore his hair parted in the middle and plastered down with pomade in a fashion that hadn't been seen in a good many years. His waxed mustaches were equally anachronistic. Georgi thought he looked like one of the store window dummies that might have stood in the department store in Zagreb.

Georgi smiled and slouched on the countertop. He was determined to conceal himself a good deal better than he had with the whore.

"Your brother said I should look you up if ever I needed help with any travel plans."

"Yes," Barta said, and smiled. "Which brother would that be? I have one still living, and one that only just lately passed away."

"Were there more?"

"We were seven brothers altogether. Seven brothers and a sister. All dead now but my brother Dushan and myself."

"You once owned a department store in Zagreb, didn't you?"

"I was the director of it after my oldest brother died just after

the war. Then everything as large as our enterprise was nation-
alized. I stayed on for a while, but after a time the officials
decided the store was better run by a workers' commune.''

"Was it?" Georgi asked, and winked.

"Well, you know. Some say yes and some no. What does it
matter? There isn't a wide variety of goods anymore the way
there once was in my father's day.''

"Your father started the business?''

"Oh, no, it was started a long time before that by my great-
grandfather. My father was the one who put it all together in
Zagreb.''

"Your father was in politics, wasn't he? He was in the legation that petitioned the Prince Regent of Serbia to rule the new
nation of Yugoslavia, wasn't he?''

"He was a patriot," Barta said proudly. "Did Dushan tell
you all this?'' Something flashed in Barta's eyes. Suspicion.
Wariness. Caution, even after all these years and changes, as
instinctive as the taking of a breath.

"No, Ivan.''

Barta crossed himself in memory of the newly dead brother.

"Do you ever wish for the old days?" Georgi asked.

"Well, I was only a child. What do I remember about
them?''

"I don't mean the old, old days. I was thinking of the days
just before the second war when King Peter was on the throne.''

"I don't have much to do with politics. Never did. I was a
merchant. I still am a merchant in my heart.''

"The Communists took it all away from you, didn't they?''

"Listen, I don't think we should go on talking like this.''

"What's the matter?''

"Well, it could get to the wrong ears. Someone might report
us to Ozna.''

"Ozna? You mean the State Security Service?''

"Call it whatever you like.''

"Hell, this is nineteen sixty-nine. I don't think the Secret
Police are going around arresting people who feel nostalgic
about the old days under the monarchy.''

"Why take the chance?" Barta said. "The Croatian Separat-
ists are still active. I wouldn't want to be mistaken for one just

because I was born in Zagreb and once owned a department store." His mouth trembled.

There were casualties everywhere, Georgi thought. No matter where a man lived, no matter when in the history of the world, there were things to terrify him. There were events that scarred him. Some were as small as the death of a brother, some as large as a war that killed millions, and some were nothing more than the loss of status or possessions.

"Did you come in to book a journey?" Barta asked brightly.

"I'm making a pilgrimage," Georgi said. "A memoriam to a brother who was killed in the war."

"If you know where he fell, you're luckier than most."

"Well, I don't think I'll be able to find the exact spot. But I know the general area of the battlefield. The battle took place in December of nineteen forty-one beside the River Drina, near the town of Priboj."

"I know it," Barta said in some surprise, as a person will react when a miraculous coincidence comes into one's life. "My brother Ivan fought there."

"Yes, I know," Georgi said.

"That's how you came to be a friend of my brother's?"

Georgi nodded. "I myself was scarcely old enough to fight until the war was nearly over, but I asked questions around the veterans clubs."

"And met Ivan?"

"And met Jan. Met Jan Horvath," Georgi said.

Barta's expression changed. He was no longer cautious and fearful. Georgi had proved himself to be a very close friend of Barta's brother, indeed. Barta leaned on the counter, bringing his head closer to Georgi's. He lowered his voice in a confidential manner though there was no one around to overhear.

"Your brother fought with the Chetniks then?"

Georgi placed his hand over Barta's hand.

"Well, it's not over," Barta said. "When Tito goes the whole thing falls apart. Croatia gets her independence."

"I don't have much to do with politics," Georgi said again, and winked.

"Was it my brother who told you where the battlefield was located?" Barta asked. "You're sure about the town?" He started taking out maps and railroad schedules from the drawer behind the counter.

"No, it was someone who survived it. His name was Bosa Kvadir."

The name that had never been forgotten since the day the mountain man sat at the kitchen table and recounted the death of Otto and the capture of Stephano fell out of Georgi's mouth like a plum.

Barta, his eyes on the timetables as he ran his finger along the columns, nodded his head.

"You know the name?" Georgi asked. "Did your brother ever mention Bosa Kvadir?"

"Oh, yes. I don't know how it came about, but he told me more than once that he'd saved the life of a man with that name."

= 31 =

The old man dipped the crust of bread into his soup before taking a bite of it. He had no teeth, except for two that grew in his lower jaw like fangs. There were some mountain men who looked to be much younger than their years. Bosa Kvadir was one who looked much older than the fifty-five or so he might have been. What would he have done if Bosa Kvadir had died in the intervening years? Georgi asked himself. Would he have taken it as a sign that he wasn't to pursue the rumor? Hadn't he always known that one day he'd be confronted with the mystery of his brother's death and would have to do something about it?

"Tell me what you can remember about Stephano Merin's death," Georgi asked a second time.

Kvadir looked up from his soup with rheumy eyes. He was the kind of man who cultivated the look of a poor creature, avoiding any chance that anyone would find him dangerous and perhaps step on him. He managed to alienate everyone in this way, those who should have been friends and those who were newly met.

"You know that it was a long time ago?" he said in a querulous voice.

"Yes, I know. I've already said that I know. But I trust the power of the incident to jog your memory. The men who fought in that battle are known to have been heroes. You're a hero. You'll remember."

Kvadir grinned and nodded to the beat of Georgi's flattery.

"It was a fight, yes. Those damned Chetniks outnumbered us four to one. We took their measure and cut them down to our size. But it was too late by then. Our bullets and grenades were gone."

"A good many Partisans dead?"

Kvadir nodded, remembering the old battle in a way that was probably nothing like the truth.

"Otto Merin dead," Georgi went on hypnotically.

Kvadir continued to nod.

"Stephano Merin dead," Georgi said.

Kvadir blinked, and paused with a sopping bit of bread halfway to his maw. "No, no. That's not the way it was. Stephano Merin was still alive at the end of the fight. He was captured along with the rest of us."

"Oh?" Georgi practically whispered. This wasn't the way he remembered the story as it had been told nearly eighteen years before.

"You say you were captured?" Georgi said.

Kvadir thrust the bread into his mouth and chewed on it furiously. His eyes darted everywhere. He knew that he'd said something wrong, but he didn't know what.

"Along with the other Partisan heroes," Georgi went on softly, pretending by his tone to be the voice of Kvadir's spirit that so wanted to have been brave.

"That's the way it was. We were tied up like chickens. There was a Chetnik officer—a captain—known to Merin. Stephano told me he'd seen the man execute a fellow Yugoslavian on a battlefield in Spain."

"What was the captain's name?"

Kvadir shook his head. "Be sensible," he said. "How can you expect me to remember such a thing after such a long time?"

"Little things that happened even during a big thing stick to one's brain like bits of wet paper," Georgi said. "You only have to turn a light on them and dry them out. Then they float free and reveal themselves before your very eyes. Close your eyes. Try it."

Kvadir closed his eyes, pressing the lids tightly together with a real effort.

"No, no. Gently. Take it easy. You'll only give yourself a headache that way," Georgi said soothingly.

Kvadir did as he was told. He sat there with his head slightly thrown back, mouth half open, eyes closed, his face in repose. He was a gentle man, Georgi thought, damaged by guilts about the past. Surely he had wanted to be a hero and had failed. It was evident in everything about him, except now, when he seemed at peace with himself.

"Napica," Kvadir said. "That was the name the captain gave me when he questioned me. Napica."

"Was that the name by which he was known to Stephano Merin?"

A slight frown reappeared between Kvadir's eyes. Then the lids popped open and he grinned. "Lukac. Merin said the man's name was Lukac, and that he'd known him slightly when he'd gone to the University of Zagreb."

"Please close your eyes again," Georgi said. "I want you to describe the field of that battle to me."

"Now, just wait a second," Kvadir protested, though he did close his eyes, "you're being far too hopeful now."

"Just imagine the field of battle. It was along the Drina, was it not?"

"Yes, yes."

"Were there any trees?"

"A grove in a sharp bend of the river."

"When you were taken prisoner how did they keep you?"

"In a rough stockade they built of tree limbs and wire. There were guards and we were tied up."

"You were interrogated?"

"What?"

"You were asked questions?"

"Yes. By the captain. He was in charge of that."

"Who was questioned first?"

Kvadir laughed.

"I don't mean the name of the man," Georgi amended. "I mean to ask if you were questioned before Stephano Merin."

Kvadir began to tremble. It started in his feet so that the nails in his heels tapped gently against the wooden floor of the kafana. Then the tremor traveled up his legs. His thigh made the table chatter.

"Did you tell the captain what Merin had told you about him?"

Kvadir placed a hand on his stomach. His chest heaved in a series of short convulsions. Sour soup dribbled out of the corner of his mouth.

"Did the captain let you off the hook because you betrayed Merin?"

Kvadir's shoulders shook. His chin trembled, driving his jaws together with wet, smacking sounds. Water ran out of his eyes.

"There was a huge tree stump beside the fire where the captain questioned me. When he sent me away to his tent I heard someone scream. I knew it was Merin. I heard things that turned my blood cold. I knew that the captain was using the stump as a place to break Merin's bones. To butcher him."

"How did you know that?"

"I had such a stump at home. It was used as a place to slaughter goats and sheep."

Georgi went to the house of his sister Tessa and her husband. His mother still lived with them. He told them as simply as he could what he believed had happened to Stephano, and why his father had been haunted and diminished after his journey to Belgrade.

They traveled in a truck that Georgi secured to the place that had been described on the Drina near the village of Priboj. The grove of trees in the river's bend was still there. The great stump was still there.

They made a camp. The women cooked while Georgi and his brother-in-law dug test holes here and there, using the stump as a starting place. It wasn't too difficult to find the grave. The bones of the legs were broken. The front teeth had been shattered and wrenched from the jawbone by a blow.

They passed the skull from hand to hand. Even the sister touched it. Even the mother held it. There was a gaping hole above the eyes. No one cried, not even the women. They simply stared at Georgi. On the way back to the village, a sack containing his brother's remains rode on the bed of the truck with his brother-in-law. Georgi held the skull wrapped in a flag against his chest while his sister drove and his mother stared at the road ahead as though she were staring down a corridor with walls made of tears. He didn't speak a word.

= 32 =

"A pin in a haystack is easier to find than a raindrop in a cloud," goes an old peasant saying. The reason is clear. There is no single drop of rain in a cloud until the molecules of water coalesce around a grain of dust, and begin to fall.

There had been a suspicion in Georgi's heart about the death of his brother. He'd lived pretending to believe that his brother had died of battle wounds. Now he knew that his brother had been tortured before being murdered. He'd suspected that his father had been thwarted in some task he'd set himself when he'd gone off to Belgrade years ago. But he'd had no inkling of the nature of his father's mission. Now he was certain that the information that had come to him by way of rumor had been known to his father.

Zoran Merin's mission to Belgrade may have been for one of two purposes. First, to kill the man who killed his son. Second, to set in motion an investigation into the post-war history of that murderer. Georgi used his power to make discreet inquiries and discovered the letter of accusation written by his father twenty-two years before. Why his father had not tracked Horvath down as a hunter would do, delivering his revenge with a pistol shot or a knife thrust, Georgi would never know. Had Zoran intended summary vengeance, no amount of security his quarry might have placed around himself would have done any good. Zoran would have simply waited for the moment, walked up to the man, and without the exchange of a single word, killed him out of hand. In mountain vengeance there was no room for psychological matters, no intention of confronting the killer with his guilt, no desire to see any light of repentance in the eyes of one's victim. It was simply the repayment of a blood debt.

Perhaps his father had wanted more than that, Georgi mused. Perhaps he'd wanted Horvath to suffer public condemnation and humiliation, to be exposed as the cowardly, dishonorable villain that he was. In all the tales and legends of war throughout the Black Mountains there was not one story of such a monstrous murder. Never had a mountain fighter killed a wounded, bound prisoner, even if it was a despised Turkish soldier. Zoran Merin's hunger for revenge had not been hot, but as cold as the winds of the mountain passes, blowing through a man's flesh and turning his heart into a ball of ice.

But when his father had failed to bring the murderer to justice why did he return to the mountains to mourn his impotence, to sicken and die? Why had he not transferred the debt of honor to his youngest son, Milan? Was it simply because he'd lost two sons and had no desire to risk a third?

Whatever the father's reasons may have been, fate had determined that the blood feud should not dry up and blow away. Gossiping tongues had stirred up a whirlwind. The weight of the shame of it oppressed Georgi.

He looked at his wife. He looked at his children. His oldest daughter, Zeina, wasn't beautiful but she was pretty and so sweetly natured that when she called him Father his heart squeezed for love of her. Gara was eleven. She'd only recently started to grow so that her legs were like a colt's, knobby-kneed and clumsy. Georgi often laughed to himself when she came to him complaining that chairs and stools were forever getting in her way and tripping her, as though they were living creatures with minds of their own. Whenever he hugged her he was startled at the force and speed of her heartbeat. He could feel it with his hands on her back and her chest against his chest. He wanted to do nothing that would jeopardize their lives, the pleasantness of their existence.

It was Vinko who made his heart lurch the most. Vinko was six, and childishly merry, but it was the startling effect of his brother Stephano looking out at him through the child's dark brown eyes that always gave Georgi pause, casting him back into the past. If he failed to seek vengeance against Horvath he would be placing his own dishonor on the head of his son.

= 33 =

Georgi wanted to be careful. He'd no intention of accusing and condemning a man with no more proof than gossip. The testimony of an old veteran who might well remember things that had never been, or remember them in such a way that the truth still lay buried, wasn't enough. He searched and cross-checked files, tracked down witnesses, and questioned them meticulously for a full year.

One thing led to another. He searched his own records. The Secret Police had audited the case as a matter of policy. In the abbreviated language of the professional, the drama of one small investigation of a war crime out of thousands was briefly outlined. There was a reference to the investigatory panel that made recommendations concerning court-martials. He read the list of names. He read the name of Magistrate Anton Trevian. A spurt of anger and dismay shot through his heart. Then he smiled. How was his old friend Judge Trevian to know that Senior Investigator Stevan Georgi had once been Milan Merin, brother to a dead hero murdered by a war criminal masquerading as a respectable citizen known as Jan Horvath? The principal investigation had been conducted by the KOS into a war atrocity committed against a captured Partisan band on or about Christmas week of 1941 in a place within the valley of the Drina close to the town of Priboj. The investigation had been conducted in the year 1947 at the request of Zoran Merin. It had been given to the Military Counter-Intelligence to do because Ivan Boreta had been an officer in the KNOJ and his case was considered an internal matter.

247

Georgi censored the documents, removing all references to his father, but allowing the accusative document to remain in case anyone were to look for cause one day.

Stevan Georgi applied through regular channels to the office of the military prosecutor, and to the KOS, for copies of 1947 evidence and depositions. The office of the military prosecutor flatly stated that no such investigation had ever been conducted. The KOS claimed that an accusation of alleged crimes had been filed against Major Jan Horvath, but that a special investigatory panel had reviewed the evidence and come to the conclusion that there was no basis to the charges.

Georgi contacted a man who worked in the central files of the KOS whom he'd suborned in case of need long before. An occasion for his use had not arisen until now. The delivery of the file was easy enough. It was very complete. It told a good deal about Zoran Merin and his family. Even Georgi's uncle and father-in-law was named. One day someone might look into the file and make the connection. He destroyed the file, burning it in the fireplace at home. He went back to his double agent in the KOS, who was terrified when Georgi ordered him to vandalize the microfilm reel. His fear of Colonel Bim paled when he heard the horrors that Georgi threatened.

Georgi traced three men still alive who'd fought and been captured in the battle along the Drina. One remembered the screams of a man who was tortured and shot but couldn't remember the name of the victim or that of his executioner. Another remembered names for both, but time had altered them. The Partisan martyr, the old soldier said, had been Stevan Orlic, and the Chetnik officer a Major Vajda. The third remembered both names more accurately and confirmed Kvadir's story, except that he thought Kvadir had been the murdered man since he'd never returned from the interrogation. Twenty-eight years was a long time to be asked to remember such matters.

Finally there were no more files or questions. Georgi went home. His wife was out shopping, his children at school. He went to his lockbox and opened it with a brass key. He took out a package wrapped in a small Spanish flag. When he opened its folds the Spanish pistol brought back from the civil war by his brother lay in his palm. He put it into the pocket of his greatcoat.

The next morning before it was light he left his sleeping wife and children and drove to the gardens of Kalmagden on the outskirts of the city and fired the pistol into the underbrush to test it. He drove back to Belgrade and parked his automobile on the street where Jan Horvath lived. It was very cold. In front of Horvath's apartment house a custodian was scraping a path in the snow.

Georgi turned off the engine. In a short time it grew very cold inside the automobile. His breath deposited frost on the windows and effectively obscured him from casual view. From time to time he made a spyhole with his thumb placed on the windshield. He thought of his wife and children. He was in terrible doubt. He drove off, but after a mile or so thoughts of his brother and father came flooding back and he returned to his place of vigil. The janitor was gone, the path clear but icy. He saw Horvath leave the front door of the apartment block and begin his careful passage along the icy walk.

= 34 =

The Policeman: 1970

Karel felt miserable, torn by guilts. Guilts that were being thrust upon him by the two women in his life. He'd gone home the night before to find Dika asleep. But the next night she was awake and waiting for him, demanding another of the interminable discussions that she was determined to thrust upon him. It had been a bad session filled with her rage, tears, and at the end, worst of all, her self-recrimination.

It was absurd, and too dramatic, and filled with terrible despair.

He left the house when she flung herself on the bed, and would have gone to Marta's except he feared that she would work herself up into a frenzy of impatience and hope, demanding to know what chance was left for him to solve the case of Jan Horvath and get them the means of freedom.

He was early into the office. Konjic and Terzic were working the last shift. Anybody killed after midnight waited until morning before anybody began to search for their killers. The uniformed police bagged the bodies up and trotted them off to the morgue.

Karel didn't bother to remove his coat and hat but sprawled in the chair behind his desk, already feeling as though he'd put in a full day.

There was an envelope on his desk. He pushed it idly about with his finger. Then he hunched forward over the stained blotter and opened up the sealed flap. There were two sheets of paper inside. One was a facsimile copy of a recommendation for one

250

Ivan Kosho to a post with the Yugoslav Red Cross. The other had a single line printed on it in black ink with a bold hand.

It read, "Stevan Georgi is also Milan Merin."

So this is how it was to end for him, he thought bitterly. After all the searching and questioning, a nameless, faceless informer would settle the matter of the murder of Jan Horvath.

= 35 =

Of all the distasteful and difficult tasks a law enforcement officer is ever called upon to perform, the apprehension and arrest of a fellow professional is the most difficult. Of all the dangerous administrative duties one is called upon to do, the accusation and arrest of a member of the Secret Police is the one most fraught with danger.

Karel had been right about the vendetta. There was no doubt that Senior Investigator Stevan Georgi was Milan Merin, nor that Jan Horvath was the Captain Ivan Napica of the Chetniks who'd tortured and executed the Montenegran Partisan Stephano Merin. Why had Horvath acted in such a brutal fashion toward that particular Partisan? Had it something to do with his identity as Ivan Kosho back at the time of the Spanish Civil War? It was the sort of thing policemen never satisfactorily resolve. The principal actors were dead.

It took Karel two weeks to walk the same path that Georgi had trodden, questioning Natalia Jova, Barta Lukac, and Bosa Kvadir, terrifying them all over again. He understood the damaged document in the file given him by Borodin. Georgi had sanitized his trail as he searched out the facts in the twenty-eight-year-old war crime, but had failed to invade the files of the SJB. Why had he committed the oversight? Had he unconsciously wished to be caught after he killed Horvath to let the world know that he had, at long last, avenged his hero brother?

Karel sighed. It was nearly over for him. He'd make his arrest. He'd turn Stevan Georgi over to the Office of the Prosecutor and, theoretically at least, would have no further interest in the outcome. Whether Georgi would be charged, brought to trial, convicted, or exonerated was supposed to mean nothing to him. His job had been honorably completed.

The burden of justice would have passed from his hands. Had Borodin managed to get jurisdiction in the case for his Public Security Service, would he have used the evidence as a means to damage the rival Secret Police, or would he have employed it as a sword over Georgi's head? Colonel Bim's KOS had claimed jurisdiction for the very good reason that Horvath had been one of their own. Had it been given to them there was no doubt that the case would have been buried in the dead file again, this time with a tombstone of security clearances piled on top of it to make sure that no one would ever again disturb the skeletons. Had the Secret Police been given the case it would have certainly been handed to Georgi himself to investigate, and that would have been the end of that.

But the examining magistrate, Trevian, had assigned the case to the Municipal Police. The case had landed in Lutesh's capable administrative hands, and he'd turned it over to Michael Karel, an officer with a name for intuition and a record of success.

Karel straightened up in his chair. Yes, his colleagues were right when they accused him of thinking too much about the philosophical aspects of the job they performed. He must learn to curb it. Then he realized he wouldn't have to bother his head about such things very much longer. Soon enough he'd be on his way to Rome with Marta Barkai to begin a new life.

He went through the papers lying on his desk. The documents necessary for the apprehension and presentation of charges against Stevan Georgi were among the bits and pieces of the investigation, file copies of certain documents, scraps of papers with notations to himself, and Horvath's address books. It would all have to be looked over a last time, a decent and accurate report must be composed. But for the time being the blizzard of paper would have to wait until he went to arrest Georgi.

First he should respect protocol and courtesy and inform the examining magistrate. He placed a call to the Courts of Justice and was told that Trevian was at home with a spring cold. Another call to Trevian's home got Doder on the phone. After Karel identified himself he asked after the judge's health.

"Not well," Doder said. "He's in bed where he should stay. He went out yesterday without a hat even though I warned him that warm spring days could make an old man sicker than any winter wind." Karel expected that Trevian was nearby, sitting up in bed or in a chair by the fire, accepting his old servant's oblique scolding. "But he's a stubborn old fool and . . ." Doder rambled on.

"This is an official call," Karel interrupted. "Let me speak to Magistrate Trevian, if he's available."

"He's not able to come to the phone," Doder said.

Trevian's voice could be heard demanding Doder to tell him who was on the other end of the line. Karel could hear Doder tell his master that it was the policeman Karel. Trevian ordered Doder to hand over the phone or risk going to prison for obstructing justice. When he spoke into the handset, Karel could tell that the old man's cold was settled in his chest. His greeting was harsh and labored.

"I wouldn't have disturbed you when your clerk at court informed me that you'd taken ill except that I'm about to make an arrest in the case of Jan Horvath," Karel said.

The silence on Trevian's end was as empty as a cave and dark as a shadow. Finally he said, "Yes?" as though it needed a great effort.

"I've every reason to believe that Senior Investigator Stevan Georgi of the Secret Police killed Jan Horvath because of the murder of his brother, Stephano Merin, during interrogation following Merin's capture after a battle between the Chetniks and the Partisans in a valley of the Drina. Do you want me to present my evidence to you before bringing him in?"

After another long silence Trevian made a sound like a wrenching sigh. Then he said, "If you have the evidence, bring him in."

= 36 =

Stevan Georgi acted as though he'd expected Karel to be coming for him. He acted with a particular kind of quiet cordiality, putting Karel at his ease, forgiving him in advance for what Karel was about to do. He was not at all afraid.

"Senior Investigator Stevan Georgi," Karel began a trifle stiffly, "you're also known as Milan Merin, are you not?"

Georgi smiled. "Only among my family and a few friends," he said, smiling.

"Yes, of course. Do you carry a weapon?"

"No, I do not."

"Do you have a weapon at home or in this office?"

Georgi opened the drawer of his desk. He began to reach in. Karel took a step around the desk. "May I do that, sir?"

Georgi stepped back as Karel picked up the old Spanish pistol. He raised it to his nose.

"It's been fired," Georgi said. "On the morning of Horvath's death, I took the pistol to the Kalmagden gardens and fired it."

"Because you intended to use it later in the day?"

"Yes. Because I intended to kill Jan Horvath, who was once Ivan Napica, the . . ."

"Yes, I know," Karel said.

"I congratulate you. You've done a very good job. I thought I'd covered the trail and destroyed the evidence. But there's always some little thing one overlooks."

"I doubt that I'd have ever uncovered your secret if I hadn't been pushed in the right direction by an anonymous informer."

Georgi smiled. "But there you are. That's the one thing we

255

always overlook. There's always an informer somewhere. Sergeant, I said that I *intended* to kill Jan Horvath but I didn't do so.''

"You were in the automobile parked at the curb?"

"Yes. I was waiting for him in the cold. I sat there looking at my breath forming ice on the windows. It made me think of time. Of how the years pile up opacities of facts and feelings until they become dim. Only blood and vengeance are bold enough to be seen after a while. Even love takes on a pastel hue. Not today's love. That's vivid, of course. Today's loves and tomorrow's hopes. I started to think of my wife and my children. What the killing of Horvath would do to them if it ever became known that I committed the murder, even if no harm actually came to me."

"You had good reason to kill him . . ."

"Oh, there was good reason," Georgi said. "Horvath was a murderer and a war criminal. But I've just told you I decided against killing Horvath. What good would it have done anyone? I started up the car and drove off, returned and waited, but finally drove off for good. I went home. I was in time for breakfast with my wife and daughters."

"You'll have to come along with me all the same, I'm afraid," Karel said, putting the Spanish pistol in his pocket.

"I understand," Georgi replied, and went to get his hat and coat.

Karel sat in his office. Georgi was being held in a security cell. He'd not yet been booked. The examining magistrate and the Office of the Prosecutor wanted to look into the information as carefully as they could before taking the next step.

Karel thought again, as he had earlier in the day, that it was no longer his concern. He might be called to give evidence but that was all. He'd do so to the best of his ability, trying not to speculate upon what the judges would determine from it. Now, he had to look at his own life. The conference in Rome was six weeks away. Could he maintain the shaky neutral relationship with Dika for so long? Would she force a decision from him about divorce? And would that prove disastrous to the ruse he meant to employ for taking Marta out of the country with him as his wife?

He shivered. It was more than a chill. The trembling continued on for quite a while. He feared that his nerves were giving way. He was suffering terrible indecision and unexpected reluctance. If he went away with Marta, it would mean that he would never again be able to come home. He might never again be able to work as a policeman. He suddenly knew that it was really the only thing in his life he'd ever really cared about. The violent attraction of sex with Marta must surely fade once it became always available. How could it be otherwise? Besides, could a life be based upon sexual madness?

He picked through the papers on his desk, trying to still his mind, to deflect it to other things. He read Ulica's report on the names and addresses in the green book. Nothing of importance there. He scanned the three lists. Friends, acquaintances, and legitimate business connections; contacts necessary for his shady enterprises; girlfriends and possible prostitutes. Ulica had made no attempt to draw differences between the two.

Karel's eyes moved idly down the list. An electric charge snapped in his chest. Marta's name, address, and telephone number leapt from the page. There it was as well on the little lined page inside the green book, written down in Marta's hand.

= 37 =

The Judge: 1970

The arrest of Stevan Georgi had come as a terrible shock to Anton Trevian.

Two days later he sat in front of the fire, wrapped in a shawl, a scarf wound twice around his neck. He sat there in spite of the fact that Doder had nearly fought with him to make him stay in bed. Trevian didn't want to do so. He feared that he might die there from the shame he felt. He'd conspired to allow a brutal murderer escape justice. He'd bargained for his own life in the most dishonorable way. He'd used his position to stop a trial.

Then fate had decided to play one of her ironical tricks. She'd made him the examining magistrate in the murder of the man who turned out to be Ivan Boreta, and Ivan Napica, and who knew how many other monsters? What had prompted him to give the case to the Municipal Police? He could have easily assigned it to one of the intelligence organizations or to the Secret Police, where the evidence would probably have been repressed.

Doder shuffled into the room through the door at Trevian's back.

Without turning his head to look, Trevian pettishly told him to leave him alone. "I don't want any goose grease or lemon in hot water."

"Do as you please," Doder said. "I just came in to tell you that Prosecutor Lazar is here."

Trevian turned himself around in his chair to see Lazar standing next to Doder. He was taking off his coat and scarf.

"I didn't hear the bell," Trevian said.

"There you have it," Doder sniffed. "Getting deaf along with everything else."

258

Lazar handed Doder his things.

"Bring a whiskey for Prosecutor Lazar," Trevian said. "And one for me."

"Hot. I'll bring two hot toddies."

"And make one for yourself, you old fool!" Trevian shouted after the old servant as he left the room.

Lazar pulled up a chair a little closer to the fire. He put out his hands and rubbed them briskly.

"It's warm out, or isn't it?" Trevian said.

"Old blood," Lazar grunted.

"It's a very bad thing. I don't mean our old blood. I mean the bad blood that proved itself out in murder."

Lazar didn't reply but simply stared into the fire as though Trevian's remark had nothing to do with him.

"That was a bad day when we made our bargain with Ivan Napica at Chetnik headquarters," Trevian said.

Lazar turned his watery eyes to his old friend. The look he gave Trevian was not affectionate.

"All these years. You've made me suffer for wanting to do you a favor all these years."

"What are you talking about?"

"The girl. The French prostitute on Corfu. I forget her name."

"Felice Marchand. At least that's what she called herself when with me."

"There, do you see, you never forgot."

"Perhaps not. But I haven't tried to punish you for that. What we are faced with here has to do with the inevitable consequences of a dishonorable act."

Lazar leaned forward as though he meant to attack. "That's nonsense, a lot of rot. You've always gone through your life looking for evidence of sin, for stains left on your soul because of the slightest undignified act simple human nature led you to commit. You set standards of behavior for yourself, and when you didn't want to live up to them, you invented penances and punishments for yourself."

"I don't know what you're talking about."

"I'm talking about such evidence as the fact that you've never married. What excuse did you concoct? First, that a trusted friend betrayed you into loving a whore and then prevented you from jumping into a hot stew. Second, that the right woman for you, the one that would have made up for the foolish passions of a young man, refused you, even though she took you into her bed.''

"She told you about that?" Trevian said, aghast.

"We both loved you as a friend. Why should we not talk about you?''

They fell into silence.

"And you, why haven't you found happiness with a woman?" Trevian finally said.

"Plain bad luck or some flaw in my nature," Lazar said, and shrugged as though he hadn't time to consider such trivia. "Certainly not the punishment of destiny. Retribution does not inevitably follow transgression.''

"It would seem that this fellow Boreta—Horvath—dogged our trail.''

"I never said that life wasn't filled with persistent demons and apparent design.''

"Did you kill Horvath?" Trevian said. His voice had the flat dry quality of a stick smacking wood.

Lazar stared at his old friend as though he'd gone mad. "What in God's name are you talking about?''

"You said once that you wouldn't allow Boreta to blackmail you again, that you would kill him if the need arose.''

"A braggart's boast. Besides, what do you think this Horvath, this petty intriguer and trafficker, could have asked of me of late? What influence would an old wreck like me have that would be useful to anyone? What a question to ask me, Anton. What a question.''

Trevian stared at Lazar as though trying to read the truth in his eyes.

"I fear for my friend Georgi," he said.

"What do you expect will be done to him? Nothing. He fulfilled the demands of vengeance. It's an unwritten law like the killing of the man who's bedded one's wife.''

= 38 =

The Policeman: 1970

"The Spanish pistol is missing," Karel said.

Trevian did not react.

"You don't seem dismayed, sir," Karel remarked. "The gun was an important part of Georgi's defense."

Trevian pinched the flesh between his eyes at the bridge of his nose. He sighed deeply, a man too weary to go on much further.

"Do you see something I do not?" Karel asked.

"Georgi is a clever man and the Secret Police are very good at clandestine affairs," Trevian said. "Suppose Georgi turned over the Spanish pistol as a plant, having killed Horvath with another gun which was then hidden or destroyed. Then one of his agents steals the Spanish pistol so that it seems a plot has been mounted against Senior Investigator Georgi. The innocent gun is not there to exonerate Georgi but stands as evidence of a plot against him, becoming a defense in and of itself."

Karel shook his head.

"You don't put much belief in such Byzantine machinations, do you?" Trevian asked.

He thinks me naive, Karel thought, and remembered the intricacies of his reasoning in the case of the carpenter and the deadly nail years before.

"Or it could mean," Trevian said, "that the government intends to make an example of my friend Stevan Georgi."

"Sir?"

"The government condemns vendetta. The official policy is

261

to impose the rule of law on all such ancient customs and beliefs. They are unsuited to the modern state we are trying to construct. Besides, there are circumstances surrounding this case that are embarrassments to certain people in high places. It would seem that a good deal of people in the past conspired to protect a murderer and a war criminal.''

= 39 =

According to criminal procedures under the law of Yugoslavia there is no trial by jury. The number of judges named to sit upon a case depends upon the severity of the crime. In the prosecution brought against Milan Merin, also known as Stevan Georgi, five judges of the Federal Supreme Court heard the case *in camera*. The trial was conducted away from public view because it was said that sensitive material possibly bearing upon the security of the state might be entered into evidence.

The case against Georgi was presented by the public prosecutor, a middle-aged man who'd once been one of Lazar's protégés. The defense was allowed to examine witnesses but there were none called. Magda, Tessa, and Tessa's husband, who'd touched Stephano Merin's skull, were never called upon for testimony. The court deemed it too emotional and therefore prejudicial to the orderly pursuit of justice. After that decision, Georgi clearly saw the handwriting on the wall and acted in the only honorable fashion open to him. He stood mute, never testifying in his own behalf, allowing the government to have its way with him. The trial took three working days.

Georgi was sentenced to thirteen years in Foca Prison.

= 40 =

It was like living with a watchful ghost. Dika rarely spoke to Karel. She stopped making meals and never seemed to eat. He never saw her take so much as a glass of water. He slept on the couch. His dirty socks and underwear piled up in the clothes hamper until he understood that she'd no intention of washing them. She acted as though she lived alone or with a cat that was independent enough to care for itself. She remained in her bedroom. From time to time he would hear her weep.

Yet it seemed that every time he turned a corner or looked up from his newspaper, went to the bathroom, or made himself a cup of coffee in the kitchen, Dika's shadow had just that moment disappeared around a corner. Dika's eyes seemed to be looking at him accusingly from every reflective surface.

One night, a week after Georgi had been taken off to prison, one week before Karel's journey to Rome, he came home to find a supper on the dining room table. Dika had cooked a goose and stuffed it with dried apples. There was a fresh loaf of black bread and a bottle of white wine. He took off his coat, hat, and gloves and went looking for her. She was nowhere around. After half an hour he sat down to eat. He was afraid the meal would grow cold if he waited any longer. It was a great puzzlement to him.

As he chewed a last bite, Dika came into the room. She was prettily but not seductively dressed. She wore a long shawl around her shoulders and warmed her hands in its fold. She sat down at the other side of the table.

"You didn't light the candles," she said.

"I was waiting for you, and then I went ahead . . ." He stopped because he found his tongue stumbling over his explanation so that it sounded like a guilty apology.

"I'm not hungry," Dika said. "The meal was for you. A fancy meal. Do you like it?"

"Yes," he said with a rising note of concern in his voice.

"Sure you do," she said. "It's the sort of thing you dreamed about when you were a farm boy, isn't it so? A pretty wife and yourself sitting down to a candlelit supper every night. Earning money and collecting things."

"It's what a good many people want," he said.

"Oh, yes. Well, there you are," she said. "Your supper. Your last supper." She laughed a little.

Without haste she took her hand from beneath the shawl. It held the service revolver he scarcely ever carried.

"You have no intention of coming back from your trip to Rome," she said.

Karel's chest felt tight, his breathing shallow. But his voice sounded calm and composed when he asked her what made her come to such a conclusion.

"What are you talking about? What trip to Rome?"

"Lutesh called."

"What about?"

She dismissed his question with a wave of her free hand.

"It might have been important," Karel said. He got up and started toward the telephone.

"Stay where you are, please," Dika said. There was a sharp, hysterical edge to her voice. "He asked me if I was excited about going along on the journey."

"I didn't tell you about it because it would make no difference," Karel said in a very patient manner. "I was going to tell you the day before I was to leave. Now that Lutesh has told you, there's no need."

"He didn't tell me when you were going," Dika said.

"Didn't he?" Karel said calmly. "Well, I leave in three days."

Dika laughed shortly as though bitterly amused. "Lutesh thought I was going with you. Why did he think that?"

"When the offer was made some time ago we hadn't resolved

anything about our future yet. The matter between us hadn't reached a crisis. I suppose I still thought we might be together when the time came. Perhaps I thought we could go to Rome together and find a new life for ourselves."

"Foolish. Romantic and foolish. Broken marriages aren't made up on holiday."

"I agree."

"It's your chance to get away from me," she said.

"I have no reason to *escape* from you," Karel said. "There's no hope for our marriage anymore. It's over. Neither one of us meant for it to happen. But I don't have to leave my country and my job just to break it up between us. And you don't have to kill me. Divorce isn't difficult."

"The shame," she said.

"There's no shame in it. You can go home to your father's house. Make me out the villain."

"That makes it easy for you," she said.

"And for you. It's just your honor you want to save if you can, isn't it? What else could you want? I'm no good for you anymore."

"Nor me for you?"

"As you say."

She put the gun on the table and stood up. A trembling started in his stomach now that the immediate danger was past.

"This is very good," Karel said. "Won't you have some?"

"No, thank you," Dika said. She walked toward the hallway leading to the bedroom. He watched her go. She stopped in the doorway and turned to stare at him.

"I may not be done with you yet," she said.

"What do you think she'll do?" Marta asked Karel.

"I don't know."

"She could ruin it for us. She could arrive at the airport to confront you before you leave for Rome. She could see me with you and make a scene. Or worse."

"She could, but I don't think she will. I've taken care to make sure of that."

"How?"

"We're not to leave for a week. I told her I was going in three days. I'll watch to see if she goes to the airport to force some last confrontation. If she does, we won't be there, and I'll do what I can to prevent her from trying to interfere with us. If she doesn't, then we can—"

"She should be silenced," Marta interrupted. Her eyes seemed to be protruding from her head as she stared at him.

"What? What did you say?" Karel asked incredulously. "What are you suggesting, that I kill her?"

"Isn't that what you meant?" Marta said.

"My God, no. What kind of madness is this leading us into?"

"I misunderstood. How could I ask you to murder your wife? I'm not a monster or a fool," Marta rattled on.

"Then what were you saying?"

She moved toward him. "I was asking for your reassurances."

"No," he said, disposing his legs so that she couldn't sit on his knees. "Don't try to settle everything with your ass."

"Ahh," she murmured, and nudged him over on the chair with her hip so that she could sit next to him. She put one hand on his sleeve and put her arm around his neck. She kissed him on the cheek. "Don't be angry with me. It will be all right. We'll leave, won't we? Nothing will go wrong?"

"Nothing will go wrong," Karel said. Suddenly he remembered that Lutesh had called him at home. He was about to pick up Marta's telephone and dial headquarters when he was overcome by a need to get out of her presence.

Lutesh was otherwise engaged when Karel reached headquarters. He was told to come back in five minutes. Karel went back to his office to add a new shaving kit to the new suitcase he'd purchased for his trip. There was even a new suit and a new pair of shoes packed in the canvas carryall in spite of the fact that Marta insisted that the tailors and bootmakers of Rome could make him a silk suit and soft leather shoes at prices that would amaze him.

Lutesh came into Karel's office.

"I was just coming back again to see you," Karel said.

"That's all right. No bother. I called your apartment."

"Dika told me."

"When I asked her if she was excited about the trip to Rome, she tried to cover up her confusion, but I could tell that she knew nothing about it."

"She's not going," Karel said. "Things haven't been good between us for a long time."

"I understand, I think," Lutesh said.

"Yes, well, I didn't tell her I was going to Rome. There was no reason. There might have been quarrels."

"There are flight tickets and hotel reservations for two," Lutesh said. "For you and your wife."

"Yes," Karel said, and regarded his friend and superior as steadily as he could.

"I'm not to ask who's going along," Lutesh said.

"I'd consider it a great favor if you didn't."

Lutesh shrugged. The matter was Karel's to deal with.

"I called to tell you that there's been a new development in the Horvath case. Judge Trevian wants you at his house."

= 41 =

The Judge: 1970

Trevian sat in the chair by the blazing fire. He seemed diminished, the massive chest caved in as though something resident inside the old man had vacated the shell of the body. He merely raised his head when a much concerned Doder showed Karel into the room. He neither smiled nor greeted the policeman, as had been his habit, with the relish of a man upon the hunt.

Karel took the chair on the other side of the fire without being asked. He leaned forward and waited. When Trevian failed to utter a word for a long time Karel cleared his throat.

"Sir," he said, "Lieutenant Lutesh informed me that I was wanted here."

Trevian raised his head again like an old turtle bothering itself to discover who it was intruding on his stretch of beach.

"Sergeant?" he murmured.

"Sir."

Trevian smiled. "Good of you to come," he said, as though Karel were visiting him in a hospital.

"Are you all right?" Karel said.

"All right? Yes, I'm all right. Doder is terribly upset of course. A double tragedy."

"If I might inquire."

"My old friend and associate Enver Lazar died last night of a stroke. It was peaceful enough, I think. At least, the doctor said there probably hadn't been much pain."

"I'm very sorry."

"How is your pretty wife?" Trevian asked, as though Karel's remark had brought some comparison to mind.

"She's well."

"Remember me to her."

"She will be honored. Sir? You said a double tragedy."

"You were right, you know," Trevian said. "Horvath's killing was an affair of honor."

"Will you tell me about it?"

"My friend, Lazar, and myself knew Horvath."

"Did you know him very well?" Karel asked, hoping that the old man was not about to tell him that he and his friend had been involved in Horvath's petty schemes.

"Not very well. In fact we met him only . . . three times."

Karel's quick ear caught the hesitation that preceded what was probably a falsehood.

"During the second war, Lazar and I were asked by Tito himself to perform a service. We were asked to infiltrate the headquarters of Draza Mihailovic. Horvath, who then called himself Ivan Napika, was an officer among them. We were recognized by another man who reported us at once to this Napika, who apparently was in charge of headquarters security. Napika was an opportunist whose loyalty could be temporarily purchased for the price of anything that might aid in his survival. We, Lazar and I, were no better. We gave him information that would make it possible for him to turn his coat and he gave us our lives."

Karel was about to say something to the effect that such an act of self-preservation might be understood, if not excused, forgiven, if not forgotten, but held his tongue. Any attempt to mitigate the old man's sense of dishonor would only add to his distress.

"In nineteen forty-seven the father of a Partisan soldier, tortured and murdered by this Napika, petitioned the authorities to investigate a man then known as Ivan Boreta. By this time he was an officer in the KNOJ. I was serving as the senior judge on a board which advised the Office of Military Counter-Intelligence in the prosecution of members of the armed forces accused of war crimes. Lazar was a government prosecutor.

"Perhaps the KNOJ was embarrassed because they'd allowed such a man as Boreta into their organization. They prided themselves on the thoroughness of their investigation into the backgrounds of any candidates. Perhaps Boreta had something on one of their top people. It would seem likely. In any case he came to me and forced me to protect him and when I urged that the case be dropped, the KNOJ was quick to embrace the decision as the proper one."

"They must have rid themselves of their embarrassment soon after," Karel said.

"Oh, yes, Ivan Boreta left the KNOJ. When he resurfaced he was an officer in the Military Counter-Intelligence and his name was Jan Horvath. Later, when he retired, he started a good many enterprises and enjoyed a great deal of prosperity. But, of course, you know about that."

"Yes, sir."

"I should say that you know much but not all. Besides all the traffic in icons, paintings, jewels, family treasures, and blank documents, Horvath sold influence and provided protection against prosecution whenever a war criminal or a corrupt official was exposed. He had a very important judge and an equally important prosecutor in his pocket, do you see?"

The old man fell silent as though he were worn out from his confession.

"You must excuse me, sir, but I find it very difficult to believe what you tell me. I can imagine you performing the first act in the attempt to save your life and that of your friend. I find the second act of blackmail less easy to believe. And I find the picture of Anton Trevian allowing his honor to be repeatedly abused beyond reason."

"I had a responsibility to my friend."

"Ah. Was it your friend who killed Horvath? Is that why you waited until Lazar's death to confess this, even though you had to stand by and watch an innocent man condemned to prison?"

"I was struggling with the thought that I had to protect Lazar from the consequences of the cooperation we'd given Horvath through the years. I don't think I would have allowed Georgi to go to prison even at the cost of exposing Lazar along with myself. But he did not kill Horvath. I did."

"No," Karel said impulsively.

"Yes. I am afraid so. I had an old pistol from the first war. A souvenir. Horvath had made an unusually brazen request of me—it would serve no purpose to tell you the nature of it—and I decided that I'd had enough. I acquainted myself with the man's habits. I waited for a cold morning when I could reasonably expect that not too many people would be about. I made my way to Prince Michael's Street on foot. I timed my arrival to coincide with the moment that Horvath would be leaving his apartment block. Do you remember the old man with the cane? I was that old man.

"So, that's the end of it. I wanted to tell you first, to let you know that you did a better job than a man could be expected to do with the examining magistrate standing by ready to obstruct him if the need arose."

"Will you need an escort?" Karel asked, rising to his feet.

"I placed a second call to the office of Chief Prosecutor Pantelic. He's sending a car."

The bell at the door sounded just then, distantly, like a fragile echo of a bell at the end of a long corridor of time.

"What will become of you?" Karel said.

Trevian smiled. "I'm a very old man. They won't do much to me. A quiet hearing. Censure. Forced retirement, of course. But it's time for that in any event."

= 42 =

The Policeman: 1970

The international airport at Belgrade had nothing of the glamour and excitement possessed by those of New York, London, Paris, Rome, or nearly any other modern nation. It was drab, the waiting room oddly Spartan as though the government intended to waste not one dinar on a showcase entry to the country, and even less on making the exit area comfortable.

Karel and Marta sat on the molded plastic chairs with the same peculiar look of stunned patience common to people in waiting rooms the world over, no matter how luxurious or plain the decor. Their suitcases were at their feet. Marta carried one or two paper-wrapped parcels in her lap. It seemed to Karel that nearly everyone going east to west carried such bundles. Coming back to Yugoslavia their newly acquired gifts and purchases were carried in canvas totes of a hundred different kinds, advertising everything from Japanese cameras to the ubiquitous Coca-Cola.

Every once in a while Marta roused herself and looked around with the eagerness of a child touched with fear, as though she expected someone would come along to prevent her going away. She shifted in her chair and tapped her feet, smiling and prodding Karel to make him join her in the rage of joy and expectation she was feeling.

"Why are you so gloomy?" she teased. "Are you thinking that you've made a bad bargain? Are you thinking that I might not be such a prize on a full-time basis? Are you having doubts about finding me in your bed for the rest of our lives?"

Karel looked at her exactly as he would have looked at a

child and shook his head. "No, no, nothing like that," he said seriously.

Marta stopped smiling and grew serious as well.

"I didn't really think you would. I was teasing, don't you see? But there's no doubting how sad you are. How troubled. Are you thinking of Dika? She'll be all right."

"I wasn't thinking of her."

"Of your job. Of leaving Lutesh and your friends."

"I was, just that moment, thinking of Magistrate Trevian."

"I didn't know he was such a good friend."

"We aren't good friends. Not socially. I mean, we don't go out together or share an evening unless there's a case to discuss."

"You came to like him when working on this Horvath matter. I understand. Now the old man has confessed, and at the very least, it means that his career will end in disgrace."

"No. Nothing will happen. Nothing will change. The confession has been refused."

"Can they do such a thing?"

"The conviction of Stevan Georgi will stand."

"What will Trevian do?"

"What can he do? He's been told that in the opinion of the government Georgi is guilty of abusing the powers of his office. The wrongful sentence—if indeed it is a wrongful sentence—will be punishment for that. They don't see that justice will be better served by putting aside the sentence and trying Georgi again for malfeasance."

"What a curious justice they serve out," Marta said disdainfully.

"Perhaps. They told Judge Trevian that if he tries to make a public issue out of his confession it won't serve to free Georgi. It will be nothing but a wasted gesture. They even hinted that they'd simply let the story circulate that Trevian had grown senile."

"And Georgi will serve his sentence."

"Not all of it. Trevian and I have been allowed to know on good authority that Georgi will serve only a little of the sentence. A slap on the wrist."

"Well, then. Things haven't turned out so badly," Marta said

as though she was glad to be at the end of her obligatory interest
in Karel's professional concerns.

The flight to Rome was announced and Marta leapt to her
feet.

Karel had arranged for a room in a small hotel at the top of the
Via Veneto. They'd dined at the famous Alfredo's and watched
the proprietor toss the fettuccine with his well-known golden
spoons. Karel thought the food very poor for the price.

Marta took more wine than she was used to. The quality of
her passion when they were back in the room was of a new sort,
playful and sultry. She insisted that Karel seduce her with a
show of desire as though they were newly met and not yet
lovers. When he'd kissed her enough she went off to the
bathroom to change into a night dress.

Karel stripped down and lay on the bed naked. He turned off
the light and was bitterly amused to find that the moonlight
turned his flesh corpse blue. When Marta left the bathroom she
stood in the lighted doorway long enough for him to see the
shape of her body through the thin gown. Then she closed the
door behind her, shutting out the light, and padded across the
room to lie down on the bed beside him. She embraced his
shoulders and placed her lips in the hollow of his neck and
shoulder. When he failed to respond she raised up on one elbow
and looked down into his troubled face.

"What is it?" she murmured.

"When did you get a look at Horvath's file?" Karel said.

Marta jumped as though he'd prodded her with an electric
finger.

"What?" she said sharply.

"Judge Trevian was told that Horvath's file, much to the
embarrassment of the KOS, was missing or stolen, and the
microfilm duplicate clandestinely censored."

He knew she was staring at him with her slightly protuberant
eyes, testing his temper, weighing her chances of lying to him.

"Don't you think you should tell me the truth?" Karel said.
"We're setting off on new lives, a new beginning."

"Yes," she said, "I examined Horvath's dossier a long time
ago."

"What prompted you to do it?"

"It was part of a survey of retired personnel . . ." she said, and would have said more except that Karel shook his head and looked at her squarely.

"No," he said. "No, and no. Please don't lie to me. Your name was in one of Horvath's address books, written in your own handwriting. You examined his dossier for reasons of your own."

The corners of her mouth turned up stiffly, her chin began to tremble, and her eyes welled with tears.

"Oh, my God," she murmured.

"Why are you afraid?"

"You'll stop loving me."

He pulled her head down to his and placed his cheek against her cheek. Her entire face was trembling.

"Hush, hush, hush," he said, and continued to say it until she seemed a little soothed. "Now tell me why you studied Horvath's file."

"I was looking for something to hold over him."

"Why?"

"He threatened to go to you and tell you that I'd been his mistress."

"Had you?" he asked, leaning away.

She shook her head furiously. Her hair fell into some disarray. Another time it might have seemed sensual to him but now, with her thin, reddened nose and eye makeup smeared along one cheek, she only seemed bruised and careworn.

"I didn't think you were a virgin when I met you," Karel said. "His wasn't much of a threat."

"There were indiscretions," she said in a voice that was scarcely audible. "One or two."

"Just one or two?"

The tears spilled out of her eyes and ran down her cheeks. She looked past his shoulder, at the window and the moon, everywhere but into his eyes. He placed his face against hers again.

"Tell me," Karel murmured.

"A few times. There were pictures. I never expected . . ."

She stopped. He waited, inhaling the faintly spicy scent of her hair.

"What didn't you expect?"

"That he would use the pictures against me."

Karel closed his eyes and shivered. When all was said and done, every act of physical love could be made shoddy, pitiable, and commonplace.

"Didn't you think that there would ever be cause for him to threaten you?"

"He promised to help me get out of the country. But he was just saying that to get me to do what he wanted in bed."

"You were using him, too."

"Yes."

"In the same way that you're using me?"

She clutched the hair at the back of his head. "No, no, I love you," she said.

"Ahh," Karel said. "Yes, well, that makes it different."

"Don't you believe me?"

"I believe that you believe it."

She moaned softly, the small mewling of an injured kitten.

"I forgive you," Karel said.

She tried to get closer to him. "Make love to me," she said.

"Did the facts in his dossier give you a weapon that stopped his threats?" Karel asked.

She shook her head.

"He laughed at me. He said if I ever dared to betray him, nothing would be done to him but I'd have some wonders done to me that would haunt me all my life."

"He didn't want to lose you?" Karel said.

"He said . . ."

"Yes?"

"He said he'd developed an appetite for me."

"So you went to his apartment, waited for him, and killed him."

The silence that followed the declaration was like a door through which neither wished to step.

"I should take you back with me," Karel said.

"What are you saying?" she said with a horror that made her question sound like the slicing of a sharp knife through silk.

"I should take you back under arrest. You killed a man."

She laughed sharply. "Are you crazy? You know what kind of man he was. He was long overdue for killing."

"That's not for you or me to—"

"No, no, no!" she interrupted. "No, damn it! That's not good enough. I don't want to hear you condemn me with some ready-made, government-stamped lecture on the law. We know what's been done in the name of survival. In the war and after. You know that I had to do what I had to do. I was alone. I had no one to care for me. And I was a Jew."

"Please, I don't want to hear that again."

She grabbed his face.

"You will hear it. It seems like nothing to you. Whenever I tell you that there's Jew-hating and Jew-baiting everywhere, you tell me it's not so, the constitution doesn't allow it. There it is, equality for all, in black and white. Well, I feel the hate every day. And one day it will get out of hand again, as it's done so many times before, even in the countries that were thought to be the safest for us. I was prepared to use any means, or anyone, in order to find safety, to find a home."

"Even if Horvath deserved killing," Karel said, "Georgi doesn't deserve thirteen years in prison."

All at once Marta grew calm, as though she'd reached deep down inside her soul and found a dignity, a strength, and a formidable acceptance of fate and whatever it might have in store for her.

"I understand. You have your profession. You have your honor. I have my share of that as well. I won't trick you with tears or sex. I won't tempt you into making love with me. I've acted out of an honest need in me to find safety and security. I've become a problem to you, a matter of moral, ethical, and legal considerations. You'll have to work it out for yourself."

She left the bed. She put on a robe and went to sit in a chair near the window, in the moonlight. She placed her elbow on the sill and her chin in her hand, and looked out on the Roman streets.

Foca Prison: 1983

Karel's foot crushed the thin hard crust of ice covering the snow in the gutter. He started the walk that had begun for him thirteen years before when he'd returned from Rome knowing that, for honor's sake, he should go to Georgi and tell him all that he knew, and all that he'd done.

They'd made love after all, Marta and he, in the rented bed in the hotel room overlooking the noisy, crowded, wonderful nighttime streets of Rome. He'd left for Belgrade the next day without her. What else could he have done? Could he have condemned a frightened woman to prison? Could he have lived knowing that the body, heart and mind he'd loved was shut away? Could he have stayed with her? No. That was equally impossible. How could he have profited by her crime? How could he have accepted love and a new life at the cost of his honor?

His steps grated against the snow. He knew that he was leaving footprints in his wake as dark as a trail of sins.

Why had he accepted the counsel of first Judge Trevian and then Lieutenant Lutesh? He might have known what they would advise.

When confronted with his own self-sacrificial gesture, Trevian had explained it away as the last useful act of an old man who'd had more than his share of good life, a gift to a friend who had acted out of a deep sense of traditional honor. But Karel, Trevian said, was a young man with a brilliant career ahead of him in the service of the people. He had no right to throw that benefit away on a vain and hopeless attempt to rub the government's nose in their mistakes.

Lutesh had heard him out and simply said, "You'll have to work things out for yourself in the end, of course, but if it were in my power to do so, I would order you to forget the entire affair. You can do no good, but you can still do a great deal of harm."

In the end Karel had decided to make a reconciliation with Dika, an attempt at a new start in his marriage, his penance. But Dika, dim as she was in so much, must have intuited the essence if not the nuances of the feelings that led him to the attempt, and would have none of it. She divorced him and went home to live.

Karel felt alone and vulnerable crossing the road.

He'd been alone for a long time. Then one day he'd met a woman who was attractive to him and to whom he was attractive. Her name was Anya. After a brief courtship they married. The second marriage was blessed with children and was much better than the first in every way.

Georgi raised his eyebrows above the rims of his spectacles as Karel stepped up onto the walk.

"I'm Lieutenant Michael Karel," Karel said.

"I remember you."

"I asked permission to meet you and drive you back home."

"My wife and children, my grandchildren?" Georgi said.

"Waiting for you."

"This is kind of you," Georgi said.

"No."

"And unusual."

"I wanted to see you alone. I wanted to tell you something."

"Can you tell me in your automobile?" Georgi said. "The cold."

When they were well on their way and the car had grown warm they removed their hats and opened their coats. Georgi settled himself in the corner of the seat, his back against the meeting of cushion and door.

"Yes?" he said.

"I know you didn't kill Horvath. I knew it soon after you were convicted and imprisoned."

"I see," Georgi responded in the calmest of voices. They might have been talking about the weather or the latest film.

"Don't you want to know why I didn't act upon the knowledge?"

Georgi chuckled as though Karel had said something mildly amusing. "You haven't come all this way *not* to confess yourself to me."

"Confess?" Karel said spontaneously.

"Isn't that what you intend to do? Confess that you allowed me to lie in prison for thirteen years when you might have done something about it? Who brought pressure to bear upon you? Was it Borodin? He never much liked me. Perhaps it was Colonel Bim?"

"It wasn't like that."

"I see. Just a departmental punishment. A little lesson about the use and abuse of power. Government policy."

"Judge Trevian made a false confession hoping to free you."

"Yes, I know."

"The murderer was a woman."

"This is too absurd," Georgi said. "Did I spend thirteen years in Foca Prison because of some quarrel between a whore and her customer?"

"Not a whore. A woman who'd first been promised hope by Horvath, and then had it snatched away."

"This woman was known to you?"

"Yes. She became my mistress after she broke it off with Horvath."

Georgi said nothing to that. They drove in silence for a while.

"I didn't let her go because I wanted to save her. I let her go because I knew there was really no way that I could prove what she'd done, and no way to effect your release. You were in the grip of the government."

"And you have been in the grip of your conscience all these years."

"Yes."

"Then you weren't so very sure that you were helpless in the face of fate. Not so very sure that you might not have at least tried to save me."

It was Karel's turn to be silent.

"You came for my forgiveness," Georgi said.

After a moment's hesitation, Karel nodded his head.

"I won't give it," Georgi said. "You'll have to live with it."

He settled himself more comfortably in the seat and faced ahead, watching the barren landscape pass by. After a while there were buildings, and then the outskirts of the city.